Fire of the Blood

Jasmina Coric

LITTLE LION PRESS
First published in the United Kingdom by Little Lion Press
www.littlelionpress.co.uk

Copyright © 2021 by Jasmina Coric
ISBN 978-1-8384843-1-6

First paperback edition October 2021

Book design by Jasmina Coric
Cover art by Tom Roberts

To my incredible
grandfather for helping
me pursue my dreams

She's mad but she's magic. There's no
lie in her fire.
　　　　　　- Charles Bukowski

Table of Contents

Beings of Sundalev

Dragovik: a species of dragon shape-shifters.

Angeleru: a species imbued with some of the powers of the angels that live on Earth.

Caelitai Umea: a faction of the angeleru with all the powers of the angels.

Jaeitsi Bataruce: the children of the caelitai umea, who exert control over deabrueon.

Deabrueon: the children of the jaeitsi bataruce, who come in various forms.

Bellatoja: a faction of the angeleru who have increased strength and speed, making them the warriors of the angeleru.

Onyevaras: the governing body of the dragoviks on Earth.

Hirutere: the governing body of the angeleru in the City Between Earth and Sundalev, Miesarinda.

Vaerdiexes: the god of fire, whose familiar is the phoenix.

Alastor: the god of water, whose familiar is the basilisk.

Illarion: the former king of Dragovicia, whose actions resulted in the creation of the dragoviks.

Vernis Lanin: a grouup of dragovik insurrectionists run by Thaddeus Velemir.

Part I

Chapter I.

It didn't start with fire and blood.

It started with a man drinking alone in a bar, thinking about a woman, and whether or not to kill her.

* * *

Isabrand has spent the early evening successfully poisoning his liver with tequila and attempting to poison his thoughts against the person he has been asked to kill next.

The others who fill the bar he finds himself in most nights are like him; they all owe their lives to someone or other who has decided their life's price is death. Now they sit around this grotty shithole, wondering when their lives will stop being worth the number of bodies they cost. The answer for self-serving scum like them? Never, Isabrand always thinks.

His tongue flicks out across his lower lip, catching the residue of his last shot.

Never. That is what he would have said until today. But he has finally reached that number. Or, rather, that person, one who he cannot bring himself to kill. He knows that in denying those who own him this death, he will bring about his own. This is the predicament Isabrand finds himself in while sitting in a bar with a group of mad men and killers. This is why, when the bartender asks if Isabrand wants a refill by means of his customary grunt and nudging the glass with the bottle, Isabrand ignores the swelling wooziness that presses like an autumnal fog on his temporal lobe. He taps the side of his glass once and watches the glass fill near its rim.

It isn't that he knows the victim particularly well. Just the odd fond, distant memory. He snorts, downing the shot. He had hoped to divest himself of his sentimentality by drinking, yet here he is, thinking of his target as a victim. He has never done that before, not even the first time. Yet more proof that nostalgia is holding him far tighter than his own self-preservation. He has always had a lot of the latter. Hell, one doesn't end up in his line of work unless they're one of those desperate, base creatures that will do anything to keep their claws dug into the bedrock of existence. Sentimentality has never been his problem. That is how his bosses like it. That is how he likes it.

But now it is sown, the seed of plants like hesitation and fear, growing in his chest. He has tried to drown it but it seems nothing can uproot the beast once it takes hold.

What of her? Will she suffer the same concerns if pitted against him? He stares at himself in the mirror behind the bar. Chalky hair, gaunt cheeks and pale blue eyes few are willing to meet except in the moment before death. He looks exactly as he did the last time they'd met. Yet there is no possibility she will remember him. It will make it easier for her to kill him. He's heard she's gotten quite good at that herself.

See, she's just another pathetic creature willing to do anything to stay alive.

This is yet another of his ill-born, half-hearted attempts to turn himself against her, made by whatever part of him is not yet resolved to die.

Enough.

He sets his glass down with enough force to draw a resonating thud from the bar top. Anywhere else, this would startle, but here it is another wastrel fighting with himself because there's no one left to push away. He gets up, his hand searching in his pocket for his wallet, when it goes limp. Why should he pay? Every man sentenced to death should get his last meal. If he had thought about it sooner, he would have got some Pad Thai, not stale bar peanuts. But life's a piss-take like that.

He's slow to rise, his joints unsure of themselves after all he's drunk. He steadies himself on a bar stool. This isn't like him, no matter how drunk he is. Upright once more, Isabrand makes his second attempt to reach the door. This time, he is stopped by the bartender's over-eager latest hire. The help doesn't tend to last long here.

"Hey you need to pay! Do you know how much your tab's up to-"

No one else looks up at the glint of the absentmindedly thrown knife, nor the dull thud it makes as it cuts the young man off. It lodges in his throat, severing his vocal cords, which have been considered the most irritating aspect of him since he arrived and said hello. He slides to the floor as Isabrand stuffs his hand back in his pocket.

The bartender nods at Isabrand with utter gratitude and all the emotiveness of a dead, glassy-eyed fish. He takes up the mop, though he's known for quite some time that mopping while his employees are still bleeding doesn't do much good. Instead, he positions the mop over the young man's head so he won't be overcome with the urge to kick his protegee's idiotically shocked face. What had he expected in a bar full of those whose job is death? Had he not told his employee that his customers always brought work into the bar with them? Not in so many words of course.

Isabrand exits onto West 4th. No one sees the building he comes out of; no one wants to. But they notice Isabrand. Four girls who will all reek of vomit, short-lived love and quickly forgotten heartbreak by the end of the night are plotting their course on an effortless night of alcohol induced fun by a lamp post when he steps out. The one farthest away spots him first. How could she not? His ghostly features illuminate him like a young angel amongst so much neon and dark that crowds the street. He looks like the sort of guy that makes you think you should cross the street, yet leaves you too intrigued to do so. She nudges her friend to the left, the one she'll complain to about their other friends later. Soon they have all caught sight of him, observing as he turns the collar of his wool coat up against the chill that has little to do with the weather. The girls quickly begin to establish by way of eye contact who has dibs. The first girl, obviously, an eye roll says. A quick sideways glance at the fourth from the third contradicts. The fourth has just gone through a bad break up. She needs this. The three are still arguing through glares when the second speaks up.

"Where'd he go?"

Indeed, they may notice him, but Isabrand's mind is too fully occupied by another girl to notice them. He's walked on, and now passes Christopher Street Station, only minutes from her apartment. No, he's not resolved himself to kill her in the minutes since he left the bar. But he's decided, if he must be killed, she'll be the one to do it. He knows it's the only way he's willing to go and, besides, he's died for her before.

His choice is not all selfless. He could just refuse to harm her and his bosses would finish him off. That would be a greater act of defiance. He would be the last body on the pile that bought the twenty-five years of his life. But he wants to see her again. Seeing her after all these years will be a good time to die. And, hey, a dying man may as well say it: he wants her hands around his throat. Call it perverse, but the alcohol and all the feelings he's repressed for the past sixteen years during which he has not seen her are going to his head.

He turns onto MacDougal and curses himself almost immediately for his own stupidity. The street heaves with people shouting over each other about whatever event is about to begin in their bar or comedy club. Everyone else in-between is either too drunk or too stupefied by

the number of choices to know where they're going. Isabrand, however, does, and he wants to get there before his
resolve weakens. In his irritation, he shoulders past one
of the louder individuals on the sidewalk, almost pushing
him to the ground face first. The man stumbles, catching
himself on the hood of a parked car.

"You okay?" his friend asks, before nodding and
grinning at some potential patrons of his comedy club.
"Come on in, first drink is on us for anyone who does
open mic, and the jokes are on everyone."

The customers disappear inside, amused by what is
clearly a well-rehearsed line.

"Yeah, must have slipped or something," the man
says.

Isabrand continues, unseen by either of these men.
That is how easily he turns to shadow. He is grateful to
emerge on the somewhat quieter Sullivan Street, until he
spots the door of her apartment building. Suddenly he
wishes someone would push him into the street, prefera-
bly in front of a speeding vehicle. Can he really in good
conscious put his blood on her hands? There's a Thai
restaurant a few doors down. Maybe he could kill a few
hours, have that Pad Thai.

Kill a few hours. Murder time to put off murdering
her. He's reconsidering now. Not genuinely. It's a last-
ditch, furtive effort made by what little sensibility there is
in his brain. It fails.

He walks up to the door which, thankfully, someone
is just emerging from. Springing lightly up onto the sidewalk, he catches the door and holds it open, much to the
wide-eyed surprise of the girl. New Yorkers don't hold
open doors. She would be suspicious, were it not for the
soft upturn of Isabrand's lips as he tells her to have a
lovely evening. British accent. The English really are so
polite. The girl is assured of this by the two weeks she

spent there five summers ago. She's only just moved into the building, but makes a note to introduce herself to her neighbours over the coming week in the hopes of meeting the lovely British man again.

Down the hall is the sound of two yapping dogs. Isabrand goes to the third floor, from which said dogs can still be heard. He stops on the landing, not to catch his breath, but because the air upstairs is hot, stoked by memories. They radiate from the last apartment in the corridor, making the space between him and it change from distance to an impossible temporal chasm. The chasm all her memories of him crumbled into. Once he goes to her, he will never be able to restore the nostalgia that keeps her safe. She will be moulded anew in his mind by the cold unrecognition with which she regards him.

Still he goes to the door. He's begun to sober up but his head is by no means clear. Clarity in the face of death? That's some bullshit. He brushes the scuffed brass handle with his fingertips, as if it's her hand. The door is unlocked. Why not, it's a safe neighbourhood. Besides, anyone or anything that really wanted to get into her apartment wouldn't be deterred by a locked apartment door. She doesn't need the protection of one anyway.

He hears the hundred sounds of the city sitting uncomfortably on the thick layer of silence that holds steady. He tries to hear her through it, her breathing, heart beating, but his ears are too full. He stays his hand a moment before slipping in.

Despite having believed her long dead until recently, Isabrand is not remotely taken aback by seeing her alive for the first time. Unlike an unreliable rumour that is to be doubted by the one who wants to believe it most, if only as a means of self-protection when it is revealed false, Isabrand's confirmation of her had been certain. He had woken in the night, though usually a sound sleeper, his heart thundering and the coldness that had been in his heart since childhood lessening. Ghost arteries that had lain dormant beside the cold-blooded ones he relied on roared back to life, like a forge relit. It had been like stepping into an old life, an ill-fitting skin. There was only one person who could light the fire of his blood, long gone out, like that.

Here she stands, her back to him, soft and subtle in her movements. Each is imbued with a humanity he has been unable to animate her with in this imagination. There she had been mechanical. But she has always been the most human of their kind. Her mother had wanted her that way. An antithesis to that man. Thoughts of him always make Isabrand uneasy. As if she hears of whom Isabrand is thinking, the young woman's back stiffens instinctively. She pauses, and it is only in her stillness that Isabrand observes what she had been doing before he entered. There is a suitcase open on the sofa in front of her. Whether she is packing or unpacking is unclear, but in her hands is a wooden box. Isabrand doesn't need to get any closer to know what is engraved on the box.

A phoenix, gazing at the moon. Her mother had had it made by a carpenter at a craft's fair they had all gone to. He recalled how pleased the young woman, then a little girl, had been with it. She had been equally pleased by the strawberry and basil jam they had smeared on scones later that afternoon. Her lips were sticky and red by the time they went home, her breath sweetened by the bits of Isabrand's scones that he had passed her beneath the table when her mother wouldn't let her have any more. But that was before they had both died. She'd long forgotten him when she woke up.

He makes no sound but something stirs her to his presence. There's no perception of a threat in how she turns, slowly, casting a cursory glance over her shoulder.

Acknowledgment without recognition. He had hoped one such look from her would close his heart to the little girl he knew, that it might betray no piece of that child was still a part of her. She's stronger than her lithe body gives the impression of being. Her power is not one seen until it's too late. He waits for her to unleash it on him, the stranger who's entered her apartment with no warning, evidently just to gawk at her.

But then he really looks at her, and there is nothing cold in that face. She effuses warmth and it drips off her lips sweetly when she speaks the one word he has never expected to hear from her.

"Isabrand."

She says it and knows him as he never imagined she would. He becomes aware of his exhaustion, the strain of believing he was forgotten by the only person he loves breaking through the barricade he had unknowingly built. He wants to lay his head in her lap while she runs her fingers through his hair. He wants to listen to the childish stories she had told him in pillow forts or while hiding high up in trees so her mother couldn't find them before they ate all the cookies made for Mallory's fifth birthday. They never had a chance to celebrate.

Do you remember that, Mallory?

It is at this moment, as he takes a step closer to her, that he is struck by several disturbing realisations.

The first, that the box Mallory is holding is not at all as it was when he last saw it.

The second, that Mallory's sweater and jeans are spackled with blood.

The third, her suitcase contains only books and an assortment of weaponry.

The last, that it is absolutely impossible that she remembers him.

Unless he's being set up.

There are creatures, in the unseen world Isabrand inhabits within the human one, capable of spinning out of air what you want so desperately you will walk into its open arms, knowing it's a trap.

He reaches into his breast pocket, withdrawing another knife. If this were Mallory, the knife would be useless. But this thing…

"Who the fuck are you and where is my sister?" Isabrand demands.

She smiles at him grimly.

Chapter II.

Isabrand. How do I begin to tell you about your sister and where she went?

* * *

"Tell me what you see, Mallory."

"Me," I answer, and the mirrors that panel every inch of the octagonal room's walls answer the same. Me, infinite echoes of me, like the ones that fill my head at night; each one is useless, each one is too agonising to look at. Yet I stare at my pathetic body's reflection, stripped and shaking. No, I'm not staring at myself. I'm looking for the door, that imperceptible thing that should break a ripple in the surface of the glass, but instead leaves me drowning in my own reflection. Finding the way out would do me no good anyways. I would still have to exit. I would still have to exist, even if only in the singularity of a self with no mirrors. One of me is already more than I can bear.

"Yes. What are you?"

"Human."

The mouth that belongs to no face sighs by my ear. The air is warm and yet feels as far from lifelike as dust. I feel it tingle in my ear and the heaviness of the breath is almost more than the pain that's to come. Humans should not be still long enough to feel the dust of lost time collect on them. Yet the amount of time I have lost to this room over the years wells up, a continuous stream of unforgettable encounters written on my body, only to be erased by forgettable lapses of time spent between. It's a span of time long enough for dust and decomposition.

"Are you?"

The mouth has a woman's voice wrapped around its tongue today, but that's not always the voice it chooses.

Sometimes the faceless one speaks to me in as much multiplicity as the voices of my dreams. I have no doubt she's versed in those voices too. But this voice, soft yet with a strength to it and sharp as lightening cracking words on a tongue, I know it well. She favours it. It stirs in my mind the image of a face clouded in the vagueness of abundant detail, a compilation of every feminine feature I know. Thin lips of aged disappointment from the face of the woman who stands by our classroom door with the needle that sends us to sleep if we misbehave, even if we don't mean to; the deep cupid's bow of a full youthful mouth, my own when I have seen it. The features take turns on the ever shifting face I make for her.

"Mallory," she says in a warning voice, "I asked you a question."

My lower lip quivers but I am resolute in my silence. Again, a sigh, further now from my ear. The air beside me stirs and my whole body yearns to collapse into the space it makes in the swamp air that clots my lungs. Then -

- my skin is torn apart by the whip, like land on a map. There's no regard for how nature's rivers fall, where the Earth has spent eons raising mountain ranges. There is only the splitting of things. In one harsh motion I am made two opposing nations: one which begs me to give her the answers she has not yet asked for and one which holds my lips fast. The latter is loyalty and it won't let a scream, no not even a whisper, escape. My teeth obey its will, crushing my lower lip to stop the scream. Yet it cannot prevent my knees from dipping towards each other, a plummeting bird, as they buckle beneath the lashing. I beg for the crash, the breaking of bones that comes from falling off a precipice, but before I have the chance to touch the ground, large hands catch me by my arms.

The faceless woman does love having us saved only to torture us again. We will not die by her hand.

I'm held by a guard who has caught me on the faceless woman's wordless order. My body sags like an albatross, but those who deserve to bear the guilt for my pain do not carry the weight of me. Eventually I am set upright.

"Don't look at the floor, look in the mirror," she orders.

My stomach lurches at the thought, and the rest of my body follows suit, trying to escape the hands that hold me. They're strong but I thrash, wild and slick with my own blood. Is that disappointed woman by the door now? Does she have that needle ready with a lullaby? Better sleep than this. But the faceless woman catches my jaw with her slender fingers and I'm limp.

"Please no," I whimper, "I'll be good."

"Look."

She jerks my head up, holding it in place so I cannot avoid meeting the monster's eyes in the mirror. The crystalline pools of ice that envelope opaque windows swallow my gaze before spitting me up. How I revolt my own sight. My hair is in short, somewhat uneven patches of stubble where it was hastily shaved by the guard moments before the faceless woman arrived. Where the skin beneath is revealed, it appears a sickly grey shade in contrast to the black fluff, like the downy tuft of a baby bird. A thing that will die young. A thing whose every minute spent still breathing is unforeseen time it was never supposed to live.

Oh how I envy it.

Tresses of hair that fluttered to my shoulders are partially engulfed beneath the congealing blood of earlier lashings. The curls appear as black extensions of the trails of dark liquid that roll down my shoulder onto my chest and back, as if my own body agrees with land divisions made by the invading people and seeks to extend them. They're everywhere, the man-made territories of my body outlined by deep scarlet fissures.

My face alone they leave. After all, no one would want me if they knew what was done to me in preparation. No external marks, but again a site of rebellion. The hollowness of my cheeks gives the appearance of cheekbones so sharp they'll pierce through my skin. Even from the inside I am torn apart. My own bones do not wish to hold together such useless flesh and oxygen.

"Are you human?"

"No."

I don't stumble on the monosyllable. How can I when it's verity is so evident. The merged tear tracks on my cheeks draw downwards like the lines of blood. Wisps of black hair have caught in the dried smear of tears I attempted to wipe away, only to be reprimanded by further lashings. I should know by now not to move an inch more than I'm given.

Another sigh. The hands leave me to stand on my own.

"Whose idea was it?"

I start to shut my eyes. If I fold the world out of sight beyond my eyelids, perhaps it will disappear. Though I should know that that doesn't work and, even if it did, would I want to trade this world for the one that exists behind my eyelids? A hand cracks against the soft skin of my face.

No, even this is preferable.

Catching me by the chin, the hand digs fingernails into my jaw until they draw blood. I start, my eyelids fluttering open. She has broken her rule. But these scars will heal, they all do. Deeper still she goes. I bite the inside of my cheeks, as if pain can be dulled with the application of more pain. As if fighting on a new war front means that you're not still being attacked on the other side. In

the hazy confusion of my sight, I see her other hand resting on her hip, fingernails painted a dull red, like smatter-
ings of my blood made molten before hardening.

"I didn't say you could stop looking."

I redirect my gaze to the mirror and the hand pulls
away, smearing traces of blood along my jaw line, down
to the tip of my chin. She doesn't wipe her hand clean,
though I see a handkerchief extended to her from another guard made bodiless by shadow. Another tear slips
free and the blood on my face is diluted. It drops fast, the
once crystal bubble now given veins by my blood, which
diffuses through it.

"Whose idea was it?"

"It was both of us," I insist. I read the shape of this
lie on my lips in the mirror, just as she must do. Of all the
things she taught me, lying to her was not one of them.

"You're lying to me, Mallory. Do you want to know
how I can tell?" she breathes, the softness a leonine men-
ace before the pounce. "Because immoral creatures like
you lie."

"I'm not-" I stop, my silence the price of preventing
her now raised hand from coming down across my face
again. She waits with it still upraised, appraising whether
I will speak out of turn again. The hand comes to rest on
my shoulder.

"Do you want to be immoral?"

"No," I whisper.

"Good girl." It's not said as a croon, the gentle uttering of a mother, but as words to an obedient hunting dog.
It's accompanied with the underlying warning that, while
this time I've done well, it doesn't protect me from future
punishment. 'Now tell me whose idea it was.'

I catch the inhuman eyes of the thing that watches
me from every mirror. It wildly begs me not to betray my
loyalty.

"You may not be human, but that doesn't mean you can't try to do the right thing."

She's crouching beside me now, as if urging a stubborn child, but I dare not turn to look down at her.

"I suggested-"

The whip comes down again to catch my lie. It sings with my blood as it swishes through the air and bites into me for another taste. I fall but the ground doesn't give way. In a pocket of a parallel universe, it would bend into itself with its endless elasticity. It would draw me deep within the Earth, out of sight and reach. The dirt would cool the heat of my wounds, which feel as though a new heart has blossomed beneath each one. They all beat out of time, their dissonance dizzying my already pounding head.

The large, rough hands from before don't bother pulling me up this time; they must know how close I am to cracking. One wraps around the side of my throat and the thumb presses hard against my chin until I look back up into the mirror. A heap of limbs and blood darkened flesh. I'm gasping, and loyalty slipped from my lips during the fall and dropped to the floor.

"It was Lilith's idea."

The words are not mine. The voice, even, sounds so unlike my own. It's a guttural cry of the animal within me possessed with desperation for survival. My pupils dilate in horror; my moral compass' inability to stop base survival instinct has cost my conscious. The hand lets loose my throat.

"I see. Mallory, you understand that what Lilith did was very wrong, yes?" Is she stroking my head? I don't feel anything but the knots of sickness and shame in my stomach. She waits in silence until I nod in affirmation. "She deserves to be punished; wouldn't you agree?"

"No! She didn't mean any harm," I cry out before

the protest can be stifled by self-preservation. "Please-"

A boot to the rib cage. I sprawl across the floor and the back of my head smacks the mirror behind me. Shards fall, a rain that cuts like diamonds, coming to rest across my body like water droplets. I glisten refractions of light, disappearing beneath reflections of everything other than myself. An armour against my own existence. Yet still she sees me, and I her. Eyes gold like no manmade metal could ever replicate. They hold me down.

"She didn't mean any harm?" She rises, face gone to shadow again. "What other intention could she have had? You think she tried to take you away from me for your sake? No Mallory, she did it to hurt me and for her own gain. She was using you to escape, even if it meant exposing the world to what you are, even if it meant putting innocent people in danger. She would have abandoned you as soon as you were far enough from us. Does not such selfishness demand reprimanding?"

"She wouldn't have left me. She wouldn't have let me hurt anyone," I falter in my assurance, "She won't try again."

This time it's not just a flash in the mirror. I see the whip coming down in front of me. Turning my face towards the floor, I hear the clatter of glass shards falling from my body as I cover my head. A starburst of pain erupts in my forearm and blood falls thick on my cheek.

"You know that she must be punished, Mallory. Tell me so."

Her voice grows louder as she comes closer but I answer only in sentiments of pain, crying out and cradling my arm close to my body. She catches it, embedding the sharp points of her nails into the new wound and dragging me upwards into a crouched position. I howl, the world falling from my eyes in bits, giving way to the dark. Please, world, let me fade with you.

"If she really cared about you, do you think she would let you shoulder this punishment while she is the guilty party?" The nails press harder and my forearm is twisted away causing the tendons to tense unnaturally. She pulls at skin, pulls at my faith. "Say it!"

"Yes, she deserves to be punished!" I scream.

In an instant I am released, free to fall to the ground beneath the pressure of all my agony. The simultaneous thud of my body and hissing of the whip behind me as it is dropped open up the room to silence. I shudder with sobs I cannot give voice to and claw at the floor until I feel my nails break with the urgency of my motion. It's not until I go limp that a hand is placed on the unopened skin that's stretched thin across my shoulder blade. The act is the ghost of tenderness, the dust of lifelessness that I wish to brush away.

"We mustn't let misdemeanours go unpunished simply because we believe we care about those who commit them," she says.

A heavy set of footsteps approaches, another guard I hadn't known was here. The intimacy of my suffering cracks and bleeds into the memory of yet another. It is meaningless, something they see every day. Thick fingered hands drag me to my feet. I don't have to be told to find my reflection. The tunnels of black in my eyes have flattened, leaving no trace of human dimension and only the slenderest ring of icy blue.

"Tell me what you see."

"Me."

"Yes. And what are you?"

"Nothing."

If only.

"Correct. Now, you will stand here until I come and get you. If you move an inch, look away from the monster you make of yourself for even an instant, you will be punished accordingly," she hisses.

"But I was good! I told the truth!" I cry in a rising panic, looking over my shoulder for her.

The breath is knocked out of me as a muscular forearm slams into my lower back. The concrete floor greets my knees once more as a guard pulls my arms straight behind me and the other forces my head down with the bottom of his boot. From the periphery of the room comes another figure whose skirt dusts the floor. She crouches in front of me and places her hand on one of the open scars on my back.

"Kehpas, isuazko, saoele, udiyat etev dvesmeel, niekedrei atrier, cits sklier akalt."

The wound burns anew as if its genesis had been half-hearted. If I could scream until I went deaf I would. Yet my throat goes raw too soon.

"You are used to my tolerance, my leniency. You think because you heal you can forget the lessons I teach you? If that is so, now you will never forget. As for being good, you are not human, therefore you are not capable of goodness or truth. Besides, betrayal of those you call a friend is not an act deemed good," the faceless woman says as the other's hand slips from my back. I hear the door open and my arms are let go, a reminder that even without them keeping me in place I cannot escape. "But I suppose you know nothing of friendship, or loyalty for that matter. Now, get up."

Chapter III.

Every minute of the past falls heavy on my mind, like a guillotine affirming my guilt. If I was the sort of person who had friends with who to make jokes, I'm sure there'd be a pun to be made there – guiltotine perhaps. But I'm not and even when I did have a friend, I couldn't have imagined making a joke to lighten the mood. What right had we to brighten things when we brought so much of the darkness?

Do you feel that weight of what is gone and cannot be recaptured too, Isabrand?

In the night the sentiments of regret are amplified by the surreal churning of dreams that draw my breath like a vacuum until I wake up, gasping. Some of what I dream was fantasy but most of it is the truth. Most of it is what I have done, what we were made to do, and what I have seen done. And when I sleep, the conviction that it is all my fault is so strong that, were I to wake with the same certainty, I would hang myself from one of the high-up sconces on the wall with the spare set of sheets in the bottom left drawer of my dresser. I would climb atop my dresser, barefoot, wearing the pale nightgown I was issued, fit myself with the noose I have tied a thousand times in my thoughts, and just fall. There would have been no collision, just the slackening of my body. It would be wretched and pathetic, but I deserve it. But I always remind myself just in time that it is not all my fault. At least that's what the new people tell me and the hundred others who feel the same as me.

Despite all they have done to convince me as much, I don't trust those seconds between sleeping and waking to know the difference between survivor's guilt and rightful blame. So, I took to wondering through the halls of the Academy, the halls I hadn't known as a child, far from the room I was enshrined in for the better part of seventeen years. Far from that sheet and the sconce whose light is so tempting. In those halls don't linger ghosts of memories, swirling mist beneath the wall lights. Instead, are the human shapes of my fellow non-humans, shifting past me. What would we say of ourselves to one another, if we dared to speak?

I have been alone too.

I am a tortured creature, just like you.

Silence is better than the risk of association. It is better than the realisation that our pain is not one in a million. If our suffering has no meaning, how quickly we would have become meaningless. All we are is suffering.

Sometimes I come across another, standing still, and I paused too, leaving us in a deadlock in which neither can pass through the hallway for fear we'll overlap. We'll overlap and our histories will be so similar that we'd lose pieces of ourselves in each other.

It has been this way for almost five years by the time I turn seventeen. Ever since the faceless woman and her brutal guards abandoned the Academy and the new people took over. Someone must have found out what she was doing, but none of the new ones say anything about it. They are on the periphery of everything. They must have known when they first arrived that the Academy was ours, the creatures who were made in and by it. I don't know how it came to be that they started running the Academy, but one day the doors were unlocked and the next we were allowed the illusion of freedom.

I remember that morning because they knocked on my door. I had thought they might be…well, it doesn't matter who. I thought they might be someone else. The only other person who had knocked on the door as if the room and all that was in it, including me, didn't belong to someone else. By the time I realised that it wasn't her I was already halfway to the door. But the knock was wrong. The force with which they knocked, the height at which they touched the door, it was all wrong. I slunk back towards the table adjacent to the window.

"Mallory."

My hands had flown to my ears and I fell to my knees beside the table. Until then, the faceless woman's people had left me alone for what must have been days. I wasn't used to such a luxury as that. Even when the guards didn't come to torment me I could feel the heaviness of their presence outside my door as if it could tilt the floor. And when they would come to get me, I clung to anything to keep myself from tumbling out the door. I would dig my claws so deep into the woodgrain of the table that I could feel it biting back under my nails, or I would grip the post of my bed. But eventually they would yank me free. Eventually my palms, slicked with sweat, would betray me. Then they'd be sure to declaw me, lacerate my hands, ensure I had no way to keep myself from them.

But in those few days, with no trace of the guards, I had had dreams of opening the door and finding no one else in the Academy. I had thought there would be no more blood. No, I prayed there would be no more, no more blood.

Why is there always blood?

Shh, it's okay.

I coiled my arms and legs around one of the table legs, pressing my forehead to its surface. The voices burrowed in my mind had reared their heads and begun to whisper.

Found you.

"Mallory?"

I lifted my head. If it was the faceless woman or her people, she wouldn't be asking for me or knocking. She knew that this is where I was always to be found, where

I was kept. If it was her, I would already be down the hallway, dragged by two men three times my size but only just equal to my strength.

The door yawned open.

No, if it was her there would be no slowness in the act. I peeked from behind the curtain of my unruly curls. In the doorway stood a tall woman I had never seen before. Her blonde hair was pulled back in an unruffled bun, sleeked down across her skull. Every strand appeared perfectly parallel with the others creating a smooth reflective surface that glinted steel under the light of my room as she entered. She spotted me soon enough, crouched low to the ground like some beast.

She glanced over her shoulder at the two men who waited in the doorway and indicated that they should stay there. They weren't dressed like the guards, though they were built like them.

"Hello Mallory," the woman said, entering the room. I went limp, waiting for the inevitable, when she would beckon those men to take me. But she didn't. She looked to me for an indication.

Of what?

She eased closer, her slowness not out of reluctance but caution. Was she afraid? She wouldn't be the first.

"We're here to take care of you."

The words were acid burning up my stomach. I wanted to be sick.

Take care of him, won't you?

Blood rain on a beige carpet.

Strung up, feet first.

Yet, despite my body's innate fear, my mind relaxed. We're here to take care of you. At last, liberation. I wanted to crawl eagerly into its maw, curl up as a small snack in the mouth of death, that necessary beast. It would not have to drag me.

"Diane Thorpe is gone," she offered, trying to draw me from my apparent vacancy. But the name was a drop, was nothing to me then. This was all before I knew the weight names could carry, and how they could sound like ash when spoken. "We're here to take over your care."

She held that last word in a moment longer, tasting its unsavouriness. How inaccurate a word it was for how we had been treated. Care is a soft blanket and a body sheltering your own, not a whip breaking skin or a child's cold body in bed.

My spine curled, rolling my shoulders up until they were hunched around my ears. Care is the exact misnomer the faceless woman would have used before having us beaten.

"It's alright, we're not like her. We're not going to hurt you."

Like her? Then she knew of the faceless woman. I wanted to say something, but we were taught not to speak. I opened my mouth and half closed it again before managing a yowl like a sickly lion cub. Without a moment's hesitation, one of the men made a move toward us. My body slackened, ready to be taken to that octagonal room.

"Don't," the woman ordered.

She didn't look away from me but, when the man faltered, I knew it was not me she was speaking to. Still, I shuddered. Her tone of voice reminded me that she could just as easily have told him to beat me where I sat. His immediate response to her command told me he would have done it. And she said she wasn't like the faceless woman.

"Are you sure?" the man asked.

"Trust me."

"Alright but be careful. From what I've read in the records, this one's-"

"I know what she is."

Did she? Then why did she step closer? The man eyed me with distrust and contempt, but I was used to a hundred sets of eyes looking at me like that all at once. I was used to my own eyes looking at me like that in the mirror. And Lilith's. The thought of her sent me howling softly.

"Mallory, we've taken over the Academy. Diane Thorpe will no longer be in charge of your care. She's gone."

Her words hit me out of context, a sudden kick to the gut. She's gone. But I already knew Lilith was gone. She was long gone before these people came.

Diane. It came now as a bell, ringing clear through fog shrouded memories.

A guard dipping his head in apology to the faceless woman that night Lilith and I tried to escape. His body, a heap in the middle of the room as she turned to me, golden eyes lit in the dark, all cruelty and enjoyment. The last words he spoke still struck my ears in the electric air.

"Please, Diane."

Diane Thorpe, the faceless woman now with a name, and gone. Or so said this woman.

She had come here, with a gentle voice and promises of no more pain. But she had spoken to the man with the severity Diane -

my body shuddered to think her name. I had no right to call her by a name she had not permitted me to.

- had spoken with. I looked up at the woman who was offering delivery from the past twelve years and saw her face was in earnest. Yet still I hesitated in my belief. I had seen things that could have been yet were not real before. I had seen things that should not have been yet were, as well.

Unable to bear looking at either the uncertain ex-

pressions of the men or the certainty of the woman before me, I pressed my head to the table until the pressure
became pain. She couldn't be gone. Someone like the
faceless woman did not slip between the cracks of the
world unless she wanted to. In doing so she had discarded
us. It was her final act of reminding us how worthless we
were, even to her, our maker. Lifting my head and trembling, I began to unfurl myself from the table leg.

"Get out." It sprung from my throat, scratchy and
with no authority. Yet the woman jumped back all the
same. She hesitated halfway between the door and where
she'd been. "Get out! Get out!"

They did.

No one came for some time after that. At least, no
one who came was seen. Non-existent beings slotted food
through the hatch in my door as had always been done.
I had half a mind to starve myself then, but I didn't have
the stomach for it. My body was always ready to devour.
Each time I heard the shuffle of the tray and the snap of
the hatch, I poked my head out from where I sheltered
myself under my blanket. I crawled out of bed, hands
first, palms flexed. With the new people came new food.
It had different smells to it, and tastes. I only reared up
when I reached the door, snatching the tray before dropping low to the ground and slinking beneath the table.
There I ate, watching the door, waiting for it to burst
open.

When weeks passed and no punishment came, I
began to believe at last. I had been abandoned. That
thought came unprecedented amongst all my hatred for
the faceless woman. It came like it would to a motherless
creature, yearning for its lost parent.

One night, under the hood of darkness, I slipped
from my room. I had been right in believing there were
no guards outside my door, nor any along the hallway. I

was struck by two odd sensations as I stood in the doorway. The first was being alone, as I had not been permitted since Lilith and I had tried to escape. The second was that, for the first time, I was leaving my room of my own accord. I was choosing to place one foot in front of the other and watching them sink in the split-lip red carpet fibres. I crept along the hall. There was no boldness in this reclamation of territory. I was all fear softened flesh, shaking. I reached the end of the hall, but couldn't bring myself to raise my head and look left or right. My oesophagus drew shut, tugged by the drawstring of terror at its lip. I turned and ran back to my room. As I shrouded myself in the blanket once more, I thought how dog like we must all be, how well trained. In fear, we rush to the familiar, no matter how brutal.

Again, I waited for reprimanding. Days past and I spent it all staring at my hands in the dark, hoping my body would take to its oblivion. I waited for the guards to come as they always did: silently despite their heavy boots. Wrenching me from my bed, they would drag me down that same hallway I had dared to walk, reminding me that it was theirs, as was everything. They would take me to that room, the one full of screams carved out of me. But still the food that made my mouth ache to think of came, and there was no pain other than that in my head. So, I began to go out every night.

At first, I could only manage the halls closest to my room. I never paused, pacing up and down. I was still worried someone would round the corner and I would have to run.

Restless nights prevailed, weaving me through the labyrinth. They taught me to follow thoughts of leaving, which I had lost with Lilith years before, all the way to the front doors. I held the handle and its cool metal gave way to my warmth quickly. There I stood at the threshold

I had crossed once in my life, but could not remember. My hand gripped tighter, yet the handle did not yield to my will to leave. More accurately, my body did not. It knew I wasn't ready, likely would never be, and turned me back to the halls of the Academy like a stranger returning a pet. I prowled the halls until a form turned the corner ahead of me. My body shot like a released spring, outstripping my would-be pursuer with ease. Yet, when I came to my room and looked back, there was no one there.

The next day she came to my room again, the woman with hair like metal. I was kneeling on one of the cushions by the table. I had expected her. I had realised I had no need of fearing it would be my guards at the door when I woke still breathing. Still, when she entered, I bit the inside of my cheeks and bowed my head. Just because she wasn't the faceless woman, did not mean she was kind. One should never go easily into trust. She came only as close as was necessary to be in my periphery so I would know she was there. As if I hadn't heard her from down the hall.

"Hello Mallory. May I sit?"

The question was asked with the same intention as she had had when she knocked: to tell me that this room was mine, and she was the one trespassing. I was unsure of whether to be suspicious or thankful. I nodded, still not raising my eyes to hers. She smoothed her skirt beneath her and sat across from me, tucking her legs in a v shape.

"I'm sorry I didn't introduce myself last time I visited. I'm Doctor Lindberg."

I learned later that she always spoke her name first when meeting one of us, offering it as a token of familiarity. I dared to look at her and found her face wasn't soft as I had first thought it. It was sharp, all intention but no malice.

"I've heard you've been going out at night." My shoulders began to curl in again, collapsing my chest. "We thought, after our earlier meeting, you would do better leaving the room in your own time. I'm glad to see we were right. However," she paused, looking up from the clipboard in her lap. Her gaze snatched my breath, left me unable to move. Looking a superior in the eye was a sign of insubordination. Insubordination must be -

Take care of him, won't you?

- "before you wander off through the front door, I hoped to have another conversation with you."

Did she smile then? Retrospect and sentimentality tell me she did. But Doctor Lindberg was not such a person as to soften herself like that. I tilted my head, cradling it on my raised shoulder. She was so blunt, her intentions laid out in every word. Nothing at all like the faceless woman and her constant multiplicity of meaning.

"Most of the other individuals at the Academy needed time like you. Very few wanted to come out when we first approached them."

That was because leaving our rooms usually meant something unspeakable was about to happen.

"Few spoke, either," she added, "it seems my predecessor wasn't one for questions."

No. Questions meant broken bones, split skin, starvation. If you played your cards right it could mean death, but that rarely happened. It was best to stay quiet.

"But she is gone now. My team and I are here because we want to help prepare you for when you do leave. There's a lot that you don't know about the world outside these walls. Humans aren't what you've come to know them to be."

I thought of the door handle that didn't give way; could she make it? Would I even want it to? Where would I go? I had been at the Academy my entire life. No doubt this woman believed getting as far from here as possible was best for us. But there was nowhere else.

"We're doing our best to find as many of your families as we can. If that fails, we'll endeavour to teach you what you need to know to live on your own."

Families? What was she expecting to find here? She had said she knew what I was but how could she if she would risk exposing the world to that?

"We can't live out there, we don't belong with humans." My voice was weak, shrill from being used for little else but screaming.

"Whatever Diane told you about what you are, you need to know that it wasn't true. You're not monsters."

"That's the only truth we know."

I said it as plea. I realise now I was begging her not to take my beastliness from me because the other side to it was my attempt at humanity. Lose one and I'd lose both. Then I really would be nothing.

* * *

I don't know what they were expecting when they put us in a room together. Much less that room, of all the ones in the building. Of course, they had had no way of knowing what it meant to us. It was all I could do not to stare down at the beige carpet beneath my feet when they had led me in.

We were sitting in one of the Academy's classrooms, out of the order the faceless woman always insisted we sat in. The chairs were short, made for children, but they were never the seats of childhood. The larger bodies of the older members of the Academy looked grotesque squished in those small seats. Their faces were terrifying. Wide-eyed, wild things. Just looking at them told me there would be no hope of the rehabilitation Doctor Lindberg had spoken of. I wondered if she would kill them. It would be kinder.

Uneasy, I looked at the younger faces instead. We still had a chance of being remoulded. We would retain all the parts that the faceless woman had made, cruelty, terror and the like, but they could take new form. Those aspects could be pushed to the core, hidden away beneath our youthful softness.

One of the men who had accompanied Doctor Lindberg to my room was there, along with four others. Their expressions told us what their stun guns had spoken the second they entered the room: they did not trust us. And, unlike Doctor Lindberg, they did not betray even the slightest hint of care.

The doorway filled again, another of Lindberg's men leading a little girl into the room. He was dressed differently from the others, all in pale linen and soft soled shoes that made no sound when he walked. More noticeably, he carried no weapon. The girl was so slight, younger than me no doubt, and she held the man's hand firmly. Looking at their interwoven fingers, the small comfort taken for granted, made my hands feel as though every muscle in them was knotted in tension. Some of the older ones shut their eyes or looked away. The man led her to a seat near the window and crouched beside her to say something. Hers was the only face in the room with a smile on it. She held his gaze the whole time he spoke to her and didn't flinch when he lifted his hand to pat her head as the rest of us would have. She could have only been at the Academy a matter of weeks before the faceless woman had left. That's the only explanation for how her faith in people was still intact.

What happened next was indicative of what I had observed of Doctor Lindberg's people. An air of entitlement in how they existed, bruising their surroundings with a careless insouciance. They were confidant whenever they touched something. They didn't consider the fact that moving something had consequences. I didn't think they would have understood me if I had tried to explain that, just because something was there, didn't mean it was theirs. They never treated us this way, but all the small things, like a glass or a blanket, were insignificant to them.

As the man in linen, who had spoken so tenderly to the girl, walked towards the door, his shoulder brushed a painting, skewing its angle. I don't remember what it was of, though I had been in that room all my life. It appears dark when I think of it, though maybe that's all it was. Darkness was the faceless woman's art after all. I try not to remember most things, but some moments stick fast in my memory. Their skeletons collect in cobwebs, strung from one side of my mind to the other, catching all the most unpleasant of memories.

I remember the sound of the gilt frame scraping against the wall. It was like splinters in my heart and a cold breath on my back. The man to my right groaned, dropping his forehead to the table. He caught his head between his hands and it began to loll from side to side. I feared it would loosen from his neck and roll into my lap, though I knew that's not how you lose your head. A girl slightly older than myself hissed, slipping under her desk.

It was one of the older ones who actually stood up. He dwarfed everyone around him, built like the beast most of our delicate frames disguised. The acuteness of the sound took the wildness with no direction from him. Death returned to his gaze. He wasn't hungry for it, just its subordinate. With his behemoth paw, he cupped almost the entirety of the left side of the man in linen's face. Then, with a movement of expert precision and strength, he cracked the man's temple against an ornate rose that protruded from the painting's frame. I groaned when I heard the sound. My eyes slipped upwards, rolled out a film of black before coming to rest on the chandelier above.

Strung up, feet first.

Across the room the young man lay at his killer's feet, his once clean clothes and the beige carpet reddened with his blood. Doctor Lindberg's other associates moved all at once. Two began to corral us into the hallway, starting with those closest to the body. As if we'd never seen one before. The other three moved slowly towards the enraged man, whose hand was outstretched as if he was still holding his victim. No hands jumped for weapons. They just crept towards him. I wanted to tell them that wouldn't do any good. They would die just as the young man had. I stumbled to my feet, past the desk. In the seconds it took me to get halfway across the room, it had already happened.

Thick black tendrils whipped across the room. They were ghostly until they made contact with their intended target, turning opaque and corporeal as they gripped the beastly man. They held him by the side of his head and thick, veined neck. Then they twisted.

The little girl was standing when her dark magic returned to her, faster than the second corpse could hit the ground. She walked to the body of the man who had held her hand, knelt beside it and curled up with her head against his shoulder.

The three who had been prepared to subdue the man who had killed one of their own, looked between each other. They hadn't the faintest idea what was to come. None of us ever did.

I lifted my chin and stared at the twist chandelier directly above me. Its five chrome limbs split, thick as the black tendrils and just as deadly.

Why is there always blood?

Though I didn't look away until, at last, someone led me back to my room, I felt his gaze on me the entire time. I felt his anguish as if it were my own. Because it was.

Chapter IV.

It was a few hours after the incident before Doctor Lindberg came personally to check on me. Unlike those who had returned us to our rooms, she hadn't seemed shaken. It was then I realised why she hadn't been afraid when she first came to my room. She had known exactly what she was getting herself into each time she came near one of us. When she seated herself across the table from me just as she had done the day before, as if nothing had changed, I felt I could meet her eyes without fear. I felt what I would come to know as respect.

"I'm sorry you had to see that, Mallory. It's unfortunate that our first lesson had to end in such tragedy before it could begin," she began, "Rest assured, we'll be proceeding with greater care in the future and will likely work in smaller groups until everyone's more comfortable around people."

Right there, that was the real problem. Of all the things they could teach us of the outside world, they couldn't teach us how to be at ease around each other, let alone others whose experiences were so far removed from ours.

"The little girl," I managed. She looked at me, her eyebrows dipping in the middle. It wasn't confusion that crossed her face.

"What do you expect me to say?" Her words soaked me in dread. What limited hope I had had access to slipped away. She read the fear on my face. "Mallory. She'll be fine. We won't punish her for something beyond her control. How could she have known any better?"

"Because killing people is wrong. It's what monsters do."

"You told me yourself that believing you're a monster is the only truth you know. No doubt the same stands for her. Besides, you don't consider why she acted."

"No? She reacted to anger."

"If she did, it was anger because someone she cared about had been hurt. Is that not human? She did it for the same reason you got out of your chair without knowing what lengths you'd go to to stop the man who had just killed someone. To protect people. That's not monstrous."

"For someone who just lost a friend to one of us, you certainly have a great deal of faith," I countered.

"We know the risk we run. It doesn't matter though; every life is worth saving."

"Even Diane's?" I spoke her name, cutting a temporary edge in the endless expanse of fear she inspired in me, like rust on a blade.

"Yes, if only to bring her to justice for what she's done to all of you." She stood up, ran her hand across the surface of her hair as if one would dare to be out of place. "We have every intention of resuming lessons, however we'll understand if you'd rather not. Will you join us tomorrow?"

"Yes."

She left then, no smile of satisfaction. I had agreed to try and it felt like breathing. It wasn't the laborious breath of a chest full of broken ribs, but that didn't mean it wasn't terrifying.

* * *

After feeling his gaze in the classroom, I expected him all afternoon and evening, but he didn't come until night. Those were the hours we were most comfortable moving in after all. I wasn't surprised he managed to find me despite the labyrinthian challenge posed by the Academy's extensive halls. Truth be told, I would have been surprised if he hadn't slipped into the records room on one of those first nights after Doctor Lindberg arrived and found out which room I was in. We were the only two left from our class. I don't think Doctor Lindberg would have kept my location from him if he had asked. But he had never needed permission to go places he wasn't supposed to. At least not from the people in charge of them; it was the faceless woman to whom he heeled. Besides, what explanation could he have given Lindberg for wanting to see me? Would he have told her the story of how we knew each other and reopen that body of our personal apocalypse?

I was gazing out the window when my door opened, soundless at his touch. But we knew how to sense each other in the silent dark. We would always know one another. We had never been alone, never been to one another's rooms. It was likely they were identical, right down to the dark souls that inhabited them.

"Mallory."

Though we knew each other's names from Diane's lips, we hadn't been allowed to address each other. He spoke mine so softly, like something fragile that he could only give the slightest slip from his tongue, else it might break. Or perhaps it was out of fear that, if he spoke too loudly, it would become an invocation for what Diane had made of us. I would strip off the peaceable form I'd wound myself up in for Lindberg and deteriorate to the animal, kicking and screaming, that he knew me to be.

"Zach."

We found each other in the middle of the room, objects in gravitational orbit. My chest warmed, urged me to draw closer, but the thought petrified the rest of my body. He looked at me, eyebrows drawn down and cheeks sucked in. There was something frantic in his eyes, like I was the last tangible thing in our world which had been pulled from beneath us. I was the only proof he had that everything he remembered had happened. Reality was a slick being in hands such as ours.

Despite our proximity, he appeared only as a grey shadow in the lightless room. I had always found those shades suited him better than his gleam of his blonde hair. When our class had been led from classroom to the gymnasium, Zach and I stood side by side, never speaking but always snatching glimpses of each other in our periphery. Now he stared at me and I at him as we had never been allowed to do before.

He opened his mouth and it was as if I could see the clamouring words in the back of his throat. There were questions, memories, people who had fallen by the wayside. The latter made up the bulk of this body of thought. But it couldn't be expressed. His eyes dimmed. What words had we to exchange beyond our names? All our shared experiences were better left to silence.

"I always thought it would be me who would die in that room."

In retrospect, it doesn't matter which of us said it. We were both thinking it.

We laid on the floor, our hands brushing barriers of conditioning that kept us from holding one another. He didn't have to ask me if I remembered this moment or that. It was comfort enough to know that we existed together.

The morning after, I woke and found him gone. I was in bed, covered from toe to chin by my blanket. He had even taken the time to tuck it beneath my feet before he left. Breakfast came and went. I noticed a clock on the wall by the door. When had they put it up? Perhaps during the lesson yesterday. We had never been allowed to keep time. It was the faceless woman's, and hers alone, to command. I studied the clock as if time had emotions, but its face never changed expression. It ticked on until a quarter to nine when someone came to collect me.

"Good morning Miss Mallory," said the woman. She was scarcely taller than me though she looked older than Doctor Lindberg even, "I'm Anya."

Just as they didn't fear their surroundings, Doctor Lindberg's people did not fear words. They directed them at each other carelessly, whereas I hid my words of response in my throat. Sometimes even my mind did not know them. Anya smiled at me though I was certain I looked like some deep-sea creature with my mouth hanging open.

"Don't worry about it sweetie, you'll get used to it," she said.

My eyes widened when she spoke the endearment. We arrived at the door of the classroom, a different one from the one we used the day before. How many deaths would it take before the Academy would run out of rooms to move us to? It probably already had.

Anya nodded me into the room, giving me no indication of where to sit. I saw Zach seated towards the front of the room but he didn't acknowledge me. I don't know how we came to the mutual, unspoken decision that it was for the best we take no notice of one another. After all, it was contradictory to Doctor Lindberg's aim for us to grow accustomed to people. Yet there was something about how we knew each other, the way we were getting to know each other, that demanded clandestine meetings only. I went to a desk in the back corner of the room just as Doctor Lindberg entered.

"Hello everyone, it's a pleasure to have you all here at last," she began.

It's a pleasure not to watch someone's head be split open against a picture frame.

"I'm certain you have questions that we've failed to

answer. I understand that you may not be ready to ask them. Our aim is to help you reach a stage where you'll be comfortable doing so, as well as doing a variety of other things that will allow you to function in the world outside the Academy. We understand that at the moment it's hard to imagine that world but we hope with time you'll not only be able to imagine, but also experience it."

For all her perceptiveness, she got that part wrong. It's not that we couldn't imagine the world. It's that we had seen pieces of it and it scared us.

Past Doctor Lindberg, out the window, the trees of the all-encompassing forest were thrashed senseless by the wind. The little girl wasn't in the classroom. Nor were the older ones. They had already been given up on.

* * *

Zach visited my room every night. We lay close until I fell asleep and, though I knew he'd move me to my bed before leaving, I could never bring myself to leave his side on the floor so long as I was awake. A year had swallowed twelve months since he first came. It was around that time that I found myself wanting to ask him what his room had been like. Not the one he slept in, but the one they had taken him to when he had done wrong. Sometimes simply because they felt like it. We all had one and, aside from my own, I had only ever seen…I shivered despite the night's warmth. It must have been summer. It was so rarely warm at the Academy.

"What about Lilith?"

There was her name again, tugging loose every rope I had used to tie down memories of her. It didn't matter in what context she was mentioned, the result was always the same. Every memory of her, at her best and at her bloodiest, came back to me. I nodded in affirmation of his assumption.

"You never stop thinking about the people you lose, do you," he said.

"How can I when it was my fault?"

He had been gazing up at the ceiling, flat on his back, until I said this.

"You'll believe that until it kills you," he replied, as if it was an answer. "What happened to her?"

He said it scarcely louder than a zephyr creeping under a door. Sometimes I forgot that he knew Lilith too. That she had been behind us as we were marched in pairs from room to room. He knew we had tried to escape, too. Everyone knew that. We were the reason guards had been posted at all our bedroom doors, the reason they took every opportunity to put us in our place with a kick to the back that dropped us onto all fours.

"In my imagination, every punishment imaginable. In my heart, I know what happened to her." Now it was my turn to gaze upwards, anywhere but at him.

"I remember the first morning they brought you to class after you broke out. All the bruises and cuts were nothing compared to the look in your eyes. I couldn't help thinking-"

"-you'd seen it before." I heard him swallow, breaths went shallow.

"Every day." We locked eyes, mirrors of guilt.

"Take care of him, won't you?" the faceless woman had said.

Blood rain on a beige carpet.

One.

Two.

Three.

"Perfect work Mallory."

"That wasn't your fault," I whispered to Zach, "We should have helped you."

"We didn't know how to help ourselves, much less

each other. And I'll forgive myself for that when you forgive yourself for Lilith."

"Then never."

"That sounds like a guilt riddled eternity you're proposing."

"Do we deserve anything else?"

"Yes," he assured me, "we deserve so much more
than that."

I don't know if he meant something better or a punishment far worse. I never asked.

* * *

Zach's forehead was scarcely a centimetre from
mine. Two years had elapsed. The barrier between us
had thinned out to clingfilm. We only realised it was still
there when we tried to reach past it.

We could speak with greater ease, but the things that
most needed speaking about we left in their graves. We
helped each other bury our darkest moments with superfluous talk. When another member of the Academy's
family was found and they were sent to be with them,
there was a great deal to talk about. What would we do
if our families were found? Would we be taken from one
another so easily?

"They didn't want me then, why would they want
me now?" he said, looking up at me through his eyelash-
es. His voice had grown deeper over the years. It better
suited our whispering tones than my piercing voice.

"We don't know why they left us here," I lied. They
had left us because we were monsters.

"No," he said, shaking his head. I wondered, in those
days, whether he had come to be able to read my mind.
"They're the monsters if they could leave us to Diane."

"Maybe they didn't know what she was. Maybe they

really had no other choice."

"They could have let us die."

Though Lindberg's lessons were intended to have the adverse effect, somehow he had managed to harden more with time. His eyes were flint, and only very rarely did I break through them to see the boy who had cared enough to find me. Still, I knew his scars as if they were my own. So, even when he tried to shut me out, I saw right through him. And in that moment, I saw his resilience fading.

"We're stronger than that." He snorted but I pressed onward. "After they caught Lilith and me, they took us to our rooms. They kept me there, broke me until I told them it was Lilith's idea to leave. And when I gave her up, they left me this to always remind me of how I failed her."

At this point, I had rolled away from him so he faced my back. I lifted my shirt revealing the long welt that ran from my right shoulder to the left side of my lower back. Of the hundreds of wounds inflicted on me, it was the only one that had never healed. I heard the flutter in his breath when he saw it, and I imagined his disgust.

It came like the churn of air created by the slowing beat of wings. Soft and dancing, his fingers on me. They pressed to the scar as if he could draw it out of my body through his fingertips and take it upon himself. They tiptoed the length of it. His muffled sob broke into the carpet. Letting my shirt drop down again, I turned back to him and slipped my hand beneath his cheek. I drew him to face me.

"I survived that. I survive the memory of my greatest wrongdoing every day. You do too. Being here, being alive, is an unspoken refusal to be subordinate to guilt. So yes, I could have kept my mouth shut. I could have drawn out my torture until Diane got bored and let us both go. You could have fought harder to save him, taken out the guard. But we didn't do those things because we know that any other outcome than the one that came to be is impossible. Yet we're still breathing. Wishful thinking doesn't undo time, nothing does. All it does is waste the time we're granted by surviving."

His eyes were cracked by red veins then, pinked by the tears he'd shed silently while I spoke. It was then that he pressed his lips to mine and tried to convince himself I was worth living for.

We began to lie closer together in the night. It was the most innocent of intimacies, an excuse to get used to holding someone. I rested my forehead against his chest and he wrapped his arms around me. His fingers were always climbing the ladder of my scar. We didn't speak anymore. Sometimes he whispered to me but I wouldn't reply. Sometimes I was the one who whispered. He would have frantic bursts of energy when he'd kiss my forehead, dotingly, as if I was something to protect and not to be protected from.

No, wishful thinking does not undo our past. But action can end our present and wipe our futures off the map.

Chapter V.

I cannot yet build a bridge between those moments with Zach and what came next. The waters of memory rush too fast at that point in my life. They threaten to sweep me away forever if I even dare to dip a toe in. All I can say is that one morning tore up the roots of all the good that had been planted in my soul since Doctor Lindberg had arrived and, with them, whatever part of me that had told her I was willing to try.

I remember a body. Running back to my room. No one followed me. They must have known what it meant.

I dropped to my knees, felt my chest burn and heave until only my mind swam in the emptiness of my body. Hours later I awoke in the same spot. I must have passed out. The burning stench of my vomit struck my nostrils immediately, and I wouldn't have been surprised to find out that that was what finally roused me. The day had passed, night's claws sunk into the skin of the sky. The ends of my hair were crusted in the sick. I could have gone and washed it away, but I didn't. With what limited strength remained, I pushed my dresser in front of the door, crawled into bed and fell asleep.

For days I was tossed in and out of sleep by a dread that filled my dreams and reality in equal measures. I would wake with relief that whatever sick concoction my subconscious had spun out was over, only to remember with such detail those lifeless eyes. I fumbled for the bed's edge, drawing support from the sturdiness of the wooden frame before leaning over and vomiting again. In a cold sweat I fell back to my pillow, panting, and only breathed easy when sleep came. Then it started all over again.

Food came but I took no notice. It would have ended up on the floor anyways.

Eventually there was a knock too, but I could hardly

lift my head up for weakness at that point, let alone answer.

There was a great length of time, or perhaps it was brief, in which I knew I was alive but couldn't feel anything.

The next thing I remember was standing shin deep in a puddle in the dark. But it is most likely I dreamt this, for the moon shone above me yet when I looked in the puddle it didn't hold the moon's reflection. Only me. Its coolness swept over my bones until, at last, it calmed my fire, and I woke.

Let me taste the fire of your blood.

My eyelids fluttered open, my mind's voice quieted by the reigning silence of the room I found myself in. It wasn't my own, I knew that instantly. The air had a current to it, whereas mine was stagnant. I looked about me but there was no one. The room was occupied by two rows of five beds opposite one another, all of which were empty aside from the one I was in. I sat up and felt the movement in my head like a hurtling object making impact. Moaning, I lifted my palm to my forehead and felt a gentle tug on the back of my hand. A tube ran from me to an IV drip. The tape holding it down had come loose to reveal the point of entry in my skin, yellowed by a fading bruise. I hated the sight of it. Scarcely knowing what I was doing, I yanked it. I didn't even feel the pinch of the needle as it came out.

"Mallory."

Where was the voice coming from? I could never be certain as to whether it was in my head or not. I didn't know which would be worse.

A hand took one of mine in its own. It was freckled and had a light mole on the skin pulled tight across the protruding bone of the wrist. It was so fragile. That made it all the easier when I grabbed and crushed it.

I heard the scream as if through water, distant and secondary to my immediate situation. I didn't consider that the sound came from a human being and that it was a result of my inflicting pain. The bones crunched, punctured through skin. They burst out like newly erupting volcanoes, blood spilling from each knuckle. With a twist, I snapped the wrist attached to the hand my madness had disembodied. There was a thud as I let go and got out of the bed. I tried to find the ground but it kept rolling beneath me. Lifting my gaze from the undulating linoleum floor, I found his face. It was distorted, an overlay of multiplications made in my dizziness. I took hold of either side of it, hoping to make it steady.

"Help!"

They always said that.

Then I was in the dark again and the puddle was not water, but blood. I was all fire.

* * *

"It's alright, it's me, Doctor Lindberg."

She was sitting beside me when I woke and panicked at the sight of a hand holding mine. But it was smooth, not marked by aging freckles and I knew it to be hers. I snatched my hand away for fear of breaking her. *Why would I be afraid of such a thing,* I wondered.

We were back in my room. The smell of sick was gone and in its place was the scent of my recently cleaned hair, saturated with apple shampoo. There were pieces of a dream, of a man. I had broken him. No, he had split of his own accord, a too ripe peach better suited to the wildness of loose bones and blood than bound flesh.

"Where is he?" My words hardly sounded like words at all in my sore throat. A stinging pain shot up my oesophagus.

"Here, drink." She pressed a glass of water into my hand and I downed it all. It's easy to follow commands when they make you better. The sudden intake made my stomach churn, but at least I could breathe without air whistling down my throat like knives.

"Where?" I asked again.

"We're in you room," she replied.

Was that really what she thought I was asking? It wasn't what I thought I meant. What did I mean?

A broken hand in my own. That man.

"Oh, god," I moaned. I leaned over the edge of the bed, my stomach pressing boiling liquid up my throat.

"Doctor Ayers is alive. We found him right as you were about to," she faltered as I hadn't known her to before. Apparently, the act had been too gruesome for even her to speak. What had I done to that poor man? Sinking into the sheets which were made hot and damp with my sweat, I felt a strangled sob wrench itself from my chest. It burned, tearing through my fragile throat.

"I tried to kill him."

"You tried to do worse than that."

Her voice was severe, cold. When we did wrong, the faceless woman's voice always had a glinting edge to it. There was cool delight at the prospect of the punishment she would deliver and it shimmered in her every word. Doctor Lindberg would take no pleasure in my punishment, yet it must come all the same. What would she have done to me now?

"Will you kill me?"

"You think I would do that?" I raised my shaking body and found her looking at me.

"You said you wouldn't punish that girl yet she hasn't been seen for two years."

"She hasn't been seen by you, but that doesn't mean she's dead. We simply found an alternative way to carry out her education," Doctor Lindberg said, leaning forward, "When we took you to the infirmary, you were delirious. Doctor Ayers was told not to go in there on his own but he did so all the same when he heard you cry out in your sleep. That was his mistake."

"You can't blame him for what I did."

"No, but I can blame him for being careless when he knew what threat you posed. This doesn't have to mean the end for you. You can take some time away from the other students until you're better. You understand that, in your present condition, you could be a detriment to their progress."

"No." I had steadied myself and sat up straight, imitating her equal. My back ached with the effort. "You shouldn't let me near them at all."

"Mallory, this isn't something you'll never recover from," she assured me. I think that's what she was trying to do by holding my hand, as well. Reassure me. But I had felt her disbelief in the weakness of her grip.

"No, it's the last in a long list of things I can't come back from," I replied, "You found an alternative means of education for that girl. That's what I want."

"You realise that means private tuition, no other students."

"It's better that way." At best, if I remained with them, I'd fail to save them, like I did so many of my classmates. The worst case was what I was about to do to Doctor Ayers. I could feel his skull between my hands, a phantom kill, and it made me shudder. "I want my studies to be self-guided. No tutors, at least not without protection."

"Very well. Someone will check your progress once a week but you'll be left to carry out your own studies. With your capabilities, I have no doubt you'll be up to the challenge. All the facilities available to your classmates during the day, gymnasium, track field and so forth, will be open to you at night."

"Don't call them my classmates. That's what she, Diane, called them. But we weren't classmates, just inmates."

"You're not inmates anymore. No one's forcing you to stay."

"No one's giving us anywhere to go either."

"We're trying. We're looking for your family."

Family. Family was Zach. Family was Lilith, who I betrayed to the most sadistic person that Earth has spat out of its own hell fires for fear. What kind of monster would give me any more family to destroy? Instead of telling her this, I looked up at the ceiling. In the low light, I could almost imagine I was speaking to Zach.

"They didn't want me then, why would they want me now?"

She rose to leave with no reply. Was she disappointed? The door shut behind her before I could ask.

* * *

Textbooks were delivered to my room by a tall, thin man. He left the door open as he strode in wordlessly. He had probably been hoping I was still asleep, but I couldn't sleep much those days. Setting the stack down on the table, he beckoned me to join him with a sharp flick of his hand as he sat at the table.

"I'm Professor Carl Stewart and, as has been discussed with Doctor Lindberg, I'll be carrying out your private tuition."

I was scarcely listening. My hands were so eager to reach for the books that they trembled. Tightening them into fists, I pressed them against my thighs to cease the shaking. I read the titles as he went on, listing my responsibilities as a self-guided student. There was a study schedule, allotted amounts of time for each subject: History, Math, Science, English…I raised my hand as we had been taught to do in class. Not in Diane's of course. Questions were not welcomed there. Why invite more of her unwanted attention and wrath? This fear of questioning had gripped me since, and I had never used the gesture before. My voice remained inoperative in large groups anyway.

"Yes?"

"What about the practical knowledge?"

All we had learned until then was information about or skills for functioning in the world outside the Academy. Now he was speaking of subjects that, aside from general interest, didn't seem to me to have any use.

"This is what Doctor Lindberg has instructed me to give you. Perhaps she no longer believes you have a use for practical knowledge." He spoke the last two words with relish and I knew what he meant. I would never leave. Suddenly the books seemed like closed doors rather than open ones. I shrank back from the table. "As I was saying, you'll be administered weekly quizzes and monthly tests to check your progress, culminating in an end of year exam. This education is the closest simulation of the type you would find at any other school, albeit accelerated as you're quite far behind."

He said it as if it was my fault, like I had chosen this upbringing. My voice loosened itself from my tongue and went slack in my dry mouth.

"You'll be expected to maintain your physical health by making use of the Academy's facilities for an hour at least three times a week. They'll be open from six in the evening until the same hour in the morning for all my students. Yes?" His lips puckered at the sight of my hand raised once again.

"There are more students like me?"

"Of course there are. You thought Doctor Lindberg designed the course of study especially for you? It was designed from the beginning for those who were ill suited to our rehabilitating classes." Again, there were two meanings to his words, laying side by side. One was found simply in the words and the other in his tone. It was the second one that told me what he wished to say: I was a failure. I hadn't needed him to tell me that. "You'll begin your coursework tomorrow and I will visit you again at the end of the week."

He rose, regarding the cushion he'd been kneeling on as though it were a personal offence. From that day forward there was always a chair kept in my room for his visits.

"Do you teach the little girl?"

"What?" He stops just short of the door.

"The little girl who left after our first day of class. Is she one of your students?" I wished I knew her name.

"It doesn't serve one well to ask questions about things that are not their business. You would do well to remember that."

My tongue divested itself completely of my voice, which I swallowed. It tasted of nothing. How Carl Stewart had never come into the employment of Diane I have no idea. Though, I suppose, death never had need for academia.

"Very well," he huffed, shutting the door.

I slid the books across the table, wrapped them in my arms like a prayer to hold to my chest. The chart he had left dictated two hours of tomorrow morning be committed to reading for literary studies. I reached for the book atop the others, more compact but with just as many pages as any of the hardback ones beneath it. Its cover had been pure white but already I saw trace amounts of the world cluttering it. Fingerprints, dust, flattened particles of dirt. At its centre was a skull, not bone dry but waxy on the slick paper. For many, the skull is death. But bones picked clean cannot begin to encompass the concept in its entirety. A bone is something that's been made smooth by time, long soothed in the cradle of a dead man. It's a neat package viewed at the end of a comfortable length of time. Death is now. Death is flesh. It's bloated arteries slowing but not yet fully stopped, eyes losing their ability to recognise though they still see. It's the body ceasing.

I turned to the first page.

You will rejoice to hear that no disaster has accompanied the commencement of an enterprise which you have regarded with such evil forebodings.

Why leave until tomorrow what can be done today? I set to reading without changing out of my nightgown.

Four hours of my life were written on those pages and, in return, the book wrote its story in my mind as a memory. I didn't cry, I was long passed such a capability by then, but each loss was still my own. And the monster slipped away from retribution, just as Diane had, the waves sluicing over him until he turned to nothing. But that didn't mean he was gone. And I shouldn't have assumed she was either, yet I did.

Though Carl had said that the track field would be open to us at six, I lingered in my room until even the darkest traces of purple had been pulled low beyond the horizon. I hadn't wanted to risk seeing anyone else, even those who had chosen isolation such as mine. In my dresser were the black leggings and tank top fitted for jogging. I laced up my sneakers and left my room. The lights had been turned out in the halls as we had no need for them. I snaked my way through the building, past the empty gymnasium, out the double doors to the fenced-in race track. All around, the forest sipped the carbon dioxide from my breath and exhaled its ancient recipe for life.

The ground tumbled behind me as I shot along the track. The force of the movement hit me in the chest until I steadied my breaths. With my speed I made my own breeze. It grabbed with silk hands at my bare shoulders, trying to chill my skin. Yet, I burned with all the energy that had been bound inside me, only to be released when Diane commanded it so. I thought, as feet melted to miles, perhaps I could wear myself out so much that I would never be strong enough to hurt someone again. But my stamina wasn't something that could be depleted. Though I hurtled at speeds that all but blurred the forest, sipping on the well of energy within me, I didn't tire.

Dawn cracked her lazy eyelids open, blinked and yawned light into the sky. In the distance I saw what had been on the track all night without my noticing. A lone figure, keeping pace with me so as to maintain our distance. We continued like that until I knew that soon the track would no longer be ours. As I sprinted back to the pair of doors that would grant me admittance to the Academy, the cold caught up to me at last. Or that's what I told myself when I began to shiver.

So, the years came to be filled, studying, running and wandering the Academy as if there was something I was still looking for in there.

Part II

Chapter VI.

Isabrand is still poised to attack when I finish speaking. There are moments, when I tell him of the little girl or Diane, that I think he might try to slit my neck, clip the throat of elucidation. As much as I can hardly bear to tell of it, he cannot stand to hear of the life I was left to when we were separated. As if I drew the short straw. Who left those scars on your cheek, brother, the two curls of whiteness that underline the corner of your eye?

Of course, he makes no such threatening move towards me. The fear he pretends not to notice stays his hand. When he thought me an illusion there was no betrayal of panic on his face; he was ready to kill me because we're used to people trying to kill us. Survival instincts overtake morals more often than we care to admit. The prospect of me being exactly who he came looking for, however, has terrified him. Am I not what he hoped to find? Or is it that, against better judgement, he had hoped he'd find a happier picture than the one I've just unfolded?

He's heard of the Academy, no doubt. It's notorious and some of the monsters it created even more so. Does he see that when he looks at me? As if I would lay a hand on him.

The past sits, stuffed into the gap years apart has left between us. I have been calculating in what I've divulged. There's a great deal he doesn't need to know and even more that I am not ready to tell. But underneath all these stories lies the call made unanimously by my words: I am your sister and the hundred other things that have happened to me since that last day we spent together, playing by the river. I don't mention that day though. I can already read his guilt regarding what came to pass that afternoon that changed everything.

He rocks back and forth slightly on his feet, inclining towards me only to pull away. I want to catch him, hold him steady but that knife in his hand gets between thoughts of comfort and my ability to act on them. His eyes are fixed on the box I'm holding.

"It's different," he says, gesturing to it. Then he inhales deeply, as if that first act of speech, disconnected from all I've said, has enabled him to gather the energy to say more. "How did you end up at the Academy after I left?"

"Our mother," I reply. The relief brought by answering a question, comparatively so much simpler than all those he could ask, is welcome. But of course, families are never that simple.

"That bitch."

Our mother, that bitch. Those would be synonymous to Isabrand after she chose me over him. In fact, she never chose him at all. Not even in those years before she could imagine me.

"Isabrand," I say.

His name has more effect on him than any spell I could cast. His eyes widen, are able to meet mine without fear. Then the clarity of our familial connection dissolves back into the overwhelming confusion of our reunion, and he shakes his head. The dagger disappears back into his coat and he puts his hands in his pockets.

"Let's not talk about her. I'm starving, is the Thai place down the street any good?"

"The best."

Without turning from him, I set the box on the sofa and grab my coat off the back of one of the dining table chairs. I move toward the door but he comes between me and it, all while maintaining a safe distance. Perhaps he's changed his mind. But he makes no movement to take his knife from his pocket again.

"Um Mallory, you might want to change."

I glance down at myself, but already I know he's referring to the blood on my sweater. In my rush to pack I have completely forgotten about it. No wonder he pulled a knife when he first came in. But this draws my mind to another pressing matter. The suitcase in my bedroom isn't packed yet and the others will be here to meet me in an hour. How will I begin to explain Isabrand to them? I haven't told anyone about him yet, not even Kyle. Worse yet, how will I explain them to Isabrand? If I tell him too much too fast, the existing fault lines of our relationship will give way. And I'm not willing to lose him so soon.

"I'll be right back."

My bedroom is small, mostly occupied by a mattress on which lies the completely empty second suitcase. Through the window I can see the light is out in the apartment across the alley. As I shirk my sweater, I consider what this might mean. Either someone is dead, or someone is coming to murder me. Or both. But there's no time to worry about that now. That assassin can wait; the one in my living room is all that matters.

I open my cupboard and the first thing I see is the camel-coloured turtleneck Inerea gave me. It's swinging gently on its hanger as if to beckon me, despite the stillness of everything else, including my heart. After that summer, there were so many things I had to shelve to survive. I finger the hem, the loose thread that I use as an excuse not to wear it. It's warm in my hand and I feel that unwelcome sting in my eyes. Did Isabrand ever meet Inerea before he was sent away? I doubt it. Inerea would never have stopped looking for him if she had known about him. Just one of the many things our mother lied about to Inerea, just another of the many people she lied to. It was usually Isabrand and I on both accounts, so this isn't surprising. No wonder Isabrand calls her a bitch. I pull the sweater over my head.

I take this moment, sheltered from his gaze by the open cupboard door, to slip my phone from my back pocket. I need time, though I know asking the others for an hour was already more than we can afford. Any more might cost my life, especially given my present company. The screen lights up, three texts unanswered. My thumb hovers over the second down. I know I'm not supposed to reply to him but the desire to do so is almost impossible to resist. I busy myself texting Kyle instead.

Need two hours, something's come up. All's well.

I put the phone back in my pocket and close the doors on the clothes I should be cramming into that suitcase as fast as I can. But I was never able to prioritise when it came to Isabrand's whims. That's what got me killed in the first place.

From the doorway I observe him. He's guarded even when he thinks he's alone, hiding from himself. Still, he gives his curiosity away by letting his eyes rove over the entire room. What he makes of what he sees I cannot tell. I will have to be an open book to him before he'll give even the smallest part of himself away. When he hears me enter the room, he starts towards the door without looking up. I lock up slowly, trying to keep my hand steady by tightening my grip on the keys until they dig into my palm. I can hear Ellie's two dogs barking, waiting for her to return. Usually, I take care of them when she's away, but today's been a busy day. I'll miss them when I leave.

It's warmer outside than when I was out earlier, but that could have been the chill of knowing that it would be the last time I returned to my apartment. I leave my coat draped over my arm; the restaurant is only a few doors down and it's always stuffy in the small, overcrowded space. Luckily, it's late enough that we've missed the dinner time rush. I'm not sure what two estranged siblings waiting in line for a table would talk about. My limited social experiences haven't exactly prepared me for this. I do, however, know that every conversation is made easier by food. Kyle taught me that. I glance at my phone screen, but he hasn't texted me back. Still that second notification nags me.

We're seated by the window, far from the counter behind which all three of the waiters have crammed themselves. They pay no attention to us and I'm thankful for the anonymity appearing to be a young couple affords us. Isabrand unfolds the laminate flaps of the menu, slouching into his seat as if to be absorbed by it. He doesn't seem to have any intention of speaking first this time.

"How did you know where I live?" I ask.

"I looked up your address through your university's student database when I found out you were…are alive. They don't protect their student data very well."

"I think their locks are to guard against run of the mill breaking and entering, not that of the supernatural." He shrugs off my comment.

"Anyway, I didn't really have a good reason to drop by until my bosses put a hit out on you."

"I get that a lot. Duck Pad Thai, please."

Isabrand is temporarily confused by the latter statement until he spots the waiter who's just appeared by his elbow. It's not like someone such as Isabrand to be caught off guard like that. Whatever composure he's regained since we left the apartment is clearly only surface deep, and it's taking so much of his focus that he's distracted.

I glance out the window as Isabrand looks through the menu hastily. By now all manner of creatures will know we're together, and I can think of two dozen off the top of my head who won't like it. Any one of the people out on the streets, seen and unseen, might have been sent to keep us apart. If Isabrand's not on his guard, he might get hurt. I tap my leg where I had a holster strapped only thirty minutes before. I left it in my suitcase, but that doesn't matter. I won't let anyone near Isabrand, even if I have to expose us. Human memories are erased easily enough, I tell myself, but the hardening lump in my throat tells me I won't be able to do that to the wait staff.

"I'll have the same as her," Isabrand says to the waiter, passing our menus over his shoulder. He waits until the man scratches our order onto his notepad and leaves before speaking again. "You don't seem concerned that someone sent me to kill you."

"Like I said, I get that a lot." I shrug, feigning insouciance as he does. Is this what family resemblance looks like? Two people with the same colour eyes unable to look at one another, slouched in chairs. How underwhelming.

"So much in common." For a moment I think he's read my mind, but am soothed by the thought that we're not the kind of beasts that can do that. "You like Thai food, I like Thai food. You have people trying to kill you, I've been asked to kill you."

"I don't think that would fit on a tote bag. Maybe we can get t-shirts," I suggest.

"I'm pretty sure there's a store in Soho that already prints those."

"No, it's in Brooklyn, haven of the graphic tee." He snorts, staring down at his hands intertwined in his lap.

"And here I thought all they taught you at the Academy was misery 101."

"Common misconception. We took the advanced course as well," I say. He smiles, a mirror image of mine were it not for the single dimple on his left cheek. Like that he looks so very like his father. That recognition grips me and twists my stomach until I have to look away. "Do you have any intention of following orders?"

I thought I knew the answer was no, but as the words

leave my lips, I know it's a genuine question. One he's still asking himself.

"Not sure yet."

"It's a big decision to make on an empty stomach."

"That's the truth. Why don't you tell me the rest then, to pass the time," he suggests, just as our food arrives.

"The rest of what?"

"Of the touching tale you started in the apartment. How you ended up in New York. Tell me what I missed little sis."

His glibness cuts through the sense of security familiarity had lulled me into. There's mockery saturating each syllable. *Little sis.* I dig my finger nails into my leg. I tell myself he's only being like this to reassert the predatory dominance that he's used to and will put him at ease. This must be how he toys with his victims. His eyes are so full of hunger, ready to devour me. He reminds me so much of his father and it terrifies me.

"Okay, I'll tell you."

He grins, an unsettling act of expressiveness on his closed off face, and turns his attention to his plate.

"Noutsumar letai kokku ni saviski isuazko'caz makun," I whisper beneath the roar of a passing truck. I feel the hilt of my dagger shimmer into existence within my grip as the spell unravels itself from my tongue, my blood. I would die for my brother. But right now, that's not who Isabrand is. He is as much what his employers made him as I am what Diane made me.

Chapter VII.

My reality is equal parts sentience and perception, hallucinations and dreams. They overlap all the time.

None of the children would look towards my window as they were marched across the courtyard in a neat line. Of course, their gazes would shift aimlessly, catching a peak of it in their peripheral. But then, as though a spirit had painted its frightful face on the opaque glass, terror flared in their eyes and they would stare straight ahead until their irises dulled once more. Wherever the faceless woman was having them taken was not so bad as what was behind that window: me. We expected cruelty from her, but there are ways only someone we trust can hurt us. That was why she enjoyed turning us against each other so much. She was a trickster lighthouse, misguiding us with notions of salvation until we crashed, obliterating the ones we loved, who she had placed in our path under the cover of the deceptive dark. Yet we always fell for it, and we never seemed to realise that it was her fault.

Sitting by the window, I would press my hand to the stone wall as if the other children's footsteps might reverberate through the earth and into the foundations of the building. But the walls gave off nothing except a feeling so cold it seemed as though it might burn my skin. Everything was just out of reach: other people, the wind, a glimpse of the sky. It was all on the other side of that glass I stared out of.

Such were the days following our attempted escape of the Academy. After my beating, I wasn't brought out for any classes or assignments, which was both a blessing and a terror. I had expected to be killed after I turned Lilith in. Never had I really believed my confession would afford me any clemency, and I was right. It ended up being the most painful part of mine and Lilith's punishment, and a self-inflicted wound. But instead of an end I was granted solitude that seemed a new torture in itself.

Human shapes shifted in and out of my room on occasion. But I knew they could not possibly be human, else they would not go about cleaning as if those were not blood stains they scrubbed from the floor, or a child's body they slung over their shoulders so unceremoniously. None of their presences made me feel any less lonely. Before, the thought of Lilith would be enough to make those hours survivable. But such a thought only made me feel more like an open wound.

I tried to imagine a family in her place but couldn't conjure anything. I assumed I had parents, but we were never formally introduced. They were concepts, shadowy figures who had sent me to this place as soon as they could. I never had the chance to be their daughter so I thought of myself as their creation. This dissociation from any form of a nurturing relationship comforted me and helped me begin to close myself. I had taught myself to hate every imaginable form of the people who had sent me to be enshrined in this room. But I began to understand that they must have seen back then the monster I revealed myself to be. Could I begrudge them a life free of that?

There was one other person, without whose kindness I would likely have gone completely numb: my caretaker. She came to ready me for class in the morning, though now she would simply be getting me dressed to sit in my room. She used to sing to me, and it was the only music I ever heard during those times. She would brush my hair out and braid a crown neatly around the back of my head. That was always the same, as all the girls wore their hair like that so long as we hadn't had our hair shaved off recently. But her melodies were rarely repeated. They cracked the monotony with their sweetness. I never replied to her soft songs, but I don't think her intention was to draw me out with them. They were a blanket of care with which she could measure how I was feeling.

Saturdays were my favourite. She repeated the same song every Saturday, one she had sung to me for so long it preceded any other memory. The door would crack open and, even though I didn't smile, I knew she could sense my happiness. My body leaned towards her of its own accord as if she were sunlight itself. I remembered the first day she came after I tried to run away, and dream of it often. It is not the sort of dream in which I observed from the periphery. My present conscious exists within the same body as my younger self, unable to control motor functions.

There was a knock on the door and the lock turned but I didn't stir from my seated position at the table. I had been sitting there for a couple of hours in my nightgown. I didn't think to kneel despite my dress. Legs crossed, fingers interlaced as shackles around one another, I had been awaiting her in the confines of my mind. The other children wouldn't pass through the courtyard for some time.

"Good morning little angel," she said, her voice all warmth and fluid curves. There were no edges to her on which I might snag myself. "I missed you."

My heart was eagerly waiting; it jumped at her words as if they were someone long lost and well known, come home at last. It was selfish to indulge in the relief her kindness brought, when I knew I didn't deserve it, but I could not help it. Her love was a parent's, given even when it was undeserved. She took my hand and led me to the adjoining bathroom. She ran the bath, holding two fingers under the tap until it was warm enough. While it filled, she pulled my nightgown over my head and folded it as carefully as if she was going to put it back in my dresser, though it was bound for the wash.

"Carefully," she said, as she did every day, helping me into the tub. I lowered myself until the warm water kissed me all the way to my collarbones. There was no hair for her to wash, just a shadow of the small strands beginning to grow. She lathered her hands in soap then began to scrub my arm.

"What should I sing today? Ah, but it's Saturday, how silly of me to ask." She moved around the other side of the bath. The moment she lifted my arm, cradling my hand in hers, her voice changed. It gathered air and sweetened it like the fragrance of a delicate flower.

"We're so beautifully human, so beautifully pure
unknown to mankind, hidden in their folklore.
They like to tell stories about all their worries
and if they could go back in time, they would unwind
the mistakes they made that led to the future,
cold and unyielding, what's become of your feelings?
Time can't you reverse, take back your wicked curse?
I don't know what we've done that's left us on the run.
But I won't stand for this, no we won't take this.
It's not in our nature to be bound or lost,
it's not in our nature to let ourselves be double crossed.
Beautifully human, so beautifully human we are."

She had gone around behind me and stopped, three verses left to be sung. I wanted to urge her to finish. Maybe if she had I could remember the words so long lost. Instead, she swept her hand along my back. I fell still as her hand came to rest on my new scar, then fell away. Minutes passed but she did not stir from behind me. I had forgotten the scar Diane had left on me. Of all the things that had happened, it hardly seemed important. I swam back from my state of shock, returning to my senses, and that was when I heard her.

You can always tell the difference between those who cry because they are sad and those who simply want attention. While others sob to be heard and seen, ones who are truly afflicted by sadness cry as quietly as they can, into their hands or a pillow, or through stifled gasps that only occasionally break their silence. Listening to the woman who had shown me genuine, unfailing kindness, who had never faltered in her happiness, I could recognise her pain. The me who dreams this is all claws, trying to tear its way out and hold her. The me who dreams this knows what sort of suffering it takes to make a person cry like that. A chord had snapped somewhere in her heart, pulled by cruel hands. I felt a warm tear land on the back of my neck.

"I'm so sorry, little angel," she breathed. I felt the warmth of her fingers radiate on my back as she reached, as if to wipe the scar away, but she hesitated just shy of touching me. "So very sorry."

Her words came and her tears followed, sliding onto my neck as she leaned over me. For the first time since I had lost Lilith, the black core that hung in my hollow chest stirred. It was hard as stone, yet it cracked and unfurled ever so slightly to hear her cry. What fell away was only one flake of the rock that encased my heart, but the weight it bore as it sunk sent a shock running through my veins to my limbs. Animated by the effusion of feeling from within me, my arms acted on their own accord and I turned to embrace her, sloshing water on the floor. A wavy curtain of brown hair fell around my face. I bowed my head and rested it on her collar bone, out of reach of her warm, shaky breaths. I felt each one rattle up from her lungs, a train shaking the earth as it flashed by.

"Please forgive me," she whispered, wrapping her arms around me. "I've left you alone so long."

"It's alright."

I heard her breath stop for a moment, shocked to hear a monster's voice and find it so quiet. Perhaps she had expected a knot of growls, rooted in my throat. But not all beasts roar. Sometimes silence is all the better to sneak up and slit throats with.

"I don't feel alone when you're here."

Her arms were gone from my back and she began to pull away. The mass of black rock within my chest started to pound. I'd scared her. Would she, like all the others who had come and gone, move like a shadow? The thought of her face made vacant by apathy, passing over me with a sliding glance that wouldn't acknowledge my presence, covered my emptiness like a shell. I leaned back and looked up to find her smiling.

"I wish I could be with you always. You're so brave. I never want you to forget that, no matter who tells you otherwise."

I nodded, even though she was wrong. How could I be brave when it was fear that chained my tongue down, rendering me unable to thank her? It was fear, also, that held me prisoner in this room, not some wooden door. Lilith had been the bravery that finally allowed me to realise that. Without her, I was trapped.

My caretaker understood my silence. She read it like a passage memorised from a book, scarcely needing to skim the words to know the meaning. Lifting my chin so our eyes met once more, she bound me in my place, unable to redirect my gaze. Her eyes were mismatched, one emerald and the other the shade of the clean earth outside.

"It isn't fair, but you can never depend on anyone else to save you. No one can hurt you, so long as you stand up for yourself. After all, you cannot burn flames and you cannot make fire afraid."

In the moment before she stood up, I believed her. But that belief was swiftly snatched from me. Her soft hand was gone from beneath my chin. She took the folded nightgown and left me in the lukewarm water. I watched her leave, then turned to stare at the white tile across from me. We were never meant to be left unattended in the bath. I wonder, looking back, if she was giving me a way out, a way to drown the flames she claimed I had.

She never came back. The next morning a new caretaker came to my room. She didn't say where the other had gone and I could not ask. She was cruel in her silence and my heart was wrapped once more in loneliness. I told myself I couldn't forgive her for leaving me behind but that was a lie. I had long known she didn't belong in such a place as this. She was too gentle and well-intentioned. But there were many things she had lied about as well. For one thing, of the two of us, I was never the angel.

This dream of the past dissolves, and my conscious slips from my younger body into an old haunting of my mind.

"Don't cry, don't cry. It will be over soon," she whispers, smoothing the baby hairs at my hairline. They spring back up as soon as her hand is gone so she repeats the action over and over.

Blood. It soaks my clothes and the arms holding me. It consumes my every thought. I scrub them clean only to have my hands bleed over them with the effort.

"You must be quiet. He'll find us."

The words are like a reprimand, but the tone is pleading for my sake. It's me, not herself, she wants to keep safe. If I could only turn to look at her, maybe then I could stay calm. But I know I will never see her face. I have never seen it in all the times I've dreamt this dream.

I am determined not to disappoint her this time, because I know the consequences for her if I do. Outside our cramped hiding space, the silence is cracked beneath the whip of a cackle. It begins like a scratchy cough then bubbles up. Our breaths cease to nothing.

"Come out Regan. Let's not play games anymore," a voice calls. It would be pleasant, deep and warm, were it not for the hissing undertone, as if the voice were drowning in the wetness of its owner's throat. Despite knowing better, I lean closer to the sliver of a gap between the doors of the cupboard we're in.

The hunched over figure in front of me looks as mangled as the corpses that scatter the floor. It rolls its shoulders back slowly, righting itself in a fluid, serpentine movement. A sword gleams under the light the red moon emanates through the window. Even the night sky is drenched in the massacre. From the blade come gouts, thick and steady. Blood. Why is it everywhere? The wood floors are saturated with boiling pools of it, spat from split bodies.

A cry of panic rises from the other side of the room. I turn in time to see someone attempt to scramble to their feet. They claw their way upright, grabbing on to a counter for support. But as soon as they let go, they slip, their hands and feet slick with the red liquid. The figure is a small hunted animal, bound to the same fate as all but one in this house. It knows as much, making no further attempts to escape. It lays still, enacting the death it knows will come. The looming man, drawn to his full height, throws his head back laughing with such violence I think he might break his own neck. He lunges forward.

I shut my eyes but there is nothing to stop me from hearing the sickening sound of flesh being pierced. I've come to know it so well this night. The whimpering stops. Unable to help myself, I look again as the limp body slides off the blade. It makes a wet thud as it hits the floor. The man raises the sword in front of his face, his eyes reflecting its glimmering red, his lips still parted from laughing. He runs his tongue along its flat, gleaming surface, then curls his rouged lips back in a smile.

"Regan," he says, "I'm bored now. Everyone else is dead. Please won't you come out. I'd quite enjoy killing you too."

I don't think the word 'enjoy' does justice to the pleasure he would take in the act. He turns toward us without knowing he does so. One foot crossing steadily in front of the other like a feline moving towards prey, he moves with grace amongst the corpses he's dropped like stones. Still, there is measurable caution in his movement. Just because he has the sword, does not mean he is the only thing to be feared. Regan holds me to her, her chest swelling against my back with each shallow breath. There's power in her too. But he is what I fear, and the erratic beating of my heart reminds me of this. He turns back towards the window, walking away.

"Let me taste the fire of your blood."

I gasp.

Regan's hand moves swiftly to cover my mouth, but it's too late. His eyes take their time tracking the small sound, revelling in the suspense. There's no amount of time he could take that would be enough for us to escape. Forgetting his calculated movements, he bounds over two of the bodies heaped atop one another. Their limbs are an indistinguishable tangle and I'm certain not all of them are still attached to the bodies. He's taken his murderous art to another level.

He lands, crouched a few feet from our hiding place, then lifts his head. I see his face, one I always try to remember, only to wake to forgetfulness. His wild mane of hair casts a shadow but I see the distinct shape of his features where the moon's light catches their edges. His lips are cracked, pink crevices in a red range. As a drop of blood rolls from the corner of his mouth, his tongue slivers out, all too eager to catch it. He's so close I can see the glistening saliva on his tongue when he does so. His eyes are such a shade of gold they make me think of a cat or a serpent.

"Silly Regan. You always did like hide and seek when we were little. You would have done well to remember I always found you," he says, righting himself. The arms around me squeeze me tight once more while he speaks.

"Goodbye. Be strong for me," she breathes in my ear.

She sets me aside, safely hidden behind the right door of the cupboard, before pushing the left one open with the bottom of her foot. As she slides forward, the moon light strikes her face, but it is just beyond my view. She nudges it shut with the back of her leg, feigning stumbling out. I know this is her last act to protect me. I crawl back to the gap and peer through. He freezes in place as she unfolds herself, drawing her spine straight.

"It looks like you've finally learned to be obedient. Did our last meeting teach you that?" She winces at his words. His eyes pull her strength apart, see parts of her she doesn't want anyone to know. Her fear is animalistic, a creature that's been beaten down.

"I will never kneel to you."

"No? But I'm sure you look so pretty on your knees." Then he swoops forward.

I know to look away. I have seen this moment so many times and I know what comes next is the end of everything good. But my eyes don't move because I can never look away from the sacrifice she is making for me.

Her body goes rigid as the blade pierces her abdomen. As she begins to fall to her knees, he towers over her, his hand on the small of her back to ease her to the ground. He doesn't withdraw the sword. The gravity of it in her body is all that is keeping his hand steady while the rest of him shakes. Then she goes limp and her head lolls backwards like a doll. Even in death she draws away from him.

He moans, a sound loud enough to cover my own whimper. I don't think it would reach him through his sadness anyway. Letting go of the sword, he cups his hand around the back of her head as he kneels and pulls her to him. His face disappears in her hair. He nuzzles her neck as if he is trying to bore into her skin. Violence is what it's always taken for him to get close to her.

The firmament rattles as he drops her with a roar. His eyes are burning fires that put the sun's fury to shame. But then his voice crumbles, shifting once again to that maddening laughter. I cover my ears, hoping if I can block it out this time, it won't follow me into my waking hours. It bleeds through my hands and seeps into my mind.

His body begins to contort. He falls forward over her crumbled form, heaving with his whole body and digging his fingers into the floor. His shoulders pop backwards, jerking him up with the force of the transformation. Bones snap. He lifts a hand to his face to watch, curling his fingers that now seem more like claws. No, not seem. They are. The whites of his eyes, pink in the moons red gaze, turn a violent shade of vermillion and the rest of his body follows suit until it seems blood seeps through his pores to colour his skin. He falls onto his elbow with his face pressed to the floor, torn between hysteria and screams of pain. His body continues in its unnatural buckling, moving further from a human form and growing as it does. The ceiling shudders, attempting to accommodate his stature, but it only takes a few seconds of flexing his back like a cat before the strain rips the roof apart. The air is clotted grey with debris but his new body shines, encased in scales like armour made of massive rubies to protect the fragile human within. Shaking the ceiling rubble from his back, he flicks his large arrowhead tail to smash open the wall.

Bricks and mortar pour down the side of the house like a waterfall. I yelp, bracing myself against the side of the cupboard. His movement is swift for a beast so large. He blinks, a moist film sliding over his eye, followed by his eyelid. Then it's open again and he's looking directly as my hiding place. He snorts, burning the icy air to steam. I can feel the warmth all the way from here. Then a call goes up in the night. He lets out an unearthly roar that sends tremors through the very foundations of the house, before launching himself into the open sky. His wings unfurl and he dips before soaring upwards, out of sight.

My body is thrown forward, as if only this physical motion could pull me from my nightmare. Sometimes I fear it is and, if my body were to forget that, I would be lost in the blood and fire of my dreams. My clammy hands twist the fabric of my sheets. Sheets. The dresser. The sconce.

It is not your fault.

I lower my chin to my chest. I don't believe that, but it grounds me long enough that I become afraid and am unable to run to the arms of death. Pushing the covers from my burning body, I find I'm shaking. The fitted sheet adheres to my sweaty legs so I peel myself out of bed. The air is colder outside of the alcove my bed is nestled in, but it does little in the way of cooling my nightmare boiled blood. Crossing the room, I press my forehead to the window's winter chilled pane and fog it with my breath. A sign I'm no longer dreaming. It's quiet out in the courtyard, the one I watched those children walk through while I was locked away, but I do not fear silence as I do not fear the dark. The latter is merely the unknown in its most frequent form and I have been conditioned to not be afraid of such things. It is the known, to be known, bright lights and loud noises, that are to be feared.

The sun has long since vanished, handing her chariot over to the moon. It leaves my chest so cold that I feel weak and helpless in its presence. As if I didn't already feel that way enough all on my own. I wonder why others fear the dark when there is something so much brighter and colder out there, always watching. A cyclopean eye, bereft of an iris' colour or a pupil's darkness in the milky cataract blindness. Tiresias was blind yet a prophet, and to see the future can be more terrifying than to see all of what happens now on Earth.

I draw away from my window and dress myself in my running clothes. I drop the sweat drenched night-gown in the laundry hamper by the door. The invulner-able air hangs heavy all around me as I make my way to the track. I fear its weight less than a conversation with anyone. Silence cannot lie, it only gives your mind time for introspection. Though that can be equally dangerous. The lies we tell ourselves are the ones we are most likely to believe.

Outside the Academy, the air is so icy it cools me completely. I see that hooded figure on the track in the distance, as it has been every night since the first I came out. Occasionally I have seen someone else through the vast windows of the gymnasium, but we are the only of Carl's students who use the outdoor running track. Whether the others prefer the indoors or are afraid of us I don't know. I haven't been close enough to ask them.

I wait until my companion is on the opposite side of the track before setting out. I match his pace perfectly. My dream sill has footholds on my reality; how can it not when I've had it so many times it feels as much of a daily ritual as brushing my teeth? I bite the inside of my cheeks, needing the discomfort to remind myself of physical pain

that staves off complete numbness. I have not felt suffering's corporeal hand in years and that is something to be
thankful for. I have felt it in other ways though. Its hand
is always around my heart, squeezing at it with the force
of memories until I cannot breathe. I pick up speed, hoping to leave my thoughts in the dust, and my companion
follows suit. We orbit one another, simultaneously chasing
and running away.

No, I do not fear the silence, just the thoughts it
brings.

Chapter VIII.

The man who watches over me while I take my test is not Professor Stewart. This guard has a gun in a holster on his hip and his hand never leaves it. Nor does the look of contempt leave his face. The former is a precaution I requested. It's been years since Doctor Ayers but if I were to ever lose control again, the guard would be able to drop me from a safe distance without killing me. But panic could make him slip. It could also be the perfect cover to hide an intentional kill. I think the same thought has crossed the guard's mind on occasion.

The faceless woman used to say that guns are impersonal. They made the act easier on the killer because there was no need to be so close to the person rendered a corpse. There doesn't have to be a huge mess either if you shoot point blank. She liked the mess; blood sends a message. Guns almost always spelled death and she preferred torturing, maiming, and scars. She would never let any of the guards use guns, though I'm sure they enjoyed using their hands anyways.

I scrawl out the last sentence of the short essay, reading it through once, before setting my pencil down. This is my wordless signal that I've finished; almost all of my minimal social interactions are made up of such gestures. The guard leaves his post as unwillingly as though he is magnetically bonded to it. Avoiding looking at me as I do him, he collects the test to take to Professor Stewart, who will come in an hour. He'll discuss my results and errors, though there never are any, much to his chagrin I suspect. He always seems to have particular difficulty saying I've received full marks though any reprimand during our lessons regarding my handwriting or posture comes with ease. How can he expect me to make a mistake when all I do is study? I have always taken the fluid words from pages or mouths and turned their facts to crystal in my memory.

The man with the gun closes the door behind him but doesn't lock it. He may as well as I'm not going anywhere. At least then he could let his hand fall from the gun as he walks away. He wouldn't have to worry that something in me has snapped and I've decided to tear his throat out. But locking doors is against Doctor Lindberg's policy. I asked her if they would do it as another precaution but she refused. It would remove the illusion of being able to leave. My words, her unspoken thought.

Since the day I told her I wanted no part in her classes or rehabilitation, I haven't seen Doctor Lindberg. I can't blame her, after what I did. She said she didn't think it was my fault but I believe she would have said whatever she thought might encourage me to come back to class with the other students. I don't think she could subject herself or me to the false trust she would have tried to maintain in my presence. We were both too smart to know trust was a possibility between us.

None of her associates look at me the same after Doctor Ayers, if they look at me at all. Even Anya, who had called me sweetie and smiled, now only stares at her own hands when she brings me my food, as if a stern look could will them to stop trembling. It doesn't help that I never speak, not even to say thank you. I'm just a statue they wait upon. Without Zach to confide in, my voice has fallen into disuse. Professor Stewart is the only person I interact with and he rarely leaves me the space to say anything. I have seen the way his nostrils flare and his eyebrows dip in disgust whenever I ask questions. Over time we wordlessly reinstate Diane's policy not to ask questions.

I feel tight in my skin, sitting there waiting. I wish Carl would hurry, though I know the monthly test days mean longer waiting periods than quiz days. But with my test results comes my new workload and coursebooks. Though the weekend is supposed to be leisure time, that is better suited to those in the Academy who have managed to emulate friendship and want to spend times in groups so they can forget the isolating singularity of their existences. All I want is the next book I will be given for my literature studies. I want the opportunity to comb through my growing catalogue of books and compare themes and characters. And when I've finished, I'll savour all the rest of my work just as much, because if I don't convince myself it's worthwhile and enjoyable, I'll go mad.

There's a perfunctory knock on the door. So soon? It can't have been more than a few minutes since the guard left. But it's not Professor Stewart. He always raps twice, briskly, a gesture of impatience. The door opens and the light of the hall bleeds into my room, which I keep lowly lit.

"Hello Mallory."

It's been a few years but they've drawn no new lines on her face. Her hair retains its metallic sheen, turning whatever grey hairs she may have grown silver. Her bun peeks over the crown of her head and I wonder whether she's plagued by a perennial headache from the sheer tension of her hair being drawn as tight as bow strings across her scalp.

"Doctor Lindberg."

She sweeps in, dismissing the man with the gun who has just returned from delivering my test to the professor. I cannot tell if he's pleased to be rid of me or disappointed at losing the opportunity to shoot me. As for myself, I'm glad to see him gone. Behind Doctor Lindberg is a tall, lean figure, all pale skin cast over by blue shadows of his dark hair. He's unlike any of the other people I've ever seen working for her. To begin with, he appears far too

young to have been working for her when she came here
five years ago. For another, though he doesn't greet me
with words, he smiles at me. My gaze darts from his face,
the intimacy of eye contact burning fear in my chest. I'm
so used to being avoided or, if acknowledged, reviled. His
gesture of goodwill makes me want to break my bones
and fold into myself.

"You've made good progress since we last spoke,"
she says, as if it was a matter of weeks.

Have I? It seems to me I'm exactly where she left
me three years ago, only even more reclusive, if that's
possible.

"You've not only caught up with public school curriculum for students of your age but surpassed those taught
at elite schools as well as some universities."

"Have I."

The words have a delayed release from my brain to
mouth. They're like cardboard, failing to convey any sub-
text or even the intonation of the question I intend them
to be. I scarcely know what she's talking about anyway, I
just feel I need to say something or else she'll stop speaking and I'll never know why she came.

"I can't say I'm surprised." Her companion shuts
the door behind them and follows her as she seats herself
across from me. His proximity at the side of the table
between us makes me slightly nauseous. "We've always
expected such success from you."

"Three years is a long time to wait just so you could
say you told me so."

I don't know where the bite in my voice comes from
but it shrivels as soon as I've spoken. Still, I feel its root
beside my heart, forcing it to beat faster.

"That's not why I came, Mallory. I wouldn't waste
our time like that."

What then? Why come now, and with this stranger

who smiles rather than flinching at the sight of me, but does not speak? Does she believe that if she was right about my intellectual capabilities, she was right to believe I would someday choose companionship over isolation? Perhaps that's why he's here, to act as a recipient of a false and practiced friendship. If that's the case, Doctor Lindberg will find herself wrong. The vehemence in my voice a moment ago is proof of that. Her eyes are blank, refusing to give intention or emotion away, and it only makes me more upset. The nausea converts to acid, spitting up anger.

"So, you've come to tell me I've successfully progressed to the next stage of my education."

"Something like that, yes," she replies.

"Is this your idea of education, how you rehabilitate your students? Do you have them sit in a circle and practice friendship in that hopes that, if you find their families, if they leave, they won't be lonely? We will always be alone, no matter how much family or how many friends you surround us with. We are here because those same people spat us out. Why would we be any less miserable around them?"

It's as if my throat is parched for speech, gasping at last for relief and taking its fill. My uncommon effusion of words stirs her from stoicism. She exchanges a look with her companion, who lowers his head so I cannot make out his face or expression.

"Mallory," she starts, but I shake my head.

"Those people you think you're helping by finding their families, you're destroying them. All they have, all any of us have, is the illusion of a family. An ideal utterly impossible but soothing, which you take away when you confront them with reality."

"Would you have me lie to them then? Would you choose for them a life of self-deluding?"

"If it kept them from killing themselves."

There it hangs, an accusation I never intended to make. The last time we spoke, my mind was too undone to know it blamed her for the dead body that sent me spiralling. Not having to see her allowed me to pack that thought away, but the years only compounded a loathing I did not know myself capable of. Now it springs out of its box, saturates my bones and my blood with fury at the woman across from me. Diane might have inflicted whatever torture she wanted on us, but it was expected of her. Disappointment can breed more resentment than fear.

"Mallory, I know it is easier for you to blame me-"

"When you came here, you said you were here to help. You should have saved him."

None of us speak but the room is far from silent. It screams with everything that has happened over the past seventeen years and all she's been made guilty of by what's implied but unspoken. Doctor Lindberg, who has always been reserved and unflappable, now seems only to be able to look anywhere other than at me. The young man, however, stares at me, drawn out of the reclusiveness he adopted the moment he sat down. Another indicator that he is not part of the Academy; any of Doctor Lindberg's men would have jumped to her defence by now. He is an outsider, brought for some other purpose. But if he's not a part of her rehabilitation classes as I thought, who is he? I meet his gaze, still burning with the ferocity of my anger towards Doctor Lindberg, until even he breaks under it. He turns back to her.

"Perhaps we should move on to why we're here?" he suggests, his voice scarcely more than a whisper.

"Yes, perhaps…Mallory I can't convince you."

She stops herself and sighs, then reverts to her usual blank expression. It is not made of an absence of emotion as I had thought, however, but of sheer exhaustion. She works herself endlessly to do what she believes is right, only to be berated by one of the people she seeks to help. I pity her, and it is a strange feeling. I have had cause to be sad, heartbroken even, for others, but never have I felt benevolent pity.

"We found them."

She says it as if these three words supply perfect clarity, but, instead, they leak confusion.

"Who?"

The pair exchange another look, and I feel my muscles tense. The look on their faces is so much like the one two of Diane's less willing guards would exchange before carrying out her spiteful orders. Has my outburst finally cost me the limited freedom I have in this room?

"Your family," she replies, as if after seventeen years of not knowing them, it should be the most obvious thing to come out of her mouth.

She speaks reluctantly, still not looking at me as she does so. Her words are ice, freezing rationality. They wash away the self-possession I held in my anger, leaving me vulnerable to a part of me I haven't let take control since I last saw Lilith. From amongst the cracks in the glacier of my thoughts purrs the prehistoric creature of self-preservation that I have long kept quiet with monotony. It rolls back its shoulders and flexes its muscles, made hard from years of taking beatings and sheltering the softer side of myself.

"Pardon?" it asks, twisting around my tongue like a ghost. It spools itself out through my blood stream to take possession of my arms and legs, ready for action.

"It took us some time. We couldn't find any record of your parents' names in the Academy's files so we looked through public records for anyone with your surname. When that didn't lead us anywhere, we found the maiden names of anyone who married into the family within ten years of your birth. Finding your mother's maiden name was quite the challenge; she kept it off of all public records. We had stopped looking for a few years. It wasn't until we had access to an associate's private archives that we found her."

Now I'm certain I'll be sick. She scrubbed all records clean of herself to hide from me. As if leaving me at the Academy didn't send a clear enough message that she wanted nothing to do with me. Did she really think, if I ever found myself free, I would try to find her? Even when I was young and dreamed of escape with Lilith, I was not naïve enough to believe my mother would play a part in that life.

"You found my mother. And?"

"No, we didn't find her. Your grandmother, Inerea Ovira," she says.

A grandmother. A family member that had been out there all those years but hadn't existed in my concept of family until now. Why hadn't she come for me either?

"When we found her, she confirmed that her daughter had married someone with the surname Thiel only a year before you were born though she had no idea they had a child."

"But my parents, you must know who they are now?"

No, I plead with the idiotic part of my brain that asks this question before I can shut it up. I don't need to ask to know why she's glossed over them. They still don't want me-

"They passed away."

I try to gather my thoughts from the dark places that lap at the shores of the small islands of my sanity. Doctor Lindberg's face is impassive. She's managed to pull herself back together but surely, she must know that every new piece of information is pulling me apart.

"How long ago?"

As I ask this, I feel something change in her look. Her eyes are on me like a concentration of all her energy. She's pleading me not to go down this road but both the creature within and I need to know about them. I had sealed tight the part of my mind that thought about them, but now the door has opened I'm falling, grabbing at any piece of information that can fill what feels like a never-ending hole made of my ignorance.

"It's been years, Mallory. You would have been too young to remember." What she doesn't add is the *even if you had been with them.*

"Were they the ones who sent me here?"

She looks uncomfortable, an expression I couldn't have imagined her capable of before today but now seems permanently stained on her face. Her eyes are on her companion, as if he's the one with the answers. If so, he refuses to offer them.

"I'm afraid we can only speculate. As I said, their names weren't written anywhere in the Academy, so it's possible you were taken without your parents' consent or after they passed away. On the other hand, it's wasn't uncommon for those who brought their children here to withhold their names. We can't discern whether you arrived before or after their deaths because there's no record of when you joined the Academy. We can make a sketchy timeline based on the documents Diane left, but many of them were destroyed before we arrived here."

That sounds like Diane. Even in retreat she made one last move to erase our biological families and remind us that she was the only family we would ever have, or deserve.

"When you told my grandmother about me, what did she say?"

"That they want you to come live with them."

After stringing itself tightly to bear the pressure of all

this news, my heart goes wild.

"They?"

"Your mother's sister and her husband, Celia and Milton. They've been declared your legal guardians and, if you choose, you'll be moving to New York with them to start at a private school, Blackburns, in January. You would spend the remaining weeks of the winter vacation with them in Aplin Hollow where your grandmother lives so as to get to know one another before you start school."

An aunt and uncle. Another branch sprouts from the family tree that has begun to grow in my mind. It's a tender sapling with svelte limbs grown from a root someone failed to remove. My mind is gone, spinning in the hurricane of questions that all demand priority.

"I have a choice? Can't they make me go live with them as my guardians?"

That's what happened to Zach. His parents were found and they decided to take him away without asking. They had no idea what they were doing to him.

"Yes, but they understand that you've grown up at the Academy and they don't want to uproot you. As far as they're aware, the Academy is a private boarding school where you've received one of the best educations possible. They don't want to take you away from your home."

I can't help it and I don't understand where it comes from, but I start laughing. Quietly it comes like a scratching sound. I swallow it back.

"This is what we've been preparing you for. It's entirely up to you. They'd like to meet you though, even if you don't live with them."

She's done to me the exact thing I said ruined lives moments ago. She cannot look at me because she knows that but felt obligated to tell me about my family despite how much I yelled at her. But now those words have been spoken to me, it all seems different. *We found them*. And they didn't know about me, they didn't choose not to know me. They're not the monsters I wanted to imagine my family to be so that I could hate them. They're thoughtful enough to give me a choice. Without ever meeting me they've shown me more consideration than most.

"Yes. I'll go. I want to go."

I don't know if it's me or the creature of self-preservation, at long last found its way to escape the Academy, speaking. All I know is the words come out of my mouth and they're true. Doctor Lindberg nods and I think she smiles. My eyes are stinging as they haven't in years. She was right again, after all. Even after all these years, I haven't given up as I thought I had.

"We'll arrange for them to come and collect you. For now, we'll leave you. I'm sure you need some time to yourself. Come, Kyle."

Time to myself is all I've had for the past three years. What I need right now is something to hold onto to keep my feet on the ground, and a tethering post for my mind. Kyle rises first, and the light through the window illuminates the features he kept hidden. In that instant he cannot seem to help that his gaze, drawn by some innate gravity, turns to me. His eyes are full of anguish, distilled by compassion. I wonder how someone whose face had been full of the light of an angel, in the form of a smile, could deteriorate to such grief. I wonder how someone so unblemished as him could traverse that spectrum of emotions on my behalf, having met me but minutes ago. He holds open the door for Doctor Lindberg and doesn't look back as he closes it. Perhaps I imagined that look in his eyes.

The anger and shock take their toll as soon as they're gone. My body, exhausted from the weight of keeping itself composed and upright, sags. An aunt, an uncle, and a grandmother. I unwrap the words in my mind, ironing out the creases where they've long been folded in disuse. They are not the ones who left me here and they never knew there was a me to find. Now that they do, they want me. Would they have come sooner had they known and raised me away from here, ignoring what must have been my parents' wishes to send me to the Academy? Even if I had come here after their deaths, my parents must have made the arrangements for that to happen. A sigh slips from my lips and becomes part of the warm air that presses on my chest, confining my breaths to tight, jagged gasps.

Why did they keep me a secret from the rest of family? Was it for this exact reason, so that they couldn't retrieve me from the Academy? Had my parents been protecting them from me? I suppose even in a young child there can be seen trace amounts of their future wrongdoings. I wonder what they saw written in my infant eyes that made them so afraid.

My heartbeat is erratic. The sounds of human motion are outside my door again. Please don't come back in. Not now. Not while I'm like this. I lift my head and focus on the wall opposite me in an attempt to ground myself despite the rising panic.

What I find in my line of sight is worse than my thoughts. It's fear made manifest.

When Doctor Lindberg first arrived, our rooms were rearranged. They didn't have the space to move us all to new rooms, so instead they replaced all our furniture in an attempt to strip away trauma, which exists as much in the corporeal as our minds. They gave us things we never had, but didn't stop to consider that there might be a reason we didn't have those things before. Clocks were kept from us to keep us from trying to measure our sentences in the Academy. Everything existed in a never-ending expanse of meaningless hours. Mirrors were never hung on the walls so we didn't come to know ourselves. But Diane had taught me of my reflection, which was why, when they hung that gilt framed mirror above my dresser, I had covered it with one of my dresses. I never asked anyone to remove it. Doing that would give away too much. Besides, only two people had come in here regularly enough to see the makeshift cover, and neither of them cared enough to take notice.

I know that I shouldn't, but my body moves itself. It's that creature in my bones, in my blood. The siren's call wants to drown me in still glass. I stop before the covered mirror, short of pulling the dress from it. I reach for the pins in my hair and feel the weight on my scalp as my braid uncurls itself from around my skull, falling back over my shoulder. Pulling the tail of the ribbon that holds it, the same frayed one my caretaker had used years ago, I watch it fall like cut tresses of my hair, like black blood. I rake my fingers through my hair, working it free of the braid I restore it to each morning like an offering to my caretaker's memory. Only once it's loose across my shoulders do I pinch the bottom corner of the cloth draped over the mirror. It feels like midnight: velvet and utterly unknowable. I tug it down.

In the same instant I shut my eyes and rest my chin on my chest, regretting the decision. Behind my eyelids it's as if I'm still staring at the black fabric. I squint at the ground before opening my eyes fully to stare at the curled ribbon on the floor. The cloth is still in my hand and all I want to do is rehang it. But to do that I'll have to look up. I'll have to see the mirror and myself. To look up now just so I might hide my reflection again is the safe choice. To look it in the eye, that is brave.

Little angel, you're so brave.

I lift my head and, as if the mirror's image exists seconds ahead of my movements, my own eyes await me.

They're unearthly pale pools of liquid sapphire, still fluid and rushing beneath a sheet of ice, just as I remember them. I feel their coldness prick my skin and my body hums a tremble. If I look too long, the ice will crack and I'll be drowned in the torrent that feigns stillness.

Of course my parents sent me away. A beast that can masquerade as human might be able to survive in the world, but I cannot master the art of masquerading. My face is too sharp, all angles that give me away. High, angular cheekbones pull the skin of my cheeks taut with the help of my diamond jawline. Arched eyebrows express haughty irritation when all I feel is fear. There's nothing to be read on my face but anger, even though that's not what I intend to write.

I touch the places on my jaw where the faceless woman's nails had sunken in. I curl my fingers up like hers but can't bear to dig them in. Those scars have faded into the unblemished surface. I learned to be obedient. The scar on my back remains, however, and I don't need to look upon my back's reflection to remember what it looks like. Diane was right: it made certain I never forgot my failings. I run my fingers through my hair, which retains tactile softness but is also wild in appearance. It spirals in untameable curls that haven't been cut for years. Again, I find my own gaze. My heart asks me with sorrow in my eyes: why?

Why not, my reflection replies. It is no longer just my physical self-reflected, but all the multiplications of being in my mind.

Why not abandon you here? Why not inflict innumerable tortures on a body as beastly as yours? Why not enact every cruelty imaginable on someone so far from goodness?

I turn away in an attempt to shake my reflection loose, but my memories bite, holding strong. Thoughts make me weak again and I sink to the ground. The rough carpet pricks the bare skin of my knees, unwilling to yield to the weight of my sagging body. It imprints its transitory memory on my flesh, forcing blood back so my skin pales.

Cry, I command myself. That's human. My caretaker cried that Saturday so long ago, so why can't I? Perhaps I am one of those who wishes to cry because I believe it will be reassuring rather than a genuine act of catharsis. I have no right enacting that ritual of human pain.

Poor thing, you're all alone.

My breath is snatched from my lungs by a gasp when I hear the voice. It is not my own, nor the creature within's, which now rears its head at the disturbance. We both know it so well. I scramble to my feet, grabbing the dresser for support.

Where is she? There's no one else in the room, yet I'm certain I heard her. The faceless woman. Diane. The thought strikes me: what if all this news of a family that wants me is a trick played by her? The eight years she's been gone could just as easily be another of her illusions as they could be real.

Shh, it's okay.

I spin around when she whispers, as if just by my ear. Now it's the voice of my old caretaker. But behind me I don't find her mismatched eyes and glowing smile, only my own face in the mirror. It's the face of wild terror.

A wave of laughter rolls over, flipping my stomach. If laughter could be a sickness that poisons its host, this would be it.

'No,' I whisper.

The walls ooze, porous and dripping. Blood, why is there always blood? My hand clamps down on the dresser more and I feel the wood splinter in my hand. I claw at it, feeling it come apart under my fingernails. I watch as the blood begins to run down my fingers but I cannot tell if it's mine or an illusion. I slide to the ground, shutting my eyes and pressing my hands to either side of my head. For that's the source of it all, that's what's drawing this curtain of fantasy repeatedly over my reality. I feel the warm slickness on my face where my blood covered finger tips are, but don't care.

We'll never leave you. We'll keep you forever, a voice promises. But don't tell anyone. They'll get angry.

The mirror is shattering, though then again, it may not be. It's raining down crystalline tears, just as it had done in the octagonal room.

I'm so sorry my little angel.

The laughter breaks again, cracks my skull open and sips sanity from it. The other voices scream, a near unintelligible mass of shouts that all translate roughly to save us!

Save us, they now plead in unison. Do they read and enact my thoughts or do I command them? Too late to ask. They're dragged away and silence dawns. It's not a peace offering but a threat. If he can do that to them then-

You would have done well to remember, I always find you.

Chapter IX.

Mallory!

"No," I groan, emerging from darkness at last. I blink, hoping to admit light, but still I see nothing. The voices grab at me, trying to drag me back to him.

Mallory!

The insufferable cacophony of my mind breaks beneath the roar of reality slamming on my ear drums. I cry out as the pain of my injuries is restored to my body. There's a banging on my door, the loud sound that drew me back to myself. My dresser is upended, its drawers and contents scattered across the floor. One of the former is wedged against the door, preventing it from being opened. The blankets and sheets have been ripped off the bed and shredded to pieces, which are strewn like the snow that sometimes falls in the courtyard.

Where am I amongst these sounds and corporeal forms? I feel conscious, yet it's as if my body has been snatched away. My hand hovers in front of my face, then is lowered to my abdomen, which is exposed by my rolled-up shirt. The skin feels distant and numb, like ringing in ears after a tremendous noise. A radiating pressure undulates in my chest, building tension in a space that seems to be growing smaller and smaller. It pulses so hard I fear soon I will be unable to breathe.

"Mallory!"

I know that voice, though it's newly admitted to my memory. Kyle? I press my hands to my ears. I don't want to hear it. I can't know for certain if it's really Kyle or if it's -

I had pushed my dresser against the door thinking, if they couldn't get in, I'd be safe. But the door shook beneath the beating of their bodies until it gave way. Guards' hands around my ankles as they dragged me away.

- I shiver.

The door shudders stubbornly before it, and my vision, splinter. Bursts of colour, nebular spots, appear. I feel the movement of my fingers as I claw at the carpet, but my nerves fail to pick up the reciprocal touch of fibres. The waves of energy in me have moved to my stomach and I roll onto my side, ready to be sick. Clarity is restored to my vision just as Kyle steps in. He sees me and the veil of shadow lifts from his face. Panic. Dropping to his knees he reaches out to support me.

No, please don't touch me.

"Don't," I whimper, managing only the one word of my thoughts before my voice gives out to dry heaving.

He jolts away, my word an electric command. I arch my back, leaning forward and supporting myself on trembling arms, but nothing comes up from my stomach. Slowly, I begin to breathe normally.

"I'm so sorry, I didn't think. You just looked." He doesn't finish, but I know what I look like. I saw in the mirror exactly what I look like moments before I fell apart. A shudder runs through me. "I heard a crash from out in the hall."

Why he feels he need offer an explanation like an apology I don't know. Were it not for him knocking on the door, I don't know how long I might have stayed blacked out for. The gutted dresser could just as easily have been a person had I left the room. But how am I supposed to say that to him? Thank you doesn't seem appropriate. The exposed skin of my shins grates against the carpet. Untucking my legs from beneath me, I stretch them out.

"Your fingers," he murmurs, spotting the blood all across my palms.

I had all but forgotten about them, distracted by the presence and proximity of someone I don't know. Besides, these are hardly of any concern when physical

healing comes as easy as it does to me. Not wanting to of-
fend, I suppress a shiver as he draws close to inspect them.
He's careful to keep his palms firmly flattened against his
thighs, a promise he'll heed my request not to be touched.
As he turns his attention to the rest of me in search of
further injuries, I manage to steal a glance at his face.

Up close, everything about him is lighter than I first
thought. His hair, which had seemed as dark as mine,
is actually brown, though it has no highlights of red or
blonde to be caught in the low light. His back is a curved
bow, shoulders taut with muscles that don't present as
obvious on his relatively slender frame. He retains that
part of his boyishness, though he's outgrown boyhood.
His eyes are an inky blue I had mistaken for black, and
he takes me by surprise when he turns them to my face
with no warning.

For once, I don't feel as if I'm being weighed up in
another's eyes, or playing a secondary role in the unveil-
ing of myself. He doesn't study me in an attempt to come
to any quick conclusions about who or what I am. Of all
the ways I've been regarded, this is the most unnerving
and, simultaneously, comforting. Then he frowns, and my
stomach drops.

"There's blood on your face. Did you hit your head?"

I shake my head, unable to lift my leaden tongue. I
could speak to Doctor Lindberg earlier though he was
in the room because there was a torrent of emotion that
couldn't lay dormant in me. But, in light of what Kyle's
just walked in on, exchanging words with him seems impossible.

"Is it from your hands?"

I nod, casting my gaze to the floor.

"Well, we should get the splinters out and clean them
up. I can get you what you need to do it yourself but it
might be better if I do it, so you don't push any of the

splinters further in by using your hands."

"Okay."

He smiles, not as full and friendly as when he came in earlier, but small and privately, as if meant more for himself than me. He goes into the bathroom and I can hear the tap running and cupboards opening.

My bedroom door is still wide open, leaving the mess of my room in full view of a pair of passing guards. They come to a stop immediately, surveying the damage until they spot the cause. I recognise one of them as the man with the gun, except now, they are men with guns, both of which are half out of their holsters when Kyle returns. He has a bowl of water in one hand, a towel draped over his arm and a pair of tweezers. He doesn't notice them at first but I can tell by the shift in his expression when he looks at me that he knows something is wrong.

"Are you alright Mr Caverly?" one of the guards asks. They both have their guns aimed at me but, for some reason, I feel no need to move from their line of fire. Instead, that unfamiliar urge to laugh begins to form in my throat again.

"What the hell do you think you're doing?"

I'm caught off guard at how Kyle's tone has changed. The gentleness he spoke with earlier, formed of a nurturing nature, is transformed to severity. The guards are alarmed too. Their gazes, which fear should train on me, jump to him.

"I don't know what Doctor Lindberg told you, but this one has a habit of lashing out," my usual guard says. He lacks conviction as he says it in a slightly whiney voice, like a child trying to justify himself.

"Oh, of course." The guards look relieved, turning their attention back to me. "You see a few drawers on the floor, her injured, and jump to the conclusion that she attacked me? So, what, you thought you'd shoot her? I've never felt safer in my life. If I knock something over in the hall later, will you point a gun at me too?"

"No, Mr Caverly but, this one's dangerous." The first guard whispers the second part as if to keep me from hearing. Kyle doesn't laugh at the idiocy he's already pointed out. His expression doesn't change. He simply takes a few steps, placing himself between them and me.

"Get out."

I can't see their reactions but I hear the scuttle of footsteps and grumbled apologies. Kyle sighs, setting the bowl and towel beside me.

"Utter morons," he mutters, sitting beside me.

"They're trying to keep you safe," I reply softly.

"I'll do without the protection, thanks." He shakes his head then reaches for my right hand. "May I?"

I nod and he flips my hand so the palm is upwards. He dips the towel in the water then begins to dab away the blood, removing any splinters with the tweezers as he goes.

"I know it seems ridiculous to an outsider, but they were right to protect you. I am," I pause, chewing the insides of my cheeks as he pulls out the first two splinters, "dangerous."

"To that dresser maybe. But you wouldn't hurt me or anyone else for that matter."

"Don't be so sure, you don't know me."

"No, I don't, but I'm good at reading people. You would rather do this to yourself," he says, gesturing to my bloodied hands, "than risk putting someone else in danger."

He doesn't say another word as he concentrates on the task at hand. I want to speak to him but don't dare interrupt his silent concentration, taking the opportunity to try to make sense of the past hour. He finishes, wrapping my hand up in a bandage.

"May I ask what happened?" I nod and he waits but I don't reply. "Alright, I can ask but you won't answer. Do you take everything so literally?"

He smiles. Are we born with lips that do that on their own? If so, I was never gifted with such innate knowledge.

"Let me rephrase then. Will you tell me what happened?" It's not his question but his tone that encourages me to speak.

"You'd think I'm insane."

"Maybe. Maybe you've seen more than the average person could comprehend. But what's to say I haven't too?"

"Seeing isn't experiencing," I counter.

"Sometimes seeing the people we care about suffering is enough for us to feel as though we've gone through it ourselves. Empathy can be a singularly excruciating gift. But I won't push my luck with you," he says, "here, I'll clean this up."

Before I can protest, he's on his feet, balling up the tattered sheets to squish them down into the rubbish bin. He heaves the dresser upright and slots all the drawers back in.

"There, looks a little less like bigfoot trashed it now. I'll leave you to put the clothes away, I'm not much for rooting through women's dressers."

"You've done more than enough already. Thank you."

"It was the least I could do after uh, well." He glances at my door. I hadn't even noticed earlier, but it's been busted off of the top hinge. Did he do that? "If there's nothing else, I'll go find someone to repair the door."

I don't reply so he starts towards the hall.

The voice blossoms unlike any of the others, as a bud that has been planted unnoticed in the back of my mind for years. It's warm and ripe, full of sunshine despite the dark corner it's been forced to grow in. Its roots dip down into my heart and run through every vein, circulating its will.

"Wait." I expect the voice to tell me what to say next but it leaves me to flounder in the silence that follows my request.

"Yes? Do you want me to get Doctor Lindberg?"

Sounds scrape at my throat, demanding to be vocalised, but none of them are words. I stare at Kyle, the man who's light where there should be darkness, and I know what to say.

"How is it I've never seen you here before?"

He scrutinises me with his head tilted ever so slightly. His eyes narrow and, though it's not done out of contempt, fear plays out its familiar song with my heartbeats. What was I thinking?

"I wasn't under the impression you saw much of anyone."

So, he knows. He's kinder than Doctor Lindberg's other associates, such as Professor Stewart, but that's simply because he's better at hiding his revulsion. He had rushed to my aid, yes, but he did so as a benevolent protector.

"From what I've been told, you study independently and the Academy isn't known for its mixers. So, it's not surprising we haven't met. Besides, I don't work here, I'm only visiting."

"Oh. Holiday?" He lifts his eyebrows and smiles, but I don't know why.

"I'm not sure this could be considered a holiday destination. Work, on the other hand," he starts, pausing before explaining himself, "Doctor Lindberg reached out to various communities in the hopes of locating families of some of the other students."

"You helped her find someone?"

"Yes," he replies but even I can read his hesitation.

"Sorry, I didn't mean to pry, I'm sure all of this is confidential."

"No, not at all, it's just – it was your grandmother."

Oh. Once again, I am humbled to the reality of my inability to gauge people. He didn't want to create an obligation of gratitude. He didn't want anything in exchange for the good he'd done. I'm struck by the revelation that someone could be so selflessly motivated.

"Thank you."

"It's just what I do."

Just. He's so reductive of his contribution to this life changing event. He hadn't seemed the sort of person who would need to avoid acknowledgement. Yet the way he shrugs and turns his gaze from me to the floor when moments ago he had no trouble making eye contact, it's as if he's trying to pass along the achievement of finding what no one else seemed able to. Before he had seemed a mystery but now I've seen him, I find his emotions are so obviously woven into the fabric of features. And the discomfort he now wears is so plain, I expect him to go. I don't want him to.

As if the extremity of emotion that this thought is founded on is known to him, he is jolted from his bashful stance.

"Doctor Lindberg told me you like to run. Do you want to go to the track with me?"

I'm startled twice fold, both by the nature of the request and how intimate it feels. Running has become so habitual over the years, as commonplace as a daily prayer, I had scarcely thought on it when I got changed each evening. It's only when something tries to interpose itself on that prayer that we realise how sacred it is. Bringing someone running with me feels a violation of something private.

"Why?"

"Well, I would say to swim but that might prove something of a challenge without a pool, so how about to jog?"

"That's not what I meant." He laughs, and I'm quite certain it's at me.

"I know, I was just playing by your overly literal rules. I find running helps to clear my head."

It would take an awful lot of running to clear the voices circling my head. They ought to pay me rent for the space they take up.

"Even with someone else there? Surely that's counterproductive."

"I suppose it depends on the person."

"Don't you have more work to do with Doctor Lindberg?"

"You are an awfully suspicious person," he says, laughing again. It doesn't seem mocking, rather radiates a mollifying quality that begins to put me at ease. "No, I don't. I told you, I came here for you."

"You didn't say that."

"Perhaps not in such plain terms as you like to express yourself, but it was heavily implied when I told you I was here about your grandmother."

Is he mocking me? Any second some part of his face will betray his intentions. The corner of his mouth will dip or his eyes will dart aside for a moment. But any second doesn't come. He simply waits for my answer.

"Alright."

His smile broadens and I'm certain I've never seen such light in one place, nor could I have ever imagined my company being the cause of it.

"Loafers don't tend to make the best running shoes, so I'll just go change. Come to think of it, might need to give the entire outfit a rethink," he says, giving himself a once over, "I'll meet you out there?"

I'm all out of words following the effort it took to agree to his offer, so I simply nod. On his way out, he pauses by the broken door.

"I don't know how big you are on exhibitionism, but you might want to change in the bathroom."

Once he's gone, I root through the disorganised swamp that is my dresser to find my jogging kit. Later tonight I'll put everything back in its right place, as if nothing happened. But in this moment, chaos has brought me something I never thought could be found in its rubble: the possibility of friendship.

I take my clothes into the bathroom and change. It's strange knowing my door is ajar, ready to admit someone, like an open wound leaving the body susceptible to infection. Anyone could walk in. Anyone could get hurt if I lose my grip on reality for only a moment. I tremble, sliding my leggings on. What am I doing? Even if I don't hurt Kyle, what am I supposed to say to him? It's been years since I've had conversations with anyone, and what I spoke of with Zach can't be brought up to anyone else. The thought of Zach sends me crawling back into my shell.

I can't do this.

Yes, you can. You just did.

That voice like summer whispers to me again and supplants all my concerns and drops its own seeds in their place. They'll take time to grow but, for tonight, knowing they're there will have to be enough. Even if I find my tongue roots itself to the bottom of my mouth, Kyle is too generous to be cruel to me for my inability. He knows I've been on my own for so long, and is giving me the opportunity to learn how to be near someone before my aunt and uncle arrive.

Those two words are so foreign to my thoughts they

travel slowly along my synapses. I had hardly conceived of having parents when I was younger, forcing away thoughts of a family existing happily without me. Having extended family was never even a possibility. Yet I do have them, and it's all because of Kyle.

Leaving the bathroom, I follow the winding corridors of the Academy to the track. Usually I run later than this, when the sun can no longer hold its head above the surface of the horizon and drowns in night. Still, the light is low early during winter months and there's no one to be seen in the halls. The day has disappeared in the wake of Doctor Lindberg's revelation.

I find Kyle leaning against the rail that encircles the track, his back to me. My usual fellow jogger is nowhere to be seen yet, but it's still early for him. I move quietly towards Kyle but he must have heard the door open because he's already turning around. He hitches up his trouser leg slightly to reveal his sneakers.

"I knew I had to have something other than loafers somewhere. Shall we?"

He gestures for me to go ahead. The sensation of having someone follow me onto the track is unsettling, even though I know who it is. I try not to overtly glance over my shoulder, but gaze instead far afield to my right so as to keep Kyle in my periphery. I feel the tension unfurling from my muscles as I walk across the familiar clay coloured tartan. Before I know it, I've set off. I run just fast enough that I can feel the swell of burning energy sigh and rush through my legs, without outpacing Kyle.

"You're putting me to shame," he says as we start on our sixth lap.

It's a meagre attempt at conversation and a downright lie. He has kept pace faithfully by my side and his breath has remained steady despite the exertion. Still, it's more of an attempt than I've made, unsure of what conversational ground is safe to tread upon. I'm thankful he's chosen something as impersonal as possible.

"Hardly. You must do quite a bit of running yourself?"

"It's part of what I do." What an odd use of the phrase.

"You said that before. I'm curious what exactly you might do. Clearly something in which running and finding strangers' long-lost grandmothers' play integral roles. Something that means Doctor Lindberg would trust you."

He laughs, clearing the air of any seriousness my inquiry might have contained.

"I merely offered my services. Doctor Lindberg didn't seek me out."

"Here I thought you might be world renowned."

"For my grandmother recovery skills?"

"Who knows. The Academy has a way of drawing all sorts of odd individuals to it."

"A blackhole for the bizarre," he agrees, "no wonder I came here."

"And who knows where we'll end up when we come out the other side."

"Alright Neil deGrasse Tyson," he chuckles.

"Who?" We pick up our pace a little.

"It was a topical reference, I promise."

"I'll take your word for it I suppose," I sigh.

The sky is a page of inky blots interrupted by clear parchment stars. Kyle's form has given way to the darkness around him and he moves as an indeterminable shadow beside me.

"Are you nervous to meet them?"

His voice rises as if from nowhere. It drags up with it a subject I'd hoped not to speak of. Why did he have to tread there? A place I haven't dared to go since he found me in my room earlier.

"No," I lie. It sings out of me, easier than honesty, which hides behind gritted teeth and averted gazes.

It is late enough now, yet still my running companion has not joined us. I had hoped for the comfort of our solidarity one last time. Perhaps they have found his family too and he is gone. Perhaps it's time I go too.

Chapter X.

The week tires beneath the heft of my anticipation. The last days move like the worn wheels of an old cart that can scarcely manage to drag itself along a path frequently travelled. Of course, for me, there is nothing familiar about that week. My room, my evening run, my beastly heart, all find their routines punctuated by fresh thoughts and occurrences. For one, while my anonymous companion has disappeared, Kyle is sure to be waiting for me at track in the early evening for our jog. We speak, superficially still, but at least my heart makes no attempts to batter itself raw against my ribcage.

On the day before my departure, he comes by my room after lunch with a duffle bag. Into it we pack what little clothing I own, leaving aside my clothes for the following day. My last day. I don't tell him it's the only bag I have ever owned. Such a comment would probably seem banal to him. Setting the bag down beside the door, Kyle surveys the room.

"What about your books? I'm sure I could get a box for them," he suggests, nodding at the books that have accumulated in piles next to the dresser.

Despite the volume of them, no one in the Academy has ever taken them away, nor have they brought a bookshelf on which to store them. They are organised only by a system arbitrary to anyone other than me.

"They're just my course books," I reply, so reductively. They are the thousand lives I've lived. "They're the Academy's, not mine."

He shrugs and we say no more of them.

That night, after I've showered, I kneel beside them in the dewy blue moonlight that diffuses a watery sheen on all things. Considering what would become of my books hasn't occurred to me since I had found out I was leaving. It makes me feel guilty, as if I've neglected something helpless. When I had been weak, they poured their strength into me leaving them with none of their own, based on the assumption I would protect them. They may have hardcovers, but their insides are mollusc soft and mutable in the hands of an inattentive reader.

I take one from the top of the nearest stack and open it, careful not to crack its spine as had been done with mine. Suddenly unworthy of the contents, I find my eyes can't hold the sentences. They fall apart like dry bread but don't make a path I can follow. It is all circles and confusion that lead back to nothing. The dark shapes of incomprehensible letters bloat and blur as my eyes fill with tears. I close the book just as the first tear falls. They will be well used and well loved by someone else in the Academy now. I restore the book to its place, then curl up beside them and sleep.

Morning comes and I find my charge unharmed, safe behind the barrier of my body. It comes as a relief following my dream in which they had gone up in flames while all around me came peels of his faceless laughter.

Let me taste the fire of your blood.

He had licked their pages clean, devouring my many lives and leaving only me, raw and exposed to the fire. Down his chin had dribbled crimson that filled all the books with his history of death.

I press my hand to a cool leather-bound spine beneath the morning's unobtrusive light. Everything held together through the night, still and tightly bound by the single thread made by a re-emergence from nightmares into day. I sigh and then realisation loosens that thread. Today is the day. The seam of my world goes lax and all its contents slacken. How to keep it from falling apart?

I roll from my back and push myself to my feet. I'm on my way to the door to go I don't know where, when it opens. Kyle steps in, his presence stopping me in my frenzied tracks. He falters too. Whatever train of thought that had brought him in here is held up.

"I thought I should check if you were awake," he says, brought back to his reason for being here almost immediately. "But it seems you're already up and about like a woman on a mission."

"I had to," I start, but am too unsure of where I'm going to finish.

He peers at me, eyebrows heavy with curiosity. He clears his face of the intrusive expression.

"Get ready, of course," he says, covering my own tracks for me, "they'll be here soon. Doctor Lindberg will be there when you meet them."

He leaves out the *just in case*.

"Yes, getting ready." My verbal response is ten steps behind my mind and our conversation but we both pretend not to notice.

"Is there anything you need?"

"No, thank you."

He nods, eying the unslept in bed, then leaves. I'm beyond wondering what he must make of that. I undress, leaving my nightgown on the floor where it falls as I head to the shower.

As it has done for as long as I can remember, the shower head drips twice then pours like a sudden gasp, like so many words kept back. Its roar falls around my ears, cloaking the sound of my breathing. It feels safe enough in here to speak to myself, even if that's only because I can block the world out, not because the world cannot hear me.

At first, I merely mouth the words, a forbidden mantra I've wanted to say all week. But I've been afraid to speak it, as if all the magic it's held in my mind will be expelled in each exhalation, disseminated in each syllable.

My lips press the words into form and soon my tongue does to.

"Celia, Milton, Inerea."

Their names don't turn spectral as I'd feared. No echo takes them up in my broken voice. They hang, shimmering in the steam that goes dewy on my skin. They are breathed, effervescent, into my pores and write themselves on me. When I get out of the shower to dry off, I am imbued with the warmth of their names, which will protect me from even them. Or, rather, the worst versions of them I've imagined.

Dressed, I sit on the edge of my bed, awaiting the arrival of someone unknown. Will it be Kyle or Doctor Lindberg who takes me to them? Or will they be brought there? I hope it's not the latter. I don't want their first impression to be of me dwarfed by the crushing history of this room. Better to meet on neutral territory, some room I've never been in. If only I'd thought to ask Kyle what Doctor Lindberg's intentions were.

There's a knock at the door, Kyle's knock, and that's all the reassurance I need to know that nothing horrible can come of today, so long as he's involved.

"Come in."

He enters the room alone, which I find comforting as well.

"Are you ready?"

What satisfactory reply can I possibly give? He realises the impossibility of the question he's asked and picks up my bag.

He leads me down the hallway. My once intact world disappears with each step, giving way to the vagueness of memory with every second. I won't see that room again, the track field either. The thought doesn't fill me with sadness but something does pull on the ropes around my heart as we leave it behind. I find we're tracing a path I once wondered on one of my night walks, one I remember well. We emerge from the hallway into the atrium, directly opposite the large pair of double doors that turned me away. I cannot imagine anyone coming in through that door. It has only ever seemed a potential exit to me. But instead of leading me to the exit, Kyle opens a door to the left for me.

"Doctor Lindberg is just speaking with them and then I think she wants to talk to you before bringing them in here." He doesn't follow me in. "I'll take your bag to the car."

I turn to watch him go and see, over his shoulder, someone headed towards the exit with a box heaped so that I can see the covers of some of my books peeking out. The ease Kyle's presence engenders dissipates.

"They're taking them? Where to?" My dream rushes back to me, fire pulling down the foundations of my mind contained in those pages.

"I know they're just your old course books but I thought perhaps you might want to take them with you," Kyle says.

Overwhelming gratitude frees itself from the dormancy I have kept my emotions in all morning.

"Thank you, for seeing through me."

"You're not quite the mystery you make yourself out to be."

"Clearly you've made out more of me in the past week than I have in almost two decades. Goodbye, Kyle."

He sucks his cheeks in. Had he forgot that this would be the last time we saw one another? The thought of parting with him had been playing on my mind after every run. I had known from the first time we went that our friendship would be limited by my departure. Perhaps it was only this certainty that had made it possible for me to accept his invitation in the first place. He nods in acknowledgement of the farewell he seemingly cannot reciprocate and shuts the door.

The room is empty save for a large circular table with no chairs. This is a place of comings and goings. The gentle pastel colour of the flowers on the table invites me towards them. It's a pink with a diluted saturation, as if they've been worn by time. Of course, they're likely one of the youngest things in the Academy. Diane never seemed the type of person to go in for flowers. The vertices of the petals peel backwards, pointing towards the door.

I circle the table a few times, studying the wine-coloured carpet. It has no history of stains to read and remains an uninterrupted canvas from wall to wall. Outside the window, the sun is blanketed heavily by so many puffed clouds that even its light doesn't have the strength to blanch them. Grey hangs stagnant. My mind becomes a vacant sky, gazed up at by the vulnerable and unknowing. Any moment the storm could hit.

What if they change their minds?

What if my Celia and Milton exist only in the conjuring of my thoughts and they are an illusion soon to be wiped clean? Because despite all my attempts not to think of them, they've begun to grow in my mind. They're not clear forms, they have no edges of characterising definition. All they are is shimmering warmth. I tug absent-mindedly on my hair, twisting it around my finger until the door opens, audibly grazing the too stiff carpet fibres.

Doctor Lindberg shuts the door behind her. She walks towards the table as if to admire the flowers before halting. I think she's drawn the same conclusion as I, that they are uninviting in their sharpness.

"I'm sorry about what happened to you here."

Had I expected anything of our last conversation? No. But this, this was beyond imagining.

"Why are you apologising?"

"Because the people who should have didn't. They never will. I don't know everything about your time here but I've seen enough to know that-," she breaks off. She moves her shaking hands from behind her back and holds out a small wooden box. "This was discovered when clearing out some of the disused rooms. It was in a drawer labelled with your name along with notes on you."

"Thank you," I say, unsure whether I am thanking her for not mentioning more of my past or for the mysterious box. The top has been carved into a high relief of a phoenix staring up at the moon. Why does it look so fearful?

"There's something else. I know you're sceptical of the reality of going to live with your family. For all your reading you're weary of romantic notions. It seems an impossibility to move forward from where you've been, and to back track to the naivety of childhood in which you can blindly trust someone just because of shared DNA, well, that's absurd even to the well-adjusted mind. I was sent here to help reintegrate everyone into their families where possible. But, should a time come when you find this isn't right for you," she pauses, clearing her throat.

Suddenly she's come to stand so close to me I wonder if she's going to hug me. She takes my hand in hers and, in no particular order, memories stir themselves from the bottom of the darkness.

A voice in my ear.
Hands dragging me from my room.
Heavy footsteps. No, they were light. They trod air.
Unwanted hands on me.
Raking my nails over flesh, into flesh.

I don't remember how to fight. I don't know how to free myself or breathe. But then she detaches from me and air dives itself down my throat. I look down and find a small piece of paper with ten numbers scrawled on it.

"It's my phone number. It's not really common practice to do this."

"Then why?"

"Mallory, I never stopped looking for your family even when you believed you weren't worthy of them. I'm not going to stop looking out for you just because they're here. Besides, you may one day find you need someone to talk about what happened here. Now, shall we?"

Following her out the door, I fold the piece of paper and slip it into my pocket. I glance around for Kyle, hoping one passing look may fortify me before I meet them, but he's nowhere to be seen. We cross to an identical door across the atrium and she twists the handle.

Part III

Chapter XI.

Here something happens, my brain feigning conti-
nuity even though there is a gap, as when blinking, during
which the past drops out of sight and I forget it was ever
even there.

* * *

"Mallory, you're working far too hard for a second
semester senior," Chloe says. Brushing off her comment
with a smile, I finish reviewing the last slide of our presentation. "Oi, boring one."

"Just because we've gotten into university already
doesn't mean we can show up without anything for our
final project," I remind her

"Actually, it does. It means that we should finish off
early today so we can go get ready for the bonfire. Please,"
she says, feigning a whine, "it's your first one, we've got to
do this right. Do it because you love me."

"You're totally overvaluing your stock there," I laugh.

"And you're both overestimating how much fun
there is to be had at these bonfire parties," Connie pipes
up, "it's always the same people, and some drunk guy will
inevitably try to feel you up by the keg."

"On that charming note, I think I'll give it a miss."

"No! Don't let misery guts trick you. She's just bitter
because she's a lightweight."

I raise my eyebrow at Connie, who lets out an exasperated sigh, shrugging her shoulders.

"Yeah, that's fair." She flips to the next page of her
magazine and lifts her feet onto the table.

"Besides, maybe the cute new librarian will show
up?" Chloe giggles, glancing over her shoulder into the
stacks.

"There's a new librarian?"

"Of course, that's the bit you think is important. I'm sorry, you come to the library every day, how have you not noticed?"

"Not everyone comes here to gawk at the librarian, creeper."

"Maybe I should go ask for that book you're always recommending – what's it called again?"

"*A Tale for the Time Being*. And while the prospect of you checking out a book would be cause for a city-wide parade, it actually being read is as likely as hell freezing over. How about we focus on the task at hand," I say, attempting to refocus on our assignment. Chloe doesn't seem to hear me, her attention now on the broad-shouldered back of a man re-shelving books. "The man in question?" I whisper to Connie.

"Shh!' Chloe hisses"

"Oh, very good audition for a job here!" I laugh.

I see her launch her pen at me in my peripheral. Lightning fast, my hand snatches it out of the air and there's a rush of blood. It's a sensation that's become all too familiar in the months since I arrived in Aplin Hollow. My head spins and it's all I can do not to double over with the sick feeling blooming in my stomach.

"Nice, very cat like," Connie says. My mouth feels too dry to speak so I just smile at her.

"Okay he's gone now. Thoughts?" Chloe asks. I swallow hard, gripping the underside of the table.

"Very nice back. Man can fill out a shirt."

"Boo, that's all?"

"I assessed what I saw, which was his back. Oh, and very handy with a book."

"Which is probably a massive turn-on for you."

Connie laughs, but all I can think about is how to get out of here and back to Inerea. She always knows how to help with my dizzy spells.

"Alright, you want to call it for the day?" I ask

"What's this? Miss Perfectionist is willing to stop working? Connie, can you believe it?"

"She just wants to go home and fantasize about your librarian."

"You got me! Don't worry I'll finish the project. Consider it my early graduation gift."

"Bless you and every second since you arrived in this god forsaken middle of nowhere town." Chloe's already out of her seat as she says this. She crams her books in her bag and slings it over her shoulder. "Want to come back to mine and help me pick out an outfit?"

"I'd love to but I've got to run an errand for Inerea. Want to meet at mine in a couple hours and you can show me the prospects?"

"Perfect. Then I can prevent whatever fashion catastrophe that's waiting to happen on your end. Tell your grandma hi, and that I miss her more than her pancakes, though only marginally."

"I might leave that last bit out but, I will."

"See you in a bit."

"See you!"

This should give me enough time to pull myself back together. This should –

Shit.

The edge of my vision darkens as Chloe and Connie walk away, like someone pulling a drawstring. Light tunnels, narrower and narrower until I cannot see or hear and I don't know what happens next -

* * *

I'm still sitting in the library. That's good. I can't have lost too much time this blackout. My laptop screen has gone dark and the other nearby desks have been emptied of books and occupants. I root through the mess of my handbag for my phone and start typing out a message to Inerea before pausing. I don't want to worry her with another one of my spells. And it's only a quarter past five so it didn't last more than twenty minutes, maybe?

Shutting off my laptop I glance around and notice that the books I had meant to check out are gone.

"Shit," I mutter.

Chloe's librarian must have done away with them while I was out of it. I can hear the trolley's wheels a few bookshelves over. Hopefully he's still got them. Stuffing my possessions into my bag, I follow the sound. I make out his shoulders from the narrow gap between books and the shelf above.

"Um excuse me?"

He goes rigid, his hand raised to put a book away. He quickly draws it back to himself, tucking it against his chest as if my appearance portends danger to its pages. Anything but, I want to tell him. He turns and stares at me. I have seen hints of gold feathering the edges of blue eyes, or drawing lines of light in brown eyes, but his are hard shimmering gold, rimmed with black. He has shaggy dark brown hair, tucked behind one ear. He's older than I would have imagined based on how Chloe gushed about him, but not so old that he shouldn't still be handsome.

"Sorry to bother you, but I, uh, wasn't done with my books, I think you might have picked them up?" I say, shuffling my bag further up my shoulder.

"Oh." Does he look disappointed? What did he think I was going to ask him about? He glances down at his trolley. "Which were they?"

"*Death of a Naturalist* and *Beowulf*," I reply.

Restoring the book in his hand to the shelf, he deftly

plucks my two from his trolley and offers them to me.

"Thanks."

"Of course. You enjoy poetry?"

"Um, occasionally, I prefer poetic prose."

"Have you read Calvino's *Castle of Crossed Destines*?"

"No, I keep meaning to, do you have it here?" His eyes flicker slightly, seemingly pleased by my interest.

"I can get it for you if you like?"

His voice trails off with the question, as if expecting me to decline. Why does he seem so nervous? Perhaps he's just the typical bookish introvert as I was when I moved from my old boarding school to Aplin Hollow's high school.

"Yes please."

He smiles pleasantly and I'm fully aware of why Chloe's infatuated. He's extremely attractive in a non-overly maintained way. And the fact he knows his books? *Probably a massive turn on for you.* Damn you Connie. He gestures for me to leave the row first then leads me to the right. Suddenly I'm seeing his back in a whole new light. He really can fill out a shirt.

Mallory what's gotten into you? I admonish myself. This isn't like me at all. Must get brain out of gutter.

"So, when did you move here?" I ask.

"How did you know I just moved here?"

My cheeks flush with colour and I can see him glance at me over his shoulder as I avert my gaze to the floor.

"I'm a bit of a regular and I hadn't seen you here until a few weeks ago."

"I noticed you were here almost every day. Full disclosure, I saw you looking at some of Calvino's other books the other day. It's one of my favourites."

Oh dear lord the gorgeous man has been noticing what I've been looking at.

"Well, I guess we should just both be glad I wasn't

looking at Fifty Shades of Grey," I say as we come to a stop in front of one of the bookshelves, "that would have come across as a truly bizarre recommendation."

He laughs, and I feel the warmth rising in my cheeks again.

"You're not really of the demographic to whom I'd recommend that."

"Dare I ask who is?"

"Are you sure you want to know how easy it is for librarians to read people?"

"Likely as easy as reading a book." Again, he laughs. Gone is the nervous little smile, as he flashes me an easy grin.

"I knew you would have such ready wit."

He scans the shelf and slips a thin black book off with his long fingers.

"Really? How so?"

"Anyone who reads that much does. I'm convinced you don't sleep the number of books you go through."

"I'm ninety percent water, ten percent coffee. I've overcome the need for sleep. Thanks," I say, taking the book from him.

"No problem, it always nice to meet one of our biggest customers. Do you need me to come check those out for you?'

"If you don't mind."

I follow him downstairs to the front desk and he scans the barcodes and my library card.

"All done."

"Thanks." Where's that ready wit he just spoke of? No doubt gone out the window the second the gold of his eyes turned molten, darkening slightly.

"I hope to see you around again soon."

"Biggest customer, remember? You'll be begging me to leave in no time. Have a good day."

"And you."

I feel his gaze on my back as I leave the building, putting the books into my bag. As I step out into the yawning lazy sunlight of early evening, my phone begins to buzz. Inerea. I've missed two calls from her while I was checking out my books.

"Hey Inerea."

"Hi little angel, where are you?"

"Just headed to the antique store to pick up your book."

"I tried calling you earlier."

I know what she's going to ask.

"Yeah, sorry my phone was on silent."

Her silence says she doesn't believe me, though she'd never say that.

"You didn't make it to your therapy session yesterday, did you?"

"No…"

"Mallory, I know they're tedious but they're important."

"I know, I know, I'm just swamped with all my school work and applying for housing at university. There's still so much to sort out and time just seems to be running out."

"I'll help however I can. Just promise me you'll go to your appointment if I book another one."

"I promise."

"Good. Now, shall I come pick you up from the antique store?"

"Isn't it a bit far?" Again, silence. "You're already on your way, aren't you?"

"You didn't answer your phone, I was worried."

"I'm fine," I sigh, "nothing's going to happen in the library. I should go before the store closes."

"Okay."

"Love you."

"Love you too little angel."

The line goes dead and I shake my head to myself. Surely it does her more harm than good to be this worried about my well-being. I swear she has a way of knowing when my blackouts happen before I tell her. I glance each way, crossing the empty square, and turn off the main road onto the street which houses most of the town's limited number of shops. I duck into a narrow store with a dark green awning. Inside, the lights let off a warm yellow glow over a darkly veneered wooden desk and glass cases holding jewellery and other trinkets. In the middle of the room is a table covered in a thin lacy cloth that has begun to yellow with age. Despite all the cars parked outside, there doesn't appear to be anyone else in the store. Between the staircases leading upstairs and downstairs is a sign indicating furniture below and books above.

"Hi Mallory," Mr Bowen says, righting himself from behind the desk, "you here to pick up that book for Inerea?"

"I'm thinking of starting a delivery company," I reply.

He chuckles then glances beneath the desk.

"Just a minute it doesn't seem to be here. It must be somewhere downstairs. Why don't you take a look around, this might be awhile?"

I nod as he retreats, then follow the spiral staircase up the curls of its spine.

Upstairs the store is much darker, lit by fewer lights and smaller windows, which hardly infiltrate the crowded rows of bookshelves with their light. The leather spines of books look dull in the darkness, though occasionally one with a gold or silver design glints. I follow the straight path between an entire forest worth of bound pages, running my thumb freely across their buttery leather. Every day I go to the library, am exposed to beautiful literature. But never is it presented as exquisitely as in Mr Bowen's shop. I slide a green leather-bound book from where it's wedged snuggly between its brothers and begin to leaf through the pages. I hardly examine their contents; it's the tactile experience of the moment I seek. I'm far more interested in the weight of the book contrasted with the light kisses of the paper on my fingers as I move between pages. The potential for that to turn into a sharp bite that draws blood. A few minutes pass before I'm overcome with that familiar sense of being seen but not seeing.

I'm not sure what I'm expecting when I turn between the dashes of my heart, but the small girl, who I would assume was ten were it not for the sharpness composed in her expression, comes as a surprise. She's short with a delicate looking body and full cheeks that add to her childish appearance. Her eyes are filled with a brown that brings out honey tones in her golden waves and give the overwhelming sense of a cold crypt. I've never seen her in town before and certainly not at school.

"Can I help you?" I manage breathlessly.

"I need that book," she drawls, indicating the one in my hand.

I hold it out and she takes the proffered book. I wait, expecting her to leave with it but she just begins to read the opening inscription. I study her carefully and the initial softness that I had seen in her features fades. Her lips are pinched, as if forever angry at the world, and her button nose is ever so slightly upturned, betraying the same sense of arrogance I had detected in her tone. Despite these outward signs of cool dislike, there's something in her that provokes a sort of warmth in me.

"Hello, I'm-"

"I would listen to your little introduction but I don't care. Go be pleasant elsewhere," she says, waving dismissively without bothering to look up. Her cold voice takes me by surprise, so much so I find myself apologising before I can tell her off.

"I'm sorry, I didn't mean to bother you," I whisper, stepping away.

"Of course you didn't," she sighs, shutting the book, "but I'll tell you how you managed to anyways. First: you're stupid. Second: you're extremely idiotic. Third: you're revolutionarily and comically moronic."

She leaves the row of bookshelves that we stand in and disappears back down the stairs. Eventually her footsteps fade out of earshot. Fully aware of the fishlike manner in which my mouth hangs open following her verbal ambush, I stare at the place she disappeared.

"Mallory?"

Mr Bowen's voice draws me back to myself.

"Um, up here."

He peeks around the corner of the bookshelf, then comes into full view once he's spotted me.

"Sorry that took so long."

"No problem. Any idea what this one is?" I ask, taking the book wrapped in a thick linen cloth.

"You don't read them?"

"Inerea's very protective of the manuscripts you get her. They're the only thing in the house that's off limits."

"Hm."

He regards the book in my hands warily now, as if he regrets having handed it over.

"Don't worry I'll respect her wishes between here and the shop door. She's meeting me outside anyway." The look of concern dissipates as he laughs. "Do you know who that girl was?"

"Who?"

"The one who was just up here. I don't think I've seen her at school."

"That's Robyn Caverly. Her grandparents live here but I think she and her brother live in New York. Probably visiting for the summer. Why do you ask?"

"Just wondering. Thanks for the book."

"Of course."

We make our way back downstairs and I wave to him before leaving. Inerea's car is idling outside the shop, and I can just make her out through the opaque glass. Ducking into the passenger seat, I put my bag on the back seat.

"Hey grandma," I say, leaning over to kiss her on the cheek.

Her wiry grey hair brushes my cheek bone as I draw back and click on my seatbelt. Even in her oversize beige cardigan, she still appears slight. I'm always taken back by her petite and soft look, concealing a lithe sharpness. The strength of her youth still resides in old bones. She watches me with a catlike unblinking gaze, eyes exceptionally large on such a small face. They're an unnerving shade of grey as pale as my own, and I know lying to her about my blackout under their surveillance will be a difficult task.

"Hi little angel."

Her voice sings like air whistling through a metal tunnel, clear and cutting. But beneath that is always an authority, ready to be evoked.

"Thank you for picking that up for me."

"Thanks for picking me up, but you really didn't have to."

"Well I didn't know if you were in a state to get yourself home considering…" She trails off, glancing at me sideways as she pulls away from the pavement. Here we go.

"Considering what?" I reply, feigning innocence.

"Chloe wasn't with you at the library to give you a lift home."

"You called Chloe?" I gasp. Blood rushes to my cheeks as I'm swept by embarrassment.

"You didn't answer. But I see now there was nothing to be worried about."

I know this admittance is more of a testament to her willingness to let me get away with my secret than my acting.

"Sorry, I just got caught up looking at the books. Speaking of, are you finally going to let me take a peek at one of these?" I ask, hoping to change the subject and tapping on the cover of her new book.

"Absolutely not. They're not for your eyes."

"Hm, begs the questions, what's in here then. Something tawdry." I wink at her and she laughs.

"Mallory Theil, I am eighty-two years old."

"Never too late I guess."

She gives me her best attempt at a withering glare though the effect is diluted somewhat by the smile that plays at the corner of her lips.

"I hear about these sweet dutiful granddaughters from all my friends. What went wrong?" She pulls the car out, glancing over her shoulder.

"Dutiful? What should I be waiting on you hand and foot?"

"No but you could give me a foot rub now and again. These old toes need some love."

"Tempting but I'll pass. Besides, I think Chloe's coming over to practice a bit before we go to the bonfire."

I can tell Inerea is raising her eyebrows when she doesn't reply. How can she disapprove so thoroughly of a life she introduced me to?

"I promise it's only light stuff, I know my limits."

"I know you do, but that's never stopped you from testing them."

"You're referring to the candle incident."

"Candle incident is a generous way of putting what I would term a small fire."

"No more fire magic! I promise."

"I don't know what Chloe was thinking with that spell. Even at her level she shouldn't have been doing it."

I bite my lip, kicking myself for the lie I told a few weeks ago. That it was a spell to create living fire when really it was simple Earth magic and, once again, I hadn't been able to maintain control. Ever since then Inerea has been wary of Chloe, but Chloe had convinced me to keep it a secret. Better Inerea blame her than forbid me from practicing altogether, she had said.

"We'll be more careful. Only Inerea preapproved spell books from here on out." She snorts in disbelief. "What don't you trust me?"

"Trust a witch? Never."

She turns up the drive, and the car bobs down for a moment as we roll onto the gravel. Ahead, I can just make out the clearing our home is nestled in. The lights which twinkle warm yellow at night are strung up on the aged branches of trees surrounding the cottage. The front of the house is drenched in dripping bunches of mouse eared petals, whose tendrils have been coaxed up trellises. Each petal is slightly curved to shelter their soft white and yellow bellies. In their bunches they loom over the windows like curtains. The woodwork of the porch awning is entwined with the same lights as those in the trees, which are wound down the thin wooden columns supporting it. They cling as tightly as the flowers to the vines. Rusty chains drop from the roof to hold up a wooden swing Inerea and I newly veneered only last week. I glance at the time on my phone screen. Chloe will be here soon and, thanks to my lost time, I haven't had a chance to think about which spells to practice.

We climb out of the car, Inerea tucking the package

under her arm, and I fall in step beside her. Growing up I had no idea what I was. It wasn't until I left the Academy and came to live with Inerea that I learned the women of the Ovira family had been practicing witches for generations. One of the downsides of being an orphan: you don't really have anyone to tell you family secrets like that. A fair few families like ours and Chloe's live in Aplin Hollow. Celia, however, had moved away, refusing to practice in case it put Milton at risk, but Inerea always said she was particularly gifted growing up. I wonder where I had gone wrong. I haven't managed to get my magic under control yet, though Chloe says I've come far in a few months.

At the top of the stairs Inerea turns into her library, closing the door behind her. This is regular practice whenever she gets one of her new mysterious packages. It's one of the only times the library door is closed to me. It's not a large room but it's packed to the brim with the most amazing collection of books. My own from the Academy were added when I got here, though a couple permanently reside on my bedside table.

Rummaging through the closet, I grab a blue summer dress with white flowers patterned across it. I toss my clothes into the hamper in the corner of the room, slipping the dress on. Sweeping up my hair with one hand, I twist it round into a bun and pin it in place with a pencil from the pot on my desk. Just in time. Downstairs I hear the door open and Chloe calling up.

"Hey, your ride is here!" She comes up the creaky staircase and pushes the door open. "Very Little House on the Prairie."

"Shut up," I laugh, lobbing a pillow from the little reading nook on my window seat at her.

"I'm teasing, you look adorable as ever."

She shuts the door behind her and procures a bag of

potential outfits as well as a bouquet of flowers.

"I didn't realise this was a date, so sweet of you to bring me flowers."

"They're for the spell, though I'd be honoured to take you out anytime. Clothes first though." She pulls out a pair of black jeans and a white crop top, a gauzy white dress and a black skirt and blue blouse. "Thoughts?"

"Hm, swap the tops and go with the skirt. More casual than the dress but still very cute."

"As you say, so let it be."

She grabs the skirt and top before going into the bathroom. While she's out, I leaf through the slender spell book she's brought with her. It's a new translation, with most of the instructions and descriptions of the spells in English, while only the spells themselves are in the ancient language. I'm still learning it, though luckily I've managed to pick most of it up relatively quickly. The spells are all simplistic, and I finally find one involving flowers. I groan to myself.

"What do you think?" Chloe asks, emerging from the bathroom.

"Picking petals off a rose again? You're killing me with the mundanity," I say, reading through the spell.

"Well, you're welcome for the careful planning I do to increase your control of your magic but I was referring to the outfit." I glance up.

"Forget what I said about casual, you look like you're going to a club. In a good way. It's chic rather than cute which is much more you."

"Thank you," she says with a wink, "Shall we?"

Gathering the supplies from the bed, we sit across from one another on the floor. She removes one rose from the bouquet and lays it between us.

"I want you to try it on your own. I'm just here to give stability and support if things go tits up again."

"Thanks for the faith."

"Remember the candle incident?"

"You mean me almost burning the house down? I dimly recall."

"Ready?" I nod and glance down at the words in the ancient language. *One by one, undo what nature has wrought.*

"Cri tsi cri, pritaiyar valja tefet endaava natrabar."

The rose hovers steadily before me, an improvement from the past few times I've done the spell. It stops at eye level then rotates clockwise until its vertical. One by one, the petals are plucked by the spell. They catch as if on a pocket of air for a moment before dropping serenely to the floor below. The first few come off slowly, but it's not long before the flower begins to vibrate with the hum of my magic.

"Deep breaths. You're pouring too much of yourself into it," Chloe instructs.

How to hold myself back? Think of something else perhaps. Like Chloe's librarian. The flower trembles even more, the petals dropping rapidly. Maybe not. Think about how she'll be excited for every detail of my encounter with him. The tremors become less and less violent. Perfect. Think of the bonfire. How nice it will be, the last week of school coming up and then off to university.

The last petal floats gently to the ground, the stem lowering itself after it.

"Amazing! You did it!" Chloe launches herself across the space between us and gives me a hug. "Bet your grandma wishes she'd seen that."

I smile at her, wiping the small bead of sweat from my forehead.

"So, what next?"

"Well, we've still got a bouquet left. It's all about consistency," she adds, when I groan.

Chapter XII.

"How was this not the first thing out of your mouth when I got to your house?" Chloe demands.

She's reversed the car into a space between two others in the clearing and refuses to let me out until I've given her all the details of my exchange with her librarian.

"Because believe it or not the admittedly very sexy librarian is not the most pressing matter on my mind," I reply.

"He is sexy, isn't he? So, tell me everything."

"He took my book, I had to go ask for it back."

"And."

Damn her perceptive nature and my inability to be a closed book.

"And he recommended a book based on what he's noticed I've been reading."

She emits an unearthly squeal, leaving me covering my ears and cowering in my seat.

"Oh my god Mallory I am so jealous. He's actually been checking you out. I mean of course he has, you're gorgeous but oh my god."

"Or he appreciates a book nerd," I suggest, but the memory of his golden gaze tells me otherwise, "okay yeah, he was checking me out."

"Look at you, grinning like a moron. You're stealing my man and I'm so okay with this because I've never seen you look that way. I think you're the one who appreciates a book nerd."

"He just seems, I don't know, thoughtful. Most people are so careless, just in the way they move or speak. And if not that, they're calculating. He's just different."

"I'm melting. I cannot wait to tell Connie."

"And you mean just Connie, right? No running around to the entire school?"

"I may be a notorious gossip, but you and Connie are sacred territory. I would never." She squeezes my hand and squeals at a more human decibel. "Come on."

I follow her along the short path from the parking area to where we can see the bonfire flickering.

"Ugh I've missed this. So glad I get to be here for your first bonfire. Oh, there's Connie. Connie!" As if the register at which she's called our friend's name isn't enough to get her attention, Chloe starts flailing her arm and I can't help but laugh. I give her a hug from behind and dot a kiss on her cheek. "Well hello sailor. What's that for?"

"You're the best, you know that?"

"Hm I am aware of my magnificence, yes."

She wraps her arms around herself and holds my hands as Connie makes her way over with three drinks.

"You two are cuddly, what'd I miss?"

"Mallory was professing her undying love for me."

"It's true, I'll never love a one like her."

Connie passes us each a cup.

"First rule of bonfire, take the punch slow because it will knock you on your ass out of nowhere."

"Not a problem," I say, gagging on my first sip, "that's is rank."

"It gets good around the second cup."

"You mean when I've become a complete booze hound?"

"No that's really a title saved for fourth cuppers," Connie says, taking a sip. She swallows and sticks her tongue out in a sign of disgusted solidarity.

"Weaklings. Okay, Connie I have to tell you Mallory's gossip."

"It's so not gossip, it's just news. If that."

"Hush, now it's my turn to tell someone your good news."

I roll my eyes. As Chloe fills Connie in, I continue sipping on my drink and surveying the clearing. I recognise just about everyone there from school, except for the odd individual who must be here visiting family. Speaking of. I spot the girl from the antique store earlier today.

"Chloe."

"Not now! I'm getting to the good bit."

"Do you know her?"

My inquiry into another gets her attention. If anyone knows anything about Robyn it will no doubt be Chloe. She looks around to see who I'm indicating and nods.

"Snooty bitch. Spoke to her once briefly. She comes back here with her adoptive brother every summer to see their grandparents. Now he is gorgeous. Hasn't been back the past few years though, which is a shame because he really only saw me pre-puberty and that was not pretty. Why do you ask?"

"Just didn't recognise her."

She can tell I'm lying but I'm also right in thinking she won't push it in front of Connie. I down the rest of my drink and repress a shudder. "I'm going to grab another."

"I think you may in fact be a booze hound in the making."

"All in good time pet."

I skirt the edge of the clearing to reach the table with the massive punch bowl.

"Seconds already? Didn't take you for a drinker." I turn around.

"Delightful," I sigh. I can already feel the alcohol clouding my head. Robyn stands with her arms crossed. "Listen, you made it clear how charming you find my presence so how about removing yourself from it, so as not to be an impediment to either of us enjoying of the evening?"

She raises her eyebrows.

"Another surprise." She leans past me to grab a cup.

"How so?"

"Didn't take you for the type to stand up for yourself." She wonders off into the crowd.

"Snooty bitch indeed," I grumble, refilling my cup. As I make my way back to Chloe and Connie, who are both looking at me with excitement following Chloe's undoubtedly embellished version of my encounter, I feel someone shove hard into my shoulder. My cup sloshes in my hand, the sticky punch dribbling down my hand.

"Watch where you're going."

"Says the person who just walked into me," I reply. I glance up to see a tall guy, slightly older than me with glowing gold eyes. Unlike the librarian's, they're cold and hardened. He ignores me and pushes past. "What a shocker," I whisper to myself as I see him join Robyn and another guy. Her face has lit up in the other's presence, who's in the midst of animatedly telling a joke.

"Jeez who was that guy?" Chloe asks.

Connie's disappeared in the brief seconds between catching her gaze and being bulldozed. I spot her talking to her boyfriend Dean. They're off to the side, her head bent down as he speaks.

"I thought that might be the oh so handsome and charming brother of Robyn."

"Nope, never seen him before." The other guy walks away from the rude pair and disappears into the forest.

"This evening's been weird thus far, to say the least."

"I know. I saw Robyn speaking to you." She doesn't intone it as a question but I can sense what she's leading to.

"Yes, I met her before. I was picking up a book for my grandmother this afternoon and to say she was unpleasant would be an understatement."

"Awe I'm sorry boo." She wraps her arm around my waist. "You've had an eventful day. Drink up."

We down our drinks at the same time and I find she was right, it really does taste better the second time.

"Alright the eternal question of bonfire night lays before us: do we bother with boys or do we get absolutely wrecked and make absolute fools of ourselves?" she asks.

"Fools," I say, tapping my empty cup to hers.

"Let me get you a top up then milady."

She takes my cup and heads across the clearing. I see her get stopped by a small group by the bonfire and she glances at me to check I'm okay on my own. I nod and give her a grin, the exuberant nature of which is fuelled by the drinks. I look around to see if I can find Connie and Dean but they seem to have disappeared. Shuddering in the cold, I wrap my arms around myself. Chloe and Connie were welcoming but it's a small town and I moved here part way through senior year so, while I can smile and wave at people passing by, there aren't many to stop and talk to. My stomach does a revolution and it dawns on me that I am imminently about to be sick.

"Fuck."

Spinning around I start stumbling into the forest. My head is spinning, far more than it should be after only two drinks. One and a half if you count the fact that asshole dumped half of my drink on me. The sounds of the party fade behind me but I keep going, propelled by some desire to dissolve completely into darkness before-

My body heaves itself and I grab onto a tree for support just as I double over. The acrid taste burns my throat, coating my tongue and the back of my teeth. I hear myself being sick as if from a distance, my head spinning ever faster. When I'm done, I press my forehead against the tree to find stability. I wait until I finally feel I won't fall over, then I right myself but, for the life of me, I can't remember which direction I came from. The air is enclosed by the thick foliage of ancient trees, barring out the moonlight, and sealing me into their darkness. Out of the white glare of the moon, the darkness of night doesn't invoke fear in me. So, what is it that lights the hair on my neck with terror? Survival screams in me, urges me to call for Chloe, but I know she won't hear me. I pick up my pace, eager to find my way home now.

Brushing aside a branch I step forward only to lose my footing as my toes catch on something hard. My body jerks forward and, with my hand still raised to move the branch, I'm unable to catch myself. I cross my arms over my face to shield it as I fall onto the slanted earth. Before I can get a grip on anything to steady myself, my body gains momentum, allowing fallen twigs to scratch the bare skin of my legs. I tumble down the hill, fingernails digging into dirt fleetingly only to be uprooted. As I'm tossed down, I hit a rock, hard, shattering pain through my rib cage. The ground plateaus and I come to a halt on a soft pile of moss.

Even with my body's increased resilience of pain I can still feel it stinging with the sharp pricks of nature's floor. My nose, buried in the wet greenness, fills with the damp smell of the moss. With shaking arms, I push myself up into a kneeling position and squint to see in the dark now that I've lost all light. The forest records no echo of my fall to play back, as if it had never happened in this place time forgot.

I brush myself off, preparing to return to my path home. But looking at my indistinct surroundings that assume altering shapes as shadows enlarge their natural forms, I'm at even more of a loss as to which way to go. Perhaps if I can find the small hill I fell down I'll have some idea of which way to go. I pat the area around me, searching for where the ground begins to incline. The earth is swollen with water, making it soft and compact beneath my hands. I stand up and search with newly adjusted eyes. It appears as though I've fallen into some sort of crater, the ground all around me rising back up to where I fell from. I start my ascent when, as if lit on fire, the whole forest bursts with a single sound behind me. The snapping of a twig. It's just an animal, I insist to myself. But my breaths become more raggedly frequent faster than I can repeat this in my thoughts. No, I am not afraid of the dark.

What are you afraid of? one voice asks

Jump, another encourages.

Shh, it's okay, a third whispers by my ear.

My body tenses. By my ear? That's not possible.

Come. Poor thing, you're all alone.

Again, I am certain that I do not hear this voice within my head. It comes from nearby. I hear soft breathing from over my shoulder. It's such a gentle sound it could be the tender breath of a zephyr's very being. Everything about it, the volume, the pace, tries to lure me into security. Everything but the fact that it doesn't belong here. My erratic heart beat knows that. Beyond the rationality that tells me I shouldn't look comes the call of curiosity. I glance over my shoulder. Whether it's too dark to see or there truly is no one there I cannot tell. The area behind me is clear of all but trees as far as I can see. Then, from nowhere, a gust of wind picks up, smacking me with a rough pinpoint precision that forces me to drop onto all fours. The voices rise, screaming over each other simultaneously. Without a moment's hesitation, I'm back on my feet and sprinting deeper into the forest to escape them.

Don't leave me. Promise you'll never leave me.

Jump!

Don't leave me.

Shh, it's okay.
He'll get angry.
Come. Poor thing, you're all alone.
What are you so afraid of?
Come. Poor thing, you're all alone.
Come.
"No!"

The scream swells from my lips, finding volume in my voice despite my fear. My reply is ignored and the voices continue, unrelenting. My feet hit the packed earth in quicker succession every time they call out to me. The wind changes direction. It no longer attempts to push me down but, instead, creates a wall that is near impossible to run against. Somehow, amongst all the darkness, a fiery light casts its glow on the forest floor ahead of me. It falls like spilt blood of moonlight, overtaking my every step. It commands me to stop, haltingly brutal in its hue. I cannot help the stillness that takes over my form as I give up the little distance I had gained and turn to face the spitting source. It burns too bright to allow the finding of a distinguishable shape within it, but I can see it writhes with life.

Come. The laughter bubbles up into a roar from within my head and the swirling red. *Come.*

I bar out the light with my arm, stumbling back. It bloats, the light accommodating the darkness I tried to slip into. Another step backward and I find myself crashing down again. I throw my arms out helplessly to catch myself. As soon as my body hits the ground everything ceases, drawn into a vacuum of stillness. From behind my eyelids, I see the red light abate and I'm soothed by the balm of black nothing. I don't hear the voices anymore. His voice, overpowering them all. Why is it so familiar? I peek through barely opened lids to be sure all is gone before fully opening my eyes. I am alone, shrouded in forgiving darkness, but find myself unable to look away from where the light had been moments ago in case it reappears.

Regardless of how much I want to run away I can't will myself upright. This is what I've come to now, hallucinations? Yet, it felt so real. The insanity invoked in that man's voice could not be feigned by my mind. I drag myself to my feet, catching my breath as I stagger towards a tree and let my body sag against it. A break in the foliage above allows illumination to reveal my trembling hands are covered in scrapes. Blood beads in small pinpricks and seams across my palms. I flatten my hands on either side of me against the tree trunk, pushing hard to gain some stability. My hands slide over its bark, made slick by my blood. It cools the searing pain. The tree stirs behind me at the newly added pressure. No. That's absolutely not right. I pivot around and come face to face with a smooth bronze surface. My eyes adjust, taking in the details, and I see it's not hardened like metal. It's not one fluid surface. Plates like those of a pine cone overlap and interlock, pointing downwards, to create a sheet of armour like flesh.

"Scales," I breathe.

Picking up the faintest whisper of my voice in the air it stirs, the thing shifts. I step away from the stocky leg to take in the whole creature. It tilts its head slightly, its great snout directed towards me. It bobs its head up and down slightly as if dazed before lowering its gaze to survey me with those massive grey reptilian eyes, sharp as steel. It encases me in that frozen, unblinking look until it moves again, moonlight rippling down its gleaming scales like water.

"No," I plead to no one.

I hear its growl start, rumbling low in its belly before it snakes its head down in one swift movement and releases its deep roar in my face. The warm breath jets out, fuelled with the residue of fire, and tosses me away easily. Pain lances through my back as it smacks into the unforgiving surface of a tree. I push myself up onto all fours and look back at the creature. Its mouth remains open, displaying the moon reflective teeth that could pierce through me like the skin of fruit. I don't look back again as I sprint beneath the cover of trees.

Encased in scales, like small rubies dotted across skin to protect the soft human flesh within.

Where do these thoughts come from? It's as though I've had them all before. I hurl my body up the hill I had fallen down, dodging errant branches as I wind my way back through the forest. I see the light of the house emerging in a small opening between trees but it doesn't give me any relief. I trample a cluster of blue flax. As if those walls could protect me should that thing come after me. I shove the door open, rushing in and slamming it shut behind me, turning the lock. Such a trivial means of protection. Now that I've come to a stop, the frightened shivering of my body overcomes me. I slump down and bury my face in my hands. Could it only have been a hallucination? I look back at the forest that is steeped in pervasive illusions.

As the shudders reside my reason kicks in. Surely there's an explanation for what I saw. Or, rather, what I thought I saw. It was the alcohol. Or someone slipped something in my drink. I felt so dreadful leaving the bonfire, that must be it.

I look down at the mess I've made of myself. I need to get cleaned up before Inerea finds me or she'll be even more worried than she already is. I go upstairs to my bathroom where I clean the dirt and blood from my hands and knees before plastering the worst of the cuts. Yes, it must have been the punch. I grip tightly at the ceramic edge of the sink, biting the insides of my cheeks until I feel the iron sting of blood on my tongue.

I can force myself away from this delirious fear with rationale. When I suffer from my blackouts my therapist reminds me routine is key. Brush my teeth. Change into my pyjamas. Say goodnight to Inerea. I need the comfort of her voice. But outside on the landing I can see the light under her bedroom door is off and I don't want to disturb her any more than my abrupt return must have done. I'm about to return to my room when I spot the lamp still glowing in Inerea's study. I go to turn it off and see the book from earlier today is open on her desk. Through the haze of fear this night has brought, my feet guide me numbly to the desk. This is what I need right now, something to distract me. I have to admit, ever since she was cagey about the book's contents this afternoon, I've been curious.

The clock on the wall reads eleven thirty. I close the book, noting the page it was left open to. The brown cover's gold detail decoration glints in the light. Tracing the patterns, I realise that some of them are overly flourished letters.

"Ildsta Mai Den Liesma," I murmur.

It's in the ancient language all spells are written in. The words sound primitive and natural in my mouth, like components of an innate language my tongue was made to curl into the shapes of. I tap the last a, the tail of which dissolves back into the golden pattern. If beautiful covers are merely disguises for dark truths than this book should be avoided at all costs. Aware of the fragile state of the cracked brown leather binding, I lift the heavy cover with care. The first page is an identical copy of the cover's patterns, the same words inscribed on its surface. A loose piece of paper has been tucked inside as well. The delicate handwriting takes form with black ink like lines of ants that could be shaken off the page. It too is in the ancient language, but is beyond my comprehension. I restore the note to its place before turning to the next page. I find it's made of a thick vellum with a velvety texture. The other side of the page is coated completely in paints that, once slick, have now aged into dryness. Unlike the texture of the paint, the images have not lost their vividness to years. Bright colours burst from the full-page prints, forsaken by any words or attempt at description. There is almost no recognisable order for the images. It's as if someone has cut out great fragments of the narrative and left no space to reinsert them. The repeated images are clear enough though.

A king, whose hood falls just above bushy grey eyebrows, is seated on a seemingly decrepit throne. Its back is engraved with the same golden pattern that outlines each page and the book's cover. A pack of wolves whose menacing nature is caricatured by their gigantic teeth and an excess of shaggy fur. Their grotesque forms twist unnaturally, as if writhing on the still page. A phoenix grows from a wrinkled lump of ill-fitting skin to a creature possessing exquisite red feathers, some of which are illuminated orange by its own burning flame. Three eggs. Three serpents. The moon. And fire. Always, on every page, there is fire.

Languishing over every page and the rich nature of the images, I don't keep track of the hour until the grandfather clock on the other side of the room chimes once. The book has allayed thoughts of the evening, restoring sanity so I feel at last I can sleep. I get up, being sure to flip back to the page Inerea had left the book open to. Blood chills like a fire abruptly doused. How could I have been so unobservant? I recoil from the book. Three eggs. Three serpents. Only serpents don't have wings. I sink into the desk chair staring at the black creature on the page, spitting fire onto an already burning city. No, not serpents. Dragons.

Chapter XIII.

I don't fall asleep for a long time that night. Even
after forcing myself to lay still in bed, I can't stop listening
for the sound of powerful wings beating the air around
the house, drumming up a hurricane. It isn't until the
sun began to blaze over the tips of the trees, like matches
lined up and lit on fire, that I am finally overcome by my
weariness. But my waking hell follows me into sleep and
coils around my unconscious.

"Remembering hurts, doesn't it?" he says.

His hands hold me firmly in place so that, squirm
as I might, I cannot pull my feet out of the fire he bathes
them in. For all the roaring pain on my skin, I cannot
ignore his burning grasp my body screams against. His
touch is worse than the suffering because, though it
immobilises me, it is gentle. He thinks he's doing me a
favour. I can feel the fire in places it doesn't touch, its
warmth blooming in my chest.

"You seem to know all about the causes of pain.
How much do you know about what it fucking feels like,"
I pant.

"All too much."

His grip tightens and he applies more pressure to my
shoulders, forcing me into the ember chasm. The world
fractures, overlaps, echoes of images to choke in. I hear
my thoughts calling to me from a distance, slipping out of
reach. His hands are gone and replaced by the touch of a
memory I cannot grasp.

"Don't worry, I'll save you."

I'm plunged wholly into the flames. They don't burn.

I don't wake with a start. I see the tips of my eyelash-
es as I blink slowly into the morning light. Sitting up, my
body doesn't groan in retribution for my falls last night.
The places where I was cut by branches are still marked

by faint white lines, but the skin doesn't feel tender against
the probing of my fingers. The fog of memories from the
night before, bathed in sheer exhaustion, unfolds itself
slightly. I remember changing into my pyjamas but my
head feels as though there's a mist pressed to it, curtain-
ing off most of the night. How much did I drink? Running my hand through the knots of my matted hair until
it's untangled for the most part, I scatter a few stray pine
needles in the process.

Despite my waking calm, I stand to find my body is
shaking. I manage to get into the bathroom before I find
I need to sit down again. I seat myself on the edge of the
bathtub and lean forwards. My legs feel new worn, so I
bend and unbend my knees a few times until the quivering feeling of disuse falters. Running the shower, I strip
my pyjamas, which have a little caked dirt on them, off
and wait for the water to turn scalding hot before I get
in. Burning kisses crack against my skin until rivulets of
water darkened by earth pour down me. I watch as one
dips inward at my navel then drips down and recollects its
drops into a stream all the way at the drain. Cold water
never feels as though it cleanses the way heat does. The
traces of my falls would disappear and the grains of soil
would mingle briefly with flakes of dried blood as they
circled one another around the drain before disappearing. But the steam hot water exhales that fills the room,
attaching itself to all the oxygen I breath, staves off the
fear that's really hanging over me.

Once the worst of the grime and natural debris is
gone, I work shampoo into my hair made heavy with the
weight of water, trying to ignore last night. The events
that led me into the forest unwrap themselves for me to
reconsider and I can't help but wonder about that book.
Why does Inerea have it and what are the chances that
she had such an interest in that matter the same night one

of those things appeared? Just like that, I see it again in my mind's eye. The way its predatory eyes had beheld me clutches at my heart again. I hastily wash the remainder of soap from my hair and stare ahead at the painting on the opposite wall. Some semblance of clarity returns and I glaze over the worst part of last night. The part I won't bring myself to recall again. I decide to attach my attention to the first thing that comes to mind.

"Shit."

Scrambling to turn the water off, I step out of the shower and wrap a towel around myself. I can feel the heavy drops of water beading from my hair to my back and know I should stop to dry it but there's something more pressing. Snatching my phone from my jacket pocket, I go to my contacts list and press the first name I see. Two rings and-

"Where the fuck did you go last night? Do you know how worried I've been?" Chloe demands from the other end of the line.

"I know, massive screw up. I just felt so sick and went to throw up then got lost."

"Wow, you're some kind of lightweight." Already she's back to her laughing self and the sound of her voice puts me at ease. "You only had, what, two maybe three drinks?"

"I know but my head was spinning and I felt like I was going to collapse. It's like I had no control over myself."

"Seriously?" she asks, suddenly very quiet.

"What?"

"You don't think someone spiked your drink, do you?"

"Who, Connie? She's the only one who had my drink-oh shit."

"What?"

"That guy who bumped into me could of. I knew I felt way too weird for it to just be the drinks." Spiked. Relief floods me. If that's the case then hallucinations aren't off the table. Maybe what I saw wasn't real. "Chloe I've got to ask you something."

"Uh-oh, serious voice."

"Are dragons real?" She pauses a moment and I'm certain she's about to ask me if I've lost it.

"Short answer or long answer?"

"Short is fine."

"Yes, but you'll never see one. I can guarantee that."

"Thank you," I sigh.

"You're so odd. You vanish and your first question is about dragons?"

"Yeah, just regular hijinks for me, you know where my mind goes."

"Not really but I've stopped trying to figure it out," she laughs. She waits, her breathing soft.

"So how was the rest of your night?" I know she's waiting for me to ask.

"Oh my god, crazy. So, after you bailed, I found out Connie broke up with Dean who then tried to get with Michelle so obviously I did a little hex so he would get some grey hairs, nothing major but I want to stress the son of a bitch out."

"Is Connie okay?"

"Oh yeah, this has been a long time coming. We both knew she could do better."

"Too true."

"Anyway, I was thinking library date to finish up our project today?"

"Since when have you been keen to go to the library?"

My train of thought fractures into spirals of images. *Mirrors.*

Towering men in thick soled boots.
Waiting in dark rooms, waiting for whom?
A rope hanging from a chandelier.
"Mallory? Mallory?"

"I'm here," I reply, just as suddenly transported back to reality. I rub my forehead. Where did that come from?

"You okay?"

"Yeah, must be the after effects of whatever I drank. My head's a little rough."

"I was saying, before your hangover so rudely interrupted me, I want to check out you and a certain librarian. You have to promise to talk to him."

"I've got nothing to say!" I exclaim, flopping on my bed.

"Have you read the book he gave you?"

"Not yet."

"Well do your super power reading thing and finish it so you can chat him up." I roll onto my stomach, gazing out the window. "You owe me after last night."

"Fine."

"And wear that blue dress with the knot in the back, he'll melt."

"You're incorrigible," I laugh, "alright I better get reading, see you at the library."

"Perfect, I'll text Connie. See you around three." She hangs up and I trot back to the bathroom, nabbing the hair dryer as I go.

Heard about last night, if you need anything let me know x, I text Connie.

Love you but I'm fine, she replies quickly.

I've just showered but something about my conversation with Chloe has got me worked up and I feel an urge to go on a run. That or maybe I just need some fresh air to clear my head. I throw on my leggings and sports bra, swirling my still wet hair into a bun.

"It's daytime," I assure myself in the mirror, "it'll be alright."

As if evil can only live at night. As if it doesn't reside in human bodies that make a habit of cruelty during the day.

What the hell? I stare into my own unflinching gaze. Where is my mind wandering?

The sky has darkened outside my window, the sun now entombed in clouds. Even though I know its light wouldn't be of any use to me once I'm in the forest, the complete obscuring of natural light seems a bad omen to me. I trot downstairs to find Inerea in the kitchen.

"You off for a run? I was going to make pancakes."

"Ah the perfect post run snack."

"Snack? I believe that's what most people call a meal," she scolds teasingly.

"It's first breakfast."

"Your appetite is a terrifying thing. How was last night, I didn't hear you get back?"

She's probing to see if anything went wrong and, for once, what she expects is the case but I have no intention of telling her about my suspected drug trip or the cascade of seeming memories I just had. When in doubt, deflect.

"Really fun, but Connie broke up with her boyfriend."

"Is she okay?"

My heart melts over her concern for my friend. I nab a strawberry from the bowl on the counter before planting a kiss on her cheek.

"Yeah, I think so, but I hear people often think they're fine after break ups until they're not. Not that I'd know," I say leadingly. She sighs.

"You know I just worry about you and dating. What if you had an episode? How would you explain that?"

"I go to school and I'm fine, I hang out with my friends and I'm okay. Why would it be different with someone else?"

She finishes mixing the batter and gives me a signature piercing look.

"Why the sudden interest in the subject? Is there someone you're interested in?"

"Oh, would you look at that, I need to go on my run." I pop my earphones in as she opens her mouth again and gives me a bemused look. "Sorry, can't hear you."

"Speaking of episodes, have you rescheduled your appointment with your therapist?"

"Tomorrow afternoon."

"Good." She comes over and kisses my forehead. "I just want you to be okay."

"I will be. Promise."

Outside, the glade has come alive again with the soft movement of butterfly wings that beat lazily with the help of a breeze. Despite the lack of sunlight, a warm misty glow ensconces the forest. It has the aura of a lullaby and, were it not for the recollection of the previous night, I would be overcome by the desire to curl up between the roots of the trees and be lost in here forever. I make my way right to the back of the glade, picking up to a light jog. The foliage shelters me, seals me in with the shade, and that's when I start gaining speed. I breathe a pent-up sigh of relief I hadn't known was in me, pressing further into the forest. Whatever daunting effect the woods have on me is nullified by the speed building in my legs as I run off path, winding between trees. Before I know it, I hear my smart watch beep and know a mile has passed. I glance around me, taking in my surroundings, which seem all too familiar. There are crushed tracks of flowers and ferns all around me. Shit, I know where I am. The hill from last night. Have I really run here instinctively?

The air around me is suddenly full of movement that does not belong to nature. A shape darts before me in a blur, too close and swift for me to react. Another body collides with mine, knocking me from my feet. We fall, tumbling back over the hill just as I had done only hours ago. Only this time, elbows and knees hit me as we continue our descent, along with the bites of the forest floor. I'm allowed swirling glimpses of my fellow falling one: a bulky figure clad in a shirt of warm storm blue and black trousers. Then I lose sight again. We reach the bottom, my body coming down second and landing on top of the other. In a wave of dizziness, I glance everywhere but at what's beneath me, because whoever this is can't be as bad as what's been in this clearing before. I half expect to look up and see it or see some massive footprints, but it's just us. I breathe a sigh of relief just before I'm flipped over and pinned on my back. My body erupts in panic that grabs hold of my vocal cords.

"Get off!" I gasp, but the hands holding me down just increase their pressure. A sharp rock pierces the skin beneath my shoulder blade, slicing pain through me. I writhe against the grip but it holds fast.

"Who are you?" a deep voice demands.

"Who am I? Who the hell are you?" I ask in return, surprised by the biting tonality of my voice given the circumstances.

Wriggling beneath his weight, I manage to extricate my arms from his hands and push hard against his chest. It's hardly enough force to actually move him but the action seems enough to make him aware of what he's doing. He shifts, moving aside to give me enough room to stand. Dusting the twigs off of my person, I eye my assailant. He watches me with dark grey eyes that force me to lower my gaze slightly. He has a Roman nose that would be too large for his face were it not for the broadness of his square jaw covered in short stubble, a shade darker than his caramel-coloured hair. The round peaks of his cupid's bow are the only feature that suggest he might be younger than I first thought.

"I'm sorry. I thought for a minute," he starts, but ends up shaking his head, "never mind."

His voice sounds like the rare and steady movement of honey. I don't reply. There's something I know in his eyes, which I can look at now he's glanced away. Do I know him?

"I said I'm sorry, can you stop looking at me like that?" he mutters, standing up.

"Sorry, this is just how my face looks all the time," I say, narrowing my eyes at him.

"Oh, I thought you were still mad."

"That someone just tackled me over a hill?" I ask.

"It was an accident, I promise," he answers sheepishly, rubbing the back of his neck. No doubt sore from the fall. I dust my hands off to remove the dirt before groaning. My head's spinning again. "What's the matter? Aside from the internal bleeding."

This guy is way too chatty for a hangover.

"It's nothing. Sorry to have got in your way."

"You're sorry? See now I'm not sure if you're just abusing sarcasm."

"I'm not, I take acts of abuse very seriously."

"Sure, because being stationary and ran into is definitely something to apologise for," he mutters coming to stand beside me.

"Is it?"

"No, that was sarcasm."

His brow furrows as he looks down at me.

"Sorry my head's just a bit foggy, bonfire last night."

"Ah the infamous punch."

"You were there?" I take another look at him but already know I don't know him from school. "You were with Robyn."

"You know Robyn? My condolences."

Before I can ask him what he means, another voice interrupts us.

"Aaron!"

I hear three sets of footsteps skittering down the hill to reach us. Soil comes loose beneath feet and outstrips them, dusting the tops of the fern leaves in the clearing.

"Are you alright?" a girl's voice calls.

That voice I definitely know. I go rigid wondering if this is another bout of imagined images and voices. I glance back at Aaron, who is now looking over my shoulder. Could it have been his voice I heard in the forest last night?

"I'm fine," he replies hesitantly, catching my gaze.

Whose ghost from my memory are you come to haunt me?

Three people descend the hill, coming to a halt in front of us. Emerging, ahead of the rest, a girl rushes to Aaron's side.

"Be more careful next time," one of the other two says, hanging back beside a tree. His eyes are like the flat, dull surfaces of tacks and don't hold the concern of his words.

"Again, I'm fine."

"You wouldn't want to harm your precious face by falling so clumsily."

Aaron makes an obscene gesture towards the leonine eyed figure and brushes off the girl who worries about him. She's a small creature, capable of gentle kindness but possessing of a lethal grace as well. Robyn. And I swear I recognise that guy as well. The asshole who bumped into me! But before I can say anything the fourth member of the party cuts in.

"Enough Leo," he says, stepping forwards. Recognition hits me within seconds of seeing his face. He turns towards me at the sound of my quiet intake. "Shit."

"I'm sorry Kyle, did hell just freeze over?" Leo yawns.

"Yeah, unnecessary profanity," Aaron scolds mockingly.

"You, you were at my school," I say, stepping instinctively towards the one named Kyle.

I recognise his eyes, a shade of darkness with barely traceable hints of blue. His dark hair, however, is no longer slicked back, and now falls in floppy curls over his head. "You worked with the head teacher."

"Head teacher? You mean Doctor Lindberg?"

"Who's Doctor Lindberg?" He stands there staring at me in awe. "Did the school send you?"

"What the hell is she on about," Robyn asks Kyle.

"Robyn, Leo, Aaron, this is Mallory. I'm Kyle," he starts, moving towards me. No. Don't.

"Charmed, I'm sure. But see, I don't really give a damn," Robyn interjects icily.

"Well you should. She's a Thiel," Kyle replies, not looking away from me.

Leo, the man with golden eyes, flashes Kyle a dangerous look that I feel would cut through his skin were he to be lying about my surname.

"Last name aside, are you following me?"

"It's not stalking!" he insists defiantly. "I happened to find out you were a Thiel and I knew I had to come to the Academy to protect you. That's why I'm here."

"And we all thought you wanted to have a nice holiday in our company," Aaron says.

"Just for the record, I would never waste my time stalking you. I genuinely believe you to be as stupid as I said yesterday. Turns out you just happen to be a stupid person I'm going to have to put up with," Robyn clarifies.

"You've known about her for half a year and failed to mention her existence on what basis?" Leo demands, ignoring Aaron and Robyn's remarks.

Locked up in a room all on my own until one friendly person finally arrived.

A running track.

All my books packed in cardboard boxes in the boot of a car when I had expected never to see them again. He did that.

"Why," I ask, to myself and Kyle, rubbing my forehead, "why do you seem two people to me?"

"Do you always talk like a dead poet from the eighteen-hundreds?" Robyn asks.

"Please stop! None of you are making sense. Except for her," I say. "What does my last name matter?"

"You really don't know?" Aaron asks.

"Told you she was stupid."

"Hush Robyn," Kyle says.

"No, I don't know," I reply to Aaron, my stream of thought on the verge of complete dissolution. "I don't know why you're going on like mad people about protecting me because I'm a Thiel or who Doctor Lindberg is or what the Academy is. I thought I was insane but you four are the very derivation of insanity!"

The air thickens to a leaden weight in my lungs. I need to get out of here.

"Alright let's just all calm down. We should probably explain everything to Mallory first," Kyle says.

"Wonderful idea. Except she's running away," Leo interjects.

"What?"

Their voices become quieter as I sprint up the hill and disappear behind the thick line of trees. A relief to be back in the forest is not what I expected.

"Come back!"

At the sound of the command, I pick up more speed, anxious to get away from them. At first the sound of their footfall nears me but I dart steadily between tree trunks.

They may be fast but I know the forest from all my runs and know I can outrun them. I thank my preternatural speed that allows me to leave them in the dust. I enter the glade behind Inerea's house, letting myself in through the backdoor. As I collapse into one of the dining room chairs, my lungs burn with a hunger for oxygen. Panting, I tilt my head back and stare through the glass ceiling at the still grey sky.

"Mallory?" Springing from my chair, I send it skidding out from beneath me. Inerea looks at me in a puzzled manner.

"Sorry, didn't hear you come up behind me." She doesn't believe me but chooses not to push it. "I should shower, then pancakes?"

"Sounds good."

"You're a queen amongst women," I call back as I go upstairs.

I shut the door and rest my head against it. What the hell is going on here? This is about my last name? As soon as he said Thiel something changed in them all. A sort of begrudging responsibility became present. I sit on the edge of my bed. What do I do, tell Inerea I'm being followed?

Don't tell anyone. They'll get angry.

Not now.

Then when, they whisper.

It's time.

Jump.

What are you so afraid of?

Stop, I command. Their voices hush. I feel myself tearing up. This can't still be the effects of last night. Something is really wrong with me. I need to tell someone but Inerea will just freak out and it's not fair to shoulder Chloe with this responsibility. My therapist, Doctor Hersch. I sigh with relief. She'll know what to do. Resolved to leave the problem until tomorrow's appointment and focus on my final project, I take a quick shower and put on the dress Chloe demanded I wear. I grab Calvino's *Castle of Crossed Destinies* and head downstairs where I hear the soft flop of a pancake onto a plate. Inerea nods in approval of my book choice.

"Something of a homework assignment from Chloe," I say, seating myself at the table.

"I didn't take Chloe as a fan of Calvino."

"Oh, she isn't and she didn't recommend it," I answer.

I start reading and continue to pour through the pages once Inerea joins me. She flicks open the newspaper and I can sense her glancing at me over the top now and again but I pretend not to notice. When we're done, she clears the plates.

"I'm just going to shower then I can give you a lift into town whenever you're ready."

"Thanks!" I watch her leave the room before glancing hastily out the window. I still half expect them to have followed me home but it seems safe for now.

It's almost two when I finish the book. I slip it into my bag and knock on Inerea's closed library door. She's at her desk, leafing through the book from yesterday. Never before have I found a book so repellent in my life.

"You ready?" she asks.

"Yup. Hoping to get everything done today so I can just rehearse the presentation tomorrow," I say, following her outside.

"That's my studious one. I can't believe you'll be off to college in a few months."

She smiles warmly and, for all her overprotectiveness, I know I'll dearly miss her presence when I move to New York.

The drive is short and, before I know it, I'm waving

goodbye to Inerea from outside the library. I see Chloe approaching, two coffees in hand.

"You're a saint," I say as she hands me one.

"Well, I come bearing bad news. Connie's sick and so you and I have to finish the project by ourselves and by you and I, I mean you. I'm going to be ogling your beloved."

"One conversation does not a beloved make."

I follow her inside and upstairs to our favourite table. It's right at the edge of the balcony, overlooking the rest of the library, but tucked behind some bookshelves so as to obscure us from sight.

"Did you finish the book?"

"Yes oh domineering one."

"Well go return it and ask for another recommendation! He's at the desk now."

I scowl at her, retrieving the book from my satchel.

"Only because I owe you for bailing last night."

I head downstairs, Calvino in hand, and can't help but notice my nerves present themselves in a slight tremor in my hand. He doesn't seem to notice me approach, scrutinising the computer with a furrowed brow.

"Hi," I say, and I'm surprised by how quietly my voice comes out. He glances up and seems to stiffen for a moment before relaxing.

"Back so soon?"

"End of the term so there's a lot of work to finish off."

Nice, mentioning school. Just remind him about that age gap. What am I thinking? He nods then looks at the book I'm clutching tightly. The corner of his lip twitches up.

"That busy but you still had time to read the book I recommended?"

"It was hard to put down. His language is so compelling," I say, ducking my head as I pass him the book.

"Isn't it though. It's hard to know what of it is him and what's the translator's doing."

"I'll stick to the idealist notion that the translator doesn't tamper too much with the original language."

"Ah but what would Ted Hughes' translation of Ovid be without some poetic license?"

"I wouldn't know but I suppose I'm going to have to find out." He stands up, his smile broadening now.

"Let me show you the way Miss Theil." Theil? How does he know my last name? After this morning the comment sends me into a panic. He notices and is swift to clarify. "It's on your library card."

"Of course it is, could I be more of a parsnip head," I say.

"Parsnip head?" he asks, leading me toward the poetry section.

"It's just a stupid thing I say." God could I be more of a moron? But he laughs and slows to fall in step beside me. "It's a bit unfair I don't know your name."

"John."

Suddenly the silence seems uncomfortable, as though we're both desperate to say something but not sure what it is.

"So, are we going to make a habit of this?" he asks.

"It's rare I find anyone who likes to read as much as me, though librarian should have been an obvious go to," I reply, before quickly correcting myself, "sorry that sounded arrogant. I just mean-"

"You like to read. And it's not arrogant. Are you going to study English at university?"

He pauses at the shelf, scanning for Ted Hughes. I can spot it from here and I'm certain he has to but is stalling.

"I haven't given it too much thought. I'm just looking

forward to having a more diverse curriculum. The school here is fine but," I trail off shrugging.

"Not suitable for one so formidable as yourself I imagine."

"I'm hardly formidable. My school before this one was just a bit more rigorous."

"Do you miss it?" he asks, abandoning his task of looking for the book.

"I feel like I should. What I recall of it makes me certain it suited me so much better, but I always have this underlying feeling of revulsion towards it."

Why am I telling him this? Despite fond memories, my old school has always left a knot in my stomach when I think on it.

"Revulsion is quite a strong reaction to a school."

"Must be that all the reading has made me hyperbolic," I joke in an attempt to deflect.

"Maybe, but you don't strike me as one for hyperbole."

He hands me the book and our hands brush. My fingers feel as though they burst into flames, skin full of screams.

Red scales, like metal lacquered in blood.
Bodies scattered across the floor like so much debris.
The moon, full, and me to wait under it.

"Are you okay?" he asks.

He's got his arm around me to support my weight as I sag slightly. Without thinking I rest my head against his shoulder, my breath scattered. His grip tightens around me. We stand for a few moments like that while I collect myself. These bouts are getting more intense, more vivid.

"Sorry, I just have this awful headache that keeps cropping up today," I whisper, but he doesn't let me go.

I'm suddenly aware of my body as I've never been before, the way his arm rests around the curve of my waist to draw me close to him. Here, after all the madness of today, in the safety of his arms, I'm overcome by the desire to kiss him. I draw back slightly and still he holds me, studying my face. Why do I feel so intensely about a stranger, I wonder? Our noses brush lightly and suddenly he spins me round and I'm pressed against the wall. The full weight of his body pins me there and it sends shocks like lightening delineating pleats of sky through me. He puts one hand low on my waist, his thumb rubbing across my hip, and the other winds itself into my hair. His roughness is not something I expected but my body responds in kind. I press my hips against him and hear his breath shake as I bite his lip. The only thought that manages to escape the sudden tangle of emotion is am I doing this right.

I hear a creak of floorboards and just as quickly he lets me go, leaning down to pick up the book I dropped. A couple comes from around the corner, oblivious to what's just happened, and walks away.

"Thanks," I say through slightly gasped breaths, "for the book."

He laughs and I feel my cheeks flush.

"So, are we going to make a habit of this?" he murmurs, stepping back towards me.

My heart is pounding in my chest as he draws near. "I-"

"Mallory?" I spot Connie over his shoulder.

Within an instant John is disappearing around the corner.

"Hey, I thought you weren't coming in today," I say, going to give her a big hug.

"Yeah, I wasn't really sick just needed some time to clear my head. What were you doing with the hunky librarian?"

"All in good time pet," I giggle, taking her by the

arm.

Chapter XIV.

In my dreams I am fire. It doesn't just cloak me to burn away my skin, it is a breath of heat on my body that cools to become my skin. I wear it as my own. Its swelter suffuses with blood cells until my veins rage with a life force surpassing anything I have experienced or even imagined. I feel wings grow from my soul, allowing me to be free of myself and human existence's boundaries.

But the first rush of power is soon overwhelmed by a realisation: I don't know how to control this new layer of my being. What started as a strengthening extension of my self now dominates me, subduing any attempt to fight back. I can feel it consuming and suffocating my body without leaving any space for my newly freed soul to escape. Wings beat hard against the burning architecture of my skeleton, the futility of trying to escape instead of being converted to ash. What takes hold is not a smoke that would chase oxygen from my lungs, but the purist elemental power itself. It erodes the thinly veiled branches of veins and bleeds fire into my body. The fire of my blood. It seeps through my pores and sweeps through me until it reaches my core. Then my heart sheds its everything as ashes of excess and I am lost entirely.

My eyelids fly open and I feel the heat already receding from my chest with this waking action, though my skin still prickles. My hair is splayed across the pillow, a swarm of night tendrils to cool me with shade. The fine hairs on the nape of my neck are sticky with sweat, as is the back of my pyjama top. Reining in irregular breaths, I sit up and rub my eyes.

Again, the sky is plastered completely together, a greasy film I wish I could peel back. I pull my duvet from my still warm body and watch the dormant sky, hoping my body will cool. Heat heaves its breaths across my skin as if to warm it again. I slip out of the bed and press my hand to the radiator, but it's off. My heart tingles when I recall how powerful I had felt in my dream. Even when I was on the precipice of burning out completely, it felt safe and worth the flash of pain just so that I didn't feel helpless. Pacing my room, I cannot shake the sweltering memory the fire left on my skin so I stand beneath the raw icy water of my shower. The drops chill my skin almost instantaneously before their cooling powers begin to work on spreading through the rest of me. I feel that faint nagging in my throat of a feeling pushing up, a fear embodied that wants to rise up into the scream. Beneath the sheets of cold water, I shiver. Once I've been chilled to a subnormal temperature, I change into my clothes and go downstairs. As soon as I reach the bottom of the staircase, I hear the front door opening, causing me to start ever so slightly.

"Morning," Inerea says, coming in with the watering can.

"And yet I feel like crawling back into bed."

"Maybe you should go on a run, clear your head before your therapy session today. I've got to go do some grocery shopping."

I bite my lip, unwilling to tell her of why I so desperately don't want to go into the forest after yesterday. But I go every day. She'll find it odd if I don't all of a sudden. And I only have to wait until this afternoon to talk to Doctor Hersch about what happened. What are the chances I run into them again? Or rather, they run into me.

"Will do. See you soon," I say, though this is more of an assurance to myself than her.

I go upstairs and change into my workout gear.

Outside, I find the morning air as cold as two nights before, though it hangs still without the slightest hint of a breeze. I start off slow with the intention of remaining within close proximity to the house. Perhaps I'll just circle the trees on the fringe of the forest a few times, keeping the house within sight. But before I know what my body is doing, my legs have picked up to their usual pace. A need to run overrides my desire for safety. Within a few minutes I've plunged deep into the forest, well beyond sight of the house. The air screams at me to slow down as it whistles by my face but I don't take heed. It bites at me in cold bursts as I leap clear over a tree stump that lies in my path.

"Look out!"

My leg extended before me strikes something hard and for a moment I fear I've tripped on the stump, or something worse. I crash atop something warm and sentient. A huff of hot breath is expelled onto my face with the impact. Looking down, I meet the gaze of mirror eyes that hold the dark grey plumes above us in perfect reflection.

"Well look who's tackling who now," Aaron says, reaching for my wrist as I attempt to dart away. "No wonder I couldn't keep up with you yesterday. You're a speedy little thing."

Pressing the underside of my wrist hard against where his fingers join, I pry myself free from his grip and scoot away from him so he can sit up. My stomach lurches as touch memory replays the feeling of his manacle grip on my skin the day before. Compacted in my throat is a knot of pressure leaving little to no space for air to slip around it.

"Don't worry, I'm not going to hurt you. If anything, I should be concerned about my safety."

"Are you hurt?" I ask in alarm, moving back towards him.

"No, I was just teasing." His smile drops. "You really

do have trouble with humour, don't you?"

"I get thrown off my game when I run into stalkers. Speaking of, are you alone today?"

"Yeah, I gave my groupies the day off. I'm generous that way. Why do you ask, intending on doing more harm?" he asks, leaning lazily back on his hands.

"I don't think I'm the one doing any harm." He takes my arm as I start to stand. Something about his touch is enough to prevent me from getting up. The structure of molecules in my legs cave and my architecture falls apart so I'm left immobile, kneeling beside him. "Would you please let me go?"

"Hm." He squints up at the sky, as if to read the answers in his own eyes from it. "I don't think I can do that."

"So, you and your cohorts now not only intend on stalking but also kidnapping me?"

"I need something to put on my college application. I hear admissions officers like well-rounded people."

"If by that you mean people with well-rounded criminal records then yes, I'd agree that you're on your way to being well rounded," I say, "now please let me go."

The shackle like way in which his fingers link around my wrist makes me feel unwell. His grip is tighter now, the intention of keeping me here clear.

"I thought you wanted to know why we're stalking you?"

"I'll stay and hear why if it means you won't touch me again."

He flinches back, a look of shock the first disruption to his calm features. But he acquiesces, freeing me from his grasp to my great relief.

"Alright. You do sort of owe me enough to hear me out anyway."

"How so?" I say sceptically, curling my limbs back to

my body and well out of his reach.

"Well, I've only tackled you once. This is the second time you've run into me, with such spectacular grace I might add. Therefore, you owe me." I feel the tension above the peaks of my eyebrows as I frown at him. "You don't remember?"

"No, I'm afraid we only met once yesterday. You must be confusing me with someone else."

"I don't think, for one second, that it's humanly possible to confuse you with anyone. And back to the matter at hand, I'm talking about the other night. I mean, sure I looked a bit different but you really don't see it?"

I stare at him before stupidly repeating, "We only met yesterday."

Yet hadn't I thought I had seen his eyes somewhere before? Not at the bonfire, he'd been too far away then. No, I had been certain. Glinting dangerously at me then as they are now. Holy shit.

"That's not possible."

I try to scramble to my feet but my body refuses, dragged back down to the ground by its terror.

"You said you'd hear me out," he reminds me, though complies with our agreement not to touch me as I attempt to claw my way upright. I still and stare him dead in the eyes. Yes, their silver sharpness is so clear in my memory now.

"But you're human. You have a face and arms and skin just like a human."

"Kyle said you knew about us," Aaron says frowning.

"Well I don't, I don't know about any of this." Didn't Chloe tell me dragons were real? "Okay I sort of do."

"You make absolutely no sense."

"Please enlighten me as to the appropriate reaction. I thought, when I saw you in the woods that night that you couldn't possibly be more than some sort of hallucination. I never imagined for one moment that you could be so," I falter.

"Human shaped?" he asks, tilting his head.

I nod. But the truth is dawning on me. If we're witches why can't there be humans who transform into beasts? In my reality, it is equally probable for what Aaron's saying to be real as it is for it to be a figment of my imagination. Despite all the danger what he says implies, I'm urged into belief. Those flashes of half-memories I had of scales in the library could only have been of a dragon.

"Mallory, are you alright?"

His voice sounds as if it's calling through a veil of roaring water and yet it is the only sound I hear distinctly.

"I just, I thought the other night was my imagination."

"That would be some imagination you have there."

"People have dreamt up stranger things than dragons."

"Yeah, the dragons but also to create me. Because all of this fineness coming from one brain is a bit much," he says, motioning to himself.

I stare blankly, his tone now more foreign than that with which he explained what he was to me. He sighs eventually, sitting upright again and dusting his hands off.

"Why does insanity make so much more sense than reality?" I ask after the long drawn breath of silence.

"It doesn't because this isn't insanity. Consider it a mere addition to the reality you believed in."

"Mere?"

There's nothing mere about the crashing avalanche of realisations. If Inerea had that book, does that mean she knew and didn't tell me? Why?

"That was a bad choice of words on my part. It's more of a universally spanning, other dimensions involving, eon lasting addition to reality," he corrects himself.

"And what do I have to do with this reality? There's a reason you're interested in me isn't there?"

"I wouldn't say interested per say. I mean, don't get me wrong, you're gorgeous but-ow!" He looks at me in surprise as the stick I throw bounces off his arm.

"So not what I meant."

"I know, but come on, let a man diffuse the tension with a joke, won't you? You've been a part of this reality since the day you were born. You're a Thiel."

"That's what Kyle said, as if there were more weight to it than five letters. But it doesn't mean more to me than that."

"Ready for a quick history lesson? There are twenty families that carry the transmogrifying abilities that I have. See how brief that was?"

I blink slowly at him, trying to catch up with the conclusion he's leading me to.

"The Thiels are one of them?"

"Bingo."

"But I've never experienced some bizarre dragon hybrid transformation," I insist.

Their existence may affirm some of my sanity, but for me to be one of them pulls humanity further from my grasp. I've only recently come to terms with balancing being a witch and a human. I'm not sure I can take this too.

"First of all, rude, we're not bizarre. Secondly, of course you haven't. Usually, only males at birth inherit the ability to transform. The women are far more powerful in different ways. It's not always so binary as that though. Sometimes our kind are born without powers at all or they might have a mix of powers, but odds are you're nog going to turn into a dragon. But, as I was going to say, if it weren't for the women's gifts, we wouldn't exist at all. How do you think King Illarion managed to get humans who could shape shift into dragons?"

"If I'm being honest, as I believe such a conversation warrants complete honesty, I've never really considered the matter. Since I've never heard of Illarion or had any affirmation of your – our – existence until now," I say.

"Well then," he begins, leaning towards me, "I should probably fill you in if you're going to join us."

I still.

"I'm not going to join you." His eyes widen to allow shock in for the second time. "It's something of a relief to know I didn't hallucinate the other night, but that doesn't mean I want this to become a part of my life."

"It's not really a choice," he says, "birth rights aren't something you can exactly turn down, especially when it's in your blood."

"In three months, I'm moving to New York with my aunt and uncle to start university. I'll live a relatively normal life with human guardians and the closest I'll ever get to a dragon again will be in Inerea's books."

"That would be a great human plan with your human family were it not for the fact that neither you, your aunt nor your grandmother are human," he replies.

"But my grandmother's not a Theil. They're-"

"Like me? Or should I say like you, since you're clearly not getting it. Your dragovik blood doesn't just come from the paternal Thiel side of your lineage. It's on your mother's side too."

I stand up but, realising I have no intention of actually leaving, I sit down on the stump. Shouldn't the world be spinning in my eyes or my mind falling apart? Everything feels so still and undisrupted by the cracks Aaron has made in my life. He hesitates, lingering on the forest floor before coming to crouch before me. His eyes hold mine, hooks for the soul, hooks to bait me and tear me apart.

"Tell me exactly how much I need to know so that I'm not torn apart by the confusion. Save me from a complete mental breakdown by telling me no more than that."

He nods, his previous insouciance regarding my reactions now gone. His face goes solemn, heavy with the weight of an ancient history he now bears on his tongue.

"Several thousand-year story short, dragoviks – you and me – are individuals who descend from a bloodline of shape-shifters. The women of our kind, you for example, are capable of great magic that allowed us to be joined with dragons. We're not human destroying demonic myths; we're still human too. Perhaps more so than any normal person because we are bound to the most primitive survival instincts of the first humans, something most people have shed as society has begun to shelter them more and more."

"Inerea, Celia, and your friends are dragoviks too?"

"Yes."

I get back to my feet, but remain motionless. How do I go back to Inerea's house with this knowledge and not speak of it? For I know I can't simply bring this up to her. She'll want to know how I found out and I'll need to know why she's kept this from me. It's not a fight I'm ready to have

"Here, let me help you home," Aaron says, evidently aware of my trembling.

"And show a stalker where I live?" I ask, attempting to employ humour as a means of self calming. But my voice shakes and I feel none the better for it.

"I already know where Inerea lives. This is a small town and, besides, dragoviks are of a very close-knit community."

"Thank you, but I'll be fine."

I feel as if the particles in my muscles are separating,

floating too far apart for me to exercise any control over them. My thoughts, my body, are in total entropy.

"You're too stubborn. But I can see that you can barely stand. If you don't let me walk you home, I'm going to have to renege on my promise of not touching you and carry you home. It will be meet cute like and mushy."

The unwelcome feeling of panic at the thought of his touch slips into my heart and doubles its pace.

"Alright. But don't go further than the edge of the glade," I say, starting back towards the house, "I don't want Inerea to see you."

"She knows who we are, we've actually met a few times. She probably wouldn't be surprised to see that we've made contact."

I ignore him, pacing ahead of him for a moment, trying to conjure the image of these two people meeting, so distinct in their places within my life.

"If she's one of you and aware that I am too, why wouldn't she tell me?"

"I can only assume, that aside from the obvious reason that you might reject her in a panic, she might not want you to be a part of this world. Inerea's good friends with many dragoviks, but the same can't be said for the Onyevaras. She hasn't quite forgiven them for what transpired years ago."

"Who?" I inquire, glancing over my shoulder and slowing so we're walking abreast.

"I suppose the Onyevaras could be considered our government. They see to relations with those who are aware of our existence and our assimilation with humans," he says. I can feel the sharpness of his stare as the house comes into view between the trees. "I'll leave you now, if you're so insistent."

I start to move away from him without another word but he reaches for me. He falls short of actually holding me still, but his fingertips brush my wrist, sending a chill up my arm.

"You promised," I warn, pulling my arm away.

"I know. I'm sorry. But I just needed to say that I saw that fear on your face the other night before you even realised what I was. It's not just us you're afraid of and running away from us is running away from your chance to protect yourself," he says. The clouds in his eyes clear and he shakes his head. He hitches the corner of his mouth into a half smile. "I wouldn't imagine forcing you to accept us. But if you need anything we'll always be here."

His figure recedes back into the forest. I stare after him. Always isn't a promise a stranger can keep. I cross the glade and slip into the house. Through the archway of the dining room, I see the massive bag of potatoes Inerea bought the other day laying out on the counter, its contents half emptied beside a chopping board. There are two large pots sitting on the stove top though the fires are unlit.

"Is that you Mallory?" Inerea calls from upstairs, "come join me."

I follow her voice into her library. Again, she's got that book open.

"What are you reading?" I'm surprised by the contempt in my voice and she clearly hears it too. She surveys me sceptically.

"Just an old book."

"About dragoviks?"

I hadn't wanted to bring it up but, now, in her presence, it seems impossible not to. The small room is overwhelmed by her secret, spilt from my lips.

She goes completely still.

"What did you say?"

"Don't pretend you didn't hear me. How could you keep something like that from me? Why lie and say we're witches, when it's already so close to the truth?"

She hesitates, no ready explanation. She truly believed I'd never find out.

"Mallory, you still are a witch. Technically. Besides, I saw how badly learning that affected you."

"But you didn't know that when you lied in the first place. I dealt with it and I could have handled this too."

"It's not that simple."

I'm overcome with anger as she piles on yet another excuse, this one more meaningless than the last in its vagueness. All I know is I have to be as far from her as soon as possible

"I don't want to hear it. I'm going to stay at Chloe's for the rest of the week."

"Mallory please," she starts, but I go to my room and start cramming things into my duffle. I send a quick text to Chloe asking her to pick me up.

"I have finals this week I need to be focused and I can't do that living with someone I don't trust. We can talk at the end of the week."

She doesn't dispute me as I zip my bag shut.

Be there in a few. Everything okay? pops up on my screen.

"I'm going to wait for Chloe outside. Don't follow me, don't get in touch with me," I say, pushing past her into the hall. I pull the door shut behind me before dissolving into tears on the porch swing.

By the time Chloe's car arrives minutes later I've managed to compose myself. I climb in the passenger seat and sling my duffle in the back. She must be able to sense something is wrong because she doesn't pry. Gone is yesterday's giddiness when I told her about my kiss with John. All I have now is the assurance that Chloe will believe me when I tell her about the past couple days, and even that feels scarcely enough to keep me together. We pull into her driveway, parking beside her parent's car.

"So, I told the parents you were a basket case about
finals and were crashing for study sessions. I hope that's
okay. I figured whatever's up you wouldn't want them to
know." Her concern drives me back over the edge and
I burst into tears again. "Oh sweetie, tell me what happened?"

I tell her everything I haven't mentioned for the past
few days: the dragon, Aaron, Kyle and the dragoviks.
That I'm one of them, as is Inerea who never told me.
When I'm done, she remains uncharacteristically quiet
for a time, her hand still resting on the steering wheel.

"That's so awful. I can't believe Inerea would do
that."

I simply shake my head in response.

"But, a dragovik," she murmurs, and I think I detect
awe in her voice.

"So, you've heard of them?"

"Heard of them? They're mythic royalty, up there
with the celetai umea." I don't ask her to elaborate on
the last bit. My head's already spinning from all the new
information I've taken in today. "No wonder we couldn't
get your magic under control."

"What do you mean?"

"Our power comes from different places. A witch
draws theirs from the power inherent in ancient language. The words summon magic. But yours is innate.
Dragoviks are, if you believe the legend of Illarion and
the phoenix, practically descended from the gods themselves. Using the ancient language augments what's already in your blood. Explains your affinity for starting
fires I guess."

In spite of the day's events, I can't help but laugh.

"It was one tiny flame!"

"That almost engulfed the curtains!" We're both
doubled over laughing for a time, and Chloe dabs away

a tear from her eye. "You know as a dragovik you're officially way too cool to slum it with a lowly witch like me."

"As if I'd ever be too cool for you. Why'd you say that?"

"It's the hierarchy," she says, shrugging, "witches are pretty much bottom of the barrel because we don't really have any magic of our own just the ability to call on the world's magic."

"Bullshit, you're an absolute witchy badass."

"Damn straight. I knew you weren't some elitist Dragovician snob." Her smile falters. "There is one thing that's bugging me though."

"What's that."

"Well, you said this Aaron guy actually transformed?"

"Yeah, why?"

"Dragovik transmogrification has been punishable by death since they were banished to Earth."

Chapter XV.

The week passes without further discussion of Inerea or the dragoviks, and Chloe's promise to keep it all secret from her family and fellow witches. Mad as I am with Inerea, she's decided to keep her heritage a secret and it's not my place to reveal that to the witch community of Aplin Hollow.

The timer at the front of the classroom goes off and there's the simultaneous sound of pencils being put down and several groans, followed by curse words. I catch Chloe's eye next to me and grin. Once the teacher collects our tests, she leans across the aisle to me.

"We're officially free. Do you have any idea how drunk we're getting at tonight's bonfire?"

"God, never again," I laugh, following her out of the classroom.

"Oh, I'll get you drunk," she insists, and I know from her tone she'll get her way. "So now finals are over, I'm once again restored to my former life as a gossip and can return to probing inquiries such as what are you going to do about John?"

"I haven't even thought of him in the past week," I lie.

Truth is that kiss has cropped up in more than a few late-night musings and unbidden during exams. Better that than dragons.

"As if with a kiss like that. Even I can't stop thinking about it. We're stopping by the library on the way home. Got your book?"

"I'm too fond to part with it, good associations and all," I protest.

She swipes it from me, waving it in front of my face.

"Well, how about a new book with even better associations?"

"Fine, that seems a fair trade," I sigh, trailing her to the car.

"What are you going to say?" she asks, as we queue to get out of the parking lot.

"Go Yankees." She frowns at me. "I don't know. It's just kind of spontaneous."

"So cute," she sighs, as we pull out of the parking lot, "why can't I find anyone?"

"Because you're too busy finding someone for everyone else."

"Well, you all desperately need my help."

"Honestly yes. I've never dated in my life and you know what a bumble fucking mess I am."

"You want to date him now?"

"I don't know! I mean like, I've never even interacted with a guy I like. I'm totally out of my depth."

"Well, whatever you've been doing apparently made you irresistible so I don't think there's anything for me to teach you. Here we are." She parks outside the library.

"Wait you're coming in?"

"Obviously! I've yet to observe your interactions. I'll wait by the front desk don't worry." I cast a weary glance her way before scanning the library for him. Upstairs I make out the broad shoulders and messy brown hair I've come to know well from our two encounters.

"Be back in a second."

Ascending the stairs, I round the corner and collide with him on his way back from the bookshelves.

"Miss Theil."

Miss Theil? As if he hadn't shoved me up against the wall last time he saw me.

"I came for another book recommendation. It seems I will be making a habit of this," I say, internally cringing.

God could I be any worse at this? He takes Hughes' translation from me then surveys my face.

"I hadn't seen you in a while so I wondered whether that would be the case," he replies, nodding for me to follow.

"Finals week, I'm officially a free woman as of this afternoon."

"I'm flattered to be your first stop. Novel or poetry?"

He seems stiffer than before, unable to meet my gaze and his voice has gone flat.

"Novel, I like to alternate," I answer.

I try to get a look at his face but he keeps it hidden behind his hair.

"Then I think this will do," he says, handing me *Circe*, "is there anything else?"

Something is definitely off.

"Is something the matter? I thought –"

"I think it's better we don't talk here."

"Oh, okay."

He takes me to the front desk where Chloe is waiting. When his back is turned, she raises an eyebrow at me but I just shake my head. Whatever chemistry was there before is now long gone. He scans my return and the new checkout before handing me the latter.

"Have a nice day."

"Thanks, you too."

We head out to the car and Chloe waits until we're on the road to start her commentary.

"Have a nice day? This from the man who formerly shoved his tongue down your throat."

"Let's just leave it Chloe."

I feel the flush of embarrassment in my cheeks.

"Well, what happened, I missed it all."

"He just wasn't interested. It was a really normal librarian encounter. No walls, no kissing."

"That's a shame, I swiped his home address from the computer too for a stake out."

"Please tell me you're kidding."

"Five Elmwood Drive. But I guess that's off the table now. You okay?"

"I'll be fine once I feel the humiliation wear off. Could use a bit of spell casting to keep my mind off of it."

"Done. I've been thinking about that anyway. We need to change how you cast. I think you should still use the verbal spells to guide your intentions but don't rely on them. Feel whatever power is natural in you to cast."

"Have you been thinking about your finals at all this week or just my lack of a love life and my spell casting?"

"You're very time consuming."

Already I feel the sense of misery lifting.

"Well thank you for thinking of me. You're my personal angel."

"Oh hell no, don't confuse me with those assholes. I'm one hundred percent witch and proud."

"I'm sorry, there are honest to god angels?"

She gives me a sympathetic look.

"So much you don't know little one."

"I don't think I want to," I sigh, leaning back in my seat.

"So, have you thought about talking to Inerea?"

This is one subject I can tell she's hesitant to broach by the way she fidgets with the windshield wipers even though it's not raining.

"I need to give her a chance to explain. I'm furious, but she's Inerea. Whatever her reason it must have been good," I sigh.

"Your life is crazy."

"Hey you just drove past your house, where are we going?"

"Trust me. I've got a plan."

Next thing I know we're pulling into the clearing we parked in for the bonfire last week.

"It's way too early, no one's even set up."

"Nope, but we're going to."

"Okay, so not my idea of hijinks. You want me to move kegs?"

"Better. You're going to start the bonfire."

"What?"

I follow her out of the car as she marches across to the clearing. I can see the ring of scorched earth piled with fresh wood where the bonfire usually burns and it's not until we reach it that she stops.

"Think about it, your affinity for fire will be perfect for this. And I'm done making you pick petals off of damn roses. Let's think bigger."

"I don't have a spell, what am I supposed to say?"

Removing a notebook from her bag, she rips out a piece of paper from her bag and jots down a single word.

"Now just, channel that," she instructs.

She takes a few steps back but doesn't look away from me as I stare at her incredulously. I turn back to the black patch of dirt piled with half burnt logs.

"Kaisma." My fingers begin to tingle and the paper in my hand writhes, licked by blue tongues of flame. I cry out, dropping it just before it burns my hand and stomping on it to put the fire out. "Well that was a roaring success."

"I'd say so," she replies.

I hear crackling, the pop of wood being spat out of flame, and, when I look up, the bonfire is glowing beautiful sheets of orange that roll in the breeze.

"Holy shit. It's not going to spread, is it?" I ask, watching as the flames draw themselves taller.

"It shouldn't do. As of now it's an ordinary fire. Witch fire is a totally different beast and I'm not ready to be burned to a crisp by you. So, marshmallows?"

"We don't have any."

"In my kitchen. A basic teleportation spell should do it. Noutsumar valja ne sav."

The air in front of her opens up and a box of graham crackers, chocolate bars, and marshmallows fall to the ground.

"You really do use your powers for evil."

We sit down on the ground and impale marshmallows on sticks.

"Kaisma," I whisper again. The white flesh pocks and smoulders golden brown before I blow it out.

"Very nicely done," she says, offering me the chocolate and crackers.

By the time people start to arrive we're both sick to our stomachs and the sky has gone dark. No one seems the least bit confused as to why the bonfire is already lit, leaving me to wonder if witches don't have their hand in every bonfire. It's not long before the whole area is packed and I once again have been persuaded to drink the punch.

"Second cup?" Chloe asks, though she's already on her third.

"How about I get you your fourth and I'll hold out for now."

"Boo, no fun," she says, pouting as further indication of her inebriation.

I cross the clearing and start ladling the red syrupy liquid into our cups when I become aware of a heavy gaze upon me. I turn to find the hollow brown eyes of Robyn pinning me with their acute look of dislike.

"Oh look, the moron's here," she mutters, walking towards me.

"Hello Robyn," I sigh, not in the mood for yet another unpleasant encounter with her.

"Do you enjoy being the damsel incapable of doing anything other than cowering and being saved? It's rather contemptible."

"I haven't asked anyone to save me."

"No, but idiocy such as yours will demand saving."
I pick up my cups and turn to leave. "And now she runs
away."

"I'm not running away I just have no interest in your
contempt," I say spinning round, "I'm staying out of
your way so why can't you leave me be?"

"Because even though you're leaving us alone, I
unfortunately do not have the privilege of being able to
avoid you."

"I grant you that privilege."

"Of course you think you have the right to do that,"
she sighs, flicking her gaze across the crowd, then back to
me, "You don't. This comes with your last name, the only
important thing about you."

"Yes I'm aware, it means I'm one of your kind."

"Oh, it's more than just that." She darts forward,
pulling me with her so we're both absorbed by the shadows. "I don't like you, which is all the more reason to
believe me when I say we need you. You seem well aware
that I have no desire to waste time with you if I don't have
to, so I think you can see the validity in my insistence."

"First Aaron, now you? I'm not going to join your
cadre of dragon-human hybrids."

Her eyes flash.

"Aaron spoke to you? When?"

"Last week, I ran into him in the forest. You didn't
know?"

She grits her teeth as if something I've said is an insult to her intelligence.

"Whatever," she hisses, letting go of my arm, "drop
dead for all I care."

She returns to the crowd in a heartbeat. I circle to
the other side of the clearing where there are fewer peo-

ple. My heart slows and my face burns with a blush that I doubt will show against my blanched face.

Drop dead for all I care.

I lean back against a tree and gaze at the trail of smoke spiralling towards the sky from the bonfire. I forget about listening to my surroundings, forget that there are at least a hundred other sentient beings in my immediate proximity with beating hearts, lives and notions of a future. Eventually I can perceive what is hidden beyond the grey smog. I imagine the stars, ornaments of the sky, sprinkling down and shattering like glass baubles. The universe, so barren without them, crashes after to consume the Earth as it has long desired to. It would crush my world too, finally rendering me into the nothing I feel I've been disappearing into for the past week.

When I blink again the stars remain, dotting the cape of darkness. After seeing this amalgamation of light and dark, how can I possibly move to New York where the night's vestigial beauty is bound to be hidden behind the human stain of pollution and skyscrapers?

"It's rather pathetic of you to be standing out here on your own at an event made for socialising."

My trance shatters and I turn to see Leo looking at me. His narrow cheeks are hollowed out further by the shadows cast by the fire, like gaps in a skull.

"You're alone too."

"No, I was just speaking to Aaron before I came to speak to the girl on her own. Unless you don't consider yourself an individual worth speaking to."

"Between you and Robyn I'm really starting to consider that to be the case."

"Wonderful, self-pity. Your ability to be annoying increases exponentially with every word you say."

I glare at the ground, my heart screaming with rapidly succeeding beats.

"You'll have to forgive me but I'm not particularly in the mood to be called pathetic or contemptible. If you'd leave me alone now, I'd be much obliged," I murmur.

I hear the soft tread of his footsteps as he disregards my request and comes to stand beside me.

"Robyn dislikes you with exception. I'm indiscriminate in my dislike."

"That's nice to hear."

"Odd. You actually mean that don't you?"

"I'll take being disliked as the result of another person's disability to like people over being disliked because of who I am," I say.

"Robyn doesn't dislike you for who you are exactly. But it's not really my right nor my concern to discuss that," he yawns, "I wonder how much you and I are alike in regards to the reasons we prefer receiving contempt for."

"I'd think it beyond you to care," I reply.

"How swiftly you assume my personality. Still, you're right. Not as foolish as Robyn claims."

"Yes, miraculous what a few brain cells can achieve."

He laughs with little mirth.

"I doubt Aaron will be too happy to see this little exchange," he says in his low monotone.

"Why's that?"

"I suspect, based on his reckless decision to talk to you last week without us, he doesn't want you looking at anyone else just yet."

"I'm not looking at him. I'm looking at you," I reply, frowning as I turn towards him.

"That's a bit more literal than the capacity to which I'm referring but I suppose you have a point."

He doesn't say anymore as he looks back towards the humming crowd.

"Then what are you referring to? I'm beyond the

help of mere insinuations. Clarify please."

"Again, it's neither my right nor concern. I find Aaron self-indulgent and you self-pitying anyway. I see it in your eyes, the way you weigh everything said to you as if it could be some sort of salvation from your pathetic existence. You're not even pitiable or worth caring about if I'm to be blunt."

His words cut me to the quick, stinging my throat with a gasp. He doesn't bother looking at me, but continues to lean beside me as if we were engaged in a pleasant conversation.

Without another thought, I abandon my place and make my way hastily into the forest. My eyes begin to prick with the unaccustomed feeling of tears. I can feel the hurt that gave rise to them in my chest as well, possessing my lungs and breaths. All I can think about is that I need to get away from these people and their seemingly insatiable desire to carve out the little happiness I have within me.

It isn't until everything falls to silence that I remember how upset Chloe was last time I disappeared. She'll worry if I leave without telling her where I've gone. I steady myself. She'll try to kick Robyn's ass if I tell her what really happened though, and I'm not sure that's a fight she'll win. I'll just tell her I'm going home with a headache. I head back towards the bonfire.

Mallory.

I pivot around but there's no one behind me. Don't wait, just run. I begin to sprint, praying I'll reach Chloe before the voice reaches me. A white hot flash explodes in front of me, blocking my path. The singed air sizzles, spitting sparks of electricity, which turn from light to a thick red liquid as soon as they touch the ground. More bursts spew out, joining together on the forest floor like threads that weave themselves into a heavy stream, oozing across the earth. It rolls over rocks as if to swallow them and they disintegrate like lumps of powder in water.

Mallory.

I can't take my eyes off of the source of this strange element from which the voice seems to emanate. Now cut off from returning to the bonfire, I begin to back away. My movement triggers a new reaction. Two cords break themselves free of the mass and twine themselves around my wrists. I cry out but in all my panic there's no name that manifests from my vocalisation, just a sound of fear. The liquid bubbles and bursts in its excess, making a hissing sound as if to laugh at me. Two more tendrils slither forwards with impossible speed. They reach my feet, biting their way up my ankles. I press against my restraints but, with the manacle clasp of my wrists' bonds holding my hands still, any attempt to escape is futile.

The harder I pull, the tighter the now solid liquid, like cooled magma, squeezes. I can barely feel blood flow in my hand and I stop straining for fear that the bonds will cut straight through my bones. The rivers that have crept up to join the ones around my ankles heave themselves up into ropes and wind around my legs. Like a spider's web they bind me fast, entombing my torso completely so I cannot even turn in place. They constrict themselves tighter with each expansion of my chest as I gasp, until oxygen becomes scarce and I can hardly breathe for the pain of their burning touch. Another cord frees itself of the almost trunk like accumulation that holds my body and curls around my neck. It forks five ways as it reaches the underside of my chin. I tilt my head back helplessly as if to pull away, or at least stop it from reaching my face.

Mallory, let me taste the fire of your blood.

My eyes widen, and the blinding light source of this unknown threat sears itself into my vision. I can scarcely see, but I feel the threads, heavy with their life-like

warmth, snaking up across my cheeks. I shut my mouth
and eyes, as if this could prevent whatever it is from
climbing within my mind to take control of my conscious.
My eyelids burn with heat as two cords of the liquid lay
to rest over them. Red hot light roars like the mouth of
a furnace through the thin skin protecting my eyes. And
despite my thoughts of self-dissolution beside the bonfire,
of the night sky crashing down to take me whole, I realise
this pain is worse than what giving up should be. I won't
surrender to it.

"Help," I whisper.

I hear the air stir behind me. Then a darting breeze
sweeps beside my body and a strangled cry of pain is
followed by a horrifying laughter that poisons my mind.
There comes a slash of steel, something sharp biting
through the nothing of atmosphere. The tendrils recoil
from my eyes almost instantly. The air's stillness is mutilated by a flurry of movements. I open my eyes, blinking
rapidly to clear the after image of the red glow.

A group of four move within the realm of the creature's light, their faces illuminated by the radiating bloody
glow of its being. Robyn hangs back to the right, raising
a crossbow and taking aim at the seeming invulnerable
light. But as one of her bolts soars through it, lodging
itself in a tree on its other side, the bright spotlight of its
gaze is turned towards her. It hisses, its limbs retreating
further from my body.

Taking their opportunity during its distraction, Aaron and Leo dart towards the sinewy stock that lies across
the ground and begin to cut through it with successive
swings of their swords. As the cord breaks beneath steel,
it comes apart with a sickening sound like parting flesh.
Kyle bolts to my side and draws a dagger from his belt.
Slipping it between my bonds with care, he presses his
thumb against the cords and eases the blade through

them. As the coils begin to loosen, I yank myself free. He crouches and cuts into those that shackle my ankles.

The light shines fiercely, blindingly bright like the mortar grounds of a supernova. It ruptures, a vein bursting beneath sharp pressure, before shrinking back into the nothing it sprang from. The forest goes dark and I stare into blackness before my sight accommodates the night. Robyn's weapon seems to have disappeared into thin air, her hands now busy with searching for any trace the creature might have left behind in the dirt. Aaron and Leo sheath their swords, glancing around warily. My vision blurs and I can feel the acute searing of the creature's tracks on my body, a stinging pain I've never known before. My clothing has been burnt through where it came into contact, as if exposed to acid. Where the tendrils attached themselves, I find my skin is engorged in dark red strips with nauseating thinly covered clots of blood threatening to burst.

"Mallory!" I hear someone yell.

I look up to see a blurred person running towards me. I notice a track of blood from an open wound on the figure's leg. Kyle catches me as my body gives way to gravity.

Why is there always blood?

My feet leave the ground just before I slip out of this reality I had clung so dearly to.

Chapter XVI.

"Leave her be. She'll be fine provided she has sleep to speed up the healing process."

Footsteps and the door shutting are the last sounds of consciousness that penetrate my mind. Please, don't leave me here on my own again. Don't leave me only to find me a mass of scar tissue in a few days. I cannot bear this. I'm gasping stifled by my own breaths.

How can they say I'll be fine? What right have they to assume the degree of my pain and my means of recovery? A choke for pure air, something other than the tainted misery in my lungs, jerks my chest upwards and I exhale a trail of gold. It spirals out of my mouth and wafts upwards like smoke. So fragile, yet bright. How can that be me? Its air like quality shatters on first contact with the ceiling, becoming a starburst of light. It consumes all above me, turning it to a textured charred black and leaving only the edges of my vision with trace gold, the last burning embers of a page. It maps out the universe without stars that I had imagined at the bonfire, but it's not the expansive dark of the sky it is attempting to replicate. I see myself in the fading image of that gold, a promise for hope that went wrong. I inhale and just as quickly the dark recedes, twisting a hurricane of itself until its compacted into a gilded façade that returns to my body. I blink and my eyelids unveil another reality. I'm standing now, outside of my room at Inerea's. I hold my ground in a circle of feeble light that makes battle with the darkness all around. It's as if I've been inverted, turned inside out and pulled into my own body so my eyes can see what is within.

You cannot run from me in here and you cannot be unbound from these thoughts. This is my home, the shadows whispers, reaching for me like hands.

"This isn't your home. It's my dream, my mind."

Once, perhaps. But even when it was your own you gave it over to me. What control could you possibly imagine to hold over your mind now that it is so completely mine? I am the corners your darkness clings to.

The voice doesn't pour forth with malice. It's as if it wants to cover my wounds with a worse infection, a silent killer. I feel the threat of the words pouring out, overflowing and penetrating the last of the light.

"Stop!"

I spin around, but there's no vein of light through which I can run. The black wave of this being swells, pours itself on me like ice. Just as the touch of the tendrils had, it calls on the primordial torture of slow life deprivation to make me suffer. Hyperventilation to battle the cold becomes false breaths that imitate the intake of life force.

"Stop!"

I feel nothing. No, not nothing. It's not as if every last feeling has abandoned me for death. I feel normal, free of this being's grasp. When I open my eyes, the shadows have retreated, now even further back than before. They don't whisper from within to rustle their fragile state. They move, delicately sinking into the light slightly, only to sweep themselves back within an instant. I hold my breath, only to hear that of another. I turn around to where I know the man who possesses this voice must be standing, prepared to see his face.

Instead, I find a petite girl, waiting readily to meet my gaze. Her dark brown hair tumbles over her shoulders, shining even in this pale light. She has a fine china face that has yet to be cracked by experience, the palest porcelain painted with bright lips. She surveys me with large brown eyes so different from Robyn's in that there seems to be a golden glow in them, as if the inner light of her soul were brimming through them. Such a small face and large features render her so doll like I'm somewhat startled when she begins to move with a fluid grace that does not lend itself to a porcelain creation.

Her floor length black gown sweeps the ground, drawing the shadows as a train. The sleeveless bodice is decorated with red flowers christened in dew that magnifies their colour like drops of blood. Their vines and squat, ovate petals seem to move of their own accord, curling and flexing as if alive. The full skirt is a waterfall of layers made with a mesh like fabric lined with satin. Their edges are decorated sparsely with the same pomegranate-coloured flowers.

"You were encroaching on the dark. That's why it tried to take you," she says.

Her voice is sweet and melodious, the unintentional seduction of innocence. Her lips are a dark shade of red that steals all colour from her face. I'm almost scared she could draw the colour of life from me just by coming close. Yet her face seems so soft I can't bring myself to move away. The conflicting aspects of her appearance leave her with a beauty so terrifying I surrender any words for a moment as I try to take her in. She doesn't break the silence but instead offers it to me with a piercing look that demands reply.

"I believe the dark was encroaching on my mind. Or, at least, the dark made manifest was," I reply. She smiles.

"Yes, him. He is quite something. But tell me, if we take in to account all theories of universal creation, which was here first in the universe: light or dark?"

"Dark."

"And yet your kind would have the world believe that with their light they illuminate safety."

"Often the threat precedes the means of protection," I counter.

She bubbles up with laughter, her face glowing with pure delight.

"Oh, you are a marvellous specimen. How captivating your mind is. What you say is true. But while that may often be the case, all your fires of destruction do is make the world burn a little brighter and a little faster." She begins to hum a melody but falters quickly. Her face falls with the tune. "Oh dear."

"What's the matter?"

My heart pounds as I move towards her. But when she looks back up at me, her eyes are reignited with heavenly fire.

"Are you worried about me? With all the dangers that surround you, perceived and unperceived, you still always look to others' wellbeing. What sin are you atoning for when you do that?"

"What makes you assume that action is born from sin?"

"All good-will is born from atonement for a sin we have enacted or seen." She silences me at this. "Your newfound family's danger concerns you because of what you once did, and now it will be what draws you into this war," she says.

"What have I done? Are we at war?" I ask her.

"Not you and I. Not yet at least. But the world is restless and a civilisation that divides itself into factions of society innately demands blood."

She hums again, skirting the edge of the light while I consider her words. As she draws nearer, I shift away. She comes to a stop before leaning back on her heels as if to prevent herself from taking another step.

"So, who's fighting who at the moment?"

"All people. They wage wars on families, friends, enemies. The list is endless," she sighs. Her eyes light up again with sudden curiosity. "Don't you find it odd that people say white is pure and untarnished? If, as you and I agree, darkness came first, then is it not the purest, elemental thing? All light is merely a scrape, a bruise on the skin of the universe, white being the most offensive of all ailments."

"Why do you insist on speaking only in riddles?"

"Am I? I intended on being quite sincere."

"So, this meeting was premeditated?" I ask

"Oh yes," she gushes, darting close to me. Before I can move away, she takes up my hands, spreading an icy chill into the tips of my fingers that freezes all of me. "You and I are going to be the death of each other. When I heard, I couldn't wait to meet you."

"I wouldn't hurt you. Or anyone for that matter."

"You mean you wouldn't hurt anyone again," she sings, her scorching eyes branding all the names I could be called by across my face.

Weakling.

Traitor.

Murderer.

I don't know why I deserve these monikers, only that I do.

"That's not me," I whisper, unable to look away from her face.

"Don't say that! How very disappointing it would be if you turned out to be just as incapable of killing me as all the others." She gives my hands a squeeze. "It would be my pleasure to die by your hands Mallory Thiel. Meeting you has assured me of that."

"Who are you?"

"Someone whose torments burn brighter and in greater number than yours."

"Then let me help you, not kill you."

"That's how you will help me," she says, kissing my forehead. "But it's not my turn with you yet." She leaves my side.

"There has to be another way." She stops, shaking her head. "Something I can do."

"Make me a promise."

"What's that?" I ask without missing a beat.

"Please don't follow him into hell before I have my chance to send you there."

As she fades away, the spell she held over the dark breaks. Her delighted laughter races with the shadows to converge upon me.

* * *

I think it's her abandonment wakes me. I can't sustain this dream without her. A long sigh follows the opening of my eyes, but it does not come from my lips. My eyelids are heavy with the weight of exhaustion. I hardly manage to open them to take in the warm light of my room.

"So, kind of you to finally wake up. And just after everyone else has gone downstairs," Leo says.

I turn my head on my pillow, groaning with the effort. He leans back, tilting the desk chair that has been brought to my bedside.

"What happened?"

"Let's see. You were attacked and eventually passed out. Then we went and bought matching turtlenecks so we could all be Steve Jobs for Halloween. After a small panic, in which we questioned our costume choice because Robyn wasn't sure her neck was suited for such a shirt, we brought you back here."

I try to sit upright, but collapse back onto the bed, gasping in pain. The bubbling welts that had been left by the tendrils are now flat patches of blackening scabs.

"She looked fine in it by the way. The same cannot

be said for you."

"Do you always say rude things, regardless of current circumstances?" I ask through laboured breaths.

"People deserve stability and consistency in times of need such as these," he assures me.

When I make another attempt to move, he comes to my aid and helps prop me up against the headboard. Unlike his words, his touch is compassionate. He's careful not to touch any of my wounds as he inspects them with great care. When I shut my eyes, it's almost like having Inerea with me.

"How long will these take to heal?" I ask.

"Not much longer, especially after everything Robyn has done to help move the healing process along. Still, were it not for the fact that our bodies are far more durable than your average human's, you'd be dead. You have your heritage to thank for that," he intones, giving me a shrewd look as he places my arm back in my lap.

I half hate myself for thinking it, but I almost regret having him let go.

"I wasn't aware this was a silver linings situation," I reply, "especially given that the cloud it lines is me being attacked as a result of my heritage. Tell me that isn't true."

"I can't when I know that's exactly why you were attacked," he says.

I sag with the relief. This isn't about me in particular, that means that whatever that thing was probably mimicked that voice from my dreams to taunt me. A demon personalising its being for an attack. How kind.

"Robyn has been resting so she should probably now have enough energy to do another round of healing spells."

"She doesn't have to. I'll heal in my own time so I'd rather not be a burden."

"Why? Because you enjoy looking like a rotting corpse or because you know Robyn will make sure you know you're a burden?" he snorts, "I can see you're barely conscious without the energy that your body is draining to repair itself. We need to know exactly what you saw and for that you need to remain conscious. For the sake of the lives at stake, make the right decision."

I bite the inside of my cheeks but nod all the same. He leaves the room and I hear him calling for Robyn. I look down at my now purplish skin again. A decaying corpse. I've never seen a dead body so long after death as for decomposition to begin, but I know enough about the process to see he wasn't too far off the mark. I hear agile footsteps darting up the stairs and the two join me.

"You look like shit," Robyn says, but her voice doesn't carry the energy of insult. "You'd think I hadn't done anything."

As I look up, I'm startled by her appearance. Her face looks weary, semi-circles of blue ill health having bloomed beneath her eyes as if it's been days since she slept. Leo draws the chair closer to my bed for her. She sinks into it, the briefest flash of relief on her face before she takes my arm indelicately, examining the wounds. I hate to have her touch me, her hands so careless and rough. Where most everyone else's touch has caused panic due to the potential for threat, I feel the threat imminently with her. Her mind is constantly shifting between the notion of helping and hurting me.

"This was the work of a powerful deabrueon. You can't expect the healing to come quickly," Leo observes, not meaning to reassure her of her abilities in any way.

Robyn seems to believe the same about his comment because she rolls her eyes and grasps my arm with a sudden tightness. I try to pull back but Leo gives me a warning look.

"Lueicht, nandirava letai nevorso ni isuzako etev udiyat," she murmurs.

She repeats the phrase while her hands' place of contact with my arm begins to glow, a white fluid cloud covering forming around it. When she's done, the dark scabs that covered my wounds have shrunk. They've changed to a very pale colour and are starting to cover over with new skin. I look at her with wonder but she takes no note. She does my other arm, neck, ankles and face.

"You'll need to take off your shirt," she instructs.

She presses her hands to the particularly thick wound on my abdomen before uttering the words again. The white mist appears again, wrapping me up in its cotton softness. It fades to leave the same pale marks. Robyn slumps back in her chair, her face covered in a thin sheen of sweat.

"I'll get you some water," Leo says, leaving us.

"You're incredible," I breathe. She rattles with laughter.

"I know," she sighs, her exhaustion depriving her voice of any sharpness.

"Is there anything I can do to help you?"

"Shut up."

"Fair enough."

We wait in silence for Leo to return with a large glass of water, which Robyn downs in a matter of seconds.

"You look worse than she did," Leo says, studying her.

"Fuck off Leo."

She seems to further wither with the effort of her retort.

"Here, take my bed," I offer.

She doesn't resist when I take her arm and help her into the still warm sheets.

"You're being nice and that pisses me off," she mur-

murs, before her breaths become shallow. Her small figure is only just visible beneath the duvet.

"Will she be okay?"

"Given some time." We stand in silence for a moment. "Do you have plans to put a shirt on anytime soon?
I'm sure Aaron would be more than delighted to see you
in nothing more than a bra and jeans, but that might
leave him incapacitated with excitement and we have a
lot of work to do." He says this without any particular
interest in the matter, just mild irritation.

"Sorry. Give me a moment."

I pull on a loose fitting sweater from my closet before
grabbing a pair of leggings. As I begin to slip my jeans off
I hear his sharp intake of breath.

"Do you have no awareness of your own body?"

"What?"

"You're just going to strip in a room with a complete
stranger?" he demands.

"I didn't really think about it."

He shakes his head as I wrap my arms around my
body. Did he see my scar?

"I'll wait downstairs in that case."

He shuts the door silently behind him. I put on the
leggings and put my bloodied, ripped jeans into the bin.
I turn off the light in my room and enter the bathroom.
Splashing cold water on my face, I stare up towards the
ceiling. How can I put off the inevitable inquiry awaiting
me? They want to know what happened but I'm still in
the dark. Of the many things I'm beginning to understand in this world, what happened tonight is not one of
them. A bead of water drips from my chin. I wipe my
face dry and am suddenly taken up with a burning thirst
that forces me to go downstairs at last. I hear hushed voices in the dining room that turn silent as soon as I enter the
kitchen. Getting myself a glass of water, I turn around

to find them seated around the table. My best tactic is to remain objective during their questioning. Avoid any personal feeling that might draw me and Inerea any further into this. Even if that's an impossible prospect.

"How are you feeling?" Kyle asks softly.

"I'm able to get out of bed, thanks to Robyn," I say, approaching them cautiously, "Thank you for coming to save me."

Aaron is up and beside me as soon as I come to a stop. He snatches my hand from my side with a suddenness that startles me from the air of distant formality I had hoped to maintain. He examines my scars. My surprise overwhelms any sense of fear, which I only regain by the time he's letting go of me.

"She could have done a better job," he mutters, "Mallory would be fully recovered if Robyn wasn't casting spells so poorly."

"Robyn did the best she could, given how awful those wounds were," Kyle says, frowning at his companion.

Aaron shrugs and I slip away to refill my glass. All of them still behind me and the relief of being able to take pause, even just to drink water, is a heaven send. Only a couple seconds conversing with them has drained me back to the bare minimum. I turn back and just like that they restart.

"Did the best she could be bothered to given who she was healing," Leo mutters.

Whether Kyle and Aaron hear him or not I don't know. Neither replies but the silence that takes hold feels like a sharp intake of breath. I make my way back into the dining room.

"You should sit," Aaron offers, glaring at Leo. I seat myself beside him wordlessly, my hands wrapped around the glass to steady them.

"I know you're probably confused and exhausted,

but it would be very helpful if you could tell us exactly what happened before we got there," Kyle says warmly.

He ignores the all but death like look Aaron is still giving Leo, who yawns in response. How can he be so calm with all their small acts of aggression in the air? Billions of people waging war on family, friends and enemies. There are two right here. With the plainest spoken sentence Leo somehow declared a war that will be fought with silence between the two. I look back to Kyle.

"I was in the forest trying to get home when all of a sudden I heard someone calling out my name. I tried to run away but then the light appeared and it took hold of me before I could move."

"It knew your name?" he asks in surprise.

"Yes. At first it sounded as if I was hearing the voice from inside my head but then I could have sworn it came from within the light. What is it?" I inquire, hasty to change the subject from the voices in my head.

"A deabrueon. By the looks of what it's already done and what it planned on doing to you, it's a very powerful one," Kyle clarifies, only to open up new avenues of questioning. I open my mouth to start asking but Aaron interjects.

"If it's a deabrueon, it's the duty of the Hirutere to deal with it," Aaron says.

"You really think they'll care about one deabrueon killing our kind?" Leo replies, though it's hardly a question. His opinion of whoever Aaron mentioned is clear from his tone and the way he wrinkles up his nose at their mere mention.

"Perhaps we should bring it to their attention," Kyle offers.

"I'm sorry, but would someone mind explaining this all to the lay person?" I ask.

"Explanations entail more information than you

absolutely require. Are you sure that's what you want?" Aaron inquires, reminding me of the conversation we seemingly had a lifetime ago, when it's only been a week.

"Right now I want to not be completely in the dark about what happened to me."

He nods and glances towards Kyle.

"The Hirutere are the governing body of Earth's angel factions, known as the angeleru. As the deabrueon are fallen angels of sorts, it's generally their duty to dispense of them when they're causing problems," Kyle says.

"Problems for humans that is. The Hirutere couldn't be less concerned when it comes to deabrueon attacking dragoviks," Leo interjects.

"We don't know it's only attacking dragoviks for sure," Kyle reminds him before turning back to me, "That deabrueon that you met in the woods seems as yet incapable of taking on full corporeal form, meaning that it's weak in comparison to its normal state. Not exactly something I'd like to see. It must have sensed your isuazko and known that it would be powerful enough to help strengthen its hold on this dimension."

"How is that with every explanation I'm able to understand even less? What's isuazko and how could something exist in multiple dimensions simultaneously?"

They all exchange a look.

"Aaron said you wanted to avoid knowing too much about us, which I understand. But if you want to fully comprehend what is happening and how you fit into it, you're going to have to give up any hope of isolating yourself from knowledge of dragoviks," Kyle says.

Do I have a choice anymore, I want to ask him? This world will draw me in no matter how much I try to escape it. It's better I enter it prepared than helplessly. I nod at him.

"Isuazko is the magical quality that runs in the blood

of all Sundalevean creatures. This next explanation will require a bit of a history lesson so forgive me in advance. Sundalev is our, and the angeleru's, native land. It's a world apart from Earth, the other dimension that the de-abrueon exist in, yet accessible from here. Millennia ago, in Sundalev, a king named Illarion ruled over a small city called Dragovicia, which had fallen into poverty due to the wars constantly waged on it. One day, while wandering through the forest, he came across a newly reborn phoenix that was being attacked by a pack of wolves. Illarion defended the phoenix and nursed it back to health before setting it free. Years passed and Dragovicia slumped further into destitution. The kingdom was all but won from Illarion by a neighbouring immortal queen who had sought to possess Dragovicia for a long time."

"But it came to pass that the phoenix reappeared, now fully grown, and it offered Illarion a reward for his services. Illarion knew there was but one thing that could ensure the safety of his kingdom so he asked the phoenix for some of its fire. He learned that no mortal body could retain such heat and, therefore, the phoenix gifted the king with three Basilisk eggs from the god Alastar's familiar. The blood of these creatures would be cold enough that when the phoenix bestowed upon them fire, their bodies would not burn. He also gifted them wings like his own, feather shaped scales harder than armour, and told the king that if he raised them, they would be the great bearers of fire who would protect his kingdom. Illarion did as he was hold. He fed and cared for the creatures, which he named dragons, as if they were his own children."

"Even though they loved him as a parent, they were innately animalistic and, as they grew older, they became more reckless. Their ferocity could not only be directed merely at enemies' armies. The people of Dragovicia demanded that the beasts be killed before they did further harm. But what parent asked to kill his child can comply so easily? In the king's desperation to protect them, he offered a place in his court to anyone who could save them. Out of the mobs of those who sought to kill the dragons came three witches, who told Illarion they could bind the dragons to men so they would have reason as well as fire. Illarion agreed and the witches turned to their husbands to be the chosen three. Now possessed of a human conscious, the three shape-shifters were able to defend Dragovicia."

"When, many years later, Illarion passed away, they were considered his only heirs as he had no children. The monarchy was shared between the three and, while at first it was feared that once they died their protection would go with them, the children of these men bore the same abilities as their parents. The females had a great hold on magic and the males were shape-shifters. The powers eventually spread through twenty families before they were forbidden to share them for fear of the danger of an entire race of dragoviks. The people of Dragovicia, however, saw this as a means to monopolise their power."

"Uniting with Queen Morenna, who still desired Dragovicia for herself, witches of Dragovicia, who envied the authority granted to their sisters married into the twenty families, cast a spell to banish them from Sundalev. Without a rightful heir, Dragovicia fell at last to the power of Morenna, who welcomed the witches into her ranks. Exiled to Earth, the dragovik families reconsolidated their power in a governmental body known as the Onyevaras. Though they could no longer protect their homeland, they knew that somewhere on Earth was a portal through which they would one day be able to return and reclaim Dragovicia. They made it their mission in the meantime to defend Earth and its peoples from demons and deabrueon until the portal could be found. Over time they formed a tentative alliance with the Hirutere, whose duty was designated as the protector of Earth's people. They helped defend the City Between, the angelic lands between Earth and Sundalev, with the promise that one day the angels would help restore them to Sundalev."

When he finishes, Kyle watches me with a steady gaze of concern I feel I recognise but have no recollection of ever seeing. Is there some sort of simple reply to all of this that I'm missing?

"And how does this particular deabrueon fit in?" I ask.

"Its relevance doesn't lay so far in the past. Aplin Hollow is home to several dragoviks, my grandparents, for example. We were up here staying in their house when the first murder occurred."

"We thought Kyle just wanted to spend time with his old friends after a year apart but turns out the whole trip was about finding you," Aaron says, though there's no resentment in the statement.

"And that person who died was a dragovik?" Kyle nods, his skin paling.

Was it one of his family members that was killed? I want to reach out and hug him but I don't know how that could make it alright.

"From that knowledge it was an obvious observation that the creature was after isuazko in order to gain strength. There was no chance it would attack us four though. It's must be targeting older dragoviks who can't defend themselves, which means it's still weak. That's why I had to upset you enough so you'd go into the woods alone," Leo says.

"You did what?" Aaron snaps, "you used her as bait?"

"I came to get the rest of you as soon as she left. There wasn't enough time for any real harm to come from it."

Aaron holds up my arm like some sort of sick scientific specimen.

"This? This is what you call no real harm?" he demands, displaying the bright white line encircling my wrist. "You saw what it did to her, right? Do you have absolutely no sense of a moral compass?"

"Aaron, let go of her," Kyle warns. Aaron obliges, grinding his teeth together as he stares at Leo with a luminous rage in his eyes. "You told us you saw Mallory going into the woods. You didn't say that you set this all up."

"Does it really matter how she got there? She's alright now."

"Of course it matters! You handled her life recklessly," Kyle says.

"So?" Leo asks.

Aaron is on his feet in an instant, snarling a litany of obscenities. Amongst their raging, I'm unable to look away from Leo. Even though he put my life at risk, the weight of the horrible things he said lifts. I don't doubt he still believes them, but perhaps with less intensity than he suggested. And knowing he said them for the better of others, so he might understand what threatens the people he tries so hard to pretend he doesn't care about, is enough to forgive him.

"He's right. It doesn't matter. Though I suggest you apologise to Robyn for all she was put through tonight to help me," I say, turning to Leo. They all fall silent, Aaron looking at me with incredulity. "No doubt you know more about what you're dealing with now?"

He nods.

"We weren't even sure it was a deabrueon to start with, nor why it was attacking our kind."

"Then it was worth it," I say to the others.

If what we learned tonight helps protect Inerea and others, it will all have been worth it.

"I suspect, however, that it will try to attack Mallory again in a short time seeing as she's untrained in how to defend herself."

"What do you suggest we do about it?" Kyle asks. He still looks uneasy but seems set on putting his qualms aside until later. He nods at Aaron who lets out a half snarl half sigh. "We can't exactly stay with her day and night."

"I volunteer," Aaron says, though the usual lightness does not accompany the words.

"Of course you do, you're a pervert," Robyn's voice interjects. She stands in the archway, leaning against its curved beam.

"I'm completely normal," he assures her.

"If by normal you mean disgusting."

"Robyn you should be resting," Kyle says.

"With this racket? A corpse couldn't sleep through it."

She sits beside Aaron. I'm thankful for the ease she brings to the conversation, even if I can still feel the tension just beneath the surface of her jokes.

"If I were under your protection, it would just go after someone else, wouldn't it?" I ask.

"Well yes. There are others in and around Aplin Hollow," Kyle answers.

"Then I want to help."

"You might be a dragovik but you don't have any training. There's little you could do to help us. It's better we just keep you safe until we can kill the deabrueon," Aaron says.

"But a little is enough in some cases. You can use me to draw it out again, can't you?"

To protect Inerea, a little is only the beginning of what I'm willing to give.

"And even though she's completely ignorant regarding spell casting, I can borrow her isuazko's energy should I need it for more powerful spells," Robyn adds in an almost complimentary tone. Though perhaps she's just trying to convince them to let me join so I'll have a better chance of dying.

"I don't think it's foolish enough to attack her again, not once she's under our protection," Aaron retorts.

"But it's desperate enough. Based on the form it took, it channelled all its energy into manifesting just enough of it to attack at her. It must have temporarily given up its corporeal form at some point and now, to get it back, it will need a lot of energy. Regardless, while Mallory would be the ideal target for the deabrueon given her youth, I believe it would be best if we check up with all members of dragovik families to ensure that no one susceptible to attacks remains alone," Leo replies.

"We can bring anyone who might be at risk to my grandparents" house until the matter is resolved. I'll compile a list of addresses tonight. Mallory, if you're certain you'd like to join us, we'll come and get you tomorrow at ten," Kyle says, "Inerea will be able to keep you safe that long."

I start at the mention of her name.

"Where is she now?" I ask

"Out apparently."

"Is she safe?"

"Your grandma can definitely handle herself."

I sigh with relief.

"Thank you."

"Wait, you're kidding right? With Mallory's skills from the Academy she'll be perfectly fine," Leo says.

"What do you mean my skills?" I ask, puzzled. All

four of them go silent.

"Your training," Leo clarifies.

"You mean my education?" Leo looks to Kyle who is staring at the ground.

"What aren't you telling us?" Leo asks.

"Not now," Kyle answers warningly, and I don't expect the sharpness in his voice. He glances at me and I can tell it's my presence he objects to.

"Kyle if this is about me, I need to know," I say, "what's he talking about?"

"I noticed it in the forest," he starts, and I can tell he resents every second of this, "you didn't remember me as you should have. And you don't remember the Academy as it really was."

"What are you saying?"

"Someone tampered with your memory," Robyn answers when Kyle fails to speak up, "you're living half of your life. I can trace the spell."

"Someone took my memories? Then that explains-" the flashes of images, not knowing who Kyle is, why my past feels like something I'm reaching for through water. "Do it," I say.

Because deep down, I already know who it is, but I need to hear her say it. She kneels beside me and takes my hands.

"Valja siezaeta maroa sa vanagemarra varasta kair letai parasus ni siezaeta." Our hands grow warm and I watch as the veins in my arms light through my skin. They wind up to my shoulders and I see a golden haze that clouds my vision. "Holy shit."

"What is it?" Aaron asks. No one else says a word because, like me, they've already figured it out.

"It's a powerful spell but even so, it required maintenance which it hasn't had in a while. It's fading in its own time so you've probably started experiencing flashbacks."

"But who did it?"

"Inerea," I say, wiping a tear from my cheek. Robyn nods and, in that moment, even she pities me.

Part IV

Chapter XVII.

"That's why you didn't remember you were a dragovik and why you could function so well outside of the
Academy? Inerea cast a spell on you." Isabrand has
paused with his chopsticks mid-air.

"She wanted to take away the pain. I would never
have stood a chance of living a normal life in Aplin Hollow if I remembered the things they made me-the things
I did there," I correct myself. My blade has warmed in
my hand and I press it flat to my thigh.

"She fucked with your head Mallory. Whatever her
reason, that doesn't make her a good person."

"I know," I whisper, "but it's so difficult to speak ill of
her now. She loved me."

"A lot of people love you, but that's not how you
show it," he murmurs. He reaches out a hand and, before
I have the chance to flinch, he gently tucks a strand of
hair behind my ear. "You can put the knife away, I'm not
going to hurt you."

"You saw right through me didn't you," I say, putting
the blade down beside me on the bench and reaching
over to squeeze his hand.

"It hurts," he whispers, lowering his gaze, "I want to
restore something we've lost over the years and I'm not
sure how to navigate this situation. But it feels like I've
waited forever for this moment, for you to know me and
want me near you. That's all I wanted."

"Of course, I want you here Isabrand. Not because you're the only family I have left," I say, reading
his thoughts, "I've built myself a family since then and I
know there are people who love and protect me. I want
you here because you listened to all my stupid stories
when we were little and you didn't tell anyone when I ate
all the cookies in the kitchen. I want you here because,

whatever happened in those years apart, you're the first person I loved."

What's come to pass that's left him so incapable of believing those words? Because I see him struggle to process them, struggle to accept my affection as part of the world he's grown up in. I touch my thumb to the scar on his cheek.

"Perova tai ne, perova tai ne noventa, recritar letai laje, remaror tais vuzels." His skin tingles beneath my touch, warming to a heat that should burn us both were we not beyond the pain of fire. Slowly, the scar beneath his eye fades. "You want to protect me from the past as I do you, but neither of us can really do that now. Just let me be part of your future."

"You were always welcome in it, little sis. Now, where were we?"

"I was about to tell you about how I met your father for the second time."

* * *

Even my unconscious seems exhausted by the previous night, for it doesn't bother me with nightmares. A relief, I would think. Yet the lack of dreams is unsettling to wake to. I'm left with an absent feeling as I knot my hand into the fabric of my shirt. Dreams are something I rely upon to be consistent. Glad as I am not to be tormented, their absence is yet another sign of exactly how upside down my world has become.

The clock on my bedside table reads nine thirty, so I abandon my useless lounging and train of thought. My skin has become smooth once more while I slept, unblemished by the damage done. I'm relieved the sickly welts are gone.

Pressing two fingers gingerly against my arm to test

if I've fully recovered, I find the skin is still slightly tender, the external wounds having left their pain behind. That should heal soon too. Leo said we had an increased rate of healing. Why, then, does that scar on my back I can't remember getting remain? I wonder if Robyn could heal the scar it, or if I even want her to.

Knowing there's little time before they arrive, I grab the leggings and sweater I had left on the floor after the others had left and put them on. I brush my hair roughly, yanking painfully through its knots before going down to the kitchen. Inerea is mixing pancake batter when I come in.

"You got home before me last night, I didn't want to wake you. But I'm glad to have you home." She comes around the counter to give me a hug but I put my hands up. "You're still angry."

"Why did you do it? I don't mean keeping secrets from me. I mean taking my memories."

She freezes and a look of shock and terror crosses her face.

"You never went to the therapist last week, did you?"

"What? What's the therapist got to do with-Doctor Hersch was the one who cast the spell," I answer my own question.

"I cast the spell. Doctor Hersch was only ever maintaining it. The spell required a second."

"Which is why you kept pushing me to go back there."

My stomach knots itself. I'm certain I'll be sick any moment.

"But you didn't. That's the only way you could remember," she mutters, more to herself then me.

"I don't, not yet anyway. Robyn told me."

"Robyn Caverly? Then that's who told you we're dragoviks." She looks furious. "She had no right ambushing you like that."

"And you had no right to invade my head but you did anyway."

"I suppose that's why her brother Kyle is here too? They're trying to recruit you."

Kyle and Robyn are siblings? They look nothing alike, not to mention the disparity in their personalities. Then I remember what Chloe said about Robyn being adopted.

"I'm going to help them. And I don't want to hear from you again until I'm ready to talk."

"Mallory." She grabs my hands and holds them firmly. "I love you so much. I am so sorry I've hurt you, just please don't go."

"Fine, you're sorry? Lift the spell."

She bites her lip, gazing at me intensely as if I'll waver; finally, she realises I won't.

"I can't do that."

"Then I can't forgive you."

I pull open the front door to find Aaron standing directly in front of me, blocking my view of the outdoors.

"Nice to see you're awake and alive," he says.

"I managed not to be assaulted in the middle of the night so I suppose that's a good start to the day," I reply, though my voice is cracking with the weight of unshed tears.

"Not that good, what happened?"

He spots Inerea over my shoulder and I step outside and shut the door.

"I'm not ready to talk about it. Just be a pervert again, please."

"I'm sorry, was that the deployment of the humour you claimed to have no skill with?"

"You're a bad influence on me that way." He grins.

"I'll have to get a testimonial from you later," he

laughs. His cheeks are flushed by the cold air and the tip of his nose is pink.

"Is it always so cold here in the summer?"

"I haven't been up here in the summer before but, given the temperature in the winter, I wouldn't be surprised."

"You must all be very close if you come up to visit Kyle and Robyn's grandparents together." He frowns at me.

"Yeah, I've known Leo and Kyle as long as I can remember, and Robyn almost as long. What makes you ask?"

"Just trying to get a handle on the people I'm going to be spending time with," I say.

"Hm. I don't remember anyone mentioning Kyle and Robyn being siblings. Are you stalking us now?" he asks. I blush.

"I didn't intend to pry. Inerea told me."

"I'm not sure I want to ask about the extent of your conversation," he says, an undiscernible tone taking root. He casts his gaze away from me uncomfortably.

"Where's everyone else?" I ask, to change the subject.

"Robyn slept in. She was still pretty drained from last. I slipped away to give you the heads up that we weren't all murdered in our sleep."

"That's a horribly macabre thing to say."

"It was a joke."

"I don't think that clears it of being macabre. It just means it was a horribly macabre joke."

"And just when I think you might have gained a keen sense of humour," he scowls, "how are you feeling?"

"My scars are all gone," I say, rolling back my sleeves so he can see.

"Not what I meant," he sighs, but takes my arm to

examine it anyways.

"I assumed as much but forgive me, I'm not really able to speak about my feelings on the subject at present." I hardly understand them myself, so what would I say of them to him?

"Just tell me, fine or not fine?"

"I'm fine."

"Really?"

"No."

"It's okay to be afraid," he assures me.

"Are you?" I ask.

"Never."

"Liar," I mutter. His mouth crooks into a half smile and I can't help but smile back.

"Not a lie at all. I get afraid, but never in these kinds of situations. Deabrueon are just what I deal with on a regular basis."

"Well thank you. For trying to make me feel better," I clarify when he gives me a questioning look. "Even if I'm not sure why, it helps to know that at least one of you doesn't completely detest me."

"That's not true at all. Kyle likes you too," he says grinning. I don't laugh at his joke this time, just stare at the floor. "Truth be told I didn't just come over here to be incredibly witty as ever. I have something of a favour to ask."

"Oh?"

My heart sinks. Why do I get the impression that nothing could ask of me will be easy?

"That first night we met in the woods. The one where I wasn't human, strictly speaking."

"I recall it, no need to go into detail," I say, hardly repressing a shudder.

I don't like the idea of associating that night, that thing, with Aaron. I'm still not sure he wouldn't have

ripped me apart in his dragon form had I not run, despite his claim that they retain their human conscious in
dragon form.

"I'd appreciate it if you didn't mention it to the others. Or anyone for that matter."

"I wasn't planning on it. This wouldn't have anything to do with it being a punishable offence, would it?"
As I ask, the sound of footsteps on the gravel draws my
attention.

"I mean if you're the one doing the punishing I'm
listening."

"Of course you're here. I should have expected as
much," Robyn interrupts.

She storms up the porch steps, glowering at the two
of us. Her hair is pulled back in a high ponytail that
swings from side to side as she comes to a stop just outside
the front door.

"Glad to see you're back to your angry little self,"
Aaron says. She doesn't laugh, but throws a furious glance
in his direction.

"We've been looking for you everywhere. We already
visited just about every family on Kyle's list thinking you
may have gone ahead before Leo suggested I come here.
Do you have any idea how," she stops short of saying
what she really wants to. She was worried. I feel guilty
now for detaining him in conversation. They've been out
there looking this whole time while I've been idle.

"And is everyone alright?"

"What?" she demands, seemingly confused.

"You said you had checked in on almost all the families. Are they alright?" he asks.

"Of course, they've formed pairs to protect one
another so no one has to come stay at ours," she says
brusquely, "that's beside the point."

"Not really. If you didn't need me to help, there's no

reason I shouldn't have been here with Mallory."

Robyn falls silent but her frame quivers with fury. I want to tell her I have no intention of taking Aaron away from her as Kyle took himself away from her for my sake.

A buzzing sound disrupts the hushed tension.

"Give me a minute," Aaron says before pulling his phone from his coat pocket. "Hello?"

His eyes narrow as if the caller could see him. It's probably for the best they can't because he's starring daggers at the moment. But the irritation dissolves away as the colour drains from his face.

"We'll meet you there."

He hangs up before grabbing my hand, steering me towards his car. Robyn follows, her previous rage now mingling with her occupation over what could be happening.

"What happened?" she demands as we climb into the car.

"It's one of ours, they've been attacked."

"You mean," she falters before she can say their names. Kyle and Leo. My heart pounds. Please let them be alright. For her sake if not for their own.

"No, they're safe," he assures us, "the last house they stopped at. It didn't look good."

He curses under his breath as he begins to drive.

"Whose house is it?"

"Theodore Wainright's. Why didn't we check on him first? I'm sure he's one of the few on Kyle's list that lives alone."

"If you have qualms with how we did things perhaps you should have actually been with us," Robyn snaps. For all the gusto with which she says this, she cowers in equal measures of fear when Aaron turns to her with a fierce look pervading his features.

"Don't," he says back in a low but dangerous voice. I

shiver and, for the first time, can see that pure predatory power manifest in his human form.

"Is the man, Theodore, alright?" I manage. Aaron takes a moment to disengage from his anger with Robyn before he can address my question.

"No traces of him as of yet. The others are waiting for us before they go into the house but apparently it's in pretty bad shape."

"So he could still be alive," I breathe with relief.

"And the deabrueon could still be there."

He slows the car for the first time to look over me. He's concerned.

"I won't stay in the car," I say.

"It would be safer."

"If that's what you think occupies my mind at the moment than you don't have the faintest idea as to why I'm coming with you."

"I don't understand your motives at all," he replies, shaking his head. He speeds ahead without another word, going far too fast for the narrow road. If another car were to come around one of these bends in the woods, I doubt Aaron could get us out of the way before we collided. I feel the unwanted weight of his glance in the rear-view mirror now and again, but I continue to stare out the window as we drive in the opposite direction of town.

"Shit," Robyn murmurs as we come to a stop.

I hold my breath, staring at the destruction through the windshield. An old house is crumpled before us, folding in on itself. The skeleton of its once sturdy architecture remains, but many of the windows have been smashed, littering the ground with tears of glass. There are holes in the drywall, as if something has barrelled straight through it without any care for the damage it would cause the house or itself. The building has been reduced to something akin to a moth-eaten shirt. I see

Kyle coming around the side of the house, and he spots us at exactly the same moment.

"Stay here," Aaron orders, "don't argue."

He and Robyn shut their doors behind them and jog up to the front door where Kyle waits. They begin to discuss something and Kyle acknowledges me by way of a glance in my direction before they disappear into the building without returning to me. Minutes pass yet all that stirs are leaves and the breeze that redistributes them across the grass. I'm keenly aware of my heart trying to work its way into my throat and beat so hard that I won't be able to breathe. I can't just sit here while they're putting themselves in danger. After everything they've done for me before I was even aware of the danger I was in. What if something happens to them? The thought slows my breathing. They said the deabrueon wasn't strong enough to take all of them on, but what if it did kill this Theodore man? He could have given it just enough strength that it's now a threat to them.

I test the door and am relieved to find it's unlocked. Slipping my seatbelt off my shoulder, I sprint up the driveway. Only once I've reached the front of the house do I slow to a walk. The door creaks, the breath of age, and the breeze nudges it open for me. A soft voice wafts from within or around me. I cannot tell anymore.

Don't tell anyone. They'll get angry.

Were it not for the sound of this voice, lined with the concern I now hold for my four companions, I might have been unable to enter. But, as my heart stands, I can never leave a place this gentle voice leads me to. I push the door open just a little more to find the interior of the house is in just as a bad condition as the outside is. Boards of hard wood flooring have been torn up in places, and the staircase's frame hardly seems able to support itself any longer. Fragments of glass lay strewn across the floor, flashing reflections from the masses of light that come through the holes in the walls and casting rainbows into the shadows.

Little angel. I missed you.

The voice beckons me to join it from upstairs. Disregarding the safety hazards in doing so, I leap nimbly up the steps, avoiding the ones that seem weakest.

I'm so sorry I left you alone so long.

As if these words were a map to lead me to the owner of the voice, my body instinctively follows their command. My feet take off and I'm running down the hall to catch the voice. My insides ache with the ferocious desire to see the face of the one it belongs to. But when I push open the door of the room from which I was certain the voice came, I step into an empty library.

It's a sizeable round room with walls lined by bookshelves. The clerestory windows above are made of opaque stained glass, bearing a pattern of images that resonate with memories I scarcely recall. Despite the mess of scattered papers across an oak table, the room is in remarkably better condition than the rest of the house. There's no intrusive object nor damage that catches my eye. And yet. The papers on the table stir in a gentle breeze, though there's no window that would allow such circulation of air. I follow the unnatural guidance towards the table. Beneath the documents I see the faintest glint of silver.

Brushing aside the thick parchment, I find a roughly forty-inch slightly curved sword. Its blade is made purely of silver, the point of which is tapered to a flat edge. It has next to no rainguard and a strip of leather wound around the grip. But this is not what catches my eye. It's the highly decorative nature of the sword. Within the bevelled groove of the fuller is a swirling pattern of vines with inlayed emeralds for leaves. This level of ornamentation

can hardly be meant for a weapon of actual fighting pur-
poses. Hesitant at first, I'm intrigued enough now to pick
the weapon up. Despite the size and weight of the precious metal and gems, the blade seems relatively light. As
I curl my fingers around its grip, a current of electricity
rushes through my arm and I yelp, dropping the blade to
the floor with a clatter.

There's a soft sizzling sound and I glance down at
my arm to see my flesh glowing white hot. The same pattern on the blade now decorates my hand, climbing up
from the right corner of my palm. The roots shoot down
my forearm, burying themselves within the inside of my
elbow. I wait for the burn mark to turn black, or that pink
colour of a sickly scar. Instead, it glows a soft sunshine
gold before the light and pain recede to a white line. As I
reach to trace it, the pattern vanishes altogether.

I crouch down, examining the weapon where it lays.
The beautiful low-relief tracery that once covered its
blade has now disappeared. Reaching out, I pause, my
fingers resting on the air around it. Somewhere behind
the bookshelves, the floorboards creak. I pull my hand
back hastily as though the blade has burnt me again.

"Who's there?" I ask, timidly.

A stupid thing to do, I realise as I straighten myself. But silence hangs like dead weight around me when
there's no reply or further movement. I step cautiously,
trying not to awaken the groans of the floorboards. A
weak moan punctuates the quiet. I bolt forward, rushing
up the three steps nestled between two bookcases which
lead to a platform that houses more bookshelves. Peeking
around the corner of one, I see no one. A rattled exhale
of relief leaves me. At least none of my companions are
hurt. Perhaps my mind has yet more tricks with which it
will attempt to drive me insane, or perhaps it's the house
itself. I turn to leave.

"Help."

As if, with the softest touch, rose thorns have been raked across my skin, I shudder. The wavering voice ends its one-word plea with a fit of wet coughing. Glancing back, I see now an older man, huddled in the corner. He's slumped against one of the bookshelves, the contents of which has been scattered about him. A thick gash hooks up from the top of his nose then runs down the side, where it appears to have been broken. Blood streams from either nostril, rouging the top of his lips. Beneath his left eye is a pink and purple line. The other has begun to swell. Beholding him revives vile and vague memories of my own body and others' in a similar state. All clamour at my mind, begging me to run. No good can come of this. Ignoring my instinct, I rush to his side, dropping to my knees. He opens his mouth as if to explain.

"Please, don't exert your energy trying to speak. There are some people who came here with me, your kind. I'll get them. They can heal you," I assure him, trying to stand so I can go in search of Robyn.

He pulls me back to him, mouthing wordlessly. Now I'm closer I see the shirt that once appeared black reveals itself to have slightly orange tints where blood stains have soaked through the fabric. They've merged to the point that I cannot distinguish their number or seriousness.

"You see now, why I cannot wait for you to return with others. There's not enough time," he wheezes, tightening his grip on me. "I found out."

"What?" I look desperately around me, pleading with whatever unreasonable god has allowed this to happen that Robyn will find us.

"I found out what it's looking…it's looking."

His eyes roll back, and the blood vessels connected within them strain beneath the movement. For a moment, I fear they'll burst and fill his waterline with their crimson agony. I've seen tears of blood before. Where I cannot say. The man gags and blood droplets the size of coins spew from his mouth. Some dribble down his chin, dripping a steady rhythm.

One, two, three…

I'm scared.

My vision scatters for a moment and behind reality I see a pair of eyes looking into me.

"Find, Leora," the man rasps.

His head falls against my shoulder as he's struck by another bout of coughs. He heaves breaths through the spider web of bloodied phlegm filling his throat.

"We mustn't let him in," the man breathes, regaining me from my mind.

"Him?" But then my head begins to pound and the dripping grows louder.

One, two, three…

"How foolish of me," the man sighs, resting his head back on the bookcase though he never looks away from my face. His eyes are lit with great pity. "He's already here."

Amongst the fear that possesses his face, a sad smile plays across his lips. Then his eyes begin to swell, the pupils consuming the irises' whole. Between the roar of dripping blood from his chin and the pounding in my head, I'm not sure if there's any sound simultaneous with what follows. The veins in his eyes burst, swallowing all their light with red. I cry out, but it falls to a whimper. I can hear him groan, still alive despite the pain.

He rattles out another breath, his eyes sinking back into their sockets as blood spills over his lower lid. Steady streams forge with his nose's bleeding, pushing the dark substance over the crest of his quaking upper lip and down his mouth. It dips inward at the crease of his mouth. I part my lips to scream but my back snaps upright in response, stringing me taut like a bow. What's happening? Clawing for a moment at the ground to drag myself away, I find my arms cleave to my sides. My body tilts and I collapse into the man's lap. The river of red falls in beads onto my face and I gag, trying to free myself from whatever has possessed me. The salty taste of blood bites my tongue as if it's been struck by an iron blade, and a gargled scream releases itself from my lips.

I try to spit the blood out but instead choke on it like my own bile until it slips easily down my throat. Reality fragments again and there are those eyes, closer than before. The man's rasping breaths are drowned out by the phantom beating of my heart roaring in my ears. I thrash from side to side as shadows pour into the corners of my eyes.

Let me taste the fire of you blood, he whispers.

Then there's dark.

Chapter XVIII.

He sips on their death. All the world's a blood bath, he's a human drain. It circles him, magnetised and drawn into his body where its power is appropriated for his use. That man is all talons, madman bound.

In his hands hangs a twisted body.

In this field of bodies desiccation makes quick work of us. Decay is hungry in this red skied world of two moons.

Where do I fit in? A body in the mass of carrion is what I feel like. But if it were so, would he be able to single me out with such swift ease?

He lets the body go and it falls into the pool of blood ready made by the cuts in it, for it to rest in. I am his next target.

"No. There will yet be more," he says, "but for now, I am sated."

He reaches out, hands lost somewhere between claws and human flesh. His nails grow well beyond a normal length, sharpened, but chipped due to their brittle nature. He takes hold of me, drawing my body towards him. I cannot define what extremity of the spectrum of hot or cold the pain of his touch resides with. All I know is I have to scream. And I keep doing so into consciousness.

* * *

"What the hell happened here?" someone gasps.

I don't move at the sound of the voice, perhaps because I can't move. They all sound the same anyway. Who's to say this isn't the voice of that madman or another I've met. My skin tingles. It feels stretched, as if someone else has climbed inside it as well and left it taut across my weak frame.

"Where is she?"

"She could have run away. Maybe she saw something and got scared."

"Unless-"

"Unless what?" another voice demands.

Yes, I'd like to know too.

Unless I've already died. And here I had hoped it would be such sweet rest to be departed at last. My body, if it ever belonged to me, feels as if it's in enough pain to belong now to death. That, or we're in the midst of the act. Pay up grim reaper and take me out of this misery. I open my eyes, but all I see is black with speckles of white, which could just as easily be the ceiling as it could an afterlife. The small action triggers instantaneous pain, as if microscopic needles are being carefully stitched into my eyes and the thread following them leaves the pin-prick wounds open.

I want to hear that voice again, to know what the person is thinking. I want to know their unless.

"I'm just saying-"

"Well stop."

If I could speak, and they hear me, that would be confirmation enough that I'm still alive in their world and not a lingering ghost.

"Let's not assume the worst Robyn."

Footsteps move away and the library door shuts. Robyn. Robyn can save me, even though I told her I wouldn't ask for saving. I open my mouth to call out to her but what it releases doesn't give way to her name. The waiting tide unfastens itself from my tongue. Screams unleash their assault on silence, snapping it in half easily. They reawaken the pain of his touch in my dream. My body joins in with inaudible cries of agony. This is far beyond what a body can bear.

"Mallory!"

Their feet disturb the wood beneath them in a rush to reach me. Even over my screaming, the floorboard's groans of protest are not lost.

"Do something!"

Cold hands take a hold of me. A searing pain shoots up my arm, draws itself back to the source and explodes again. I howl, trying to pull myself from this grip. I dig my fingernails into the flesh of a forearm.

"Shit! Someone hold her down."

Someone prises my fingers off while another pair of hands pins my shoulders to the ground and a third holds my feet. My teeth snap open and shut in an almost mechanised motion. Whatever darkness holds a place in my heart has burst out. I want to tear these people apart. I won't be touched, I won't be held down and made a slave of.

"Lueicht, nandirava letai nevorso ni isuzako etev udiyat."

I hear a hiss whistle between my teeth as the incantation is repeated. You can't hurt me, heal me and make me break again, I want to yell.

"Why the fuck isn't it doing anything?"

"I don't see a single scratch on her."

I toss my head restlessly from side to side, snarling. I won't lay down and die.

"Can you stop being so fucking useless and do something?"

"I'm trying!"

"Try harder."

I hear the call of a solitary heart beating. It's in so much agony over the cruel words it's fed. All it has now to give to others is malice.

"Nevorsona imadiava etev si kauava udi tyesta couras. Perova destoyar nevorsona baniraava avot!"

The bestial sounds that had possessed my tongue fall

to whimpers, those of a wounded animal waiting to be killed after a fatal, but not instantaneously so, shot. Quiet murmurs only partially punctuate the room's atmosphere. The air becomes a heavy blanket, clinging to my body. It shimmers around me, full of life's texture, and then begins to pour over my skin. It bleeds into my pores, rushes through my blood, my heart and is oxygen's revival in my mind. The curtains of exhausting confusion part and my eyes finally clear.

Robyn kneels beside me, slumped over and propping herself up on stiffened arms. Her head is hanging down and her chocolate eyes are hidden behind eyelids as she gasps for breath. Her expression isn't expectant of my revival. She's already given up, having drained herself to a pallor close to death. Still, she utters the strange language once more and, with the last word, the restorative air pulls away. My body begins to feel as it did not long ago, before I had come into this horrible place.

"I can't," she whimpers, "I can't do anymore."

I can't part my lips to tell her I'm alright. She's saved my life yet again. Aaron is looking at her, a fervent plea on his face even though his eyes recognise the impossibility of what his silence asks. Leo is crouched by my feet, head bent as if already in mourning. I feel the weight of hands still on my shoulders and, when I glance directly above me, I find Kyle's endless ocean eyes looking back at me. His face cracks into relief and he removes one of his hands to brush the hair from my face.

"Robyn, it worked. She's coming to."

Those hard brown eyes open to look upon me, flushed with curiosity and amazement. Aaron and Leo follow her gaze to my face. The former all but falls back onto his hands with a self-consolatory moan. He tilts his head back.

"Mallory, can you hear me?" Kyle inquires.

I mouth the word yes with my lips, unable to move my tongue. It still feels heavy with the taste of blood. The thought sickens me.

"What did you do?" he asks Robyn.

"It was a mind calming spell. It was just supposed to stop her from screaming and trying to attack us so that I could actually think about what to do. I didn't imagine it would do anything more," she trails off, giving me an odd look.

I want to laugh as she says this.

Kyle slips his hand beneath my back, propping me up into a sitting position like a delicately poised doll. As soon as he lets go, my shoulders slump forward and I hang there, limp. Calm settles like dust over my thoughts. Oxygen comes steadily in and out once again. One moment longer behind closed eyelids before the onslaught of questions begins. One moment could so easily elapse into forever. I want to fall asleep so desperately. I force alertness upon myself, slowly blinking myself from the edge of sleep.

"Why didn't you stay in the damn car?"

This time, I do laugh at what Robyn says. She looks taken aback by the ripple of sound that bubbles off my lips so easily. There's a relief in the effortlessness with which she falls back to being angry at me.

"I was worried something might have happened to one of you," I say when I finally manage to repress my laughter.

Aaron moans, running his fingers through the fine hairs at the nape of his neck. He looks at me in disbelief.

"And there we were with the exact same concern when we went to the car to find no trace of you. Rightfully so, I might add," Kyle remarks, scooting up beside me.

He's assessing me, looking for any injuries. But despite all the blood, none of it is mine. My heart rattles. All the blood. I pivot my torso and I'm only unable to scream due to the suffocating panic that fills me. The man's mangled body sags in front of me. His body reeks of putrefaction already, as if hours of decay folded themselves up into mere minutes. A clear fluid leaks from his nose and slightly parted lips, glazing the blood like a fine polish. His eye sockets are hollow, leaking black trails halfway down his already darkening skin. Bile rises in my throat, acid pricking my mouth. I dart towards him, past Leo, as if there were something I could do. No one else moves for a moment, as if they're all seeing the body for the first time as well. A small shocked intake of breath is reigned in with almost complete quietude.

"Get her out of here," Leo mutters.

The others seem incapable of movement. Aaron is still drawn into himself by whatever leaves a pained expression on his face and Robyn barely seems able to hold her own weight. I'm leaning towards the man, one hand outstretched. As I lay my palm gently on his cheek there's a strange shifting beneath it. I pull my hand away and the skin covering his jaw peels back with it. Now I manage to scream. A pair of hands grasp me around the abdomen, pulling me to my feet. Almost as though he could sense me leaving, the man's head tilts down, casting that empty gaze to the floor.

"No," I choke while being half dragged half marched out of the room, "we have to help him. Let me go back."

I try to shove my weight down to my feet, digging my heels into the ground to hinder whoever pulls me away. All I manage to do is stumble, leaving me all the more dependent on the strength of the other person.

"There's nothing to be done," Kyle says.

"No!" The hands reconfigure themselves, one griping me around my lower back and the other scooping me from behind my knees. "Please."

Just as soon as the voices resume in the library, they grow distant. Are they deciding what to do with the body? The body. A lack of life reduces a man from sentient entity to an object. My head spins, those sickening eye sockets staring at me from behind my eyelids. Had he been in the piles of dead in my dream? I feel the bump of each step rattling my stomach, and my throat itches with the burn of sick. It threatens to rush out of me with as much uncontrollable force as my screams. Just when I think I cannot hold it in any longer, a dust of wind moves across my skin, removing the blush from my cheeks. I'm set on my feet and, being unprepared, it takes all my effort not to fall to the ground. The arms don't let go of me completely. They keep me upright as I continue to tremble. When I open my eyes, I find Kyle gazing at me.

"Please don't make me leave him behind," I beg.

"You have to. There's no future you can take him into," he says softly.

"Robyn can do something. She saved me," I say.

"You weren't dead."

"But you should at least be able to protect your own kind."

"I know. I wish we could have, but sometimes it's too late."

"Then what's the point!" I scream.

My throat becomes raw with the effort of my cry and the shock of my own outburst stills me into silence. I can see the distress my own anguish causes Kyle. His eyebrows dip inwards and his eyes widen slightly as he takes me in. He waits until my chest has stopped heaving with haphazard breaths that expel more carbon dioxide than they take in oxygen. He cups the back of my head tenderly as if to support an infant and draws me against him.

"Please."

"I'm so sorry Mallory," he whispers.

I sob, tearlessly, but with all the uncontrolled shudders and breathing of someone crying. I twist my hands into the fabric of his shirt just above his shoulder blades. It feels safe to let him hold me. Even being as vulnerable as I am, there is no doubt that he's only hugging me because of some unspoken need for consolation he saw in me.

"There's no point to this death, I know."

"I want to go back up there," I say.

"I know, but not until you've calmed down. You've only just come back from a near death experience, let yourself rest for a moment," he insists.

I step back and he releases his hold on me completely so I might stand on my own. I sway lightly for an instant before grounding myself in a resolve for composure.

"How am I supposed to be calm after coming here with the hope that he would be alive, only to watch him die? All I wanted was to run. I was so afraid."

"It's only natural that death is frightening. Do you think, beneath those artifices of self-possession, any one of us wasn't just as afraid? Seeing death never becomes a sight that can be normalised. To watch something so vital slip from existence is a reminder of the price we all pay just for living, even when we haven't lived well," he says.

"That's not really an answer."

"Any attempt to give one is impossible. I can't explain how to cope with death because there's such a singular means of coping for each person."

I have never lost someone, not really. I never mourned my parents because there was nothing to mourn; they were ghosts to me before they died. I stare out back towards the car. I have not made my peace with what I've seen, but my resolve clamps down on my nerves, steeling them.

"I'm ready to go back now."

He nods. I fall two steps behind him as we re-enter the house, my feet hitting the ground a second after his until they sound like a heartbeat. I watch his figure as we ascend the stairs to the library. I can see a weary tension held in his shoulders, his muscles wrung taught to squeeze out every last bit of energy he has to give. Back in the library, our footsteps rouse the others from their hushed conversation.

"Why would you bring her back here?" Aaron demands, stepping between us and the others.

"Because she did such a good job of staying in the car last time we left her alone," Leo mutters.

"She wanted to come," Kyle replies, resting his steady hand on my shoulder.

"And I wanted a chilli cheese dog the other day but you weren't jumping at the opportunity to satisfy that want. Far less perilous as well," Robyn grumbles.

"Debateable," Leo drawls, "those are vile."

"Either way," Kyle interjects, clearing his throat, "I think it's best that she come back up before we leave so that we can ask her any questions. Within reason."

He shoots Robyn a look with his last two words.

"Is she well enough to answer?" Aaron asks.

"I'm much better. Thank you again Robyn."

"Save your thank yous. Instead, why not use that energy to not almost die for once."

"Robyn," Kyle says, inclining his head in a slight plea.

"Maybe in your time away from us you've forgotten how this works, Kyle," Robyn spits, her brother's name shattering in her mouth full of cold anger, "but we don't make reckless decisions just because of how we feel. If something had happened to the rest of us it would have been better that she hadn't come in."

The other two fall still, and seem inexplicably unable

to look at Kyle as he turns his gaze to each of their faces successively. Realising there's nothing to be gained from gauging their blank expressions, he looks away.

"All I meant by it was that perhaps you could accept her gratitude. Any mistakes she made in regards to how she's supposed to conduct herself are our fault for not making the situation clear to her," Kyle replies in a faint voice. He can barely manage to lift his eyes to meet his sister's as he says this.

"Whatever," she mutters.

I want to comfort Kyle as he did for me moments ago. But wherever he's retreated in his mind seems well beyond the reach of my words. Leo has begun to circle the room, observing it and occasionally glancing at me like some point of reference.

"Other than the blood and the corpse, is the library exactly as it was when you entered?" he inquires.

"You could at least try to phrase it with a little more sensitivity," Aaron groans.

"It's alright, really," I assure him before turning to Leo. So long as I don't have to see that man and I can just imagine corpse to refer to a skeleton of someone I've never spoken to, I can manage this conversation. "There was a sword on the floor, just there."

I indicate the place I had dropped the weapon.

"We already collected it," Leo replies, but gives me a strange look. "Nothing else, you're sure?"

"Nothing other than the fact that he was alive."

Leo stops in his tracks, looking towards the bookshelves that hide his slumped body from view.

"Alright. Did you see anyone when you came in, other than Theodore?"

I wince when Leo says his name. Human attributions are not something I want to be assigning to dead men.

"No. I was the only one in here with him. But I

thought I heard someone calling for me from in here. That's why I came into the library in the first place."

"How ridiculously unintelligent are you, you vacuous imbecile?" Robyn demands, standing up in a sudden flurry of irritation. "Less than a day ago you were almost murdered by a deabrueon that called you by name and couldn't be seen until it chose to be. But what do you do when you hear your name being called? You run towards it."

"That's enough Robyn," Kyle warns, drawn out of his self by her words.

"Seriously! You're defending a complete fool with no concept of self-awareness. All you seem capable of doing is taking her side over mine!"

"Stop it," Aaron says, placing a hand on her shoulder. She stills beneath his touch, turning her body away from Kyle and me, and towards him.

"It wasn't the same voice," I reply.

"A deabrueon can easily alter the sound of its voice, if it has one," Kyle sighs, though his remark holds no reproach. "I'm so sorry Mallory. I should have explained more to you before allowing you to come into contact with such a situation."

"No. I understand it's my fault for leaving the car. I should have listened."

"We should continue this conversation later. Perhaps somewhere that hasn't seen a recent murder," Aaron says.

"We're lucky one kill was enough for it today, otherwise we might not have been able to get to you in time," Kyle adds.

"Lucky," Robyn repeats, but the manner in which her inflection varies from her brother's suggests she doesn't agree with him at all. She shrugs Aaron's hand from her shoulder and storms past us.

From the outside, the house truly seems on its last leg.

Even more so than when we entered. The newly picked up wind pushes hard against our bodies as we cross the lawn to reach the car. It rages against the weary building, set on clearing this stage now unsuited to the living. Unlike every other part of town, nature does not spring to life here. The grass is thinned out and the earth is so dry it's begun to crack.

"Don't move a muscle."

I feel the cold of metal permeate the back of my shirt, but whoever is pressing a blade to my back isn't speaking to me. Aaron, Kyle, and Leo still.

"Do whatever you want, we don't really care about her," Robyn replies, examining her nails.

"Hush you filthy dragovik," the voice answers.

"Yes Robyn, do shut up," Leo growls.

"What are the bellatoja doing here?" Kyle asks quietly.

"You called, didn't you? To clean up your mess."

"Well, if you're here to help how about you let our friend go?"

I feel the body behind me shake with laughter before I'm jolted forward, knocked to the ground. My knees hit the earth first before I manage to catch myself. I feel the air stir behind me and roll out of the way just in time to avoid a kick.

"You're fun to play with."

The man towering over me must be in his mid-thirties, stubble covering his square jaw. His expression is a mix of amusement and disgust. *Filthy dragovik*. He knows exactly what I am and he wants to punish me for my very existence. In those next few seconds, Aaron is between us and Kyle is helping me up.

"You won't lay a hand on her unless you want your throat cut," Aaron hisses. The man narrows his eyes.

"You can't take us boy."

From the forest emerge ten more men, swords identical to his, glinting in the bright pale light emitting from behind the clouds. The man grins, lowering his blade. He has no need for it and we all know it.

"In case your thick bellatoja heads are unaware, we're not the deabrueon. So take your species prejudice and shove it-"

"Robyn!" Kyle interrupts, warningly.

"Robyn's right, if it weren't for how slow you were to respond to clean up your mess people wouldn't be dead. And we all know the only reason it took so long is because it's dragoviks that are dying," Aaron says.

"I see no problem with a few more of you heathens dying."

"Listen, I'm aware you two have history. But perhaps we could work together to get rid of the deabrueon sooner rather than later?" Kyle suggests.

"I've heard of you Caverly and I must admit, there's more to respect in you than most of your kind. But I will not be forced to work with the likes of them," the man says, nodding to Aaron and Leo.

"As if we'd stoop so low as to work with you either," Aaron retorts. I want to pull him back, out of reach of the man's sword.

"Aaron," I say pleadingly.

"Yes Aaron, listen to the little play thing."

I ignore him, stepping between the pair of them with my back to the other man.

"Let's go."

I don't add 'while they still let us', for fear it will insult Aaron's pride. I press a hand to his chest, urging him to back away, and I feel him tense. But then he relaxes, flits a lazy grin at the man and pulls me to him. Scooping me up, he tosses me over his shoulder so I'm confronted with Kyle, Leo, and Robyn's shocked expressions.

"No one touches my play things."

He spins around and the last thing I see before I'm deposited in the car is the man's laughing face.

Leo and Aaron take the front seats in the car while Kyle and Robyn slide in the back after me. Leo turns around wordlessly, handing a tightly bunched midnight cloth that juts around the angles of whatever object it conceals to Kyle. I hadn't even noticed he was carrying it. Kyle begins to coil his fingers around the bundle subconsciously, scrunching the fabric up like dark whirlpools. I peek at him through the curtain of my hair but he doesn't seem to notice as we begin to drive. Blue roots of veins run across the back of his hands, pressing hard against his taut skin. I watch his fingers curl and uncurl, working the cloth in his hands, until watching the nervous action starts to make me feel uneasy.

I find looking at Aaron no more comforting. His easy expression is gone, his jaw now clenched, and his hands have become devoid of any colour as he clutches the steering wheel. I don't bother turning to Robyn for some sense of comfort. Instead, I settle my gaze on Leo, who remains remarkably unchanged. His face is as pale as ever, his hair unruffled even by the gusts of wind that had attempted to drag us all away. He roles his shoulders back, pushing them into a stiff posture that would seem uncomfortable were it not for the self-possession that seems so intrinsic to his nature. The rigidness constricts him in a comforting way, as if he was resetting himself into the packaging which humans are taken from before entering the world.

With a slight jolt, the car moves onto a more poorly paved road. My stomach rolls with nausea and I shut my eyes, hoping it will only be temporary. That sickly acidic liquid rises in my throat again as images plaster themselves to the backs of my eyelids. I try to unstick them with other thoughts, but they persevere. A killer's face can be filled with compassion during the act. The act itself can be orchestrated from a merciful feeling towards the victim. That doesn't not make it murder, does it? But why do I ask myself this question, and why do I fear the answer?

Then I feel a near imperceptible pressure applied to my hand. My eyes open, stripping away the thought of hands so readily painted red, and the sickness is replaced by panic. Kyle's hand is resting on mine. His grip is so faint that I can't be certain he hasn't just laid it there unintentionally. Is he afraid, or does he believe I am? I don't risk looking at his face, but the sight of his pale hand wrapped around mine plagues my peripheral. I try to focus on not moving an inch beneath his touch, or pretending it's a mere itch rather than the weight of another person. But the more I do the more I begin to tremble. His grip tightens. My heart lurches furiously in my chest. I chance meeting his gaze so I might make something of his expression, but he's staring dead ahead through the windshield. His Adam's apple rises as he swallows hard. Laboured breaths roll unevenly through his slightly parted lips as he tries to regain control. As if sensing my gaze, he ducks his head down. Beneath the curls that now hide most of his face, I see his expression. He's so isolated, sitting among this crowd of five.

I flip my hand over and curl my thumb up around the side of his. He begins to move away to set me free, believing me to be doing the same. I slip my fingers between his and press the pads of my fingertips gently on his skin. I refocus my gaze through the front window, as does he. Neither of us is able to face the mirrored look of loneliness in each other's eyes. Yet my queasiness and panic both subside as I listen to his breaths.

"We need to go back to the house and clean all this

blood away before we can do anything else," Aaron mutters to Leo.

Perhaps he's speaking at a normal decibel. Other than Kyle's touch, none of these human actions seem to reach me, as if a buffer has fallen over my senses because I've been drawn into realisation. I had known and seen what we are. I have not really seen the violent attempts of danger to remind us of the precarious relationship we hold with mortality. I hadn't known the burn of a human life extinguished so close to me, not when that person should have lived on. The consequences of my life's path have been clear to me since Inerea told me I was a witch. But the consequences of what I was born to be hit me only now. Even in the forest when the deabrueon tried to kill me, it felt more about who I am than what I am. How could it not, when it spoke with those voices that seemed to know me? At present though, I sit here having come to terms with what I am, a vapour of humanity, amongst four of the greatest lies of life the world will always believe: that their youth indicates a lifespan greater than most.

Again, sickness finds its roots in me and grows. It's not a mere queasy anxiety, but a sinister heaviness in my stomach. Words ripple the air, moving back and forth. I can't hear them. I want to, so I have some sense of goings on that might distract me. All I can think of is that by now the man's blood has dried on my skin and clothes. The only thing that keeps the full fledged burst of panic waiting in my chest from wreaking havoc is the repetitive motion of picking the blood off in flakes. The more I watch flutter away, the more desperate I become to be rid of it all. Even where I am clear of its taint, my flesh feels dried and cracked by the weight of spilt life. In my mind I see him, over and over again. It's not the image of his swollen body, blood blossoming from cuts that haunts me, but that last flash of fear and realisation in his eyes before we fell helpless to the power of whatever killed him. The car comes to a stop and I feel Kyle pull me slightly, leading me from the car as I continue to be mesmerised by that dark repeating image.

"This is my grandparent's house," Kyle murmurs, his words a barely comprehensible slur through my daze.

The only thing that does draw me from it is the sense of his fingers loosening from mine. My shield of numbness drops and I'm made vulnerable to my five senses again.

Ahead of us is a large manor, kept in impeccable order as if time was something that could be so easily brushed off. We trundle behind the other three as they enter. I'm not sure what I was expecting of the inside. Perhaps some grossly obvious indication that it was the home of supernatural beings. The only thing remotely supernatural is the enormity of the entrance hall we come into. Though this house belongs to one family, it seems roughly the same size as the Academy, which accommodated more people than I will likely ever know. Before us is a large staircase leading to a balcony from which the entire atrium can be taken in. There's a hallway on either side of the stairs leading deeper into the house, and archways on opposite walls open up into vast unlit rooms.

"So, shall we resume our conversation?" Leo asks.

"Give us a chance to change out of these clothes, and perhaps rest," Kyle says in response. Not one of us has managed to avoid getting blood on our clothes. "Robyn, could you let her use your shower and lend her some clothes?"

I want to plead him not to ask but it's a bit late. She draws her bottom lip into the grip of her teeth, needling her brother with a look of great displeasure.

"Fine," she mutters, "come on."

She walks swiftly down the corridor to the left of the stairs and I follow. She doesn't bother turning on the lights as we progress and, prior to recent events, the darkness would not bother me so. But now I see movements in every corner and shapes that don't exist. I am desperate for illumination to beat back the uncertainty of the dark. Robyn opens a door on our left, finally switching on a light. Its bright glow pulses as my eyes readjust. The chandelier hangs low from the incredibly high ceiling. Robyn crosses the room, passing the bed to reach her dresser. She opens the drawers and picks out a few pieces of clothes, which she hands to me.

"I'm not sure how well they'll fit. The bathroom's through there," she says, indicating a door in the corner of the vast room, "you can shower first just make it quick. I really hate having blood in my hair."

I nod in gratitude, mostly because I've now been rendered unsure of how to respond. She turns back to the still open drawer and starts to select her own clothes. I'm inclined to apologise for the burden I've so quickly become to them, especially her, but know the words would not be received with the kindness with which they are intended.

In the bathroom, I let my body become soaked beneath the shower before taking a washcloth from beside the sink and scrubbing away the blood. Starting at my wrists, I work my way methodically up both of my arms. How can she say something so blithe in the wake of what's happened? Her eyes didn't even give the slightest hint of any emotion other than irritation when she spoke. I hope I'm wrong and that I yet know her too poorly to be able to see whatever she's hiding. But her face is always so wrought with expression, it seems impossible that she'd be able to keep any of it back. Just when I think I've cleaned most of the blood from myself, I find more faint traces of it painted across my collar bones, as if made to torment.

"Why should they harrow me, when his death was not my doing," I assert quietly to myself.

I scrub with more vigour until my skin blushes red beneath the pressure of my touch. There's no longer any means to distinguish the blood screaming beneath the veil of my human softness from his death markings upon me. Finally, I stop and just wait until the water runs crystalline over me. This will be my marker of cleanliness as calmness seems not to wish me clarity.

That initial surge of reassurance I had been filled with by Robyn's spell has since been racked into instability. Eventually I am clean enough to turn the faucet off and dry myself. I begin to do battle with the narrow jeans Robyn has left me, struggling to pull the last inch over my hips. My ankles stick out awkwardly from the trousers and the black sweater's hemline leaves a significant gap between it and my waistline. When I emerge, Robyn is sitting on her bed, eyes trained on the door.

"About time," she scowls.

"I'm sorry to have kept you waiting," I say as she shoves by. "Robyn?"

"What?"

"When you found me, I heard someone saying I didn't have any wounds. And after you cast that mind calming spell, as you called it, I was fine."

"Well thank you for that question not worded as a question. I figured you must have some injury given the blood everywhere but I couldn't find it. I couldn't exactly look for it either as long as you were freaking out and trying to rip the flesh from my arm. Whatever pain you felt must have been an illusion the deabrueon cast to keep you out of its way. Not that you could really do anything to stop it."

"Thank you."

"Whatever," she scowls and turns from me.

"I do mean it when I say it. Since that night at the bonfire, I've needed your help twice. I wouldn't be alive if it weren't for you, and you alone."

She doesn't look back over her shoulder as I speak but refrains from storming off as I thought she would have done.

"You can take a rest on my bed if you'd like. Just don't snore or drool."

She shuts the bathroom door, leaving me to the heavy fatigue of the day. It bears down on me to weaken my bones and loosen my muscles. I curl up on her bed, my skin still too warm from the shower to get under the blankets, and let lethargy sweep through me. It roots me in place and I sense that, if I stay now, I may never be able to leave again. Not this room, but this way of life. My eyes, heavy with the thoughts of days to come, droop shut.

Chapter XIX.

I see Death, but I can't describe what manifestation of starvation and plague appears before me dressed in his cloak. In an instant he'll change from a child to a grown woman, then to something not altogether human in appearance, but still clutching at the edges of it. He's waiting for me, as he has been since I was born. Yet his hands are not around my throat and he presses no dagger to my skin. He has no intention of drawing life from me just yet. He takes me by the hand, leading me through the world so I can view it as he does, or perhaps it's just what he wishes me to see.

Everywhere there is suffering and I condone it by leaving it behind without trying to help. We ascend stairs but it doesn't feel as if we're moving further upwards, just that we're further from the world. We come to a standstill and when I look left, I no longer see Death in his sable robes. Instead, a mirror stands a distance from me. I move towards it but, no matter how close I get, the glass is incapable of rendering my reflection. Resting my hand on its cold surface, I breath heavily on it, but it draws no warm fog on its surface.

"What reflection do you believe could manifest? Simply your outer being? That would never suffice. An effluence of darkness from a heart? They are no longer separate entities so that would do no good either. There is no image it could conjure to show you how deeply the roots of evil have wound themselves within you. Your skin is the cloth from which killers and demons are cut."

I turn and tilt my face upwards to gaze upon the man whose voice has been haunting me. But all I see is a shape in the darkness into which all terror is drawn. A shadow within the shadows that surround me. The only thing darker than Death. He's raw meat on bones.

"After the torment you've wrought, why are you starting to show yourself to me now?" I ask quietly, drawing closer to him.

"I will not show myself, not in whole, not yet. I wish that I had strength enough for that. But here I will be nurtured into flesh. I told you, Mallory, this is my home."

"You've said that before, yet I'm still disinclined to believe that you truly exist here, let alone have power enough to become something from this nothing."

"And yet you tremble at the very notion of it because you know it will come to pass. Still, I commend you for even having the courage to speak. You've grown stronger," he purrs, moving like a ripple in the darkness towards me. "But fear will always claim your rationality. Logic, bravery. What are those but mere words in the face of that which can truly get under your skin. And I am, Mallory. I am under your skin and the seed of your every thought."

"You are nothing more than a ghost of a memory I can't recall. A phantom of a dream bound in my mind," I say.

I cannot help but step forward again, drawn by the desire to be close enough to see him. He chuckles, not with the same mania as usual, but in a low controlled manner.

"Perhaps for now. But through your every word, every action, I await the chance to set myself free. Already I am more than I was before."

He rolls his shoulders back as he continues his steady path towards me. The shadows follow him, enshrining him in their dark worship and I find myself incapable of moving any further in his presence. Something holds me with bindings I can neither see nor fight, just like him.

"I am not here to kill you."

"You'll never be given the chance to."

"As if I need to be given the chance! You've been obedient for so long that no acts of rebellion could stop me."

"It's not me who would stop you."

His eyes glint angrily from his darkened face, burning with the trace of another emotion I can't name.

"Ah so you're under the impression that your companions will save you? That they don't have selfish agendas that bring them to your aid just as quickly as they will drive them away? You have no one. But fear not. As I've assured you, you will not die here. When I bring the end, I will favour you above all, my little angel."

My little angel. But the voice that had beckoned with that moniker had been so gentle. Surely it couldn't have been him.

"You're the one doing this. You're the deabrueon."

"You're right and wrong. But you won't know my plan until it's too late."

* * *

The lights in my mind shut off and I am once again aware of those glowing in Robyn's room. My heart is thrumming with the effort to contain thoughts of what I've just seen. For a moment, I felt so terribly sorry for him. He appeared as the paragon of loneliness. While we each carry our sufferings, they are always mixed with other experiences that show us the good in the world. He was without happiness, burdened by every type of pain imaginable. Do I pity him? The thought makes my stomach turn. It's not a question I believe I can answer. It would be so much easier to see people like him in terms of black and white, a pure evil or divine good. But I should have realised that the crazed manner in which he has always appeared to me was a result of suffering. If he's evil for becoming the product of cruelty, then are not we all? I curl my knees to my chest.

I hear the shower running still, indicating I've only been absent from reality for a few minutes at most. I can't even consider going back to sleep if that's what awaits me on the other side of my eyelids. I'm confused enough about my present state of mind without feeling empathy for him. The prospect of remaining here so that I might be subjected to a fresh bout of Robyn's anger isn't exactly appealing either, though I feel we may be on slightly better terms now.

Smoothing the sheets on the bed so they no longer hold the creases of my form, I leave the room. I make my way towards the entrance hall again, finding the dark of the hallway less chilling having had some time to rest. Through one of the archways in the entrance, I see a distant illumination coming from a pair of doors. There's a slight clattering sound, which I follow through the dining room into a spacious kitchen. I see a dusting of black waves peeking out from behind marble topped counters that serve as a breakfast bar.

"Kyle?"

He straightens himself, a large glass bowl in hand.

"I thought I heard someone," he says, setting the bowl down and smiling at me.

He looks exhausted, mentally at least. His thoughts must have been moving a thousand miles a minute since we arrived. I want to ask him what it is that makes his mind so weary but think better of it.

"Sorry if I startled you."

"Not at all, it's actually somewhat of a relief to find it's you. Feeling a bit better?" he asks. I shake my head in answer to his question. "Why don't you take a seat. I was just going to make some pancakes."

"You cook?" I ask, sitting down on one of the stools

on the opposite side of the counter.

"In a very limited capacity. Is there anything I can get you?"

He opens the fridge door and comes back with milk, butter and eggs.

"I don't think I could manage to keep anything down at the moment." He cracks three eggs into the bowl. "Is it normal that I'm still afraid to close my eyes for fear of seeing Theodore again? You were the only one who even appeared remotely as affected as I did. Robyn, Leo and Aaron seemed so pulled together."

"Seemed being the operative word," he sighs.

I study his face, the way he unwaveringly observes each of his movements with care and dedication. He's so fastidious, even in trivial matters such as measuring out milk.

"You would know their feelings better than I," I say with slight disbelieving. He glances up at me, distracted for a moment by my tone.

"Do you find them unfeeling?"

"No, I didn't mean that. Just, desensitised," I correct him.

"They've been on a lot of missions for the Onyevaras and seen death first hand more times than they can probably count."

"And you haven't?"

"When dragoviks turn nineteen they begin specialising in their training. Aaron and Leo chose battle studies, weaponry and strategy. I was far more interested in our history and the tentative alliances our position depends upon. I still continued to train to fight alongside them but my studies could only allow for so much time with them."

"Is that why they didn't disagree with Robyn back in the library?" I ask, regretting the words as soon as they come out. I hate the idea of prying into Kyle's pain. He sets down the spatula he's begun to fold the batter with and rests his palms on the counter as if for support.

"I grew up with Aaron, Robyn, and Leo as my best friends. It's not as if we were some exclusive group, but we worked well together despite all our constant bickering. Things haven't been the same since I went away. I didn't realise they'd be so cross with me, at least not Aaron and Leo, until today. I'm sorry by the way, that Robyn's been taking her anger out on you," he adds.

"I'm sorry you had to leave your friends behind for my sake."

"Don't blame yourself."

"But you're allowed to?" He smiles wryly.

"It was my choice after all."

"I think it was the choice of your morals rather than a decision based on what you wanted."

He resumes scraping the batter down the sides of the bowl before whisking.

"Do you really think I'm that good of a person?" he laughs.

I almost think he's joking, but trace amounts of self-doubt are evident in his features. How could he believe he isn't?

"I think you're more a good person than they are truly fearless. They wear masks of bravery that their experiences have given them time to perfect. Maybe it would be better for them to live in fear together and take courage from their unity rather than live in false security," I reply.

He chews on his lower lip. Somewhere within the bleakness of his thoughts, a single ray of sun, must come through because he smiles.

"What is it?"

"Just that you're better at understanding them than they are," he says, "and you give away advice that could probably be used for your own advantage."

"It would be selfish of me to keep it, knowing I won't use it," I say.

He taps the whisk on the edge of the bowl to shake off the excess batter before going to wash it.

"Well then, can I give you some advice, seeing as I have no need for it?"

"Of course."

He rests his forearms on the counter, leaning towards me. His eyes are marked with thin white lines I had never noticed before, like the beginning of a fissure in ice.

"Forgive Inerea."

I'm taken by surprise by the change in the path of our conversation. I haven't given her a second thought since this morning. Our fight seems so trivial in the face of this present predicament.

"I can't let what she did go. She took my memories."

"Mallory, I have known you for six months, though you no longer know me from that time. Throughout the duration of my stay at the Academy, after I found out who you were, I waited for some sign that you would come out of the atrophic state your heart had fallen into. I saw you at night when you left your room, on the verge of leaving, only to go back. You had all those opportunities to do something for yourself but you didn't. You were so scared and broken from the unspeakable things that were done to you. But here you are now, risking your life because you were worried something might happen to complete strangers. You came to life when you were given the opportunity to help others when you never did the same for yourself. I don't think that change could have come about if Inerea hadn't given you the opportunity to become someone independent of the Academy."

What was done to me that's so bad he thinks it's better I don't recall?

"Even if you're right, I still need time," I say, sighing,

"I did remember something today though, while I was unconscious. I don't think it was a dream. And it made me wonder if maybe you're right."

"What was it?"

But don't tell anyone. They'll get angry.

This secret, could I really tell him? My breath shatters into quiet, short gasps as I draw the courage to speak.

"It was a sense of something. That I always thought death was better than being trapped alone in the Academy. I remember one day when someone left behind a pair of scissors used to cut my hair," I start shakily, "bodily damage was so instinctive to me then that I knew exactly what to do with them. Hurting myself wasn't scary because it was so much easier than being happy. If it weren't for the guards that found me, I would have been dead at the age of seven. The only thing I regretted, for years, about that was that my attempt failed. I know that changed when I met you, even if I don't know why. The most selfish thing to think is that there isn't anything worth living for when, really, the only thing that wasn't worth living for was me."

I can't look up at him beneath the shared burden of my confession. My skin had been a chaos of blood and it wasn't long before I had felt dizzy. I curled up on the floor waiting to go. Then I heard rushed footsteps and the door burst open. I took up the scissors to defend my death. When one of the men tried to grab me, I plunged them so deep into his hand they came out the other side. He had crumpled to the floor, howling, and I skewered the blade into the carpet. After that, there was no energy left in me to fight off the others.

I feel Kyle looking at me, and it hurts. It's as if I've peeled part of my skin away, showed him the way my blackened heart rests in my rib cage with no bearing on how I act. It was so selfish of me to tell him, to leave him with no means of response. The manner in which he had comforted me after Theodore's death fails him now. All he can do is clear a space in sound for my words to sink into silence.

"You were seven," he echoes, "how can you have had such a notion of self-loathing at such a young age?"

"Apparently. I wasn't exposed to any other reaction to my existence." I look up at him. His face is fallen, shattered emotions and trust in what childhood should be. "We don't have to talk about it or try to rationalise it. I suppose I just wanted you to know that to me you're truly good. You're a reason not to die. I don't mean it as some sort of burden, just as truth."

"You'll forgive me if I don't agree. I was worried I would come back to three people who couldn't bear me after how I'd left them. Finding you was the only relief. You've become so compelling to all of us, almost bewitching, in different ways. It felt like a chance to bring us back together. Your protection was something we could all agree on."

Come, poor thing, you're all alone. But the voice doesn't speak to me. It calls to Kyle. It reaches out from my heart for him.

"Forgive yourself for leaving them if it's what you believed was necessary. They can't until you do."

"You're telling me to let go of the past when you let if interfere with how you interact with others?" he asks, cocking his head to the side.

"Perhaps, though I see the irony in it. And I promise in time I'll forgive Inerea. It will just take a while. On a less depressing note, can I ask you about those men back at Theodore"s house?"

"The bellatoja," he answers grimly

"Who are they? Or should I be asking what are they?"

The image of that man towering over me flashes through my head, his boot raised ready to kick me.

"They're a faction of the angeleru, the warrior faction dispatched to deal with deabrueon."

"Those guys were angels? Why did they hate us so much?"

"The bellatoja look down on dragovik's as a perversion of nature. We were created by magic, which, in their eyes, is an abomination of the ancient language. They're all that stands between dragoviks and a return to Sundalev."

"They keep you from going home?"

"Don't get me wrong, the dragoviks have grown very happy with Earth as a home. We've been here for millennia now. But there are some of our kind that believe restoring one of the original three families to the throne in Sundalev is the only way dragoviks can reassert themselves as a force to be reckoned with."

"They want to challenge the angeleru?"

"Exactly. There was a radical group a quarter of a century ago, the Vernis Lanin. They tried to put the rightful king of the dragoviks on the throne."

"So, you have a monarch?"

"Not exactly. King Illarion's rightful heir was disputed through bloody wars for many years before the Onyevaras was formed to maintain peace between the twenty families. A few still believed that the members of the first three families whose souls were bound to dragons deserved Illarion's throne. When the wars were being fought, there wasn't a single person who didn't have an opinion on which should be ruler. Velemir was the second oldest of the three and his descendent, Thaddeus Velemir, was the one the Vernis Lanin wanted on the throne. They planned on breaking political ties with the Hirutere and waging war on the angeleru. But Thaddeus went mad with power, killing himself, or so they say, and without a rightful king, the Vernis Lanin fell apart. Mallory?"

I've gone very silent, my head inclined.

"I remember having this dream the other night. I thought it was the first time but I think I've always had it. I'm hiding with a woman while this man slaughters innocents. I can only just see him, but not enough to make out what he really looks like. He hears me gasp but the woman sacrifices herself, pretending she was the only one there. It's only after he kills her that I find out he's not a man, he's like us. And every time he says the same words: let me taste the fire of your blood. And it's only now I remember his name was-"

"Thaddeus."

"But that's not all. When I heard the deabrueon in the forest and at Theodore's house, it said the same thing, in that man's voice. I don't know if it was doing it to scare me or if it was connected somehow but I thought I should tell you."

"Shit."

Of all the responses I could have possibly imagined coming from Kyle, this is not one of them.

"Who died?" Aaron asks. I jump at the sound of his voice as he and Leo join us in the kitchen. "Not to be insensitive to the person who did actually just die."

"I don't think anyone would ever accuse you of being insensitive," Leo drawls.

"Thank you, king of sarcasm. You're going to add passion fruit seeds to that right?" he asks Kyle, nodding at the pancake batter.

"Here we go again with your weird obsession with passion fruit," Leo mutters.

"Could you please be quiet for a moment," Kyle manages. The two glance at him with mild surprise and he returns the look, warily. He's holding the bulk of his weight on his trembling arms, which he rests on the counter. "Mallory has just told me something rather disturbing."

"She doesn't like passion fruit in her pancakes?"

"What happened?" Leo inquires. Kyle repeats what I said and upon hearing those eight words, the other two go slack.

"Shit."

"If this deabrueon is acting under the banner of the Vernis Lanin, whether they've truly remerged or not, this is bad news," Leo says.

"But what could the deabrueon possibly be trying to achieve by using their mantra if it wasn't supporting them?" Kyle asks.

"There isn't a them to support. They have no claim to the throne without Thaddeus," Leo says, "it was his right to assert leadership that they supported."

"Couldn't they find another member of the original three families?" I ask.

"Unless you're considering running, there isn't anyone who's of a reasonable age to make a claim. The Velemir line ended with Thaddeus and you're the last of the Ovira and Thiel line, aside from your aunt and grandma."

"What if they brought Thaddeus back?"

"He killed himself, there's nothing that could bring him back," Aaron says, tasting some of the forgotten pancake batter on the side of the bowl. He begins to empty a bag of chocolate chips into it.

"Alright but hypothetically. If we consider the fact that deabrueon are fallen angels, then is it completely unreasonable to believe that they could access the sort of magic that could resurrect him? If, as you once said, the Hirutere are in charge of dispensing of deabrueon, and the Vernis Lanin intended to lay waste to them to get to the portal to Sundalev, why wouldn't the deabrueon support his return? It would be in their best interest as he's clearly a leader with enough organised support and power to have a chance of winning a war."

"Supposing the deabrueon did know what to do then yes, it's quite possible."

"Say that's the case, what exactly are we supposed to do about it? We can't wait until the deabrueon's next ambush and say 'oh don't mind us but we were hoping to find out what you intend to achieve by draining the isuazko of dragoviks, possibly a ritual of resurrection for a mad man?' I don't think it's going to tell us over a cup of coffee," Aaron says.

"No one said that was the plan you idiot," Leo replies nonchalantly.

"This is speculation of course, a worst-case scenario," Kyle adds, "we don't know for sure that this deabrueon isn't just using the Vernis Lanin as a means of inspiring fear. Nothing is certain until we can get some confirmation."

"I might know where to start on that front," I remark.

"What?"

"Not what, who. And her name is Leora."

"What are you going on about?" Leo asks.

"Before he died, Theodore told me he knew what it, the deabrueon wanted and that I should find someone named Leora. I'm guessing that she knows or has what the deabrueon wants. Whatever it may be, it's clearly imperative we find her to understand what we're dealing with."

"Why is it that you almost dying has become the most convenient means of gathering information?" Leo sighs. Aaron narrows his eyes at Leo from across the counter. "Obviously I don't mean I'd be happy if she were dead."

"I know I've heard that name before," Kyle mutters to himself, "I'll go try and find out where. She wasn't on my list of dragoviks in the area but it's possible she doesn't live here. Leo, can you go fill Robyn in on what we've learned. And Aaron-"

"Say no more. I'll make the passion fruit chocolate chip pancakes. Food is the most important part of every mission," Aaron replies, halving two passion fruits and scooping their seeds into the mixture. "You want some Mallory?"

He tosses aside the outer shells. Their purple colour, dappled with sallow spots, gives the distinct image of a bruised corpse's skin.

Chapter XX.

The bell above the door to the antique store sings a clear note of welcome as we enter. It bounces up and down on its chain, roused by our arrival, and does not calm to silence for some time. Mr Bowen isn't behind the counter with the cash register as he usually is and there are no customers browsing. In fact, once the bell chimes no more, there is no sound at all save for the five of us as we spread across the shop floor. Leo goes across the room to the two stairwells side by side and peers both above and below.

"Oh, pretty!" Robyn squeals, startling me with the departure from her usual sullen intonation.

She rushes from where she had stood beside me over to a display case mounted on the wall. It boasts a collection of weapons, several of which are intricately decorated, almost as beautifully so as the sword from Theodore's house. I press my hand to my right wrist recalling the brightly seared pattern that had appeared on my arm. Leo said they had found the blade and taken it. I wonder of what importance it is to them?

"You're such a girl," Aaron says mockingly, and Robyn manages to pry her gaze away from a crossbow with a silver gilded tiller long enough to glare at him. The anger with which her looks are usually composed is only half-hearted however; an undertone of humour easily perceived has begun to take over. If only she were always so at ease as she is now.

"Are you certain this is where we can find her?" Leo asks Kyle, now circling the wooden table covered in a lace cloth that sits in the centre of the room.

"I'm not certain she's here but I believe this is the place to start. I knew I had heard the name Leora before when I remembered that I overheard Mr Bowen discussing her with someone last time I was here. Given that it's not a particularly common name, I'm hoping he can tell us where to find her," Kyle replies.

He crosses the room to a door to the right of the weapons case and knocks twice. When there's no sound indicating anyone within, Kyle tries the handle. It refuses to open.

"It's locked."

"Let me," Robyn sighs.

She pushes past her brother, perhaps with more force than is necessary and I don't doubt it's because she's still upset with him after this morning. They haven't exchanged a word since and she hardly bothered to look at him when he told us he had an inkling as to where we might find Leora. She raises her hand, cupping the air around the handle as if it were something she could hold on to.

"Knosramenthka tihzendava osav savis perova eskulerava."

Her hand trembles slightly and I see the air waver with released heat. It hisses slightly before the door handle and lock begin to glow molten red, as if to be forged anew by her command. We wait for a moment, Robyn seemingly satisfied with her work. Then, the handle flashes bright gold and a surge of heat bursts forth to return to Robyn's hand. A sickening sizzle, like fire taking a bite of matter to make it ash, spits into the air and Robyn cries out. She draws her hand to her chest, moaning, before splaying her palm to look at it. The skin has turned a dark shade of red with an almost milky lustre to it. Pink waxy blisters bubble up, with the paler ones dappling the edges of her palm. The ones closer to the burn centre darken and wrinkle slightly. She gasps, a mix of revulsion and pain, yet is unable to close her hand to hide the sight.

"Robyn!" Kyle cries in panic. He cradles her arm,

examining the wound. The rest of us draw to her side in an instant. "Please tell me it still hurts."

"Of course it hurts you moron. Exactly why do you seemingly suggest that's a good thing?" she gasps, her face turning pale with a sheen of sweat fast forming.

"It means it's not a third-degree burn," he informs her, "do you think you can heal it?"

"Without my casting hand I can't work any magic. What the hell?" she murmurs when she glances up as the door again. It glows faintly gold for an instant. "There's a ward cast on it."

"We'll worry about that later," Kyle mutters.

Leo seems less concerned with Robyn than he is with the information she's just shared. While Aaron and Kyle surround her, he moves closer to the door. He studies it as if for some mark of magic other than the traces of light that have now faded. Robyn ignores the other two's concern and turns to me.

"Do you remember the spell I used to heal you?"

"I remember," I say, the words she spoke when she was healing me flooding back to my mind.

"You'll need to take hold of my hand and repeat them. I know it's kind of disgusting." She scowls, looking at the marred skin.

"I'm not afraid of flesh," I assure her.

And I know, looking at her hand, I have seen similar if not worse burns. I know my skin has felt a flame's tongue and I feel that heat radiating off my skin as if it is burning. With as much care as I can, I take up her hand in my own. I hear the soft hiss of air from between her teeth as she tries to hold back as much of the pain from vocalising itself as she can. Even so, I can see the tension in her features. Her lips are pulled back over bared teeth, on the precipice of snarling. She presses her lips firmly back together, staring down at our intertwined hands with determination

"Lueicht nandirava letai nevorso ni isuazko etev udiyat"

The words come like sweet recompense to my
tongue, a repayment in part for all Robyn has done. I
gasp as I feel the spell even before it begins to show its
outward signs of taking effect. My heart warms and I can
feel each beat. I am aware of my mortality, both the power and fragility in it. The heat begins to travel from my
core, a small part of my life's energy detaching from my
heart and seeping through my veins and I am aware of
exactly what it cost Robyn to heal me. It moves with near
lightning speed to the tips of my fingers, which begin to
glow. I hear a slight groan escape Robyn, though whether
it's of relief or further pain I cannot tell.

Her head tilts forwards to rest on my collarbone and
small pants come forth from her parted lips. She grips
my hand tighter with each passing second, right up until the moment the light grows faint. I feel the magic as
it fades and I am all the colder for it. A part of me has
slipped away to become part of her and I daren't believe
it will ever return. I look at her with new wonder. She had
abandoned little bits of herself numerous times so they
might heal me. How exhausting such literal self-sacrifice
must be. When I remove my hands, her skin has returned
to its previous smoothness.

"All healed in one go your first time," she says, a
cocktail of bitterness and intrigue highlighting her voice.
She examines her hand as if hoping to find fault with it.
"I suppose that makes us even."

"Hardly," I reply, "I'm just glad I could help."

"Do you always have to be so sweet? I'm going to get
diabetes," she grumbles, but there's the faintest trace of a
smile on her lips.

She goes back towards the door despite Kyle's small

sound of disapproval at her doing so. She raises her hand
but doesn't touch the wood. Still drawn to her by curiosity of what she's done for me numerous times and what
I've just done, I come to stand beside her. I am overcome
by a sense of insufficiency that I never knew existed. I'm
aware of the disparity between when I do nothing and
what I can be when I use magic. I can be useful to others,
help them and heal them as I just did Robyn.

"Can you lift the ward?" Leo asks her.

"I don't think so, but I can read the spell to see what
kind of magic we're dealing with," she answers.

She flexes her fingers as she had done before casting
her last spell, but Kyle steps forward. Wrapping his hand
firmly round her wrist, he lowers her arm, shaking his
head.

"After what just happened? I don't think it's wise to
try anymore magic here," he says.

His eyes have gone black in the dim lighting, but even
in the absolute of dark Kyle's softness and love towards
his sister shows clearly.

"Why not?" Robyn scowls, childlike and indignant.

"Skin can only be healed so many times in such a
brief period of time. Even magic can tire of saving you,"
her brother warns.

Robyn seems to accept his words, because she steps
away from the door for a moment, though not without a
haughty look of irritation. Then, she yanks her arm free
from his grip and crosses the room to lean on the table.

"Fine, let Mallory try," Robyn says.

"No fucking way," Aaron says.

"Absolutely not," Kyle replies simultaneously. The
two of them are suddenly standing between me and the
door as if it posed an immediate threat to my person.

"It's not going to leap off its hinges and attack her,"
Robyn sighs with exasperation.

"Death by splinters, I'm quaking in my boots now," I quip, and Robyn shoots me a smile that screams co-conspirator. "Please let me be useful for once."

"Puppy dog eyes won't get you out of this," Aaron says in answer to the major doe eyes I'm giving him. Time for a different tact.

"Why can't I?" I demand. His nostrils flare.

"Now of all times you choose to voice your dissatisfaction," he groans, "why do you two have to be head strong."

"It's not head strong, it's logical that she try to cast the spell if I can't."

"It's completely illogical. Aside from the fact that Mallory is a magnet for absolute catastrophe, she only cast what I'm assuming was her first spell moments ago," Aaron begins.

"Excuse me, I am down with witchcraft I'll have you know." If you count my limited practice with Chloe.

Magic is not permitted at the Academy without Diane's express permission.

What the hell? My mind takes a turn and when I come back to Kyle is speaking.

"Besides, reading someone else's spell requires more knowledge of magic than you possess. It's not just about knowing fundamentals of magic. You have to be aware of its variations and the signatures of another spell caster," Kyle finishes.

"Oh for fucks sake, don't try and mansplain magic to me. I'll not so kindly remind you who the badass witch in the room is," Robyn snaps, "I know why you're opposed to me casting but stop molly coddling Mallory. She doesn't have to be able to understand exactly what she sees, just so long as she can describe it to us. Even you idiots could do that much. And she managed the healing spell. One more spell won't hurt her."

"It's not worth the risk given that we're not sure there's anything we even need in that room," Kyle replies urgently.

"We're not sure but it's very odd of Bowen to put a magic seal on that room. It's not the sort of lock system to keep out your everyday robber. I'd say it means we're in exactly the right place to figure out what the deabrueon wants," Leo comments, now standing behind the desk.

"So, Bowen mentions Leora and has a magically sealed door. Half the people in this town are magically inclined. It doesn't mean she's keeping whatever the deabrueon wants here. Like you don't keep secrets," Aaron says.

I sense the iron bite to his words, clamping down onto old bones that yet have enough flesh on them to be torn into. Leo's eyes harden, his walls of indifference rebuilding themselves. It isn't until they go back up that I realise they had started to go down. I look back at Aaron but already his face has recovered from whatever angry and almost possessive look had come over him.

"Yes, but I don't happen to be the person a dying man told us to find who also works here," Leo replies, holding up a small rectangle of worn yellow card for us to see.

"What's that?" Robyn asks, leaning across the counter to get a closer look. "Leora Winfield. It's a time card. She's been clocked in every day for the past two weeks."

She glances back at Aaron and Kyle.

"Let me see that," Aaron demands.

He takes the card from Leo and grumbles with displeasure as he reads it.

"Well I'd say that's reason enough to want to see what's behind this door. Now if you don't mind," Robyn says, taking me by the wrist and pulling me over to the door, "I'm going to get this moron to read a spell to see if our mystery girl has anything to do with this."

"What, you think Leora cast it?" Kyle asks.

"Theodore indicated she knows what the deabrueon wants and she works for Mr Bowen, a dragovik. I doubt she's human, even if she isn't one of us, so it's possible she has magic."

"If she's not a dragovik, what could she be?" I inquire.

Aaron and Leo exchange a look.

"We'll worry about that after we're certain it was her who cast the spell," Kyle says as he steps aside, his way of begrudgingly giving Robyn and I permission to use magic. The look Robyn gives him makes me certain she never needed his permission. She turns to me.

"Alright, hold your hand up about an inch away from the door. Keep it flat, as if you've pressed your hand against the wood." I follow her instructions. "Now say these words: valja siezata maroa sa vanagemarra varasta kair letai parasus ni siezata."

"Valja siezata maroa sa vanagemarra varasta kair letai parasus ni siezata," I repeat, turning from her gaze on the last word to look at the door.

The space before me deconstructs itself to take a new shape. It is an image of grace and dominance, something frightful and rightfully so. It shimmers with a clear sense of pain and outrage. There's no distinct shape to these feelings but the colour of maple leaf orange binds them together. What holds the door fast appears clear to me now. There's betrayal in its reasons, both that of information's revealing and a personal gash between two parties. I can't see past the coldness of the magic, however, to see how to undo it. The power is so unlike my own. There's no heat or feeling behind it. It's resigned to being magic without emotional meaning.

Tell me what you see.

A woman's face, resolute and sharp. She discloses nothing of her intention through those spring green eyes whose colour suggests the clarity they do not give. She fragments but I can see her in my mind still.

Yes. And what is she?

Something to be feared.

I gasp, stumbling back as a wave of darkness comes into contact with my own magic, washing it to nothing.

"Mallory? What did you see?" Leo demands.

"More importantly, are you alright?" Kyle asks.

I crouch over, hands on my knees for support. I feel my stomach undoing itself, drawing up sickness.

"I'll be alright, just give me a moment," I breath.

I see a shadow overlap with mine as someone draws near. The shadow raises its hand towards me, meant to come rest on me with comfort and care.

My body is bent as if I'm about to be sick.

My body is exposed, vulnerable to whatever new form pain assumes.

My body is a canvas for other's expressions of anger. It does not know how to be held gently.

I flinch away from the hand that reaches for me. I bump against the table, knocking over a vase of flowers. My eyes widen, accommodating all of the eyes that take me in in turn. I've made myself a spectacle. Again. Why again?

My heart screams against my rib cage, tries to find the key for its prison or simply break free with brute force. The spell has not only shown me the echoes of a cold art, but also started to illuminate another memory, seen through the strained light of my mind's confusion. I reach for it with my mind's eye, but the demands of my surroundings on my attention pull it away. All I see before it fades is that same unfeeling magic coming up against my own.

"Mallory, you should sit down," Kyle says.

He's slipped past the others while I was disconcerted, though he knows better than to get too close. The ache of the other magic is still within me, drilling a hole through my body with its keen strength. I hold Kyle's gaze as I slide down to the ground, tucking my knees to my chest.

"I told you that was a bad idea," Aaron mutters to Leo and Robyn, kneeling beside me.

"It wasn't the spell, please don't blame them," I plead softly.

I'm overwhelmed with an urge to reach for him and pull him from the anger that seems to be clawing up the walls of his chest. This need is contrasted by the rolling sickness that crashes through me again at the thought of touching someone. I cower, folding in on myself, trying to escape their proximity.

"Well then, what did you see?" Leo asks again, crouching in place.

"A woman, with light eyes. She has magic to her but it doesn't feel like ours. It comes not from a need to protect but a need to harm. There's something so cold and resentful in it," I reply.

A shiver climbs my spine when I recall how close to Death's breath that magic felt. I could feel his hands in it, reaching out with it as one.

"It's definitely not the magic of a dragovik then," Robyn says, "it wouldn't have affected you that way if it was."

"Well this might get interesting," Aaron murmurs. He lifts up the edge of his shirt slightly, revealing a dagger tucked into his belt. "Just in case."

Kyle casts a wary look to the other three while offering me a hand. I take it, but even the lightness of his touch seems more then I can bare. After holding his hand for the few seconds it takes me to raise myself, I can feel the uneasiness sinking its teeth back into my gut. Though that may also be due to the sharp glint of Aaron's dagger that forces itself into my periphery no matter how hard I try to avoid the sight of it. Has there not been enough death for today, for all time? Is the world not exhausted of being glutted with blood?

"Surely that isn't necessary. If she was helping Theodore find what the deabrueon is after then she can't be intent on harming any of us," I say to Aaron as he stands back up. He raises his eyebrows.

"Don't confuse similarity in goals with an alliance. You said Theodore only told you to find Leora. That doesn't necessarily mean she has the intention of helping us," Aaron remarks. "In fact, I'd say it's best we over prepare ourselves. Kyle, you might want to lock the door. Robyn, if you would be so kind as to help us out."

I look between the four of them, the atmosphere suddenly like lead arming their bones with the threat of what we might find. Kyle crosses the room to the front door. He peeks between the slightly dingy green blinds before turning the lock and joining the others. They join hands and Robyn bows her head slightly.

"Noutsumar letai kokku ni saviski isuazko'caz makun," she murmurs.

Pockets open in the air, rippling into form. Now strapped across Robyn's back is the same crossbow she carried in the forest and sheathed swords rest on both Leo and Aaron's hips. Buckled to Kyle's belt are two pairs of daggers, one set short and curved, the other slightly longer with broad blades. They break their circle and Kyle moves back towards the front door, nodding at me to come with him.

"Kyle, you stay on guard down here so Leora can't escape if she gets past us. We'll start by sweeping the upstairs. Mallory, for the love of all that is holy, please just stay put with Kyle," Aaron commands.

I open my mouth to speak but the memory of this morning's events and my failure to comply with his request leaves me without response. I don't have any right to argue with his order given the expenditure of Robyn's strength as a result of my wandering off.

The three of them go up the spiral staircase, leaving Kyle and me alone. I'm rather relieved it's him and not one of the others I'm left with. I haven't been alone with Leo since the night of the bonfire and I'm still left with the distinct impression that he barely tolerates me and, even then, only as a sacrificial lamb.

"They'll be fine," Kyle assures me as soon as they've disappeared from sight.

My gaze holds fast on the top of that staircase. I won't look away until they've returned safely.

"What could Leora be that would pose such a threat to be a concern to the likes of us?" I ask him.

"You're clearly under the impression that we're a lot more dangerous than any of the other creatures that have made Earth their home."

"If I am, it's only because experience has taught me so. Are there really so many fantastical beings in this world?"

A floorboard creaks overhead and my heart leaps. I can feel Kyle's body tense beside me as if it were my own. We wait but no further sound comes to indicate any harm has been done.

"Yes, and very few see eye to eye with dragoviks. Even our allies aren't overly fond of us."

"You don't suppose that says something about dragoviks do you?" I ask in what I intend as a slightly teasing tone.

I'm hoping to make him laugh even though my joke doesn't amuse me. His laughter might do some good in the way of alleviating the fear that is fast building in my chest. There are so many things to fear, more than I can count and more that I don't know the names for. My comment is received by momentary silence.

"I don't doubt it does. But I'd say being that which seeks the deabrueon to help it is far worse than being those who hunt something that has killed at least two people," he answers.

His words draw my entire body's attention. I cannot help but turn to look at him, praying I've misunderstood the social cues of humour and this comment is a joke in poor taste. His face betrays no amusement when I find it.

"Why would anyone want to help that creature?"

"It's set on killing dragoviks and, like I said, few see eye to eye with. Fewer still would be sad to see us gone."

I look back towards the stairs, all but overcome with the urge to run up them and find the others. Then I feel it again. A coldness stirring, same as the one emitted from the door's ward. It speaks a different language than the one within me as it uncurls, awakened by the presence of someone who knows we shouldn't be here.

A figure darts across my field of vision, obscured by Kyle who has moved in front of me in a heartbeat. The lithe body starts towards us and suddenly one of the sheaths on Kyle's belt is empty. There's a whizzing, driven through the air on the tip of a blade. A small gust conjured on the tips of the figure's fingers thuds against the dagger, sending it to the floor. The hand jerks up and Kyle's body slams against the wall. He struggles to his feet but with another simple gesture from the hand, thick vines covered in thorns shake themselves free from the wallpaper behind him. In yawning movements, they stir before darting around him. They hoist him up, holding his body rigid against the wall.

"Kyle!"

I dash towards him, vaulting over the desk. I claw at the vines, sinking my biting nails into their trunks. The sticky secretion within bubbles up around the punctures, hissing and stinging my flesh.

"You'll hurt yourself," Kyle protests, but I keep attempting to pry them away as the acidic liquid sings cool fire pain on my hands.

Kyle's eyes widen, urging me to get away and I feel that cold front rising again, coming towards me. A hiss slices through the room. I turn just in time to see Robyn as she leaps over the stair railing, crashing down on our assailant whose hand is still outstretched towards Kyle and I. Leo and Aaron rush down after her. I turn back to Kyle, drawing the second broad bladed dagger from his side. With some effort, I drive it through the tough skin into the meaty body of the vines. They come apart with difficulty before trying to draw back together. At last, I manage to prise them away to reveal lacerations dappled across Kyle's arms where the thorns have torn in. The cuts are surrounded by a greenish-grey tracery. Kyle sinks to the ground, his body shaking. I hold his forearms, trying to steady him. His weakened state is contagious. I find myself trembling beside him as the pattern slithers beneath the skin's surface, spreading from the wounds.

"Lueicht, nandirava letai nevorso ni isuazko etev udiyat."

"No," Kyle groans, trying to pull me off of him.

I tighten my grip as much as I can without causing him anymore pain. I already feel parts of me chipping away and I know even if I stop now they won't reattach. I don't want them to. He gives up, without the strength to remove my hands. The branch like patterns glow softly under my touch, recoiling back towards the wounds they sprung from. The same bubbling acid the vines had spat up before now oozes from the wounds, draining itself from his blood. His abdomen curls inwards with a jerk and he coils his hands into fists. The skin across his forearms goes taught, the veins pressing up against it. I wipe the liquid away with the hem of my shirt as the skin regrows, twisting like a whirlpool to cover the open wounds. My head feels as if it's filled with lead, my eyelids too. I groan, my body tilting slightly to the side. Elsewhere in the store I hear the sounds of the fight beginning to subdue. Kyle leans his head back against the wall, shutting his eyes.

"Are you alright?"

"You shouldn't have done that, but thank you. I'll be fine."

He looks exhausted and I wonder exactly what the vines' secretion managed to do to him in the few minutes it was in his bloodstream. I clutch the edge of the desk, pulling myself to my feet.

Robyn has her foot firmly on the person's shoulder, a bolt loaded in her crossbow pressed against the tender skin of the neck. The pixie like woman stares up coolly with her paisley eyes. Her short auburn hair pools out around her head like a crown of flames as she lies completely still on the ground.

"Let her go Robyn," Kyle says, coming to stand beside me.

I study the woman's long and thin face. She narrows her eyes at Robyn, like small leaves sieving sunlight to illuminate her hauntingly pale face.

"She just tried to kill you," she snaps.

He takes the crossbow from her and offers his hand to the woman. She turns her sharp gaze upon him but makes no move to take his hand. Instead, she swings her body back slightly before leaping to her feet with agile grace.

"You're Leora, aren't you?" he asks. She doesn't respond, sauntering back towards the stairs. "We need to speak to you, it's a matter of urgency."

She raises her hand to silence him.

"I gathered as much from what I heard of your conversation. However, as you just attacked me, as well as attempting to break into the store's office, I don't have time to speak to you."

Arrogance and irritation flash through her eyes. She has an indisputable faith in her abilities unlike anyone I've ever seen before. If the others hadn't surprised her, I doubt any of us would have survived this encounter.

"Quite frankly, I don't give a damn about whether or not you have the time. Make it," Robyn hisses.

"I have enough power to sense that you don't know the witchcraft to make me speak against my will," she laughs.

"Maybe not. But I have the temper."

Robyn darts forward and, though she's hardly any larger than Leora, she lifts her by her collar and slams her down onto the display table.

"Robyn!" Kyle exclaims, starting towards her.

"Don't interfere," she hisses.

Using her forearm, she pins Leora's windpipe and leaves her gasping for air. It's not enough to extinguish that glint of arrogance in her eyes.

"Is this the part where you say we can do this the hard way or the easy way?" she manages, wriggling beneath Robyn's weight.

"No. We can do this the hard way or we can do this my way."

"Oh? And how does your way go?"

"Something like me pinning you by your hands to the table using knives before I pummel you so hard the table breaks and you fall through while your hands are ripped off because they can't be moved."

Kyle's knees buckle with the burst of effort it took to move so soon after being healed. His body falls back against me and I just manage to support his weight before lowering us both to the ground. His face goes pale and his jaw slackens as he begins to breathe heavy. Panic sets into a flutter in me. Why didn't my spell heal him fully?

"Oh! Scary," Leora hisses back, "you and I both know that while you can commit such violence on an assigned mission from the Onyevaras, you have no right to do so without permission." Robyn's eyes widen and she removes her arm from Leora's throat. 'That goes for all of you and your friends.'

"They may need someone's permission, but I don't." I feel the heaviness of being watched as I look up from Kyle's face. "I have no ties to the Onyevaras. As for us attacking you, I think perhaps you should take a second look at what you did to my friend before you make such claims."

My fingers knot in the fabric of Kyle's shirt as I hold her gaze. Inflicting pain isn't something I thought I could do. But the heft of Kyle as he lays helpless in my lap tells me otherwise. There's something ticking in my muscles. Memories of how to hurt, how to kill.

"Who might you be?"

"Mallory Thiel," I reply.

She remains calm, despite her body still being pinned down by Robyn.

"Very well," she says, "I'll talk to you as soon as this guard dog lets me go."

Robyn steps back, allowing her to sit up. With one hand she rubs her neck, trying to alleviate the pain that comes with the red mark left by Robyn's arm. It burns like the scarlet of a fire against her snow skin. Her throat is so thin she can almost wrap one hand around its entirety in her attempt to soothe her skin.

"What do you want?"

Kyle stirs, seeming to recover his senses. He wipes the sweat from his brow and I help him back to his feet.

"My bag," he says to me, and I reach into the small leather bag strapped across his back. The inside is larger than it appears, and the object still bundled in fabric from earlier this morning is nestled inside. "Be careful not to touch the sword."

I remove it cautiously from the bag, unwrapping it as I do. Pulling back the fabric, I find the silver blade that branded me hours ago. My chest tightens as if a string draws it closed. I dart a glance at my forearm but the pattern is still invisible. Leora flinches as I approach her with the parcel.

"Don't worry, it's not a weapon we intend on using," Kyle assures her.

As it comes into her view, she darts further back. She needs no time to recognise or consider the significance of the sword. She eyes us with suspicion.

"You can't have this. If you do, it means-"

"He's dead," Leo interjects numbly, "and so you will be and so we all will be if you don't help us."

"Tell me what has happened and in exchange I will tell you what I know," she says, taking the sword from me with delicate, claw like fingers.

"Like hell we will. You go first," Robyn snaps.

"It's alright," Kyle says to his sister, righting himself with my aid, "We have to trust her with what we know if she's going to trust us."

"How exactly do we know we should trust you?" Robyn demands.

"You think Mr Bowen would allow me, a non-dragovik witch, anywhere near his store if I were a threat to you?" Leora says, raising her eyebrows.

It's as if someone pulls a chord attached to Robyn.

Her shoulders drag back, the muscles tensing in her upper back. The slightest movement of her shoes indicate her toes curling up. Behind her, Aaron looks over at Leo whose body has stiffened similarly to Robyn's. Kyle watches his sister as she draws her shoulders upwards, squaring them defensively, before inclining her body towards Leora's. It's like some strange show of dominance, only Leora has no interest in partaking. She already knows she's stronger.

"You pull anything, witch, and I'll have your head," Robyn hisses. Leora bites the inside corners of her lip, though it seems more to hold back laughter than out of fear.

"Come, we can sit in the office and speak."

As she says this, she turns her back on Robyn. It's not an act of trust, but her way of saying she has nothing to fear from us. And the way Robyn narrows her eyes, I can tell it's not sitting well with her. Leora raises her hand in front of the door and it shimmers gold. She reaches for the handle and it gives way to her touch. We file through into the small room, overcrowded with furniture.

In the centre of the room is a table with three chairs. Allowing Leo, Kyle and Leora to arrange themselves around it, Robyn perches on the edge of a desk cooped up in the corner. I cross the room to a bookshelf, pretending to examine the volumes while really focusing on blocking out their voices as Kyle begins to tell the story of this morning. I don't want to hear him describe what we saw, let alone the death that occurred before I joined them. If it was anything like Theodore's – my stomach turns at the thought and I rest my hand on the edge of a shelf to steady its shaking. And there's that aching still in my limbs. A real desire to hurt Leora for what she did to Kyle. That scares me more than the memories of this morning.

"So, are you feeling a little badass now that you've

told Miss Arrogance off?" Aaron whispers, coming to stand just beside me.

I'm overcome with the dizzying concern that drago-viks may also be telepaths.

"It was a petty threat and one I wouldn't have gone through with," I reply.

I look over my shoulder to see Kyle, his face now regaining colour. I called him my friend earlier and I meant it. He means as much to me as Inerea does. As I study him, the way he speaks and reaches out to Leora when her face pales on hearing some gruesome detail of someone's suffering, I realise the truth. And the truth is, I think I could have hurt Leora if she had done real harm to him.

"Well you had me fooled. You can be rather terrify-ing."

"Don't say that," I murmur, glancing back at Aaron. In the darkness of the poorly lit room, his usually bright grey eyes have hardened to a near black.

"Alright. So that's a no to complimenting you and a yes to passion fruit chocolate chip pancakes for today. See, I'm learning all sorts of things."

"I wasn't aware that calling someone terrifying was a compliment," I reply.

"In our line of work, it's one of the best things to be."

"I'll bear that in mind. That and the pancakes, be-cause it's always a yes to those." His chest rumbles with quiet laughter as Kyle stops speaking.

"A deabrueon?" Leora asks as we re-join them.

"Yes," Kyle says.

"You didn't know?" Leo's face is completely impas-sive as he asks, so why do I sense some scepticism in the question?

"Ah, we had come to the same conclusion. I'm just

surprised you managed to as well in such a short time. You're correct in assuming it has the power to revive Thaddeus," she answers.

"What?" Robyn says, shocked for the first time.

"In my research with Theodore, I became aware of vague details of what it was doing and how it could be possible. While each dragovik's body and power is maintained by a certain amount of isuazko, that same quantity is not enough to restart a body. To reanimate the dead, the new body must be made purely from isuazko. How it is harvested, how much is needed and how the final resurrection comes about, I cannot say."

"That would explain the rapid decay of the victim's bodies. There aren't even enough remnants of life for the desiccation processes to occur over a normal length of time," Kyle says.

"Exactly."

"And this is the information Theodore told us to get from you? This is all we came for?" Leo demands.

"No, not all. I have a spell. One that can erase Thaddeus from all days to come," Leora replies softly.

"Why do we need this specific spell? There are plenty I know that will work," Robyn scoffs, crossing her arms.

"You know magic that works on an enemy you can see or touch. You might be able to destroy his body again, dragovik, but a new one could be made for him. This spell fragments his soul beyond repair."

Leora narrows her eyes as Robyn crosses the room to stand in front of her.

"So give it to us and we'll take care of him."

"As if a witch as unskilled as you could pull that off," Leora laughs. Robyn's body tenses again, her face washed by a furious blush. She grips the back of Kyle's chair, kneading it with her fingernails. "I will, of course, allow you to assist me. Maybe then you'll learn some real magic. If the Vernis Lanin is threatening to return then I am already as involved as any creature that wishes to stay alive."

She goes to the desk and produces, from the bottom drawer, a black wooden box. From within she removes a single sheet of vellum, littered with black ink scrawling and swatches of purple outlined in gold.

"Where did you manage to come across such a spell?" Leo inquires, tilting his head to the side.

"The books in this store contain many interesting spells. Some of them more dreadful and difficult than you can possibly imagine. But, in this case, it's not just the spell that will prove challenging," she says, "the preparation might give you hell too. Well, only in the most literal sense."

"How so?" Kyle asks.

"Bodies, no matter how durable, are inadequate receptacles for the soul. Eventually all souls burn through the life span of their bodies, yet they still exist. While a body can be cut into a hundred thousand pieces, to make but one scratch in the soul is near impossible. To do so would require one of the Vaerdiexes stones."

"The second, if I'm not mistaken," Kyle says, "I've studied them. Well, studied what little there is regarding their existence and powers. They were lost along with Dragovicia though some say their disappearance predates the fall of Dragovicia."

"Some say they never existed at all. Some say they were lost on purpose by Illarion himself," Leora murmurs, her eyes glowing.

As she nears me to return to the table, I feel the air ripple with her gelid power. It's like a dampener on my own magic, shackling me with its chill and causing me to shiver.

"Even if they were lost on purpose, there's no way to

ask Illarion where he hid them," Aaron says, "what are we supposed to do, call out oh mighty giver of fire, where the hell did you put those all powerful Vaerdiexes stones several thousand years ago. Oh, by the way, thank you for the powers."

"Or we could go to a burial site marked in his honour and communicate with his spirit through there?" Kyle suggests.

"Channelling the dead? I don't have that kind of power. It takes years to master such magic and, even then, amateurs in such spells shouldn't try to invoke such a powerful soul," Robyn says.

"It's a good thing that I'm not amateur." Leora has procured a hefty volume from the bookshelf. Balancing it in one hand, she thumbs through the pages before a slight smile lights her lips. "I can make your witch lacking problems go away, for a price."

"What will it be?" Leo asks.

"The katana," she says, nodding over to the blade on the table.

"That's all? You're risking quite a bit by using these sorts of dark magics. The Onyevaras and the Hirutere would have your head for doing so."

"I'm an antiques collector with a special interest in weaponry. Besides, I couldn't care less what the Hirutere and Onyevaras think. They have no jurisdiction over my people," she replies.

"Very well. We'll go to the marker for Illarion at the Aplin Hollow cemetery tonight."

"The Aplin Hollow cemetery? And you're saying all we need to cast the spell is the witch? Thank you."

Aaron's arm is in front of me in an instant, pushing me back to the bookshelf. In the open doorway stands the bellatoja leader from before, and I can make out some of his followers over his shoulder.

"We'll be taking the witch as an official prisoner of the Hirutere in connection with the death of Theodore McCullen. Captain Alastair, at your – well, not so much service per say," the man says to Leora.

"You most certainly won't," Aaron says, drawing his sword but failing to step away from me.

"Don't play dragovik. We outnumber you easily and thanks to the accords, you don't really have the upper hand unless you're interested in being executed. I know I'd enjoy that."

"You'd love that, to see us all dead," Robyn hisses.

"Yes actually, it would make for a major upswing in what's been a dismally dull day of following you around. Until now. Thanks for the witch."

"Wait," Kyle says, springing to his feet as two of the bellatoja clamp handcuffs, glowing an ethereal blue, around Leora's wrists. "This isn't just about us versus you anymore. It's about Thaddeus."

Alastair stills, his hand resting on the door handle as he's about to pull the door shut behind him.

"Thaddeus is dead."

"Yes, but there are those that want to resurrect him."

"Even if there are, why should we care if he's back?"

"You can't be serious. Whatever show of strength you may want to give, you know he'll come for the angeleru as soon as he'd come for dragoviks."

"And you think we can't take care of ourselves?"

"No, I'm thinking we can stop this before it becomes a matter of defending ourselves," Kyle answers earnestly. His hand grips the back of his chair until his knuckles go white.

"What do you say witch? I know you have no allegiance to the dragoviks."

Leora's green eyes betray nothing, though I sense, as if through a cord that has been strung between us since I read her spell, the utmost contempt radiating within her as she turns to look at Alistair.

"It's the same conclusion I've come to in my own time. Whatever your petty squabbles, you would be best served working together."

He surveys her coolly, and I think he reads in her what the others cannot. What I have seen; a hunger for something akin to revenge.

"So be it. We will accompany you to the cemetery tonight."

Chapter XXI.

Amongst the stones settled for the dead,
Amongst vessels sacrificed for time,
You will find no souls, those sold,
Now seek penance for the crime of life.

"Well, isn't that ever so touching. It makes you feel warm and fuzzy inside," Aaron comments, the whisper of his breath just by my ear.

I jump slightly, having taken no notice of his approach. His gaze drops to the engraved plaque just within the cemetery gates that I stand before.

"If by warm and fuzzy you mean sick, then yes. That's a horrible thing to have in a place of mourning," I reply.

The look on his face as I say this could mean anything; it is equally possible that something haunted brushes against his thoughts as it is that he is simply curious about my thought that hardly seems a thought. It seems to me more like common sense that one wouldn't want to read such a thing about their loved ones.

"You think so?" he says finally.

"It is essentially saying we all sell our souls out for a few years of life and then go to a hell of sorts."

"I wouldn't have pegged you for a believer in any faith."

"I'm not, but of late I cannot be certain of what does and does not exist," I pause, "also, you should consider not sneaking up on people in a cemetery."

"After everything that's happened over the past few days, you're still scared of the things that go bump in the night," he laughs softly, starting to walk aimlessly away from me amongst the headstones. I fall in step with him.

"More than ever and especially of the things that

might go bump in the night in a cemetery."

"Don't worry, as much as I loath to admit it, between us and the bellatoja you're perfectly safe. Also, why would demons seek the dead? There's no fun for them to have here. You're much safer in a cemetery than you would be in, say, a nightclub. I don't really peg you as a nightclub person though."

"Aplin Hollow distinctly lacks any kind of hopping nightlife, so that's a safe assumption."

I curl my arms around my chest in an effort to stay warm against the bracing wind. My midriff is very much exposed by Robyn's too small clothing, which I haven't had a chance to change out of since I showered at her house. Despite the sweater's long sleeves, I'm unable to keep the cold from burrowing in me. Perhaps it's the notion of being in a cemetery late at night that keeps me frozen just as much as the actual temperature.

"Would you mind clarifying something for me?"

"Is it something specific or a random fact of my choosing?" he asks.

"Specific."

"By all means."

"You asked me not to tell anyone about your transformation in the forest and I understand why. But, why did you do it?"

"Curiosity. The rule was put in place during a peace agreement between the Onyevaras and Hirutere when the dragoviks first came to Earth. I was wondering what it would feel like."

"And?"

"The actual change itself was just about the most horrible thing I've ever felt. Cells rapidly altering themselves, multiplying to create a much larger being out of me. It was like being torn apart. Apparently it takes a lot of transformations to get used to but, personally, I don't see how anyone could. Once that part is over, it's the most amazing feeling. To be full of fire is worth the pain," he breathes, before shaking his head as if to clear it. "So, speaking of new experiences, ready to witness your first full on casting?"

"You mean instead of being too preoccupied writhing in pain to see what's happing? At the very least I should have a better vantage point this time."

"Sarcasm becomes you."

The wind softens in time with his voice. Air falls short of another gust without a sound. In the distance, the sharp edges of the shadowy building housing Illarion's grave marker are darkened further in contrast to the lights that begin to glow. I see the shape of Robyn's shaded body as she lights each candle, lining them along the window sill. The headstones just outside the building harden out of the ambiguity of shadows and take form.

"Looks like they have everything set up. Soon we'll know where the second Vaerdiexes stone is."

"We're not going to find it."

"I don't think that's how sarcasm works," he teases. I look up and have to squint through the glaring white brightness of the moonlight to see his face. He frowns as he takes me in. "Why do you have so little faith in us?"

"It's not you," I sigh as we make our way through the mist that seems to spill like ghosts out of graves. "Believe me, I hope we find the stone so that this can be put to an end and no more harm comes from that creature. But I don't see any likelihood of us managing to recover a relic of the ancients that's been lost for thousands of years."

"You heard Leora. It isn't lost if someone's hidden it."

Across the cemetery, in the dark, the trunks of trees appear like calligraphic marks on the parchment of landscape. Their branches are a lost chaos in the sky.

"Have you not considered that if Illarion made the effort of hiding them, they're better off lost?"

"Okay, so no more cemeteries for you." I sigh, throwing him a sideways glance as I tighten my arms around myself again. "Hey, you brought this on yourself by reading too many tombstones. Stop speaking in riddles and let's go speak to a dead person," he says.

Just then I hear Robyn's voice ushering him from within. He glances at me and I nod to say I'll be fine. The bellatoja have set up a perimeter rendering them indistinguishable from the forest, even when I squint at the tree line. I'm not sure I feel much safer knowing they're there, but the temporary alliance struck between Kyle and Alistair seems strong enough to trust they won't kill me. As for letting harm befall me, that's another matter.

"Oi Aaron, enough of the late night promenade. We'd like to get on with our lives."

"It's a shame this spell doesn't require a sacrifice, I'm about ready to chop Leo's head off," Aaron grumbles as I walk him towards the building.

"Again with the horribly morbid jokes? That was a joke, right?" I ask sceptically.

"Just trying to diffuse your aura of anxiety. This place is depressing."

"You're right, that's the problem with cemeteries, they're too depressing. We should have tombstones decorated with rainbows."

"Now you're talking."

I watch him go inside then turn back to the tree line. I see a tall figure break from its ranks and approach me. With each step closer, Alastair loosens the shroud of darkness that obscures him from my sight until he comes to pause beside me.

"Walk with me."

It's hardly a request but it's as close to polite as will

come from him. I don't sense an insolent reply would be well received so I fall into step beside him.

"You'll accept, I hope, my sincerest apology for my earlier behaviour. Scare tactics are what's recommended to us when dealing with unruly dragoviks."

I can't help myself this time.

"I wasn't aware attempting to protect oneself made one unruly," I retort. Luckily, he takes it well, smiling and squinting into the distance while nodding.

"Indeed, but you have to comprehend how unlikely and unwanted a story that Thaddeus Velemir was back was to us. He is much despised for what he did to my people."

I can hear the resentment in his voice and I don't doubt that it was every bit as horrific as he makes it out to be.

"And for that you loathe all dragoviks?" He turns to me with a curious look.

"No. Before the accords created between our people that banned dragovik transformations, we lived in constant threat. I'll appreciate it if you don't repeat these words to your companions but yours is a mighty powerful race, and I'm not sure even we could do anything if it truly came to a head to head battle. Hence the scare tactics. Every encounter we run the risk of meeting a dragovik who has had enough, who would rather transform and kill us, than abide by the accords anymore."

I think to Aaron's comments only moments ago, about the power he felt. *To be full of fire.* Such a destructive force. I wonder if Alastair overheard us. Somehow, I doubt Aaron would be alive if he had.

"May I ask you something," he interrupts my thoughts now, that look of inquiry still on his face. I nod, prompting him. "You know so little of the fundamental history of your own kind, and you're not helping with the spell. You're a Thiel, undoubtedly powerful, so you'd be of great help and yet here I thought the Thiels had died when Thaddeus was in power."

"That's not really a question."

"No but you get the gist of what I'm asking."

I chew the inside of my cheeks, wondering how much is safe to reveal to him.

"I wasn't raised by dragoviks. My parents passed away well, before I can remember them." I don't add that I don't remember much of anything that's real anymore. "It wasn't until a few months ago that my grandmother found me at the Academy and took –"

"The Academy?" His voice has grown suddenly sharp.

"The school I went to," I say. Why do I get the impression that that's not the part of my comment that requires clarification? I blink up at him. His eyes are dark, his face beyond reading. "You've heard of it?"

He doesn't answer, just sweeps me over with another glance before murmuring to himself, "You're not what I'd expect, no not at all."

"Excuse me?" But just then I hear footsteps approaching from behind me. Loathe to turn my back on Alistair when he looks so sinister, I spin around to see Kyle.

"Everything okay?" he asks me, glancing between the two of us.

"Fine," Alistair replies hastily, stepping away from me.

"Funny, I wasn't asking you. Come on Mallory."

He takes me by the hand and leads me back to the building. I look over my shoulder and see Alistair following us, one of his soldiers having joined him. As we reach the doorway, Kyle raises his eyebrows at them.

"We'll be staying for the main event, to ensure nothing goes wrong," Alistair says.

"Hush," Leora orders from the middle of the room before Kyle or Aaron can object.

She and Robyn stand either side of a large tomb. A low relief carving of a man with eerily abstract features decorates the side of it. There's no specificity to the man, he could be anyone. Atop the tomb sits a circle of newly lit crimson candles from which no wax drips. Leo speaks in a hushed voice to them and Kyle beckons us to join him in the corner.

"Why would there be a tomb dedicated to Illarion in Aplin Hollow?" I ask him.

"Illarion's buried in Sundalev, so naturally drago- viks created places to pay homage to him on Earth when they came here. Any densely dragovik populated area has one," he replies.

He opens the volume Leora had shown us earlier to a page marked by his thumb.

"Can you read what it says?" I ask, examining the page that I assume is written in the ancient language.

"Yes. Most documentation of our history is in the ancient language and we all learn it at a young age. I can translate it for you," he offers.

"Yes please."

"Alright, this first part is a requisite of any spirit sum- moning spell. It says: Death's curtain shall be parted and I shall see the dead as they see me."

"The dead can see us? Are they here now?"

I think I'm terrified but, somewhere beneath that, I feel a curious kind of hope. Those I've never met, could they be with me?

"No, they can't exactly roam about here, but they can see us from where they are. The next part is essential to specifically summon the spirit of Illarion. See, the first part acts as a general announcement, it can be heard by all spirits. It's the second recitation, one I've never seen in a spell book before, that tells the dead who is being invited into our realm. Otherwise, anyone can come through."

I shiver.

"What's the recitation?"

"Giver of safety, who procured the great fires to protect his people. Bringer of welfare, who delivered his people from the arms of Death. We seek, through the bloodline of our redeemer, an audience with he. He who can help us reclaim the salvation of our people; he who knows what ghosts whisper and people cry. Give us the words that only death has yet heard."

I run my thumb across the page, feeling the indents of the words.

"So Leora recites this and he'll appear to us?"

"Yes, though it will be Leo who address him. He can't stay in this world without great pain, and that's not something he'd be willing to take on for a non-dragovik witch."

"We're ready now," Leora calls to us. Kyle gives her the book before returning to my side. "While Leo speaks to him, you are to kneel and not look directly at him as your law demands in the presence of your creator."

"Charming," I murmur to Aaron.

"Do not jest when speaking of our creator," Aaron teases.

"Shut up Aaron or I'll gladly chop your head off," Leo says, narrowing his eyes as they kneel.

I follow their lead, bowing my head so all I can see are the tips of my own shoes and the cracked stone floor. Leora takes a deep breath, drawing all the sound out of the air into her lungs. When she speaks, her voice has grown louder than before, resonating off of the stone walls with a deep hum.

"Suyakuru ni aoisyan, qui'etai hakimaava letai osurr

kaisma kartsugar leanous namie; ciestsoru ni heaodim-
ma, qui'etai turvadaava leanous namie callanedo letai
irelka ni morvedae. Yesta motsimeravous, varasta letai isuzsusorro ni tyesta kei'atbrijaru, jutuldav aka lean.
Lean qui'etai dirava paitlider notrays kei'ircer letai paalu-
nastur'dey ni tyesta namie; lean qui'etai atzinarava valja
natuivaimka sahikstiravaz etev namie inuukawaravaz.
Suyakur paitlider letai okivaka pervo critae morvedae
pirisemaraava vema," Leora chants.

The night accepts her words, but makes no immediate reply. There's an itching in my neck, a begging to look
up to see what will happen. Then the air around us pulls
on flesh like a vacuum, dragging us towards the tomb
across the room. I drop onto all fours to steady myself.
All sounds of our breathing, my cry of panic, is drawn
from the air until we are suspended in the absolute silence
that belongs only to the dead. It's the sounds inside my
head that shatter vociferous cries. Screams for sanity and
salvation. I can tell I'm not the only one hearing them. I
lift my head ever so slightly and see Kyle's body wavering.
He grasps either side of his head. I hear the dead pleading with me as if I could free them from torment. Above
all these cries I hear another voice rise. He is pure in my
mind, the first principle. All this time he has been guiding
me and I have been so blind to believe I was stumbling
without him. The dead go quiet in his presence.

"Your majesty," Leo begins aloud through laboured
breaths, "we seek the knowledge you hoped to destroy in
order to save our kind from an enemy."

"Silence. You, my son, good though your intentions
may be, are not pure. I will not have my slumber tainted
by warriors nor by witches. I will not mingle with the living who would go to war gladly, even if it is war for the
cause of salvation. I will speak only to the ones who seek
peace. To them alone I will grant the answers sought," Il-

larion says, his voice a steady rhythm of power and comfort. I long to see the face from which the words come.
"However, there is a veil beneath which is darkness in
your midst. I will not remain exposed to it. Will you permit an exchange?"

"Yes," Leo replies hesitantly.

"Then blessed be he who knows the strength of heart
to face hell and remain unbroken."

With these words, my body turns to fire and I feel
pure.

* * *

"It's not what you expected is it?"

"No. I thought it would be either exotic or familiar.
This is-" I cut myself off, searching for some manner in
which to describe what I see. The air around us drips
thick, clots white to obscure comprehension.

"Vague," Kyle finishes, finding the word for me.

We stand, separated by Illarion, but I have never felt
closer to Kyle. I want to reach out and hold his hand
but know that the knot made in our souls by this journey
is the same connection I would be searching for. We're
bound forever now.

"You will never find the words to describe it until
your existence is wholly unhinged from Earth. This place
is beyond the grasp of the living's conceptualisation. But
I will show it to you all the same." Illarion extends his
arm to me.

I glance at Kyle but his eyes are bound by the ap-
parition of the fallen king before him. Hesitantly, I take
Illarion's arm and allow him to lead me. Kyle falls in step
on his other side.

"You're not what I expected either."

"No? Did you imagine the dead would appear as

they did at their hour of death? Old and decrepit."

"Something like that."

"Here, we are restored to what we were at the most pivotal moment in our existence. The one that, above all, bound fate to our souls."

"Is fate not there from the beginning?"

"Yes and no. There exist, within each of us, many threads of potential. With each act we pull a little on some, unthreading alternative lives, and sew others into our future so they grow more difficult to escape. There comes a time when we undo the last stich of all possibility and we find our course. That moment for me was the day I found the phoenix. So, though I died of old age, I will never age again."

He appears to be about the same age as Chloe's dad, maybe a little older. But while there is still a softness in his face, I see how circumstance has the effect of blurring years. His hair is faintly streaked with grey, the skin under his eyes has begun to slacken with exhaustion.

"And the moment you're trapped in, it's when Dragovicia was fated to fall?" Kyle asks. He seems unable to hold Illarion's gaze, to even look at his person for more than a few seconds at a time now that he's reigned in his awe.

"Indeed."

"Do you regret the steps you took to save your kingdom?" I inquire.

"You believe I should. Why is that?"

"In the end, Dragovicia was lost all the same and dragoviks were banished to Earth," I answer.

Kyle's lips part, and he looks at me. He's shocked, I can see, by how I seem to freely reprimand Illarion. It was not my intention, I want to tell him, to question your king. Just to understand. But he nods to me slowly. He knows, and Illarion's gentle smile tells me he does too.

"I have seen the choices your kind has made at times. But it was only some that chose a darker path. Perhaps I would not take the same risks to save your kind now, but at the time I saw fit to take such actions. Not only for the protection of dragoviks but for all my subjects. But come now. You seek the answers to other questions than those of history and what lies beyond death, though the ones you intend to ask me are not your own."

"No, but I doubt there's enough time for us to ask all we want to know. Only some of our questions can save lives," Kyle replies.

"You cling too dearly to mortal concepts such as time. Shrug them off my children. For now, you are immortal."

"Until we leave."

"If you leave. For if it is your joint wish to remain, this world will be granted to the both of you."

I catch Kyle's gaze, though I'm not sure what question I'm asking with my eyes. Would I want to stay, would he want to stay, could we even fathom a world apart from the people we've just left?

"Why allow us to stay? Why did you choose to bring the two of us here? I know so little of our race and have yet to even ask you a question in order to bring peace to them," I ask.

"You ask to find inner peace, to unite the contradictions between your past and the new world your eyes have been opened to. I believe once you find that you will also discover a great desire to bring peace on a larger scale, as Kyle already has. So far, you've both demonstrated an eagerness to protect others for reasons that do not lend themselves to selfishness. As for why you should be allowed to stay, it is because I fear for you both."

"Because of Thaddeus?"

His smile falters.

"Because you both have fires within you that I fear the world will put out before you can save yourselves."

Kyle comes to a halt, so Illarion and I stop as well. I see how he takes the king's words to heart, how fear holds him steady for an instant before a shiver runs through him. I want to be angry at Illarion for alighting this darkness in Kyle's eyes, but I know he means no malice with his truth. I slip my arm from his and reach for Kyle's hand.

"We don't have to save ourselves. We'll save each other," I say to Illarion, though I don't look away from Kyle for an instant. I will protect him, and all the people I've come to care about. "We won't stay here. It's not possible so long as Inerea and the others are in danger."

"Indeed, they and many others will be in peril if you two remain."

"Then you know? What is happening, what will happen?"

"Your world brushes against this one so frequently that it is impossible not to take notice of what is happening in it. And, of late, what has been happening is most disturbing."

"You mean the attempt to resurrect Thaddeus," I say.

"That amongst other things, which I cannot tell you of. But Thaddeus Velemir never escaped my notice. He burned in the same way you two do, and it consumed him."

"Are you saying we're like him?" I ask.

"Not at all. He was all passion, with no desire to allow the world respite from anger or soothe his own torment. You, in all you have done, prove yourself to be his antitheses. You rule with your heads and listen to your hearts when they prove themselves wise. You do not ignore the commands of emotion, but you are not slaves to them. Above all you will not commit violence to others even if it is the easy way to get what you want. I believe you are the balance of fire and control that can save the race I once considered my children."

"So, you will help us defeat Thaddeus?" Kyle manages, and I feel his fingers tighten around my hand. Illarion's grey eyes darken.

"I will help you find what it is you seek. Ask and you shall have it."

"We require the second of the Vaerdiexes stones' power to complete our spell."

"And so you will have it. But the stone itself I cannot deliver to you. I fear too many would attempt to claim it."

"The Vernis Lanin?"

"Among others. Even the Onyevaras would seek to have it."

"You don't trust them," Kyle says before pressing his lips tightly together.

How strange it must seem to him to have the creator of his kind question those that presently rule him.

"Indeed. Of late they have failed the helpless too many times. They have made themselves slaves to the Hirutere out of their desire to return to Sundalev. In time, they will fall for what they've done. Not naturally of course. They will be torn down by a power that rises even now."

"Is that a forewarning?" I ask as Illarion starts to walk again. This time, Kyle and I fall in step just behind him.

"No. It is a mere suggestion of what I believe to be the future. I am not a seer and I have no command over what events follow the present. Also, I note that it is not wise to assume this rising power is malevolent and must be stopped. You must let it run its course," he replies, smiling at us, "Now, I will grant you the stone's power on one condition."

"What might that be?"

"While I commend you compassion and desire to do no harm, we are on the inevitable brink of war. I wish to see you both alive at the end of it and therefore must ask that you, Mallory, permit yourself to break those rules you have held in place for so long."

I see Kyle flinch in my periphery, feel his warmth flood into coldness as he looks at me. In his face, that carefully constructed composure, I see what I've been waiting to find. Exactly how much he knows. And it's everything. Everything I don't know about myself is in him. Yet he sees me as an equal, a friend. Can it truly be so bad then? But I know, of course it is. Good does not put the flicker of fear in a man's eyes as it has just done.

"I can't. Please, to hurt another-"

"Ah even without recollections of your past you remain resolute on this matter? Yes, Mallory, I know what you do not yet recall. I would restore it all to you now but I think it best we allow for time to take its course and the spell come to a natural end. It was truly despicable what befell you. That harm done to you exceeded the retribution of self-preservation, which is all I ask of you."

"What befell me?" No, no this was nothing done to me. I know that. *My hands wrought ends.*

"Would you call it something else?"

He cannot seriously believe that it was something done to me. Not after- and memory comes like a cold light.

I've seen tears of blood before, as if one is crying about one's own death before it happens. A certain poison can leave its victim to an agonising five-day death in which the red blood cells are annihilated. Cell suicide. Then they leak their contents from every orifice. Bleeding nose, mouth, and eyes. It was snake venom. One day, when that woman was unhappy with us, she brought one

of our classmates out like a puppet in a children's pro-
duction. We sat in rows before her as she administered
the poison. Not one of us could look away, not one of us
could stop her. The image crushes my conscious, drags
my heart into a palpitating state.

Please! The boy had screamed to us. *Just kill me please,
please. Make it stop.*

That woman had stroked his face gently, nodding
along to his plea. She was waiting for us, so that we might
see how he'd die.

Please.

The boy's body had begun to turn blue from internal bleeding before anyone did anything. He quivered
helplessly on the floor before us, speaking words without
sound. Language and reason, all human constructs were
lost to him other than the salvation of an afterlife. And
perhaps even that he hadn't believed in. He wanted the
repose of death's nothing.

Make it stop.

After three days in that room a girl named Lilith had
got up, her body trembling. Lilith. Her name swims out
of comprehension but I know it means so much, holds a
universe in it. She looked at me the whole time, reminding herself and me, without cruelty, that what she did she
did to protect me from the same fate. Was it that of the
boy or her own that she feared for me?

Lilith knelt beside him, held him like a mother with
her hand cupping his cheek and his body lain across her
lap. She did the same thing whenever she was soothing
me after I had been beaten.

She held my gaze, steadying herself. And she slit his
throat.

"Mallory," Kyle recalls me to the present.

I feel as though I should collapse, the shock of the
memory folding itself around me. Instead, I remain

standing, panting slightly, beside Illarion.

"It was my own doing."

I hear Kyle's breaths rattle and I want to look at him for comfort. Illarion's eyes bear upon me with sympathy I don't want, that I wouldn't dare ask for. How can that be a memory? And yet, I am certain it is.

"Do you know what the phoenix teaches us? That even when all in our lives has been reduced to ash and there seems to be no options but to fall into fire too, hope persists. New and more powerful life is possible."

I step away from him, shaking my head now.

"I have had power before and I don't want it again. Now, you tell me I should seek it?"

"No, you should become it."

He flattens my hand and brushes across my palm with his own. Behind his touch comes a small dagger, cold and sterile as the death its very existence proposes.

"It's been a long time since you used a weapon so this should be best for now."

I shake my head again, try to drop the dagger but my fingers curl around it against my volition. I hear growling behind me and turn to find a creature of human form, with black bulging eyes and thick dark veins pressing against its skin, swelling from nothingness.

"This is a lesser deabrueon."

"You want me to fight it," I murmur. It's not human, yet hesitation stays my hand. A lingering guilt that calls to mind the splitting of skin. "You can't expect me to hurt it."

"Don't be foolish. I expect you to kill it."

"And if I don't?"

I follow his gaze to Kyle, and for a moment I fear he'll set the beast on him.

"His life is not at stake here. But on Earth, if you hesitate as you do now, someone's life may very well be the price for every second you wait. And that life may be of one you love."

On his last word, the creature wastes no time throwing itself at me, burying its decaying claws into my arm. Kyle calls my name, makes to move towards me but Illarion holds him back. Rot the colour of wet dirt packed moss blooms on its nails, scraping my flesh. I cry out, my weapon already lost to the ground.

With a heavy push, I shove its body far enough from my own that its grip is loosened. There's a sickening gurgle of blood as I fall to the ground, rolling away just in time to avoid the deabrueon as it takes a swing at me. Crouched on one knee, I spy my dagger behind it. A low hiss comes from its lipless mouth.

This is not one of my dreams, nor is it a vision. I will die if I do not protect myself. But even without my dagger I am not rendered powerless against the dark forces that have made the mistake of stumbling into a place of light. My body knows that darkness, it has been called upon by it before and it knows how to fight it. Springing from the earth, I fake left only to spin out of its way at the last moment. I plant a roundhouse on its collarbone, sending it stumbling back and giving me the time I need to pluck my dagger from the ground.

As it comes towards me again, I strike out. A gash of oozing black liquid appears on its upper arm, the creature having managed to block my attack on its throat. It wavers for a moment, eyes full not with fear but with the delicious prospect of being capable of taking down someone who has posed a challenge to its existence. It darts back before slowing into steady circles, and I match its motion. My breaths and its rasps become harmonious for a moment. I want to find in those eyes some reason to spare it. An excuse to step away from this fight. In my faltering it finds its moment. It counters its direction, shoving hard into my side and grabs me by the arms before sinking its teeth into my dagger wielding hand.

While my previous burst of adrenaline had saved me from feeling much of the punctures its claws had left in my arm, now I feel the full extent of my pain. Now I feel a scream rising in my throat as my wrist spits blood. Some of it the creature drinks; I hear the sickening slurps to attest to it. Its thick tongue with rough bulb like protrusions runs across my skin. It's so enraptured by the suffering it's inflicting that it carelessly lets most of my blood spill to the ground. I try to pull away but it bites harder and my fingers fly open with the shock. My dagger falls and I feel the veins in my hand throbbing. It's like they're trying to alert the rest of my body of the danger, as if it didn't already know. The deabrueon juts its shoulder forward, hitting me in the abdomen and knocking us to the ground. Beneath its weight I cannot reach my weapon, though I stretch my left hand out in a desperate attempt to grasp it.

I feel him in my head again. That very same voice that had interrupted the cries of the damned after Leora had cast the spell. The voice that is a balm to sick minds and has recalled me from nightmares. The warmth flows within me, eradicating the pain.

You need not steel to be a weapon.

He falls silent but does not leave me, only retreats into my mind so as to allow my conscious to be filled with thoughts other than that of his all-consuming presence. His fire is within me though, and I waste no more time reaching for the fallen blade. Instead, using my free hand, I claw the side of the creature's face with such violent force that it jerks upright. With enough of its face and throat exposed I land a harsh jab to its oesophagus. Its abdomen jerks inward slightly with the shock and its claws leap to defend its throat. I curl my legs around its back and throw my weight to the left, pinning it down.

With both my hands now free, I jab my thumbs against the deabrueon's eye sockets. It howls and I feel the flurry of its eyelids trying to shut. Applying more pressure, I crush those bulging black orbs that saw me and thought I was weak. They underestimated me, thought time could decay the cruelty my self-preservation is capable of producing. With one last press, I feel a silken warmth lick my fingers. Black liquid mingles with my own blood on my hands, spilling over the creature's eye sockets. Yet it is so unlike blood in the way it runs, as if it were still alive even without a heart to flow through. It creeps up my fingers towards my wrists as the deabrueon's spitting vines had done in the forest. Its touch does not burn as the other deabrueon's had, but I feel a tingling sensation along my skin. Gripping the sides of the creature's head, I squeeze harder. The pressure is a call and my blood sings to my fingers until I hear the simultaneous cracks of his skull in multiple places. Its head begins to cave in on itself, turning even further from the realm of familiarity than before.

I fall back from my knees, resting my weight on the balls of my feet. I lift my hands, stare at the death I painted on myself. Past them I see the loosened skin, ill-fitting, around the rearranged bones of the beast. The creature now dead, a wave of awareness as to what's been done sweeps through me. I fall to my side, my stomach heaving as breaths and sickness rise. I drag myself away from the corpse, clutching my injured hand to my chest and staring at those blood clotted holes its claws left in me. It may not have been human, but nor am I having killed it so quickly as soon as I was endangered.

"Mallory," Illarion begins, falling silent as I shiver at the sound of his voice.

Had he seen my face perhaps he would have known to never start speaking. I feel grass beneath me where a moment ago the terrain had seemed nothing and everything. It rises thickly, full of myriad colour bursts of wildflowers. I'm in the meadow behind Inerea's house. I look back but Illarion and Kyle remain in the cloudiness of this otherworld. I knot my fingers in the silken stalks of a nearby flower cluster.

"Forgive my course of action in getting you to fight. I wanted only for you to come to terms with what doing battle in the future will mean."

I hear the grass give way to heavy footsteps and nature recoils. The soft touch of this manifest memory falls away as Kyle's arms find me. I look down but the ground's slate is blank again.

"I wanted, deep in my mind, to let it kill me so I wouldn't hurt it. But I couldn't stop myself," I whimper. Kyle's tightens his grasp and Illarion kneels beside us.

"Self-preservation is not wrong and it does not make you any less human. It is what has driven humanity to exist as long as it has. A deabrueon is as far from human as can be, however, and you should pity its ever having been born, not its death." The corpse's corporeality softens and it is gone to dust before I can take another breath. "Willingness to fight aside, I thought perhaps you might miss the other point I intended to make. But seeing you now, I realise the lesson is learnt. For it is no longer just readiness to commit violence that you fear but your ability to do so."

"Power does not rest in any weapon we wield, but within the one who chooses to wield a weapon," I whisper.

"Indeed, there is no greater weapon than those which we carry with us at all times. Even in death the mind and heart protect us when a blade cannot."

"Would you not say my nightmares are an indication that my mind has no intention of protecting me?"

"On the contrary I believe they are a sign that prove, above all others, that your mind shows a great desire to protect you. It is a desire that crosses the boundaries of an ordinary witch's capabilities so that your mind might reveal to you those things that will save you in the future, so long as you come to understand them before it is too late. Now, I believe all your questions have been answered. The ones you are willing to ask at least."

Kyle nods his assent.

"There's only on more," I say.

"Ah, yes. That of he who spoke to you within your mind during battle."

"You heard him?"

"Alas, I am not so blessed nor so cursed as to hear the words of absolute truth he might bestow. Yes, I could feel his presence within you. Always I feel him burning with infinite light. If he has decided to guide you, you are indeed both blessed and cursed," Illarion murmurs.

He lowers his gaze from me for the first time. Is it guilt, shame, or mere concern that burdens his eyes so they fall from my own?

"But we're not to be blessed with the gift of his name?" Kyle asks.

"No, his name remains a curse. As for the Vaerdiexes stone, it will be sent in disguise to your world so none can find it but the two of you. When you see it, whatever form it may manifest in, you will know it for what it truly is. Now you must return before time has run out for your friends."

Kyle jolts upright, fear flashing across his already tense face.

"I thought time had no meaning here."

"It does not, but, while you have remained suspended, time remains in continuum through the fabric of your world." He draws up to full height, peering down at us.

"Before you go, I will give you one more gift. It will not save you, as now you know that you alone must do. But it will be of help during the first of many tipping points that decide your fate. Farewell."

He kisses both our foreheads and we fall, unaware of when his warm touch becomes the cold air of our reality. At first, I fear I am in one of my dreams or, even worse, have been caught in a world between the two. One in which I will never endure the pain of Earth but always carry the burden of those left to suffer it. Illarion warned me that to hear that voice, warm though it may be, was to be cursed. Perhaps the curse now begins to work its way into reality, slipping between the cracks of worlds opened by our spell.

Soon, however, I adjust to what I can perceive rather than what is imagined. The crypt that we left behind in complete silence, as if only moments ago, has now descended into a swirling of bodies and cries. Deabrueon, whose eyes seem still despite their rapid movement due to their endless obsidian colouring, gleam in the light of the last candle yet to be knocked over. Leora is encircled by the other three who fend away the creatures, trying not to break their formation but being pressed ever closer as the deabrueon advance. Leora's eyes are shut and I see her lips moving with the near silent utterance of a spell. Previously unnoticed, I take one step towards them and Leo lunges towards me with his sword extended. Kyle barely pulls me aside fast enough, giving Leo the second he needs to recognise us. Yanking on my wrist, he pulls both of us into the circle. Unsteadied by the sudden movement, I collapse on the floor beside Leora, while Kyle draws his sword and joins the others ranks.

"Where did they come from?" Kyle demands as another deabrueon throws itself at Aaron with a snarl. The muscles in his arm tense as he decapitates it with the slightest effort. I dip my head, staring at Leora's lap.

"Illarion's last words weren't intended as cryptic but as a warning of the true price of the exchange. Blessed be he who knows the strength of heart to face hell and remain unbroken. He unleashed hell on us in order to take you to heaven for a brief while," Leo answers.

The deabrueon, noticing the fall in their numbers, start to step back. Their shoulders are hunched forwards, ready to pounce, but they're waiting for the advantage. Their persistence will eventually outmatch the warriors' skill.

"Now that I don't have to maintain the spirit invocation, I can cast a shielding spell over us. It won't last too long against their attacks, my magic's greatly drained, but it will give Robyn a chance to use some battle magic while the others rest," Leora says to me. "We can hold the shield up longer if I can use your energy."

"What do I have to do?"

"Just take my hands," she says. Clasping both of my hands, she bows her head again. "Aka saviski tujoud sa iepilukor lueicht kartsugar savis callanedo uretza oelanus rahissorava."

There's a burst of heat in my chest, a flurry of successive heartbeats that resound throughout my entire body, before the warmth flashes along my arms and into the tips of my fingers. I feel my body going cold as the energy moves in such concentration towards Leora, slipping from my fingertips to hers. Above our heads is a starburst of white light, which surges over us like a waterfall until we're encased in a dome. Without restraint the deabrueon begin to throw their bodies against the shield. It shivers as they bounce off of it, cracking for a second before resealing itself.

"Now Robyn!" Leora orders. Her hands have gone clammy in mine.

"Kolamma ni ulatb verorava varasta."

A cylindrical ripple shoots through the air, impaling two of the deabrueon like a javelin. They collapse, one atop the other, stilled, and the gaping wounds in their chests begin to ooze.

"Vakier lohkiri."

As if ripped apart from either side, the deabrueon closest to Aaron splits directly down the middle. Its black blood pours out in mass quantity, pooling to the edge of our dome of light. There's a nasty thud and splash as its entrails fall from it to the ground. In the excitement of Robyn's attacks, the other deabrueon have gone wild. They claw and snarl, lashing out at our barrier.

"I can't keep this up much longer if the deabrueon continue as they are," Leora says, "my energy is still depleted from the invocation."

"Mine's not enough?" I ask.

"No, it's not that, it's just, channelling another witch's energy is more than I have the concentration to do," she replies, beginning to slouch.

"Mizahk ni letai morvedae alev inogizerava neviet lueicht!" Robyn cries out.

A flare of light illuminates the crypt for a moment. When it dies, the remaining deabrueon are covered in burn marks. They stumble back for a moment, dazed. In that instant I feel warmth flooding my body and Leora's hands slip away as our shield disappears. Without delay Leo, Kyle, and Aaron are on the offensive again, taking out the few deabrueon that managed to survive the attack. Robyn staggers, her body teetering. On my feet in an instant, I catch her and lower her to the ground. Within moments the last of the deabrueon have fallen beneath their blades and the three are left panting, swords still raised in case more appear. I look down at Robyn's head, gently resting in my lap, but her eyes are shut. After a moment, they lower their weapons and Kyle rushes to our side.

"Is she okay?" he asks, crouching beside his sister and brushing her hair out of her face with such care as not to agitate her exhaustion or pain.

"She's fine and she doesn't need to be referred to in third person," Robyn coughs, looking up at her brother. "I just feel like someone's churned my guts up, that's all."

"You'd think Illarion could have warned us about the literal hell we would be facing down here," Aaron mutters, sheathing his sword.

"He didn't really want to stick around," I say. His eyes land on my injured hand, caked in a mix of dry blood.

"Looks like you got some hell yourself."

"Nothing I couldn't handle," I reply. He rests on one knee, examining my wound.

"Just, please promise me one thing."

"What's that?"

He raises his gaze to meet mine, exuding unwavering sincerity. My body tenses to see his face so devoid of humour. The absence of his perennial amused smile ages him, or perhaps it's having just done battle that does so.

"Promise me heaven isn't full of Rottweilers," he sighs, gesturing to the bite marks on my hand, "That's not the sort of disappointment I can cope with right now."

The right corner of his lip creeps up and I expel a huff of air, the tension unravelling within my body.

"As if you're going to heaven," Robyn wheezes, sitting up.

Chapter XXII.

Why is there always blood?
For the first time, the mind does not dress these well-worn words up in another's voice, but asks me in my own.
Because blood follows death and I am death.

Is that my own answer, or another voice inside my head's? I have come to know that there was something sinister in my past, even if I cannot yet make out the shape of it. I bow my head and am grateful for the chair that holds my weight, knowing I couldn't do so on my own.

Kyle wipes away the last traces of blood from my hand, leaving five ghastly pink wounds looking up at me. Still, they're better than looking down to see that creature's blood spilt by my hand. I watch as the torn skin disappears beneath the unblemished white fabric of the bandages he swathes my hand in. I let my fingers and hand go limp, lain on the table.

"I still can't-" I start, but cannot finish.

Can't what? Believe that Illarion would make me do that? But I can, and I can understand why too. What is there that I can't believe in anymore? Kyle hesitates, biting back words as he finishes his careful work without looking up at me. As of yet he's refrained from speaking about our encounter, and I'm thankful for that, as well as his intervention when Leo sought answers immediately.

"You don't have to hold back. I trust whatever it is you have to say will be in my and everyone's best interests," I say.

"You do?"

He won't bring his eyes up to mine. I place my bandaged hand on his holding it with the same reassuring squeeze as I had done in the car, though the pressure aggravates my new wounds.

"I trust you, Kyle. Not just your words. You're the only thing I have faith in right now. You know, my past, everything I don't and you still treat me like an equal," I assure him.

He draws his eyebrows closer in a moment of agitation. At what I cannot know.

"While I wish you would extend the same feelings to the others, I'm glad that you at least feel you can trust me. I've felt the same way ever since I met you at the Academy. I wish I could tell you everything about your past, I know how it must drive you insane, but I fear Illarion's right. Not only would it be too much of an overload but I doubt you'd believe me anyway. I just want you to know that all I've done since going there and finding you was in an endeavour to ensure your safety as well as the others."

"You took care of me, didn't you?"

A cloud lifts from an evening of agony, of screams and shattered furniture. And of the solace to come from one person. It pains me to think of it, to allude to that momentary burst of insanity he had seen in me. But whatever happened that night, I meant it when I said I trusted him, and I know he won't betray the secrets of my past, not even to those closest to him.

"I took care of you that day, and I will take care of you every day to come. The way they kept you locked up in there," he falters, shaking his head. My throat tightens, perhaps with gratitude for a nameless act or perhaps with fear of the extent of his knowledge. "What I wanted to say, earlier that is, is that I think Illarion's right on another account. I'm scared for you. I'm glad you're co-operating with us, even if for now all that means is allowing us to protect you while we come to understand this situation. But whether it's your intention to or not, you keep finding yourself in these perilous situations, for the sake of what?"

"The people whose kindness towards me is of yet undue. Those who can't protect themselves."

"You shouldn't say things like that Mallory. You're just as deserving of kindness as anyone else."

"What does it matter why I'm fighting so long as I'm fighting with you?" I ask, flexing my hand beneath the tight bandages as I remove it from his. A twinge of pain shoots up the back of my hand.

"Because I don't want the cost of this cause to be your life."

He looks up from where my hand had rested on his, bracing his palm against the table to keep it from visibly shaking. He looks so pained. Unlike Leo or Robyn, Kyle makes no attempt to veil his feelings.

"The others have their own motives for wanting to keep you close. Leo made that abundantly clear when he endangered your life. They're warriors first, make no mistake, so they consider what their best tactic might be rather than the moral implications of making split second decisions in battle. Given the circumstances, having someone whose isuazko can give Robyn and Leora the ability to cast more powerful spells is the best course of action. They're not considering the other's long term needs; lives can be a worthwhile cost for victory in their minds. If you let them, they'll unintentionally help you build the path that I see being the beginning of the end of you."

"All things begun are destined to end. All I can hope is that my end does not lay so near in the future."

"Do more than hope. Fight against your end," he says, "promise me that."

In Kyle's eyes, I search for him. Out of the six of us, Kyle is the farthest from humanity's reach, but not because he is monstrous, as I am. Where we still lie in the greed of personal desires and fear, no matter how harmless they may seem, he has surpassed a need for gain. Self-actualisation, a base egocentric drive, is not the salvation he seeks. His lifeline lies in the safety of others, those he cares about and even those he doesn't know. He will never be a leader, nor will he be the strongest fighter. He will be our foundation and strength where no one sees him. If this promise is the price of his peace of mind, who am I to deny it?

"I will."

He smiles at me, returning the remaining bandages and antiseptic wipes to the small box he had brought into the room with him when we first returned.

"You're certain you don't want Robyn to heal that?"

"This little scrape is the last thing she should worry about after the ordeal she went through tonight."

"You're one to talk," he laughs, "An audience with Illarion and you hardly seem fazed."

"He wasn't intimidating."

"No, he really wasn't," he returns softly.

"Even when he pitted me against the deabrueon. I knew it was him that had put me in that situation but I didn't begrudge him that."

"No, you just blamed yourself for protecting yourself."

He yawns.

"Tired?" I share his weariness.

"I'm absolutely exhausted."

"I can't imagine why."

"Aaron's sarcasm is making its impression on you I see. Hopefully you'll avoid any other unfortunate side effects of his presence. Have you called Inerea to tell her you'll be staying here tonight?"

"I texted her before we left for the cemetery that I would likely be home tomorrow morning."

"Alright then. Leora is in the room next door and I'm

three doors down the hall if you need anything at all. If your injuries keep you up, please don't hesitate to wake me up."

"I doubt I'll have any trouble sleeping tonight. Thank you," I say.

Kyle leaves, the door falling heavy against the frame behind him with the weight of its old mahogany. I don't shudder at the abrupt sound but change out of my ruined, blood-stained clothes into the loose t-shirt and sweatpants Robyn has left out for me on the dresser. I loosen the cords that hold back the curtains on the four-poster bed, drawing them shut as I slip beneath the blanket. My eyes flicker, weary candles sputtering their last for a few seconds before sleep claims me.

Having gone to bed so late, I don't even have a chance to dream before morning comes. Its light doesn't find me behind the heavy red curtains and it's not until I draw them back that I realise it's still night. What, then, woke me? I climb back into bed, roll onto my stomach, and bury my face into the pillow. This is one of the few times I have ever longed for sleep to return. Dreamless, it is one of the few soothing experiences I have had recently, a respite from conscious and subconscious perversion. Despite my wishes, I'm not blessed with any more rest and, even in the blackout dark provided by the heavy red curtains, I feel wide awake.

I don't want the cost of this cause to be your life, Kyle had said, as if perhaps I do.

Perhaps I do. Maybe I am looking for martyrdom because I believe my life is the only thing I have worth giving to the people I care about. Years in the Academy bred instincts within me, ones I feel crawling back into my fingers, ready to spring to action. But there is one that is wholly my own. If it was trained into me, it was done so subliminally. That I would be better off dead is something

I've long believed, though I had forgotten. Even now, with a family and Kyle, the closest person I have ever had to a confidant since the girl Lilith, I still don't consider myself worth keeping alive. And yet human instinct won't let me let go. Perhaps losing my newfound friends and family will be the last thing it takes to break me. I hope it is. Eventually I'll let them down. I've done it before, I know. Yet Kyle has faith in me and this I can't understand. I have proven myself to be a liability who almost gets murdered every time she leaves the house. An insane liability. Inerea and Kyle will live through this, as will Leo, Aaron, and Robyn. I won't let this darkness take them.

Your newfound family's danger. That's what will draw you into this war.

That girl was right. The longer I stay exposed to human interaction the greater the number of people I will die for. Who is she? She's been as far from the forefront of my mind as possible since I dreamt her. And though she was a dream, I know she is real too. She promised to wait for me. She promised I would outlive this torment to meet hers. At that moment, there's a harsh bang on the door, sending me bolt upright.

"Come in," I call out.

Aaron enters at my call, his stormy eyes roving across the room languidly before finding me sitting with my legs tucked under me.

"Can't sleep? You should give the forces of evil a chance to prepare in order to stand a chance against your fearsomeness," he says, perching easily on the edge of my bed.

"Aries himself quivers before me," I answer casually, but am aware of his gaze roving over me so I draw the blanket up to my chin.

"How could he not fall in awe before you," he teases.

He leans back on his elbow, rolling his shoulders back

and looking up at me as if he were the aforementioned Aries in all his glory.

"You've not come with more pancakes by any chance?" I inquire hopefully, intent on changing the subject from any form of Mallory orientated worship.

"So, you admit you share my love of chocolate chip passion fruit pancakes! So few are willing to admit when they're wrong," he says triumphantly, "clearly you're soulmate material."

"I do believe that implies I have a soul," I say, retaining his joking tone but none of his jest.

"Soulless mate?"

"That's more like it."

I unfold my legs from beneath me and fall back onto my pillows, staring up at the ceiling.

"Want me to join you there?"

In an instant he's lying by my side and a sly smile spreads across his face as he looks at me. My body runs cold. I remember waking up. I remember the small bed felt more cramped than usual as I turned over. I remember all the blood that should have run hot in veins but had instead gone cold, caked on the sheets. And the body it came from, prostrate beside me, lain as a purposeful reminder. Do your duty.

"So I've found my way to your heart through food."

Aaron dissolves the past with his playfulness. He plucks my hand from my chest where it still clutches the blanket to my person and presses it to his lips. My stomach drops and crimson flames burst in my cheeks.

"Again implying I have something I don't," I admonish, trying to brush the agony in me aside, "You've found your way to my taste receptors, that's all."

Staring intently into my eyes, he perceives nothing of what's behind them and bursts out laughing.

"What?" I demand, feeling my face flush a deeper

red.

"I'm sorry. Seeing you nervous provokes my sense of mischief," he says, letting go of my hand and propping his head on his hand as he rolls onto his side.

"How very unchivalrous of you," I grumble.

"Indeed, to tease a lady so."

"Sexual harassment aside, did you come here for any reason?"

"Last night got me thinking it's probably a good idea for you to get some combat training under your belt, just in case we find ourselves in another such unprecedented situation. Also, I'm still wired from last night and figured you would be too."

"Given your line of work, considering such situations unprecedented seems something of a misjudgement."

"Are you always going to give me a such a hard time?"

"Sorry, it's my nature. So, will you be training me?" I ask.

"Sadly I'll have to hand your instruction over to far less capable hands. His rudeness aside, Leo is probably the best to teach you out of the four of us. He's better with general weapons knowledge whereas I prefer specialisation. Well, he would be the best excepting Robyn but," he trails off.

"She might accidentally impale me with a spear?"

"I don't think she'd bother to pretend it was an accident," he confesses.

"You're probably right. I'm convinced she'd even do a victory lap around my dead body."

"No, your dead body would be a hurdle in her track and field victory lap. We do it with all our dead. Now come on, you need to learn how to stab things properly."

"I'm not sure I'll be able to do much with this," I say, showing him my still bandaged hand.

"Why didn't you ask Robyn to heal it? Never mind, we've already been over that. Let's go see if Leora's awake. She's much more powerful than Robyn so she can heal it faster. Don't tell Robyn I said that though or I'll be another for the hurdle count."

Rolling over, he swings his legs over the side of the bed and pulls me up after him. He leads me next door and knocks on the door, waiting until Leora's summons us in.

"I figured you would be awake," Leora intones, eyeing me.

She's sitting at a table in the corner over the room, pouring over a butterfly wing delicate book.

"I can't imagine anyone's sleeping right now," I say, thankful for Aaron's body between us. Though she's helped us, I still feel ill at ease near her.

"What can I do for you two?" she asks, setting her book down.

"A healing spell for Mallory's hand," Aaron says.

His playful tone is gone and he assumes the indifference I associate with Leo. She takes no notice of his request and Aaron and I exchange a look. After a few moments of silence, I step out from behind him.

"Of course, don't feel obligated. We'd only want you to do it if you're feeling better," I insist. She snorts and extends a hand to me.

"It will take more than that to wipe me out," Leora replies.

She takes me by the wrist with a gentleness disassociated from her intonation and peels away the bandage to reveal its blood-soaked innards.

"Lueicht, nandirava letai nevorso ni isuazko etev udiyat."

A warm orb of light swells from her palm and she presses it to my wound. My skin tingles uncomfortably for a moment but when she moves her hand away, the deabrueon's bite marks have completely vanished. She inspects her work before discarding the useless bandage in the rubbish.

"Thank you," I say, as she releases me, "What's that spell? Robyn's used it on me before."

"It's our most general healing spell. 'Light, drink the dark of blood and marrow.' It serves to repair the damage of almost any physical wound, but there are spells with greater specificity that serve better," she replies, a remote interest seeping out with the words. She studies my face. "You wouldn't know much magic, would you?"

"Very little, I've only been studying with a friend."

Aaron gives me a curious look but I ignore him.

"I can teach you if you'd like. I felt the enormity of your energy last night when I borrowed it for the shielding spell. You have a lot of raw potential."

"Oh?"

"You're surprised? But you're a Thiel descended of Oviras as well."

"Yes, but I thought most female dragoviks have magical abilities, regardless of which family they're a member of."

Leora gives me a quizzical look before sharing it with Aaron.

"She's living on a need to know basis," he informs her, "We should get going."

"Alright," she says, but her brow furrows more despite her assent. As the door shuts behind us, I turn to Aaron.

"What was that about?"

"Nothing you need to know about," he replies.

"It didn't sound like nothing."

"You're the one who only wanted to know what was

necessary," he sighs.

Our walk towards the entrance is the longest period of time we've been alone without talking.

"Is everything alright?"

"Oh no you don't. Kyle told me about your conversation. I'm not being psychoanalysed and having you uncover unnerving truths about me."

"Are you saying you've something to hide? An Oedipus complex?" I ask, attempting a teasing intonation to lighten the mood. He grimaces.

"I have many things to hide but that isn't one of them."

"Oh so you're open about your desire to murder your father and-"

"I'm going to stop you right there before you leave me with a mental image that leaves me forever tormented."

I hold back. I know the weight of such thoughts.

"I don't mean to psychoanalyse. I just observe and come to conclusions."

"Except when it comes to yourself?"

"Especially when it comes to myself. If you could hear my thoughts you would know that," I say.

"I wish I could hear your thoughts. Perhaps then I might know what would persuade you not to leave us after this is over. You're fun to have around."

"Because I'm easy to tease?"

"Something like that," he says, opening the door we've stopped in front of.

Inside, the floor is padded with blue mats and the opposite wall is opened up by vast arch windows without curtains. A door to the right has been left ajar and from within comes the sound of footsteps. Leo emerges, the only entity in the large empty room.

"Are you sure you put the bolts on the top shelf?"

Robyn calls from the other room.

"Kyle was the one reorganising the storeroom. He said he put them up there," Leo answers, hardly glancing in our direction.

"Well either he lied to piss me off or he has the worst memory. They were on the second shelf," she mutters, appearing in the doorway with her crossbow slung across her back and her hand fisted around some bolts she then tucks into a hip quiver. Her eyes narrow as she spots Aaron and me in the doorway.

"Human delivery," Aaron says, lightly pushing me in front of him.

"I don't think anyone ordered that," Robyn replies, retrieving one of her recently stowed bolts and loading it into her crossbow.

"How threatening," Aaron whispers, his lips hardly a centimetre from my ear.

There's a sudden thwack as the field point impales itself into the bull's eye of one of the four targets lined up on the opposite wall. She takes her time reloading, watching us all the while.

"I'm not going to take her killing me off the table just yet," I whisper back.

"Robyn go be murderous elsewhere and Aaron go harass someone else. I need to teach Mallory how not to die," Leo says.

"Fine with me. I've seen her make an idiot of herself more than enough recently. Aaron, want to come do some outside target practice?" she asks.

"Yeah, it's been awhile," he yawns, "I'll come get you later for pancakes?"

"Whatever remains of me," I murmur.

"Out," Leo says, ushering the two out the door before shutting it sharply behind them. The two barely manage to leap out of the doorway without being hit in the back. "Obviously we don't have enough time to train you so that you can hold your own against a skilled fighter in prolonged battle. Your best chance is to conceal this and use it to surprise your enemy."

He holds out a dagger to me. It's a cold steel tooth that warms only to its victim.

"Literal cloak and dagger," I say, avoiding looking at the blade.

"This will limit the number of chances you have to hit an opponent, because once they know about the blade, they'll regain their advantage. It's important to aim for the body's weak spots."

"Carotid artery, femoral artery or the spleen. Any wound that severs a major artery will lead to death without immediate medical attention," I say, indicating his neck, groin and the left side of his abdomen as I list them with a textbook's indifference towards their mortal vulnerability. It's almost a reflex for my mind to locate these places, but I don't know why. He raises his eyebrows. "Basic biology?"

"For a serial killer maybe."

"You know them well enough yourself," I bite back, my tongue lashing back before I can think.

"I never said I didn't."

He doesn't say any more on the matter of my knowledge, but sheathes the dagger once again. I cannot look at him anymore, my mind sliding into overdrive. Why did that come so naturally?

"Here."

He offers me a blunt, polished wooden replica of a dagger and I take it quickly so he might not have a chance to notice my trembling hand. But his soldier's eyes are trained to observe the smallest indications in body language, prepared to anticipate the enemy with the slightest clue. I don't doubt for a second he's aware of my anxiety, yet with his lack of concern he is kind enough not to mention it.

"What will most likely to happen is that a deabrueon will charge you. Stupid as they are, staying alive is their first priority. Absolutely nothing clouds their ability to fight, no moral convictions, no humane concerns. Nothing but hubris. A deabrueon is lazy, it won't expend more energy than it has to on a kill. The easier the kill the better. If it believes it's going to win, that's your chance to get them. So, instead of having your blade out as soon as it comes for you, it's important you wait until the very last second."

"That doesn't sound very safe, or practical if there are multiple opponents. Once I reveal the blade to one the rest will know I have it." Where is this coming from? Leo holds his lips tight together, gazing curiously at me. "Sorry it just seems like common sense."

"It is, I'm pleased to discover you have some at long last," he replies, "it will make my job a bit easier. You're facing off with a physically powerful non-human entity, safe rarely factors into such situations. There's only safer. As for practicality, I'm afraid there's nothing practical about having an untrained individual in battle. As we plan to protect you, you will likely only ever need to fend off one attacker before we can intervene. So, as long as you hit one of the three locations I've mentioned, the deabrueon won't stand a chance. How about we practice?"

"You want me to stab you?"

"You won't actually be stabbing me. And I won't actually be trying to murder you," he says, "but I won't go easy on you either."

With a swift suddenness, he ducks down slightly and barrels his shoulder into my abdomen, knocking me into the air. I fall hard to the ground and the air is expelled from my lungs. Before I know it, he's upon me. I hit his chest with an uppercut but he catches my hand.

"You're dead."

"Why?"

"You just hit me in the breastbone. Not only am I going to be able to recover from that just as quickly as you recover from the exertion of the blow, but you've just lost your weapon. You have no chance of getting it out. Try again."

He hands me the fake dagger, which I dropped when he grabbed my hand and crouches slightly, circling me. I feel that pull from deep in my gut. The one that tries to remind me of all I'm capable of. It tells me my abilities aren't just about doing injury anymore, they're every bit as much about protection now. I turn my head to follow him but Leo is already pouncing on me. Spinning before he can tighten his grip, I throw my weight behind my shoulder, knocking him to the ground beneath me. This time I make a downwards stroke, bringing the tip of the curved wooden blade to his neck.

"Now you're dead," I breathe.

And I'm not afraid to show him what little bit of my strength I can without scaring him, without spiralling out of control.

"And I had so much hope for my future," he says. Then he grabs my wrists with one hand and plucks the dagger from my grasp. Tossing me aside, he jabs the rounded edge against my abdomen. "But now so are you. Get away as fast as you can once you've dealt a fatal blow. The only wound that would cause almost instantaneous death is a direct hit to the aorta. Understood?"

"Yes."

He helps me to my feet.

"Again."

Over and over, he attacks me, until my fear unravels completely and I'm able to hit one of the three targets without a moment of hesitation.

"Are we done yet?" I pant, standing back up after having hit him successfully in the spleen.

"Not yet."

If that's how he wants it. Instead of waiting for him to make the first move, I give him a kick in the back of his legs so he drops to his knees. Bending over him and wrapping one arm around the front of his chest, I press the false blade against his lower back, just behind the spleen.

"Dead again."

"I was hoping you might take some initiative eventually," he says.

Grabbing hold of my forearm braced against his chest, he twists it and yanks so hard that I find myself hurtling over his head. I land hard on my back in front of him, my vision spotting for an instant.

"Remember, don't give them the chance to hurt you after you've dealt a fatal blow."

"How could I forget?" I groan, reaching my hand beneath me to probe my lower back tenderly.

"I'm sorry," he says, darting around to my side, "are you alright?"

I'm almost too caught off guard by the sincerity of his apology to carry out my plan. I bend my right arm back behind my head and press all my fingers against the mat. Pushing off the ground, I throw my lower body into the air and summersault backwards, landing on my feet. I plant a roundhouse kick hard against his breastbone, sending him sprawling backwards across the floor.

"Christ, are you trying to do permanent damage?" he wheezes.

"You shouldn't check on the people you're trying to murder," I laugh.

He stares at me, his usually flat expression lit by some peculiar glow in his eyes. Out of nowhere he starts laughing to. It's a warm, quiet rumble, pleasant sounding and comforting in itself. I watch him with awe and he stops suddenly when he notices me studying him.

"Do I want to know what that look's about?" he asks, standing up.

"I've just never heard you laugh before. Or be anything other than serious or mildly irritated to be honest."

I'm worried I've offended him for a moment when he doesn't respond right away.

"Sometimes I'm extremely irritated. What, you thought Aaron had a monopoly on humour no doubt?"

His smile has disappeared but the flame is still lit in his eyes.

"I was hoping he didn't. There are only so many sarcastic comments one can take," I say. He walks over to me, taking the fake dagger from me.

"But somehow I have yet to go insane," he replies, tucking a hair behind my ear.

His gaze shifts towards a small white scar near my tragus and I duck my head to avoid his sight. I feel the scar burn as if it were the day I received the blow that left it. Taking me by the chin, Leo turns my face up towards him. He chews the inside of his cheeks as I have done so often when trying to hold back words, agony, rage, and examines the pale line.

"Do you always so blatantly observe someone's imperfections?" I ask, my voice wavering. I feel fragile under his scrutinising gaze.

"I wasn't aware the ability to be strong despite whatever pain you've been through and whatever harm's been done to you was an imperfection," he replies.

His eyes meet mine and an almost painful heat explodes in my chest. He sees a beauty in the scar, that crack in my human disguise.

"It's not strength. You of all people should know

that," I whisper back.

Of all the things I could have said, his surprised expression tells me this is not what he was expecting.

"Why's that?"

I can't bite the inside of my cheeks to hold back the overwhelming words that pour out of me.

"You have a bad habit. I don't know if it started when you were young and it's just become something you can't control. Maybe, like me, you felt lonely and pathetic so you started to put up a bold front, even using verbal abuse to keep people at a distance. Your desire to fight doesn't come from strength but from the belief that you are not allowed to be weak in others' eyes."

Where is this coming from? And why does it feel as though I am speaking as much for myself as him?

He's stilled completely before me, his hand still resting on the side of my face. Its warmth is the only lifelike thing I find in him in that moment. So I don't let him pull it away when he finally begins to breathe again. I place my hand over his to hold it to me because I'm so scared of being the one to let him go as so many let go of me. I'm so scared he'll lose hold of his humanity.

"How is it of all the people I know, even those who I have known my entire life, you are the only one who has ever seen through me?" he murmurs.

"Because I chose to believe I deserved whatever unkindness was given to me for the same reasons you started shutting people out. My resolve to fight comes from a desire to someday earn the compassion I've been given."

"So, from one emotional misfit to another, what do you recommend I do?"

"Become strong by letting others help you. That's what I'm doing by fighting with you."

"Do you intend to help me? Are you not intent on abandoning us and this life as soon as this battle's won and

you leave Aplin Hollow?" His accusation sears through
me and I can no longer hold his gaze. "As I thought. You
want me to ask for help but won't stay to give it."

He lets me go, brushing my hand aside, but with the
same tenderness with which he first touched my cheek.
He walks back into the storeroom. The breeze outside
whispers fast across the glass of the windows. I scrunch
my eyes shut until I hear Leo returning. He's recomposed
himself. He sheathes a real dagger before clipping the
sheath onto two leather straps.

"An arm sheath," he says, "this way you can keep
the dagger hidden but access it easily." He buckles the
straps around my left forearm before pulling my sleeve
back over it.

"Thank you."

"Keep it on you at all times. Especially when we're
not around to protect you," he replies sternly.

I nod, not wanting to tell him that, despite our training with the wooden dagger, I'm afraid I won't be able to
use the real one when the time comes. I can't ask the help
of him he feels he cannot ask of me.

"Now I'm sure Kyle wants to speak to you about last
night. He's been doing research since we got back regarding hints Illarion dropped. I'll take you to him."

He doesn't say another word as we leave the training
room and after how bold I was before, I'm afraid to say
anymore. Does he despise me for comparing us?

For the first time I am taken upstairs. At the top of
the staircase is a massive set of double doors that lead
into a sizeable library. There are no windows as all the
walls are filled with bookshelves. In the far left corner is
Kyle, tucked up in a large leather wing chair that dwarfs
him.

"How did training go?" he asks, perking up as we enter. He has a small, neat pile of volumes beside him, and

a black leather bound tome balanced in his lap.

"You should be on guard of your major arteries," Leo warns, hanging back by the door as I approach Kyle.

The closer I get to him the more I feel my fluttering heart calm in my chest. I want to kneel beside his chair and lay my head in his lap but refrain, seating myself in the chair opposite instead.

"That's good to hear," he says, before frowning, "sort of."

"It's good news until you piss her off. I'll leave you two now. I should probably get some training in myself." Leo pulls the door shut behind him, abandoning us to silence.

Kyle glances back down at the page, drawing his finger like a snail trail after the word he's reading. He sighs at the book, massaging the space between his brows, before shutting it.

"He wasn't too tough on you, was he?"

"Potential permanent back injuries aside, I should be okay," I assure him, but I feel my cheeks warming with the memory of the training room.

"He's hard on everyone, so don't take it personally," he says, misinterpreting the colouring in my cheeks.

"So, what have you been researching?" I ask, attempting to derail the unwanted train of thought I've been left with.

"When you see it, whatever form it may manifest in, you will know it for what it truly is. That's what Illarion said to us about the Vaerdiexes stone. I know it's useless to look at these," he sighs, gesturing to the books, "they're all about the little known origins of the stones. I didn't even know they could manifest in different forms. We can't very well go around looking at every pebble."

"Going through your driveway alone would take a few weeks at least."

He drums his fingers on his arm rest, staring past me.

"Perhaps it would be best to ask Leora more about the spell. In what capacity the stone is required."

"Do you want me to go get her?"

He shakes his head.

"She said she would come by later anyways. I wanted to know more about the spell book she used last night. Where she came by it for one thing." I lean back in my chair, leaving him to his softening voice and contemplative nature. Something about the room leaves me feeling drowsy. My body urges me to slide down and curl up in the seat of the chair to fall asleep. "Are you alright? You seemed a bit tense when you came in."

"It's nothing."

"You're sure? If Leo said something that's upset you, you can tell me. He has a bad habit of doing that."

"No, really. The whole situation is just," I pause, shaking my head at him, "it has me shaken, and a bit tense."

This isn't untrue. It's just that right now, what's really setting me on edge, it the inability to get that look on Leo's face out of my head. It was so cruel of me to speak his darkest secrets for him. I would never want anyone to do that for me and I had no right to do so to him.

"Likewise, but you're still handling this remarkably well. It's not every person you can go up to, tell her you're a mythological creature, and then have her believe you," he says, leaning across to me to squeeze my hand. The large book in his lap, left forgotten, slips to the floor where it lands with a resounding thud. His eyes turn away from me. But I know why I believed him. I've known all along.

"To be honest, it wasn't as big a leap of faith as it may seem," I start.

"Oh?"

"Remember that recurring dream I told you about?

In it, there's a house filled with bodies, and the man who put them there, Thaddeus, cannot find me. He transforms into a great red dragon and leaves me alone with the dead. When Aaron found me that day and told me about, about all of this, I was willing to believe it because I must have subconsciously remembered the dream, and my mind was trying to tell me what I was all along. It just seemed too absurd not to reconcile these two occurrences.'

Kyle doesn't reply until the book is balanced assiduously in its rightful place in the pile beside him according to its corresponding size.

"I'm sorry. I can't imagine how terrifying it must have been to realise that something in that dream might have truth in it. Perhaps it was a premonitory dream," he suggests.

"You mean it could be a glimpse at the future?"

If that's the case, then the girl I dreamt of may indeed be real. Perhaps she is truly the threat she promised to be.

"Not exact reproductions of what is to come, but abstract visualisations. No matter how precise in detail or lifelike a premonitory dream may seem, it is nearly all symbols to be interpreted. Illarion spoke of a last gift that will come to you when you need it most. Perhaps he meant one of these dreams."

"Who knows. He certainly enjoyed vagueness."

At that moment, the door opens and Leora's ribbon slim figure is illuminated by the light of the hallway. Her hair seems on fire, golden at the edges, until the door shuts behind her and it goes dull again.

"Good evening, I trust you're feeling well," Kyle says with a smile. He gestures to the seat beside me. "We were just discussing our conversation with Illarion and were hoping you might clarify something regarding the spell you have."

"What might that be?" she inquires, seating herself.

She crosses her legs and holds her hands in her lap, shutting us out with her body language. All the while her eyes move slowly between the two of us. Yet for all her scrutiny she seems softer than when I came into her room. She readjusts herself in her seat, angling herself towards me ever so slightly.

"What is the stone's use in the spell?"

"Oh," she says, and there's a near imperceptible change in her demeanour, the meaning of which I cannot interpret. "Since one cannot wield a Vaerdiexes stone as a weapon, its purpose is to imbue its energy into a weapon temporarily. After the spell is complete, the first wound inflicted by the chosen weapon will release the soul shattering power of the stone into the individual on whom the blade falls."

"Does it have to be fatal?"

"No. Even the smallest scratch will suffice, so it's important for the wielder to be incredibly careful as not to harm anyone else. Keeping it in a scabbard up until its point of use should suffice in that regard. Does that clarify everything?"

"Yes. Unfortunately, Illarion's left us with the not so small task of finding the stone. Only Mallory or I will be able to recognise it."

"Then he'd most likely hide it in a place you've been before and will go again. Our leaders so rarely make anything easy for the rest of us," she says, her nostrils flaring and lips curling upwards at the end with an ever so slight unpleasantness.

"Yet we serve them to serve everyone else," he replies.

His voice has dropped to a cool monotone. She smiles sweetly in return, an unnatural expression on her.

"Our sworn duty."

There's a moment of heavy languor, their eyes trained on one another.

"If you'll excuse me, I should speak to Leo about which weapon would be best for this spell," he says.

Leora nods at him, turning her head slightly to watch him leave. When the door shuts, she looks back at me and, though I was about to follow Kyle out, her gaze holds me fast.

"Did Illarion say anything else of interest?" she inquires.

"Not pertaining to the spell."

"You and Kyle were very quiet about your conversation with your creator upon our return. I hope you don't feel you can't speak to me just because I'm not so close to the Caverlys."

"Not at all. To be honest I would hardly consider myself the one to dispense with information, I have so little of it. But I was, however, wondering about something you seemed to know."

"By all means, ask away."

"You said that I had magic potential because I'm a Thiel, but refrained from saying anymore once Aaron spoke. After we left, Aaron seemed off."

"You're wondering what I meant by that and perhaps what has little Aaron Baeor so on edge? It's simple really. The first three men transformed into dragoviks were of the names Thiel, Velemir, and Ovira. Because of their immediate connection with the fire of the phoenix, isuazko runs strongest in their family lines. Being descended of an Ovira and a Thiel, it goes without saying that you're something akin to royalty."

"That's not exactly what I was expecting. It doesn't seem like the sort of information that Aaron wouldn't want me to know."

Hadn't they told me this already? Not in so many words but when they said I was the only candidate to take Thaddeus' place.

"Perhaps not that fact itself but the discoveries it would lead you to." Her voice is hushed to a whisper and she leans closer to me. Her eyes sweep my face. The cold drop in her voice pervades my being and a shiver runs through me.

"Oh?"

"You might begin to wonder why there are no Thiels other than yourself to be heard of. Illarion, having no children of his own, made those three men his successors. Thiel, being the eldest, was the rightful heir to the throne. Millennia later, Thaddeus Velemir desires the throne. He has an army and support, enough to take down the Onyevaras. The only ones, in fact, who could have rallied enough followers to bolster the Onyevaras' waning claim to power were the Thiels. Worse still would be if they decided they wanted the throne. So he hunted and killed every last one of them. With exception."

"He killed them over the prospect of their opposition?" I breathe.

My back is drawn taut against my spine, my entire body tense. I can't bear to look at Leora. She speaks each word with ready indifference, as if the tale of bloodshed isn't about the Thiels. Isn't about my family.

"That and it's believed he held a grudge against one in particular who married the woman he loved. It's said Thaddeus thoroughly enjoyed killing him. But it wasn't until it came to killing her that he was driven insane. Not his guilt for what he and the Vernis Lanin intended to do, but some girl who broke his heart. Men can be ever so foolish when it comes to love. But I suppose so can women."

"What was her name."

"Hm?"

"Her name."

I think I already know it. I think it's lodged in my throat and my memory where it's been held as lovingly as she must have been held in Thaddeus' mind.

"Regan, I believe. Inerea's daughter, and your mother."

No. It was never simply a dream of symbols far removed from my own life, but the shadow of a living memory. I was there that day he killed them all. I was there the day my family was massacred. I was the reason he found out her hiding place. My parents never sent me to the Academy to be alone; they gave their lives to keep me from cruelty.

"I have to go."

I hardly hear my own voice through the haze that clouds my mind. All that time I spent holding back forgiveness for the non-existent act of abandoning me.

Your parents left you. They were as sickened by you as all of humanity will be.

Diane lied. She took what breaks a child's heart most and used it against me.

"Mallory," Leora says, standing up.

I dash past her, out of the room, down the main staircase and through the front door.

She's so beautiful. One day she'll grow to be brave. Won't you, Mallory? Even if I'm not with you.

Those words. Did she speak them to me?

Regan.

My breaths overlap, unable to finish themselves before the next washes over them. Each one draws sickness into my stomach until I feel as though it can hardly hold its contents back from inching up my throat. Resting my hands on my knees, I lower my head until the moon disappears from my line of vision. He stole my family from me.

"Hey, moron, what are you doing out here," Robyn calls out. I jump at the sound of her voice.

She walks towards me, followed closely by Aaron.

"I-I-"

No, words don't come easily. Words don't come close to expressing what the guttural cry I unleash does.

"What happened?" Aaron demands, running towards me.

"I said only what I need to know. I know I asked that of you. But how-how," I gasp uncontrollably. He grabs onto my forearms, trying to keep me steady.

"Tell me what's going on."

"Get off!" I cry, the power of my voice searing my throat. I tug against his grip.

"Tell me."

"Why? You didn't have the decency to tell me about my parents!" I scream. I see his face in the white of moonlight falter like its dwindling moments before morning. He drops my arms and I step back. "You knew Leora would tell me about them if she had explained what she meant when we were in her room. You knew that and you told her to keep it from me all the same. You don't decide what parts of my own past I get to know. I've had enough fucked up people do that for one lifetime. Why? Why did you think it was up to you?"

"I didn't, I just knew you didn't deserve to find out that way. We all did. You'll notice no one else was jumping at the opportunity to tell you. Except that damn witch, and I'll kill her myself," he snarls.

His face has become livid, grey eyes sharpened to daggers. Then he finds me again, amongst all the anger we both harbour, and his face crumples in pain.

"Forgive us please, forgive me. Even though what I've done is inexcusable, it's not something I could bear to watch you find out."

My eyes widen at the softness of his voice. I never expected that of him, such anguish from one who's always full of liveliness.

"Why didn't anyone tell me?" I plead softly.

"Kyle and I thought maybe we could get through all of this without you ever having to find out. We wanted to spare you the pain of losing your family again," he whispers. His arms wrap around me and he pulls me tightly against his chest. My body fills the cage of his willingly. "So please, know I didn't mean to keep this from you for any reason other than your own wellbeing."

"Okay."

I feel his hot breath on the top of my head as he sighs with relief. I open my eyes to his collarbone. Everything of the outdoors is obscured by him. Turning my head, I rest my cheek against him and tuck my head under his chin. I need to get away from this. Just for a night. The darkness falls dewy on our shoulders and I think, surprised with myself, of whose arms I most want to be in. To feel human and young again.

"I need to make a call."

"Okay, shall I leave you?" he asks.

I nod, my throat thickening with anger and sadness. He steps away from me, drawing his arms from around me. He runs his arms from my shoulders to my hands, giving them a gentle squeeze. As he retreats into the house, I see Robyn once more. Her face is painted so clearly with hatred and it's all for me. If only I could tell her it's not him I want.

Turning away from her, I dial Chloe's number.

Chapter XXIII.

After a few rings, Chloe answers, dazed but not irritated. She can hear the nearing onslaught of tears no doubt.

"Mallory, what's wrong?"

It had escaped my notice, until then, that it was two in the morning.

"I have a bit of an odd favour to ask."

She doesn't ask why I want his address at about two in the morning. She doesn't ask what's happened because she can hear the pain in my voice and that sort of anguish explains itself.

Aaron doesn't ask why he's taking me to a different address than Inerea's home. He doesn't ask who I'm going to see and I don't know if I could tell him or explain why John is the one I want to see right now. After my phone call, we just get in the car and start driving.

Over the duration of the car ride, I'm overcome with varying emotions. Anger at the Leo, Kyle, Aaron, and Robyn for not telling me. Anger at Inerea for never explaining what happened to my parents, though I'm not surprised she kept yet another secret from me. An absolute loneliness known only to those who have never and will never know their parents. Parents who loved me; Regan, my mother, had died protecting me. I switch these thoughts off. It's the only way to survive the car journey without screaming or crying. I redirect my thoughts to John.

As I walk up the path to his front door, I settle on irritation. At myself for being so fixated on someone who made it clear he doesn't want me. At him for being so strange the last time we met. I can't help myself; in times of emotional distress, the brain will sometimes focus on that which is entirely disassociated from the situation. It's self-preservation. Instead of ringing the bell, I bang on the door. It takes some time for him to answer, unsurprisingly given the hour, but I'm done caring about coming across as a nutter.

When he comes to the door, he stands for a moment, swaying slightly in his exhaustion. He's dressed in flannel pyjama trousers and no top, his face hidden in the darkened hallway. I hear Aaron pull away as John rubs the sleep from his eyes. I fleetingly wonder what he must make of this.

"Mallory?"

Why isn't he furious I've woken him up? He only sounds concerned and it makes me unbelievably angry. I push past him into the living room.

"I know," I begin, rounding on him. He takes a step back to narrowly avoid being barrelled into. "I know I have no right to demand answers of you. But today's been more than I can take. Hell, the past week have been more than anyone could take. And I need something sane, something trivial. This feels normal."

"Coming to my house at three in the morning feels normal?" he asks incredulously, glancing around the living room nervously.

He shuffles along the wall, shutting an open door. Is there someone else here? Yet, he doesn't ask me to leave, just awaits my explanation.

"Granted my perception of normal is presently skewed. But this is a boy girl thing. Or a man woman thing? Who cares. It's commonplace."

"You're really sweeping me off my feet here," he replies, quickly regaining his wit through his exhaustion.

It throws me off guard. There he is, looking utterly gorgeous with his arms crossed, slightly perplexed and slightly amused. And here I am, a blithering idiot and I remember what it felt like when he kissed me so without thinking, I cross the small space between us and press my lips against his. In an instant his arms are back around me, reminding me I was not so mad to think he had felt for me too, that he wanted me too. He groans softly against my lips, pulls away and rests his forehead against mine, shaking his head.

"Mallory," he breathes my name, and it pillows out of his mouth in a cloud of warmth and toothpaste. "It's not a boy girl thing. It's an older man and a teenage girl thing. Even if you're eighteen, it's just."

He falters, shaking his head again but holding me tighter. We stand there for minutes, pressed closely together, until he steps back. His gaze sweeps over me and I can see it's composed of longing and distress.

"So why did you kiss me in the first place, if you knew nothing could happen?"

He runs his fingers across a newly formed stubble that was not there last I saw him. His lips part than close again.

"Why did I kiss you? You mean why did I stupidly, stupidly fall in love with you before we'd ever even spoken? You've never seen yourself read but it was something to behold, an image to fall for. I've never seen someone so engrossed that they didn't notice me, in my distraction, collide with a bookshelf. Half the room rushed to check I was okay, the other half looked up from their books but you, you couldn't be drawn back into this world. Not until you were ready. And I knew I wanted to be in whatever universe had taken you."

"Oh."

This was far from what I had expected. Call me crazy for waking him up, yes. Tell me I'm reading too much into what was happening, maybe. But falling in love with me? I lower myself onto the sofa behind me.

"Oh."

"You see now," he says, coming to kneel in front of me, "why finally being that close to you, thinking it was possible you were interested in me too, I couldn't help myself. I had to allow myself one indiscretion."

He takes my hands and kisses them. I look down at his face as he turns his earnest eyes back up to my face. They glitter, golden and radiant. As someone who has recently been in the presence of a king, I see something of that Illarion's humbled regal nature in him. How could I not crown him a king too? I slip down on to the floor with him.

"You're a moron," I tell him, not rightly knowing why.

"Is that so?" he chuckles and I want to purr, pressed against his chest as it rumbles.

"You could have just told me what you were concerned about."

"Mallory, I didn't anticipate ever speaking to you again before you went to university, let alone telling you how I felt. What were the chances anything could happen anyway? What with the age difference and you leaving town, everything seemed hopeless."

He dots the top of my head with small kisses, stroking my hair.

"And do we have to figure that out now?"

"No," he says, meeting my gaze again, "I suppose not. What would you have me do instead?"

Now I'm stumped. I want to cry in his arms, tell him what I've been through this past week. Tell him about the fresh loss of my parents. I want to pull him to me and kiss him, and finally feel loved by someone exactly as I want to be. I draw him closer, kiss him softly then pull him to his feet. This is hasty, yes. But sometimes there isn't time for everything in between. Just the beginning and the end. He's right, this goes nowhere after tonight.

* * *

Kyle calls early in the morning. Luckily, I'm already awake so I answer before the phone can wake John. Slipping into the living room I shut the door behind me.

"Hello," I say, anxiously.

I'm expecting there will be hell to pay for going off on my own last night, even if Aaron sanctioned it by dropping me off. But instead, I am greeted by Kyle's equally anxious voice.

"Mallory, I'm so, so, sorry. Please just come back and we can talk."

"I'm not mad Kyle," I say, shaking my head, "I was, but I understand. It's like you said, I couldn't be told what I don't remember, it has to come in its own time. Besides, it was Inerea's place to tell me, not yours. Leora handled last night horrifically."

"I know, I'm furious with her, Inerea too."

He goes silent for a while and I sense it's time for a change in topic.

"What happened?"

"Nothing! No, I promise, we're all fine. I was worried about you though. It's just, we found out Leora doesn't have the whole spell to infuse a blade with the power of the Vaerdiexes stone. She failed to mention she only found half the page."

"Shit, of course she did," I murmur, and I can hear John stirring in the next room. "What does this mean?"

"It means we're damn lucky the bellatoja are on our side. Alastair has offered us access to the Library Between, and hopefully we can find it there. Mind you, it's just the two of us. He's wary of the other's still."

"The Library Between?"

"The Hirutere's collection of manuscripts, books,

and artefacts. It's really something of an honour to be allowed in it, dragoviks are rarely granted access. It exists between the home of the angeleru and Earth."

"Sorry, are we travelling to another dimension today?" I ask, just as the door opens and John steps out.

He's back in his flannel trousers and his long hair is messily tucked behind his ears. He crosses the room and wraps his arms around me, kissing my forehead before going into the kitchen. I watch him, but he shows no signs of having heard my bizarre quip made moments ago.

"Yes…" Again, his voice has gone anxious. "Mallory, if I'm asking too much just tell me."

"You're not, don't worry. I will just never cease to be amazed by what we get up to."

"Okay. Well not to rush you but the bellatoja want to leave sooner rather than later."

"No worries. Aaron knows where I am. I'll be ready when you get here," I say.

John switches on the coffee machine then turns to smile at me. So much for just last night. I feel my heart turning into a sopping puddle when he looks at me like that. Must not get distracted now.

"Alright I'll see you soon."

He hangs up and I slide my phone into my pocket.

"Everything okay?" John asks pouring two cups of coffee. The steam rolls off, drawing itself up around his hands.

"Yeah, just a friend needs my help with something so I'll need to go soon," I reply, sitting down on the sofa.

He crosses over to me, spilling some scalding coffee on his hand by accident.

"It's fine," he says, brushing off my concern as he sits by me. Running his hand through my hair, he plucks my hand with his other one. "Thank you for barging into my house at three in the morning."

I go scarlet at his teasing.

"Yeah, sorry about that," I mutter, ducking my head, "It's just been a crazy week and I really wanted to see you."

"Anything you want to talk about?"

I shake my head before resting it on his shoulder. Light trickles in-between the blinds, warming my thighs. We sit curled up on the sofa until my phone dings, letting me know Kyle is outside. I throw my jacket on before John offers me my half-drunk coffee.

"Ninety percent water, ten percent coffee, right?"

"Do you remember everything?" I laugh, quickly swigging down the remainder of the cup's contents.

"Everything you say or do," he replies kissing my head. He walks me to the door than pauses. "Will I see you again before you go?"

I hesitate a moment, glancing down at his hands.

"It's okay if you don't want to."

"It's not that," I reply hastily. "I really do, it's just not something I can guarantee."

He nods, tucking a strand of my hair behind my ear.

"Call me," he says softly, "if it's something you can."

He steps back from the door, his face unreadable. Without another word, I open the door and step out into the morning light. I see Kyle waiting in the car and glance over my shoulder but John's already shut it behind me. Crossing the front lawn, I climb into the passenger seat, closing the door with perhaps a little more force than is strictly necessary.

"Everything okay?" he asks, putting the car in drive.

"Just, men," I reply, covering my face with my hand.

And then, for some inexplicable reason, we both start laughing. I snort, feel tears welling in my eyes from the non-existent hilarity of the situation. But, of course, it's absurd, amongst everything that's happening, for Kyle to be picking me up from what's effectively a booty call.

"That hardened to life already?" Kyle chuckles, as the hysteria finally dies.

"Men will do it to you, I'm telling you. Between Aaron's shenanigans and John's, I'm a shell of a woman."

"Hm, yes I noticed Aaron's apparent fixation with you. Don't worry, it should abate with time."

"God grant us time."

"It's nice to hear you say that for a change," he says, flicking his indicator on before taking a right turn.

"So, are we driving to this place?"

He rolls his eyes at my poor attempt at humour.

"One does not simply drive to the Library Between. No, we're going to the public library."

"Funny, I don't recall seeing any ancient manuscripts or artefacts at the Aplin Hollow public library," I reply.

"Every library is a gate to the Library Between if you know which book to read. The bellatoja will meet us there."

"Well, it's nice to feel so outnumbered."

He raises his eyebrows at me.

"I think they're beyond trying to pull anything. They want Thaddeus gone as much as we do."

He parks outside the library and I follow him in, grateful knowing I won't have to encounter John in front of him. It's hard not to laugh at the sight of the bellatoja. Clearly uncomfortable in such a public place without their weapons, their bulky frames seem to overcrowd the area. They huddle together, glancing around nervously.

"About time," Alistair says, shaking his head at us. He has a smaller party with him than usual, for which I am grateful. His numbers felt overwhelming when we had the other three with us, let alone now it's just Kyle and me. We follow him to the back of the library where he lays his hand on a dusty book that I don't notice until he touches it. "Ready?"

Kyle takes my hand and all the bellatoja join hands as well. Waiting until the link is made all the way from me to him, Alistair pulls on the book, and the world dissolves.

We're at the top of a sandstone staircase. Behind us is nothing but stone walls and a single wooden door. I look down to the bottom of the steps but see nothing below. My stomach does a flip.

"Kyle," I say nervously, "where are we?"

"On our way there," he assures me, but I don't see how plummeting to our certain death will get us to the library.

We trot down the stairs in pairs until we reach a small landing. One by one the bellatoja jump off and I turn to Kyle in a panic. Surely he cannot expect me to do the same? I watch their heads disappear below the landing until it's just Kyle and me left on the landing.

"Ready? Jump as high as you can."

"What? No!"

But I feel him pulling me upwards so I do as he says. We jump over the side and our bodies plummet. Oh god. I open my mouth to scream but suddenly I summersault, the wind knocked out of me. I feel myself rising, as if still mid jump, before we rise above the edge of another landing where the bellatoja have gathered. One reaches out, pulling me onto the platform at the base of another staircase. I look behind us and see the staircase we had just been on, upside down.

"What the hell," I gasp, looking back in awe.

"Only way into the library. Unless you live in the City Between. Then you can just use the front door," one of the bellatoja says.

"How novel," I grumble.

Several of the bellatoja exchange grins, which I suspect are at my expense. I follow them up the stairs to a door identical to the one on the other staircase. Alistair opens it and steps through, vanishing into a bright light.

"Ready?" Kyle asks.

"Does it matter if the answer is no?" I reply.

He laughs, pulling me after him. We're swallowed by the light before stepping out into the largest room I have ever seen. I gasp.

Towering stories and stories above us are bookshelves, ladders running closely up them. There are sporadically placed platforms in the upper levels that seem to shift of their own accord, slowly gliding along the breadth of the bookshelves. I watch as a book flaps past us before nestling itself between two others on a shelf. It is without a doubt the most beautiful room I've ever seen. Rich dark brown wood with a hint of cherry stains panels the walls and floor. The bookshelves are made of the same wood and, glancing over the banister of the balcony we're on, I see they're laid out in no particular order but seem to form some sort of intricate maze. The ladders rest on brass rails that run the length of the bookshelves.

"Holy shit," I breathe and Kyle nods at my assessment.

"Told you it was an honour."

We follow the bellatoja past a long line of bookshelves, down a set of stairs and over to a ladder which takes us to the very bottom floor of the library. Leading us over to a massive circular desk populated by several men and women, Alistair leans over it, grinning at one of the women.

"Hello Matilda."

"Alistair," the young woman replies sulkily. She has long straight blonde hair, and sharp golden eyes, not at all like John's warm ones. "I'm shocked to see you brutes in here. Not come to steal more of the library's resources?"

"Confiscate," he retaliates, "some of the darker materials."

"Like I said," she replies, narrowing her eyes.

"We're looking for spell books related to the Vaerdiexes stones. Oh, and we need two visitors passes. Absolute access."

He winks at me, inciting another dirty look from Matilda. I want to assure her I am in no way a co-conspirator of anyone who would desecrate what I can only call a sacred space but feel Kyle squeezing my hand.

"Names?"

"Mallory Thiel and Kyle Caverly."

A few of the other librarians glance up and Matilda gives us an appraising glance, tainted with mild interest.

"Dragoviks?"

"That's right."

"It must be a special case indeed that has you working with dragoviks rather than killing them for a change."

I feel Kyle's hand tense in mine.

"All the more reason for you to hurry up with their guest passes." He grins menacingly at her. "We wouldn't want any bloodshed."

She stands up, on the verge of saying something, but instead flips her hair and stalks off. She returns with two metal rectangles and passes them to us. I glance down to see my name engraved on it followed by the words imminent murder victim. Evidently, Kyle's says the same, for I hear him gulp beside me.

"Charming," I sigh, "do all of you have such great senses of humour?"

She smiles at me, genuinely amused.

"Dragovician lore and spell books are on the thirty-second basement floor. Might have to go into the restricted section for anything on the Vaerdiexes stones. And be careful," she calls after us, "those books are thousands of years old!"

"Yeah, yeah," Alistair says, leading the way.

At the other end of the hall is a gold grate in front of an elevator. We file in before one of the bellatoja pulls the grate shut behind us. Alistair swipes his own metal card before punching in the number thirty-two. With a jerk, the elevator drops a few feet, pauses, then begins to ease down. I watch floors dissolve from view as we descend deeper into the library. No one says anything but the bellatoja behind me shifts in place, shouldering me. I'm not sure the force with which he does so is an accident. Finally, we come to a stop.

"Stay here," Alistair orders two of the bellatoja, "make sure we're not disturbed." I find his order unnerving for some reason, and I'm certain Kyle does too because he draws closer to me. "It's probably best we split up."

Kyle opens his mouth to protest but I shake my head at him. He must see as clearly as I do that we're on their turf. What little negotiating power we had back in Aplin Hollow is now gone. Eager to get away from Alistair and the others, I make my way to the back corner. I'm equally as eager to get a look at some of the books, so start sliding a heap of them off immediately.

Battle Magic: How to Slay a Dragovik in Dragon Form.

"Delightful," I mutter, reading the title of the first book and slotting it back into its place.

"There's all manner of terrifying books down here, for dragoviks and angeleru alike." I jump at the unfamiliar voice behind me. One of the bellatoja is looking over my shoulder at the book I just put away. "Might want to keep that one from Alistair."

He has dark brown shoulder length hair and green eyes that light when he smiles at me. Despite his attempt at humour, I don't smile back. I feel the same keen distrust I feel with all bellatoja.

"Killian," he says, shaking my hand without invitation.

"Charmed, I'm sure," I reply coldly, deciding to take a leaf out of Robyn's book. I turn my back to him, sifting through the books in my hands before restoring them to their shelf.

"And here I thought you and Kyle were the friendly ones of your bunch."

"We are, but you really ought to consider the measuring stick you're using."

"True, Robyn's a hostile little one isn't she."

"I wonder why, what with your kind constantly threatening to stamp us out of existence." I glance down at the next book.

A History of Illarion's Great Acts.

The Legend of the Phoenix.

"We're not all like that you know."

"When I see evidence to the contrary, I'll let you know. Until then, I'll refrain from befriending any of you. Excuse me."

He steps in my path.

"These won't be of any use. It's what's in there you want," he says, nodding over to a massive barred door that looks like that of a prison cell. He leads me over and winks before swiping his metal card under a reader. It lights up blue and the door pops open. I hesitate before following him in.

"What's the point of having these doors if anyone can get in," I inquire.

"Not just anyone. My father's head librarian," Killian answers, casting his glance over a book on a podium with a fine layer of dust over it. "I wanted to follow in his footsteps but, I was born a bellatoja."

"What do you mean?" He's piqued my interest now.

"Well, most angeleru are born with the usual powers

of our kind. Prolonged life, faster healing abilities. But some of us are born with other powers that set a precedent for our place in society. I was born a bellatoja, with supernatural speed and strength. Avikas are born with something like a witch's ability, but only to manipulate reality. They can't cast spells or anything."

"So, you can't do what you want because of what you were born?" He shrugs, taking a book from a shelf. "That's totally fucked up."

Killian snorts, inhaling a large quantity of dust before sneezing multiple times.

"Thanks for that. And yeah, I'd say so. But I've got no choice. I've got to serve my people as they see fit, haven't I?" He scans the table of contents of the book before putting it back on the shelf. "Criminal records."

"Fun." I sidle over to him. Seeing as he's attempting to be friendly, perhaps I should use it to my advantage and get some much desired information. "Have you ever heard of the Academy?"

He raises an eyebrow, glancing sideways at me.

"I have. Why?"

"What – what was it?"

Finally I have brought myself to ask the dreaded question. The door to the beginning of my past has been opened.

"From what I heard you went there, surely you already know? Or do you just want an outsider's opinion?"

I nod, unable to answer. I stare blankly ahead at the spines of the books but cannot make out their titles.

"It was an institution that took and trained orphaned supernatural creatures in dark arts. Dragoviks, common witches, all manner of monster were kept there."

All manner of monster. So that's how you see me? Despite your friendly disposition. I look at his face but he doesn't seem to realise what he let slip.

"And a girl who could manipulate a black matter, command it, what sort of monster would she be?"

He freezes.

"I'm sorry, what?"

"She could conjure and manipulate a black matter, like it was an extension of herself," I say, caught off guard by the change in his tone. His voice is low and serious when he speaks again.

"You're certain?"

"Yes, why?"

"I should…I need to go," he says abruptly, scratching his stubble.

He hurries back through the door, glancing both ways before disappearing around the corner of the bookshelf. I stare at the place he vanished for some time before turning back to the books. Whatever this is about, it cannot be so pressing as Thaddeus. I reach out, rest a finger on the top of a book and let out an ear-splitting scream.

Part V

Chapter XXIV.

One day I woke up and a god was in my head. He was in everything. Mallory, listen to me. I'm trying to show you how this whole fucking mess began. I'm trying to explain that I was not born evil even if that's what I became. Was it what I became? Sometimes I doubt the malevolence others ascribe to me.

A god in one's head can lead to one of two things. You become the prophet or the mad man. And my little angel I went stark raving mad. Not at first. No, no it took some time for that. It took betrayal on all fronts.

It started with her, Regan. No, see they were wrong, I never loved her. She was a friend that was all. An old and dear friend. I'll try to make this as concise as possible, and maybe one day I'll better be able to piece it all together but, for now, this is how it began.

I woke. With. A. God. In. My. Head. It felt like the weight of a whole fucking pantheon but it was just one. And I knew he had chosen me for a righteous destiny. No, I'm not deluded. You've felt his voice too so you know this is possible. He is the first and last principle we live by. Vaerdiexes. He chose me to restore his beloved people back to Dragovicia. See it was his phoenix who Illarion had saved, his familiar, and he always honoured that kindness. First by stealing the Basilisk eggs of Alastar. No not that absolute toss-pot bellatoja. The god, Alastar. His familiar, a creature of damp and water, the Basilisk. And Vaerdiexes stole some of its eggs, imbued them with the fire of the phoenix and presented to Illarion dragon eggs. So, we came, like the sudden and violent crack of atoms, into being.

Water. Fire. Those absolute antitheses inside one beast. How were we ever meant to stay sane? Little angel, I ask you because you seem the closest to sanity in our kind I've ever seen. I'm asking! No, no you can't answer, not like this. Prostrate on the library floor, screaming as I tell you my story. It's kind of like having him in your head. Wholly. You don't know that feeling yet, perhaps you never will.

It started with Regan and how she loved me. Yes, your mother loved me. Not your dear father who pined away for her. I'll show you.

I am sitting by the river trying to think how to get a god out of my thoughts. See he's telling me I was born to rule Dragovicia and I don't want to believe it because, hand on my heart I am a simple man who doesn't know what he wants yet. But I know it's not that. The water rushes fast, glutted on a spring rain, swallowing rocks. Regan approaches. She is one of the few I have told about the god's voice. She is the only, in fact. That is how much I trusted her before. Before. *He shudders. I feel him shuddering in my mind. It rattles my thoughts.* See I'm trying to tell you but I keep getting caught up in these things I haven't thought about in so long.

She sat by me awhile then kissed me. I told her no, I did not love her. Imagine telling the most beautiful woman in the world you don't love her? Well, that was before you, my angel. I didn't know it was possible to improve on Regan's physical perfection. But she didn't have your eyes, so like the water that tempers my madness. You are the cool rushing stream I could just dive in, drown in.

She began to cry, eyes swelling with tears and I went to wrap my arms around her because, see she was a dear friend and I did love her, but not as I love you, no. Sud-

denly she was furious. She looks like you when you're angry, all blazing and fire. Wrath. There's no other word for
it. And before I knew it, I was pinned down, my hands
bound to the earth and she was unbuckling my belt and
climbing on top of me oh you think it only happens to
women but let me tell you they are just as capable, just
as capable. And she climbed on top of me and I was not
resolute no I was weak. And that is how Isabrand came to
be. That is how I came to be like this.

She left me on the river bank. My bindings did not
undo themselves until the sun was gone and they could
feed on its light no more. I didn't know how to move. No,
I couldn't begin to move. I was seventeen.

I'm telling you this because above all others you need
to understand. Try, try to understand. The truth is something I want to give you, and I can guarantee it, unlike
everyone else who has lied like it's breathing, lied cease-
lessly to you.

See, they told you I loved her, and I did not.

See, they told you I was hellbent on gaining power,
but I was not.

See, they told you I wanted your father dead out of
jealousy but I had nothing to do with his death. Nothing.
By that time, I was just a figure head for the Vernis Lanin.

I will not lie now and say I didn't kill your mother.
You remember it. I wish I could forget it. But by then I
was too far gone.

Now Regan is swollen with her child and she ac-
cuses me of raping her. Why wouldn't they believe her?

She is a good girl, a very good girl, beloved by everyone. Her mother is a powerful member of the Onyevaras, yes Inerea. Another thing she never told you. And there is me. A boy who claims to hear the voice of a god. What is one more act of insanity? They imprison me. Take me away from my mother who is the only one who believes I am good. It was my father who was tasked with torturing me.

Okay yes, I will not deny the Vernis Lanin had already been conceived by this time. Do you want to know what our intention was at first? Simply to go back to Dragovicia. I was tired of the false promises of the Onyevaras and Hirutere. They would never have let us go home. My father knew this was all I wanted, that I meant no harm and wished to go peacefully but he didn't care. Parents are not what we think them to be, are they. Your mother certainly was not.

Well he used every form of torture imaginable to break my resolve. He had avikas distort what I saw of reality until the damage was irreparable. He had witches curse me. He even brought dear, dear Diane, a friend of his, to help. But it was no good. I would not admit to the treason they accused me of, to the rape they accused me of because I had not committed them. And it was there the seed of hatred for your mother grew. And it was there I knew, one day, I would be the one to take her life.

But I did sustain myself, on the thought that I had the voice of a god telling me I was doing right by my people. Telling me that he had chosen me. And maybe it got to me. Who wouldn't be flattered by being a god's chosen one?

It wasn't until one day I woke up and he wasn't there that I finally broke. Why had he left? Everything that was once warm, the birds outside my cell, went cold. I felt obsolete. And I gave up on goodness then, as my god had given up on me.

See they had cast a spell on me, a very, very complex spell so I could not transform. But I charmed the young witch, oh it wasn't hard to persuade her to love me. I felt sick doing it, having her near me, having her lay a hand on my shoulder consoling me. I wanted to bite her hand off. And she finally gave me the opportunity. She dropped her curse and I turned to what I had never dared to become before. A beast of blood and fire.

I broke free from the prison and found that, in my absence, the Vernis Lanin had been overcome with purists. They wished to destroy those that opposed them and used my name as a figure head, a martyr. I cared not. I had but one desire. To destroy the woman who had cost me my divinity and sanity. I hunted her back to the place she lived with her husband and two children and all their servants. Yes, your mother didn't like to lift a finger for herself. She was waited upon hand and foot by the wealth of the Thiel family and your father simpered after her. So I crept into the house and slaughtered them all. No no not you little angel, I never knew you were there. And I couldn't bring myself to dispatch my own son, no matter how he was brought to being. He was just a child.

Had I found you that day what might have been different. Would your power have subdued me even then or would I have slaughtered you too?

Years passed.
You grew.

You became.

I heard of the daughter that had survived kept at the Academy. I found you and – oh, that is a story for later.

* * *

I come back to myself, gasping. I'm sprawled on the library floor and there are some blurry figures above me. One kneels beside me.

"Mallory, what happened?!" Kyle asks in a panic.

"I-"

"Here."

Killian kneels beside me as well, passing me a glass of water. I drink the whole glass in a few gulps, before drawing my head to my knees. Kyle runs his hand up and down my back.

"It's okay, you're okay now."

"We were wrong," I whisper to him, tears streaming out of my eyes. That poor man. And my mother. My stomach jumps, remembering what she did to him and I'm doubled over, sick spewing from my mouth.

"Shit," Killian mutters, "I'll go get something to clean this up."

He disappears again leaving us alone.

"What were we wrong about?"

"Thaddeus. He's not at all what we thought, oh god," I groan again, as my stomach heaves once more.

"What do you mean?"

"He-" I stop as Alistair approaches us.

"Go help Killian," he orders Kyle. He's holding another glass of water as he approaches. Kyle glances at me reluctantly but doesn't argue, leaving my side. I suddenly feel very cold.

"What happened?" Alistair asks, passing me the water.

"I don't know, I just touched that book and suddenly I remembered things, things that weren't mine to recall."

He picks up the book carelessly.

"Criminal records? Of Thaddeus Velemir's time in prison." His lips draw into a tight line. "You saw his past."

"What?"

"A person's memory can be bound to objects, either to hide them from the original possessor or to act as an active record to be experienced."

"But it was as if."

I falter, not daring to tell him it was as if he was speaking to me rather than showing me.

"As if what?"

"Nothing."

He studies me, his eyes dully lit.

"Drink," he orders, looking back at the book, "whatever was in here has gone into you now."

"So he won't remember that?"

"He might. It doesn't matter much. No one will ever know this truth."

"Truth?" My voice grows louder. "You mean they actually tortured him. But…you knew?"

He smiles grimly.

"All bellatoja captains know. Most of the Onyevaras know. The fact that Thaddeus Velemir was an innocent man is one of the greatest secrets our governments have ever kept to maintain peace."

"Why are you telling me?"

"You've already seen the truth. Besides, you're not going to have a chance to tell anyone."

I feel a heavy thud on the back of my head and slip from consciousness.

Chapter XXV.

When I wake, I'm slumped against the inside of a car door, the glaring cold of the window stinging my cheek. I blink slowly. There's a dull ache on the back of my head where I've been struck. By who? I want to move to touch the spot that hurts but am afraid indicating I'm awake will draw the attention of those speaking in hushed tones beside me.

"It can't be far from here."

"If we had a witch we could use a locator spell with the girl."

"And bring a witch into the mix? I'd rather not work with the filth if I can avoid it."

There's a rousing of chuckles.

"Do you have any idea the what's going to happen when we succeed in bringing them the girl?"

"You mean aside from the glory and fame? Immediate promotions all around," Alistair says.

That answers the question of who. My face is angled towards the window so I dare to open my eyes, only slightly. Outside is lined with tall trees on the roadside. They whip back and forth tumultuously in the wind.

"Hey faker," Alistair whispers quietly in my ear, causing me to jump. My startled expression elicits another round of laughter from the four men I now see occupying the car. Alistair grins at them then turns back to me. "Such a shame," he says, "such a pretty face belongs to a dragovik half-breed."

Without warning, he weaves his hand into the hair at the nape of my neck, getting a tight grip of me. In one swift movement, he smashes my face into the window beside me. I let out a horrific whimper which only seems to amuse the men more.

"Oh, come now, that won't be the worst of it if you

don't tell us what we need to know."

He catches my jaw in his hand, sweeping a finger over my cheek, as I try to pull away. I can feel blood running from my nose and cresting the top of my upper lip.

Little angel, you're so brave.

But I don't feel it. Staring into the eyes of this senseless violence, I'm terrified. Still, I force myself to meet his gaze. They're not cold and flat as they were before, but livened by the prospect of whatever mission they're on.

"Good girl," he purrs, drawing me close before shoving me hard in the chest so the back of my head smacks the window again. This time I don't give him the satisfaction of making any sound. I blink once and hold my gaze steady. "You really ought to have been born one of our kind. What do you think boys?"

There's a murmur of assent and for the first time in my life I am very aware of my vulnerability as a woman. I make to cross my legs but he just laughs prising them apart.

"Don't worry darling, we have more pressing issues. For now." He runs his hand down my upper thigh and a feeling of revulsion sweeps through my stomach. "Recognise where we're going?"

"No clue," I reply, my voice wavering only slightly.

"Hm, I thought that pesky memory block of yours might mean as much. We're going back to your alma matter sweetheart. The Academy."

I can't help myself then. I dart a glance out the window as if this sinister place is lurking over my shoulder, waiting to swallow me back into the halls whose darkness no one will speak to me. Still, only trees dash by our window.

"See you told dear sweet Killian a very interesting story. About a girl who could make black matter. You want to tell me about her?"

When we succeed in bringing them the girl. They hadn't been speaking of me. And I know immediately I will do anything to protect this girl from these brutes.

"Sorry," I say coldly, "no idea what you're talking about."

He laughs softly before grabbing my hair again and jerking my head down to collide with his raised knee. I can't help myself from crying out when I hear the crunch of my nose.

"You can play all you want but we'll get the truth out of you eventually," he says, leaning back in his seat. "Fix your pretty self up then, dragovik."

All but the one driving turn to look at me. He wants me to heal myself? I look at him incredulously, attempting to gauge whether he's joking but he just stares at me, waiting. Finally, I touch my hand to my nose.

"Lueicht, nandirava," I begin, but my voice falters, shaking. The men laugh again.

"What's the matter, stage fright? I know you don't remember the Academy but surely dear old grams has taught you some magic?" Alistair taunts. I clear my throat.

"Lueicht, nandirava." But I still can't get the words out.

"Looks like she didn't care enough to arm you to protect yourself," one in the front taunts.

Suddenly, it doesn't matter I can't remember the words. My hand goes warm. I hear the crack of my nose resetting itself, even feel the fast drying blood disappear and, when I remove my hand, I know my face is completely restored. The pained spot on the back of my head has even ceased to ache. A hush falls throughout the car.

"Magic without spell casting, huh. Didn't know there were many of your kind left. No wonder the Academy wanted you so much. This bodes well. Pull over."

The car slows as we pull up to the side of the road.

It's been completely empty all this time and I wonder if perhaps Alistair will take the opportunity to kill me.

"Out," he orders.

I don't realise he's speaking to me until he kicks me sharply in the shins. I open the door and spill out of the car, scampering a little distance before he catches up with me. Grabbing my hair, he twists it around his hand and draws me back to him.

"Now, now, where are you going?"

He casts me to the ground before kneeling beside me. Rolling on my back, I glare up at him, restraining the moronic urge to kick him in the chest. He'll easily overpower me.

"See I've heard about non-verbal spell casters. Magic is so inherent in your isuazko that you don't need to call on the magic inherent in the ancient language but can draw on what's in yourself. In other words, you don't need the exact wording of a spell but only a strong feeling of it."

"I don't know how to do it, it was a fluke," I insist.

I won't let him use me as an instrument to get to that girl. He rolls his eyes.

"See but you don't really need to know how sweetheart, that's the whole bit about it being inherent. I want you to find the Academy for me."

"Like hell," I snarl.

He stands up and kicks me hard in the gut. Groaning, I roll over, gripping my stomach.

"How about now?"

"Fuck you," I manage, winded though I am.

He plants another swift kick, the hard toe of his boot colliding with my soft belly.

"Listen, we're all very impressed by how brave you are, but see we've got your little friend and if you don't give us what you want well," he murmurs with a grin, "if this is what we do to someone we want something from, what do you think we'll do to someone we don't give a shit about?"

My stomach flips. Of course, they have Kyle. That bastard Killian must have subdued him when he went to help. I know I can't save them both, not the girl and Kyle. And given the choice…

"Fine." I push myself up on one arm. "Tell me what to do."

"There's a good girl. It's simple really. The Academy's location has been kept quiet for fear of what people would do if they ever found it."

"You mean what monsters like you would do?" He grins.

"You, a daughter of blood and fire, a girl who has consorted with the worst kinds of demons, call me a monster? No, I think that word is safely reserved for you and your friends back at the Academy. It's tricky to find something granted every magical protection unless you have someone who's been there before."

"I've told you I-"

"Yes, yes you don't remember. But your subconscious does. And any memory of it will serve to bring its location back to you."

He watches me and I realise he's waiting now for me to perform this miracle he demands of me. I shut my eyes and focus. A memory of the Academy? That woman, feeding the boy poison.

I wait but nothing comes.

"It's no use," I say to him.

"Not good enough. Think of Kyle."

I do. I think of his kindness and patience. He doesn't deserve to die at the hands of brutes like these because of my failure. But then, neither does this girl. I swallow hard, fully aware of the ramifications of what I do by helping Alistair. Still, I shut my eyes again, remembering the blood.

No, forget the blood.

Think instead of the wood panelled walls. Dark, made all the more so by the dim lighting. Chandelier's that only had one working lightbulb.

Remember instead the expanse of beige carpet beneath all our kneeling bodies. The platform at the end of the room on which that woman sat, illuminated like an angel by the window behind her. And through that window, the running track. I remember it now. Running side by side with Kyle as he began his journey to save me. I'll do anything to repay the favour.

It comes to me like something unfolding, or flowering. At first there is the whole world. Then it unboxes itself, peels off petals of superfluous locations. I feel as though I'm plummeting, closer and closer to a location, falling from the sky until my stomach collides with an unknown barrier that keeps me from hitting the ground. There it is. The Academy. A monstrously vast labyrinth of halls and passages connecting buildings.

"It's back the way we came. There's a dirt track with a no trespassing sign. But if you take that it will get you to the Academy."

I feel as though I have betrayed something sacred in telling him this. He reaches into his pocket and I close my eyes again, expecting him to pull out a knife to kill me now he has what he wants. But then I hear the dull beeps of a phone number being dialled.

"Yeah, turn back. There's a dirt road we want to follow. I want the damn place locked down by the time I get there." He hangs up then leans over and grabs me by the arm, pulling me to my feet. "Thanks sweetheart."

He doesn't make a move to the car for a moment, his gaze sweeping over me. My expression goes dead, not giving him the satisfaction of overt fear but he sees it on me anyways and grins.

"Like I said, there's time for that later." In one quick movement he has me over his shoulder and is marching me back to the car. He tosses me easily in the back seat then slides in beside me. "Go back the way we came, I'll tell you when to turn off."

The man in the front seat nods and spins the car round in a swift u-turn. I shut my eyes, trying to force the guilt lodged in my throat back down. Because it's dawning on me now that it's not just this girl but everyone at the Academy I've endangered. It takes about fifteen minutes before I see the no-trespassing sign on our left.

"Clever little glamour," Alistair muses.

I'm not sure what he means but the driver keeps going straight at the gate, making no stop to open it. We pass through as if it were smoke, and suddenly what once looked like a dirt road is a handsomely paved driveway. We all crane our necks to get a look through the front windshield at the vast building in front of us. It sprawls to the left and right, scarcely leaving a margin between it and the forest.

"Still, relatively transparent. That's artari magic for you."

This last comment gets a snicker from several of the men. We pull to a stop in front of the building where several vans are parked.

"Come on."

Taking me by the arm, Alistair leads me out of the car. Suddenly I hear it. Deafening screams akin to the ones I heard the night Illarion was summoned. The screams of the dead or soon to be dead. The front double doors are wide open and, through them, I see someone being dragged across the atrium. I let out a blood curdling scream, pulling back against Alistair's grip as a man's sword drops through the woman's throat as if it were nothing. He holds me steady as I squirm. There are rising cries of panic from within and the man holding the slumped body of the woman clears his throat.

"We'll make this simple. We're looking for a girl. She'd be about a teenager and can summon black matter and manipulate it."

Everything falls silent inside the building. I continue to struggle as Alistair brings me closer to the corpse. The man, sensing movement behind him, tenses and spins around. When he spots Alistair, he stands to attention and salutes him.

"Sir."

"Go on," he says, nodding at him.

The man turns back to the cowering masses of people ranging from children to adults, kneeling before him. They're surrounded by more bellatoja soldiers armed with swords.

"No one? Fine then. Where's Doctor Lindberg?"

I go still in Alistair's hands. I know that name. Oh god. I plummet to my knees so quickly Alistair can't stop me. My head is splitting. My ears fill with a buzzing sound that all but drowns out everything else. But through it I can still make out faint words.

"Not here."

"Then we'll just have to wait until she gets back. Maybe we'll give her something to come back to."

The man plunges his sword into the chest of the woman who has answered him, her defiant expression becoming her dying one. I can just make this out through the welling of tears in my eyes. Because this is the beginning of remembering. The past is beginning to unwrap itself.

"Sir."

A bellatoja approaches, saluting Alistair.

Late night wanderings through these halls. Hoping to one day get out but never managing to open the door.

"I found the file on the individual you requested. She left the Academy about six months ago."

The man hands Alistair the file, which he glances over. His smile broadens as he reads it.

"I know she did. Thought I'd bring her back for a little field trip." He grabs me by the collar of my shirt, before gesturing at the collection of people in the atrium. "Take care of this will you? And bring me this," he adds indicating to something in the file.

I hear rising screams as I'm dragged down a corridor to the right. Squirming again, I pull against his grip but he's too strong for me.

"You're a right little devil, aren't you? I mean I'd heard rumours but this," he says holding up the file with my name on the front, "this is something else. God I would have loved to see you in your element."

He drags me along the rough fibres of the beige carpet and I dig my fingers down, attempting to keep him from pulling me along. All it does is dig under my nails.

"Now where is this place? Ah I see. Right by your old room. Maybe we'll visit that later." He turns the handle of a door but it's locked. "Open it."

"No," I manage through bared teeth. With ease he hefts me into the air and tosses me clear across the hall into the wall. My vision shatters once more.

"When are you getting it through your head? You're my play thing now Mallory Thiel. When I say open the door, you open the fucking door. It's not hard."

He drags me over to the door and places my hand on it but I wrench it off.

"No!" I shout.

I can still hear screaming back from where we came and I hate to think of what might be happening. I have to help them if I can. Illarion's second gift floats through my head. If only I could remember it all. Again, Alistair takes me by the back of my head and smacks my face into the doorknob. My eyes start to run.

"Think of Kyle, Mallory," he taunts, "think of how much I'm going to hurt him if you don't do as I say."

Like that my hand is back on the doorknob and I hear a click as it unlocks. He brushes my hand out of the way just as someone approaches from behind.

"Here it is sir."

The soldier hands Alistair something but I can't see it through my broken vision. The soldier gives me an appraising look before leaving us again. Alistair shoves open the door and drags me into a darkened room. He tosses me forward then shuts the door behind us.

"This should be fun," he murmurs.

He flicks a switch and an octagonal room panelled with mirrors is illuminated. I'm overwhelmed by a sense of dread. Something bad happens here, it always does. I turn around and see Alistair reading over the file but I daren't move. Whatever befalls me here I must endure for Kyle's sake.

"Well, you won't need this."

Hooking his finger round the hem of my top, he jerks it over my head. I have just enough time to see that what he's holding is a whip before he knocks me back to the ground and I feel it bite into my flesh. I let out a scream, clawing at the floor. Tears sting my eyes as I arch my back. The pain is more than anything I could imagine and yet, it is utterly familiar. I can hear him raising his arm again and in between that moment and the whip coming down on my back, I remember.

"Tell me what you see."

"Me."

"Yes. And what are you?"

"Nothing."

My breathing grows heavier as the recollection spills out of my subconscious. Then comes the horrible draw back to reality as the whip comes down again.

"That certainly did something. Do you remember now, what you are? What you did?" Alistair asks. He crouches beside me, his face inches from mine. "This is what she did to you when you disappointed her, wasn't it? And from what I can see, you did an awful lot of that."

I cry out again as he digs his fingers into the wound on my back.

"Left you a permanent scar with magic. Now I can't do that but no harm in trying. Well, I suppose there is a little."

He stands back up and the whip comes down again.

Mallory.

Go away, I think to myself, to the voice in my head. It is warm and fuzzy, wraps itself around me.

Mallory, you have to fight back.

Why? From what little I can recall of my past I deserve this. To die in this room that saw my greatest betrayal. Poetic justice.

There are people you still need to protect.

Am I not protecting them by enduring? Kyle is certainly safer for it.

There's only silence. I hear the whip clatter to the floor and Alistair rolls me on my back. The cold floor against my wounds is bitingly painful but I don't scream. I'm right. I know it, the voice knows it. I am keeping Kyle safe. Alistair pulls on the waistband of my trousers, yanking them down.

"You really are such a pretty thing," he murmurs, pressing his weight against my hips. "You know no one will care that I've done this? The Onyevaras won't get involved especially not for an Academy mutt like you. Even if Inerea kicks up a fuss. You're all cowards. Even you in the end. You just lie here and take it."

He strokes the side of my face and the memory of what Regan did to Thaddeus resurfaces. I choke on tears, trying to pull away from him but he holds me in place.

Mallory, you were trained for this. Go save those people.

And I know he's right. I was trained for this, not by Leo but a decade before. I was trained to win, always. I wrap my legs around Alistair's waist and his eyes widen.

"Look who's suddenly going to come easily," he whispers, leaning over me and biting my earlobe. Idiot.

I throw my weight round and fling him to the ground. Startled, he grunts as I land on top of him. In a flash the whip is in my hand, I wind it round his neck, yanking both ends until its taut. His eyes bulge and he tugs at the whip.

I remember the shape of Leora's spell on the door in Mr Bowen's bookshop, pluck free the words that cast it.

"Sa rahissor, kartsugu lesti etev asias qui'etai gawesir emkaravaz'noventa, destoyar asiasous nasormka korvez-inaravaz."

Alistair screams as the thick rope begins to burn his hands and throat.

"You threaten my friends," I say, pulling tighter, "innocent people. Me. And you think I'd lie there and take it. If saving whomever I can makes me a monster so be it. Killing you will be worth it."

I give one final pull and the burning whip cuts through his neck, simultaneously cauterising the wound that kills him. His head rolls away from me. I know I should be sickened by what I've just done, but all I feel is a roar of strength, enough to overpower the remaining bellatoja. I glance over my shoulder into the mirror and watch as the lacerations on my back close themselves. I grab Alistair's sword and the whip, which warms my hand pleasantly, before darting out into the hall. I run back to the atrium but stop dead in my tracks when I reach it. The sight I'm greeted by makes me retch.

Bodies. Not just stabbed but torn apart. Guts are splayed across the floor and it is no longer clear which top halves of bodies belong to the bottom halves. It's a jumble of limbs, dripping blood. Blood everywhere. It's not just the residents of the Academy but the bellatoja too. Not a single person has been left alive. I drop my weapons and begin to wade through the gore, searching for Doctor Lindberg or the girl, but there's no sight of them. Who could have done this?

There's a sound from outside the front door and I immediately regret having left the sword behind. Still, I know now how to put up a fight. I dart across the atrium to the doorway where I'm greeted by the sight of Leo, Robyn, Aaron, and - oh thank god.

"Kyle," I cry out, running towards him.

I throw my arms around his neck pulling him close to me.

"Mallory I was so worried," he breathes, drawing me tightly into his arms. "The bellatoja took me as soon as I let you. Killian helped me escape."

I breathe a sigh of relief. Thank god there's at least one decent bellatoja out there. I cup his cheek in my hand.

"Don't you dare ever leave my side again," I order.

He nods, concern dappling his features as he wipes the tears making tracks down my face.

"What happened to you?" Robyn asks, "you're sort of missing a lot of clothing."

I glance down at myself, aware I'm in only my bra and pants for the first time since I left the mirror room.

"Alistair," I begin but cannot finish. Aaron's face screws up in rage.

"That fucking bastard. Where is he?"

"He's dead."

"What?" Kyle asks, startled, "what happened-"

He sees the look on my face, sweeps a glance over me and sees all the blood caking my thighs.

"Mallory, what happened in there?"

"They killed them," I whimper, my knees buckling beneath me. Kyle catches me before I fall. "They're all dead."

"The bellatoja too," Robyn says, coming back from having inspecting the atrium. She looks sick. "Did you do that?"

"No! I fought off Alistair and when I came back they were already dead."

The four exchange a look.

"We should get out of here," Leo says, "I'm not interested in meeting whatever did this."

He leads the way and Kyle wraps an arm around me as we walk to the car.

"I don't understand, why'd they take you now?" Robyn asks.

"She's the only one with a memory of the Academy. They must have been planning this the whole time," Aaron says through gritted teeth as Leo begins to drive, "Fucking bellatoja scum. I told you we couldn't trust them."

"It wasn't that," I say, shaking my head. For some reason, once I start, I cannot seem to stop. There's something soothing in the motion. "There was a girl. I mentioned her to Killian and he freaked out. He must have gone to tell Alistair about it, not knowing what he'd do."

"That explains why he kept saying this was all his fault," Kyle muses, "but not why they wanted to find the girl so badly."

"I told him about her magic, how she could summon black matter and-what?"

The other four are exchanging looks.

"Mallory, you really ought to have let them kill her," Robyn finally answers.

Chapter XXVI.

Following Robyn's comment, the drive home is not punctuated by a single word for at least an hour. Kyle wraps me in his coat, though it does little to preserve my decency. I sink back into my seat, wanting so desperately to both fall asleep and ask Robyn what she meant. Finally, after what feels like an age, Leo pipes up.

"We should report this to the Onyevaras," he says, not taking his eyes off the road.

"And tell them what? The bellatoja are all dead. This wouldn't look good for us. Besides, they're too cowardly to help if it comes down to us or the Hirutere," Robyn replies.

"She's right," Kyle says before Leo can respond. "Things like this have been happening more and more, which is why I left to work with the artari at the Academy in the first place. I watched similar things being covered up by the Onyevaras just to stay in the good graces of the Hirutere. I thought perhaps with time, after Thaddeus' rebellion," he pauses, glancing at me out of the corner of his eye. I still haven't told him everything I saw. He doesn't know Thaddeus is a victim. "I thought that maybe things would get better, but the Hirutere are only taking more advantage of the power imbalance."

"Right so what now?" Leo asks.

I'm surprised he doesn't argue with Kyle, as seems to be his natural disposition.

"Right now, I think we all need some rest. It's been a long day. We can regroup tomorrow," Kyle says, putting his arm around me.

I rest my head on his shoulder. My body shivers for the cold.

"I'd like to go home please," I whisper, turning towards him.

"Mallory, I don't think that's a good idea."

I'm shocked by Robyn's gentle tone. Even she's worried about me. How could she not be horrified after what they all know I've done to Alistair. I shiver again.

"I want to see Inerea."

My recent near-death experience has made it clear to me how much I need to make amends with my grandmother. No matter what she did, she did it to protect me, as I had done for Kyle in helping Alistair find the Academy. I cannot begrudge her the mistakes I myself have made. It's becoming clearer and clearer each day that I am far from innocent.

It takes another few hours before we reach Aplin Hollow, so it has gone completely dark by the time we pull up my driveway.

"Will you stop fiddling with that?" Leo snaps in exasperation as Aaron changes the radio station yet again.

"Sorry," he replies, and I notice for the first time the anxious expression on his face. "I just think someone should stay guard here, overnight."

"No, you all need rest too. Inerea and I can more than handle ourselves."

Aaron is about to protest but I give Kyle a meaningful look and he knows I'm remembering. I'm better equipped to fight someone off than possibly any of them. It's why I was such a quick study with Leo.

"That's enough Aaron. Mallory's right. It's been a long day and I'm sure she just wants some time alone," Kyle says as we park outside the house.

I can see Inerea's figure on the porch, rising from the porch swing. As Kyle steps out of the car, she rushes towards him.

"I felt it," she says to him, shaking, "all that death. Where is she?"

I slip out of the car behind him and, before I can

open my mouth to apologise, she has her arms around me.

"I'm so glad you're okay." I feel the wet warmth of her tears on my neck as she draws me close. "It must have been horrible."

She pets my hair, taking no note of my blood-stained legs or my lack of clothes.

"I'm sorry," I whisper, kissing her cheek, "I was so stupid."

"Don't be silly, you had every right to be upset. But enough of that for now. Let's get you inside, you're shivering."

She nods at Kyle, not quite able to smile, and he nods back before getting in the car. I watch them drive off as Inerea guides me onto the porch and into the house. Upstairs, she takes Kyle's jacket from me before leaving me to wash. I can hear her in my room pottering about as I climb into the shower. I expect the hot water to sting but instead it eases down my skin in gentle rivulets where hours ago there had only been the lashings of the whip. I shudder to myself, recalling Alistair's touch, the glint in his eyes as he held me down. And like that, I begin to reconcile myself to the act of death. Would he not have done the same to me? Did he not order the deaths of countless others back in the atrium and who knows how many more during his time as a captain? But there will be a price to pay for his death. He was high ranking enough to have all those men at his command and no doubt someone will track me down for his murder.

I can't think about that too much now. There's Inerea to worry about. What comes next now we can't get the spell from the Library Between? Maybe Killian would help us again? My mind strays to the young man I had met so briefly yet who had saved my friend. I need to remember him. When I think the worst of all bellatoja, I must remember that some are good. Not all of them are like Alistair.

I get out of the shower, towel myself off, and wrap the fluffy towel around myself. Inerea is sitting on my bed waiting for me. She's lain out clean pyjamas, which she's fiddling between her fingers when I emerge. Patting the bed beside her, she beckons me over. I sink myself onto the comfy mattress and know I'll fall asleep in a heartbeat when I close my eyes.

"Mallory, you've been so brave. Not just today, or the past week, helping the others. But your whole life…I just wanted to make it easier. I wanted to make it so you didn't have to stand in the shadows of your past all your life."

"I know."

"If I'm honest, as I know I must be, I don't think I will ever come to regret it. Even," she says, raising a hand to silence my protests, "though you are coming to remember. I don't think you would have ever become the person you are today if you had come to Aplin Hollow burdened with who you were. Now, at least, you have come into the world gently and you will have strength enough to live in it bravely."

She kisses my head, resting it on her shoulder.

"I hope you're right. What little I've remembered so far has been horrifying. I don't know if I can cope with a lifetime of it."

"But you already have. I just wanted to ease you into this world. Now you will have to reconcile the two parts of yourself to live in it, but I don't doubt for a second you'll be able to. And now, you need sleep."

She rises and shuts the door behind her. Changing into my pyjamas, I let out a long sigh before climbing into bed. I'm about to go to fall asleep when I hear my window creaking open. With a start, I snatch the lamp off my bedside table and hurl it across my room. There's a shatter and a thud as a dark shape slides to the floor.

"Aaron?"

"You have terrifyingly good aim." He sits up, rubbing his head. "Still, there are ways you can make it up to me."

"Perverted alien. What are you doing here?"

"I don't care what stupid bullshit you come up with, I'm staying guard tonight. I can't sleep anyway, far too wired after what happened."

He stands up, ready for me to argue.

"I know I said I wanted to be alone before, but will you stay with me tonight?" I say, reaching out to him.

"Mallory Thiel," he gasps, crossing the room, "are you inviting me to sleep in your bed?"

His eyes flicker mischievously.

"If you keep saying things like that I'll be forced to send you back to the planet pheromone."

"It's been so long since I've been to my homeland," he sighs, kicking off his shoes. He sprawls himself across the bed.

"Well you certainly made yourself comfortable."

"I figure I'll be spending a lot of time here in the future," he says wickedly, winking as I slip beneath the duvet. "Tell me, do you always invite strange men so readily into your bed?" he teases.

"Of course not," I say, flushing with the memory of John. Was that only this morning?

"Look at you, always so anxious about the subject." He lays his head back on his pillow. "I promise to be a perfect gentleman."

"I don't trust your definition of the word," I say, switching the light off. We lay in the absolute dark, even the moon's light ensconced in clouds. "Goodnight Aaron."

"Night."

The last thing I see is the ceiling, my body fully aware of the warmth Aaron's lets off, before I'm transported to a far more unsettling world. I wait for hell's scenery to rise around me, but instead I'm returned to our own world. I recognise the place I've come to, filled with relics that have been held by the hands of once living. The antique store is lit by filtered bars of light that slip between the blinds. This is my world only in sight; it is beyond my touch, which means it is beyond my saving. The thought stirs an unpleasant mixture of fear and guilt in me. I need to do something. But I am a weapon in more than my ability to fight. My dreams are the drive of self-preservation.

"So, show me how to save myself," I say.

On command, sounds begin to penetrate the silent world. First, I hear a car zoom by and then comes a quiet yet urgent voice from downstairs. Unsure of how detached from the dream my body is and whether or not I can be seen, I move with stealth down the stairs. While the rest of the store's lights had been turned out, the basement is lit with an unnatural glow, as if to highlight the exact answers I seek. In its bath of gold stands Leora, her face turned from me. Yet I can feel the anguish it must show, for it drips in her words when she speaks.

"You can't do this," she whispers, with no trace of her former confidence. No voice answers, but the shadows do. They undulate violently, progressing further into the light. Leora staggers backwards. "Stay away from me!"

"A dog that has learned to sit out of fear and not loyalty is not a worthy servant," an inhuman voice hisses, "You have done exactly as I have commanded but now your death is worth more than your life."

A red ribbon, identical to the ones that attacked me in the forest, lashes out and coils around her neck. There's a crack, the last call of life before she falls limp to the ground. The tendril brushes her skin before rearing back and plunging into her chest. It twists and her body arches as it emerges, wound around her heart. Its veins are sick with black, a poison that's been infecting her system for a long time. Raising it up to the light as if to examine it, the tendril turns the heart this way and that. The blood shimmers, rolling down in drops. From the shadows a black tongue darts out and runs itself along the side of the vital organ. My stomach lurches.

"Thank you."

I recognise that voice. The voice of Thaddeus that filled my head in the library. The voice I have been hearing all along. He steps forward, his face still clouded in shadow, and accepts the offering his servant presents, wrapping the heart in a crimson cloth. Without warning his eyes dart up to where I stand. They glint, not quite holding onto me but instead clasping the vague outline of my figure, as if he's aware of my presence but not my being. For the first time his features are revealed to me in part. His irises are an iridescent gold, full of so many thoughts that I'm shocked they can stay focused on anything for a long time. And yet he manages to keep them on me.

"You always find your way to me. I am beginning to believe that you crave the pain I promise. This is a good sign," he adds, his voice unbroken by the madness within. His hand closes tightly around the heart, hiding it beneath the surplus of cloth. "I'm all too happy to oblige."

A spasm of agony shoots through my spine. My voice has faded from this dream, leaving me to cry out a soundless scream. He studies the air in which I am held, detailing my tormented expression on its transparent skin.

"Would it make you feel better to know that I'm hurt by your attempts to stop me, little angel? I really did believe you would bow out. But this disobedience will make you all the more fun to play with. Besides, it won't happen again," he murmurs. My vision of this reality fades and all that binds me to it is his voice. In a world he controls it will surely be the last thing to go. "How sad it is that the survival of those you care for is contingent on your non-existent courage."

The echo of his last word fades, a receding tendril of night as day breaks both within and outside my mind.

My hand darts to my left instinctively, searching for Aaron. I feel his shoulder blade, his back now turned me. His shallow breaths indicate peaceful sleep. Taking him by the shoulders, I give him a gentle shake. There's no time to waste if we want to get to the antique store before the deabrueon attacks Leora. Aarons sniffs and buries his face in the pillow.

"Aaron," I plead, shaking him harder, but he still doesn't stir.

I leap out of bed, pulling on a pair of jeans and a long sleeve shirt. Re-buckling my arm sheath on, I tug my sleeve over it before trying to wake Aaron again. But not matter how hard I try, he won't wake. I grab my boots and zip them up. Racing downstairs, I run straight into Inerea.

"Hello there speedy," she says. Then she sees the look on my face and her brow creases in concern. "What happened?"

"There's no time to explain. I'm sorry to ask this of you so early but I need to get to the antique store in town."

She looks confused but doesn't protest. Taking her car keys from the glass bowl on the table, she puts on her coat. We get into her car, though I notice she glances curiously at Aaron's car still parked in the driveway. We're zipping down the main road within a minute. Nothing

changes. Not the trees lining the road, not the panic in
my heart that swells when I imagine the deabrueon hurting Leora before I can get to her. How could I have been
so foolish to believe that it wouldn't try to claim her life
force for its master as soon as we left her without protection? We've already reached the outskirts of town and
cars begin to dot the road ahead, slowing us down. I lean
forwards, trying to spot the turn off for the antique store.

"Are you in some sort of trouble?" Inerea asks.

"No it's a friend of mine. She works there," I clarify.
We pull into an empty parking spot just outside the store-
front. "Wait here. No matter what, please don't come in."

I've already brought her this close to danger, I won't
let her be caught in the middle of it.

"Mallory!" she calls out, but then her voice is lost
behind the door of the store.

After the commotion of our urgency to arrive, I feel
as if I've walked into the stillness of true disaster. The
room is completely undisturbed, but the light is coming through the blinds just as it had done in my dream,
glinting off the glass of the display cases. Perhaps she's
already downstairs, in which case there's very little time.
I am aware of the churning in my gut, a visceral sickness that can only be compared to what I felt when I saw
those bodies yesterday. I know the sight that may greet
me downstairs, the gaping hole in her chest and the unnatural crookedness of her snapped neck.

I'm about to go downstairs but hesitate at the sight of
the weapons glinting in the display case. In the centre is a
delicate looking sword. It's best to be prepared with extra
weapons. With no time to search for the key, I spin in a
semi-circular motion and strike the glass with the bottom
of my boot. It shatters, leaving me free to arm myself. I
still my trembling hand by clasping the hilt tightly until
my knuckles are bled of life, as dead as Leora's eyes had

been in my dream. The thought drains the rest of me, right to my last breath and I begin to descend the stairs, this time careful to stay in the shadows, knowing I can be seen. My heart implores me to turn away, beating rapidly against the cage of my skeleton, which cannot protect it from the deabrueon. Finally, I am close enough to the last step that I will no longer be able to avoid the sight of her body if it's already there. I blink and see -

- nothing. Maybe neither of them are here yet and my dream indicated a less immediate point of time. But this foreboding sensation within me knows that's not the case. For all I know her body has already been disposed of. I clench my hand tighter around the sword. The bell above the door rings, alerting me to someone's presence. I pray silently that Inerea hasn't chosen to follow me in. It's time to hide; who knows what the intruder will think when they find the shattered weapons case, me with a sword and Leora missing.

I step into the darkness that the deabrueon had cloaked itself in while it killed her and the likeness be-tween us is enough to bring back the primal sickness within me. Upstairs, the footsteps have ceased. It's only a matter of time before someone looks down here for whomever has broken in. Turning my head, I let the stairs into my peripheral vision, waiting to see someone descend. When I do so it's just in time to see the glint of oncoming metal.

I leap backwards and raise my sword to deflect the blow. Lunging forwards, I strike towards the hilt of the attacking sword. I feel the speed of my movement slowed as the tip of my sword comes into contact with flesh. But this attack leaves me open, and my attacker's blade pierc-es my shoulder. We jump apart only for my opponent to thrust the sword back towards me. Catching the side of the sword, I make a small circular motion, directing the weapon to a diagonal angle that poses no threat. I press my palm against the flat side of the sword, twisting their arm with it until the pressure is so much the sword clatters to the floor. The sound of the pommel hitting the cement is louder than I had expected, startling me from the quiet fear of death that had pervaded until then. Caught in my momentary distraction, I give my opponent an opportunity to dive for their weapon. But there's not enough time. I dart between the perpetrator and the sword, pressing my blade to their throat. Having finally stilled, the face of my attacker is clear to me. My stance goes slack and I drop my weapon, eyes wide with bewilderment.

"You're pretty handy with that sword," Leora says, rubbing the wrist of her sword hand, which had been twisted harshly when I attacked. "Where'd you learn to fight like that?"

"It was all instinct," I reply, "I'm sorry about your wrist."

"Don't apologize for that. On the other hand, you made quite a mess of floor room. What are you doing here? And with a sword no less," she asks.

"I'm sorry, I thought you were in trouble," I start.

"The only trouble I'm going to be in is with my boss. Mind helping me clean the mess you made upstairs?"

"Of course not, sorry about that. How exactly do you plan on replacing the case by the end of today though?"

"Witch," she answers, pointing at herself, "I can fix it." She starts up the stairs. "What exactly did you think happened to me?"

I tense. How do I explain having a dream about her dying? That's probably not the sort of information I should go about telling people.

"It was just a bad feeling I had."

She snorts.

"You're an odd person. I'll admit though, I wouldn't

want to be on your bad side," she laughs.

"Leora," I start, moving to follow her up the stairs.

The exposed light bulb above us shatters, the glass showering my skin with its still burning kisses that bite. The shadows become thick with his laughter, stirring up a wind. Abandoning her sword and not hesitating to look back at me, Leora sprints up the rest of the stairs.

"Leora don't!" I shout as she disappears from view.

I chase after her but the door slams shut between us, leaving her with no way to protect herself. At the top of the stairs, I begin to slam my shoulder repeatedly against the basement door with all my might in an attempt to get through. On the other side is a roar of whirling wind akin to a tornado. In it spiral the echoes of her screams, allowing them to seep beneath the door to me. Running back down the stairs, I snatch my sword from where I left it before swinging it at the door. It begins to splinter but too slowly.

Again, his laughter swells from behind me and, before I can turn to defend myself, the deabrueon's red vines snatch me by the ankles. They pull my feet out from beneath me and I crash to the floor. There's a sickening crunch as my nose smacks against the stairs. The raw iron scent of blood fills my nostrils as it trickles warmly across my skin. I try to roll over and lash at the tentacles with my sword, but a third swats it out of my hand. My only hope of fighting slips between two of the banister supports, clattering to the floor below.

With a sharp tug, the deabrueon begins to drag me away from the door. I reach out, trying to grab one of the supports but they're just out of reach. Clawing wildly at each of the steps, I manage to drive my fingernails into the wood. A hiss comes from behind and with another heave the creature uproots me. I cry out as splinters imbed themselves beneath my fingernails at an excruciating depth. My hands sing notes of pain as they are grazed on the un-sanded wood. The vines extend their grasp up my shins but make no attempt to hold my arms.

I writhe in their grip, trying to get a view of their source of power. But all there seems to be is an endless tangle of vines. Leora's abandoned sword is still too far from where it holds me. Then I remember. I clasp my wrist as if in pain. In one swift moment, I pull my hidden dagger out and slash one of my bindings. It recoils before the other drags me to the left and tosses me clear across the room. My body collides with the banister, smashing through it. I skid across the steps. All throughout me is the dull pain of internal bleeding, interspersed with the sharper points of external wounds. Pushing my hands against the ground I try to raise myself from the floor. But my hands are slick with blood and I slip through the gaping hole in the handrail. My head hits the concrete, leaving me without vision temporarily. In that time, the vines have already started to snake their way towards me.

Let me taste the fire of your blood.

The words awaken a fire in me. The same words that claimed Regan's life, that claimed my family's lives. I manage to heave myself up before stumbling into a crawl to reach my fallen sword. Grasping at its hilt, I find it slips from my fingers as easily as silk. His laughter reigns again, swallowing my mind with its intensity. The vines continue with their steady approach, moving slowly as if to taunt me with the inevitability of their victory. While hastily wiping the blood from my hands onto my leggings, I watch as the thick tendrils curl around the banister supports, crushing them as they go. More slither beneath the staircase, seeking to destroy my only escape route. Hand cleansed of blood, I get a firm hold of my sword and rush towards the staircase. My path is immediately blocked by a burst of bloody vines that snatch at me. I hack at them viciously. The decapitated ones retreat, while the others remain unfazed.

Within a matter of seconds, I've managed to demolish most of them, so turn my efforts back towards getting up the stairs. Here, though, I cannot recklessly swing at them, not unless I want to aid in their destruction of the staircase. With decisive blows I cut through them, the blood of each one dripping on me. Finally, there are few enough for me to take my chance to run. The deabrueon snarls, its last few tendrils shooting up the staircase after me. I heave the sword up again, my arms aching with its weight, and swing at the door. My heart picks up to a frenzied speed as the door fails to budge. I begin to beat it wildly, watching it slowly chip away. Beneath me, I hear the stairs groan, followed by a shudder. I glance back to see that the vines were not after me after all, but restarting their attempts to destroy the staircase. They encase its foundations in a deadly grip, squeezing the wood. My body hums with adrenaline.

Come. Poor thing you're all alone.

"No!"

What are you so afraid of?

"Not you. Not anymore!" I shout.

With one last strike, I throw all my weight behind the sword. The door quivers before falling from the doorframe, having disconnected from the hinges. Tossing my sword aside as not to fall on it, I dive into the shop as I hear the crash of the stairs as they crumble. The rumbling of the wood hitting the cement consumes the entire store, sending a tremor through the floor. I tilt my head forwards, resting my forehead on the floor. My hot breaths curl up around the sides of my face, warming my already flushed cheeks. The slow trickle of blood from my nose continues.

One, two, three.

My hands still aching with pain, I use my shoulder to roll myself onto the back. The ceiling at which I stare seems no different from the floor. My hands loll, palms open, rendered unusable as if someone has grated them to shreds.

"Leora," I croak, coughing up blood that has managed to find its way into my throat during the fight.

I prop myself up on my elbows, raising my upper body so as to find her. I see her figure, obscured by the table legs between us. She does not stir at my call, though the dread bleeding within me had already told me she wouldn't. I drag my body across the floor using my forearms, unable to face the prospect of standing with my body still so fragile. When I reach her, an animal like cry of anguish fills the room. I hardly recognise it as my own. Her right temple rests against the floor, though her body is tilted to the left. Eye wide open, she does not have that last look of fear as was etched on Theodore's face. All I see is that her usual self-assurance has been drained by death.

Her face has been left completely vacant and it's worse than all the emotion in the world. The deabrueon has reduced her to nothing more than a vessel that looks like her but bears no resemblance to the life force that once lived inside. With my mutilated hand, I reach out but stop short of touching her. I can't bear to lay a hand on her broken body and sully it with my own blood. I need not look at her other side to see what the rivers of blood stemming from her chest can tell me. Her heart is gone. My throat burns with the rising bile and I fall back, scrambling as far as I can from her until I'm resting against the desk. Horrible moans rise from my gut, each one producing the fearful sound of some kind of fallen wraith. My breaths are beyond control, my chest expanding and contracting quickly, unable to retain this air that is so foul.

"Mallory, what's happening? I'm worried-oh dear lord."

In all my hysteria, I had not heard the bell above the door chime. The voice sends me into a panic and I collapse in my attempt to get away. Beneath the light, which once seemed mild but now appears too yellow, like the frothy waves of a daffodil's core, Inerea's silver hair appears a sickly shade. She rushes to my side. When she first reaches for me, I flinch away, afraid to be touched.

"You need to leave, it's not safe here," I insist.

"I'll be damned before I leave you behind," she says, looking me sternly in the eye, "Whatever you've gotten yourself into, I promise to protect you."

"Please Inerea, go back to the car," I beg.

She takes my hands in her own and I feel her wrinkled skin through the blood.

"Lueicht, nandirava letai nevorso ni isuazko etev udiyat," she murmurs. The pain retreats instantly from my hands. "Dar seligpastu ni isuazko'caz tegaktka." On her command the blood fades from my hands, restoring them to normality. "Come on, let's-"

She's cut off by an invisible hand that hits her in the stomach, sending her sprawling away from me. The air in her lungs is forced out of her in a violent gasp. Her legs are bound together by the slender tendrils but with less force than those that crush her windpipe. She begins to pry at them, trying to intone another spell. Her vocal cords are crushed beyond use. She mouths wordlessly at me.

"Inerea!"

In the time it takes me to dislodge my sword from the splintered door, her clawing has become more frantic. Her eyes press alarmingly against the confines of her sockets as she chokes. The vines have sprouted from Leora's blood, twisting themselves into a sturdy base before separating to hold Inerea. I hack at the root, forcing them to retreat, my exhaustion forgotten in the wake of this fresh attack. But it is still felt, slowing down my attempts. Eventually they unwind from her legs and neck. She slumps over but continues to dig at a seemingly unseen force that still has a hold on her. It will not have a chance to choke her, not before she tears her own throat apart.

"You need to stop," I plead, attempting to pry her hands from her throat. Her eyes flash dangerously.

"Sa rahissor kartsugu lesti etev asias qui'etai gawesir emkaravaz'noventa, destoyar asiasous nasormka korvezinaravaz," she snarls.

My fingers begin to prickle, the skin blistering with the burning contact. Still I tug, trying to free her from her own hands. She ignores my attempts, finally cutting her skin open with her nails. Blood rolls from the thin laceration down her neck and collects along the ridge of her collarbone. She digs deeper, pulling her skin apart, tearing it away from herself until I can't watch anymore. I curl my knees to my chest, hiding my head between them. Shutting my eyes is all I can do to stop the spinning in my head. Even then, it only seems to stop because the dark behind my eyelids is continuous and never appears to be in motion. The sickening squelch of flesh being ripped fills the room before coming to a halt. A heavy thud follows as her body drops to the ground. Part of her falls on me and the thick spurt of warm blood on my feet tells me exactly what part it is.

The new weight becomes my tipping point. The oxygen in the room seems to completely dissipate, leaving me to suffocate on the rank scent of blood and death. Every attempt to breathe normally increases my hyperventilation. I want to run for my life but I can't. I'm being squeezed into a little ball. Everything within me is compressed to nothing. My limbs begin to tingle without enough oxygen. It feels like all my organs are suffering simultaneous instant death. As quickly as my courage had come, it flees. The force of evil I thought I could fight has proven me weak. All I can manage in this moment is a strangled whimper, a far cry from the cathartic release I need.

He promised me suffering. He promised he'd break me and now I will lose everything to his promise, one I never asked for. My skin hugs my bones tighter, smothering me. Leora's unseeing eyes seem to swallow me down to the size of a pin. I have to get out of here. I need to breathe. I stumble upright, unable to look down as Inerea's head rolls from my feet and lolls to one side. I walk towards the door blindly. I feel like I'm moving through a swamp of air that's trying to drown me. Before I can take more than three steps, the door opens.

"Hello? Someone said they heard a crash from in here. What's happen-"

The man in the doorway is trapped in motion by the sight before him. The only thing that holds him upright is his tight grip on the doorknob.

"I-I know you," I manage, taking another step towards him.

Unable to move due to shock, his eyes widen as they migrate from the blood that soaks me to the limp bodies of the two women before landing lastly on the still bloody sword I've unknowingly picked up.

"Dear God," he breathes, "what monster."

His looks at my face again.

"I said I know you. We've met before," I say dully, drooping against the table onto which I channel the bulk of my weight. "What's your name?"

"My name-I'm calling the police," he stutters, but still doesn't move.

"You're Alex. You work in the grocery store. I'm Inerea's granddaughter."

Shh, it's okay.

"But why is there always blood?" I whimper in reply.

Come. Poor thing, you're all alone. I extend my hand to the quivering man.

"Then take me somewhere I won't be alone."

"Stay away! You monster, how-how could you do this to your own family?"

"It's not safe here. Shh, they say it's okay," I say.

I try to move towards him but the combination of my already slick shoes and the blood that's pooled out beneath me causes me to lose my footing.

"You're c-crazy! I'm going to call the police," he stammers. His hands, damp with sweat, slip twice on the doorknob before he's able to fumble his way out of the store.

The police. The words get through to me, dragging me from my haggard state of mind.

It's our little secret Mallory.

Oh God. I clench my fist around the grip of my sword before steadying myself without the aid of the table. Like Alex, I find the doorknob near impossible to hold onto, my hand trembling. The tips of my fingers ache on contact, the burn of Inerea's spell having permeated through layers of skin. At last, I manage to open the door, yanking it so hard the hinges groan. As I stumble out onto the pavement, I hear a wild scream. A mother pushing a pram looks in horror upon the bloodied sword. Screams and sounds of pedestrians scuttling out of my way unanimously barely reach me through the surging roar of blood in my ear. Cars jerk to a halt several feet away as I sprint across the road. Their drivers clamber out, attempting to stop me but this only gives me the time I need to get away. I hurdle the fence that separates the pavement and a playground in seconds. For a brief moment, I find myself thankful for its emptiness before panic clouds over all my other thoughts. I dash past the swing set, leap over the fence on the other side and am lost in the surrounding forest. Voices chase after me but no one seems willing to follow me in.

Shh, it's okay.

I cannot return to Inerea's.

Just like that a blanket of rationality falls over my mind to reorganise my thoughts. I abandon the insanity of what has come to pass as a route becomes clear before me. It's as if I've marked every tree in a mental map. They are easily distinguishable. Some are useless yet others mark where my next turn will come. The voices have completely faded behind me and I gain speed that belongs only to the inhuman. I cut between the trees in what to anyone else might seem a meaningless evasive pattern. I know, however, it leads me to the only refuge left. If I am now believed a murderer as well as a freak, then I am truly one of them. The normalcy I had sought to obtain through a life with Celia and Milton is a future lost to me. The thought of the two of them is the last thread pulled from my mind and, as I break through the line of trees into the clearing in which the Caverly's house is situated, I come undone.

Gravel bites easily through my jeans and sinks its jagged teeth into my skin as I fall to my knees. But I have bled so much already that these new wounds are nothing to me. My head begins to spin, most likely due to blood loss. My hands feel heavy and utterly useless, my fingers turned pink and puffed with the new formed blisters of my burn. I rattle with desperate breaths. I am finally worn through completely. There is no more adrenaline to power me. I cannot even find the strength in myself to knock on the door or shout their names. In my mind I call out wordlessly for them, wishing they could hear my anguish through its mere existence.

The sun is heavy in the sky, drooping as my eyelids do. The sky's cyclopean eye blinks blinding light at me. I curl up upon the earth. The comfort of a mattress would make no difference to me. If anything, the sharp pain caused by the rough terrain is a welcome distraction from the continuous ache in my heart. Memory unravels itself as Inerea's spell comes undone at last and everything, everything comes back. Lilith, all that death, years of loneliness. I demand tears from myself but they don't come. This monster will not cry. I begin to sniffle. I stare across ahead, into the darkness where gravel meets the forest. I realise now, my greatest mistake. It haunts me until the sun begins to set and when the moon beams clearly in the night sky. It will haunt me until he brings the end of days. Only then do they find me, but by then I am beginning to hope they never will.

Chapter XXVII.

"What the fuck happened to her?"

"She's white as death."

"Carry her inside."

Is this what it's like to be lifted by angels or clouds? Arms are around me, arms…they're not hers. Inerea. How does this body pace its breaths? I press my hand to the chest attached to the arms holding me. Machines. What within you is not mechanised?

"Mallory, can you hear me?"

No. No your voice doesn't make sense. It pretends to care. I'm raw meat and bones, exposed veins of emotion. The arms lower me and there's a soft blanket beneath me. Hello. This is where I'll lie until death. This, this, this will be good. It's not too grand. Where are the loved ones to pity me in my last moments? Idealised notions such as those are books' possessions. Take them back, oh wait I have none to give.

"We have to stem the bleeding. Robyn."

New hands find me. No.

"No."

"Mallory, don't fight I'm trying to help."

Did Robyn speak so soothingly?

"No."

Hands outstretched to push her away. My hands? My hands. Yet I have no control over them.

"I can't heal you if you won't let me touch you."

"No more magic."

Stillness comes as the price of my rejection. At last the world doesn't move. Do I die now?

"Can you pin her down?"

No.

"Yeah I'll get her."

"No."

"You don't know what you're saying. You'll feel better in a minute."

"Stop it. This isn't the way to go about this at all."

Oh you're kind.

I reach to the voice. Who?

"It's amazing she's managed to survive this long with all her blood loss."

"Most of her wounds have closed up. She's just shy of a full fledged break down right now. If she says no magic than we listen. We give her what she wants."

Kyle.

"Kyle."

"I'm here."

"Kyle don't be stupid."

He is. He is going to try and save me, and die. I'm out of his reach.

"Let her sleep, Robyn."

Yes, Robyn. Let me sleep. Let me be...dead. Oh, please let me be dead.

* * *

Tell me what you see.
Me.
Yes. And what are you?
Nothing.

* * *

"Come watch the news."

Pause for silence.

"Shit, this is bad."

"Do you think she was there?"

"Why else would she have gone catatonic."

Leo. Did you ever wonder what it would be like if

you finally broke? Does it hurt now to see what you could have become? Here I am, your future. Come study, learn what traps to avoid. You asked for my help. I'll be your warning. Teflon hard eyes are watching me. What lies are you keeping behind them? He flinches. Does seeing yourself in my eyes hurt?

* * *

We're so beautifully human, so beautifully pure
Unknown to man, hidden in folklore
They like to tell stories about all their worries
And how if they could go back in time, they'd get us to unwind
The mistakes they made that led to the future,
Cold and unyielding where are your feelings?
Time can't you reverse? Take back your wicked curse.
I don't know what we've done that has left us always on the
run.
But I won't stand for this, no we won't take this.
It's not in our nature to be bound and lost.
It's not in our nature to let ourselves be double-crossed.
Beautifully human so beautifully human we are.
No, only you were so pure.

* * *

Later there's a hand on mine. Please don't touch me. Don't you know it's not safe?

* * *

What are you so afraid of? Jump.

* * *

Where does time go when it's waiting for us to resume? It settles in my wounds, ageing them into healing
scars. Stop. Stop making me better when your progress is
what made everything worse.

* * *

"Take care of him, won't you?" the faceless woman had said.

*The guard had grabbed the little boy by the legs, knotted the
rope round his ankles and tied him to the twist way chandelier.
Zach's younger brother. No one had to tell us. The boy's face was
full of features like echoes, diminutives of Zach's. Zach screamed
and they threw him to the floor, beat him until I couldn't distinguish
his body from the floor because it was all covered in blood. When he
couldn't move, Zach was left, the guard turned back to the whimpering child. The rest of us sat in silence as he dragged his army knife
across the boy's throat.*

Blood rain on a beige carpet.

*The faceless woman made us finish our lesson with both their
bodies there. None of us looked at them. When the child stopped gar-
gling his own blood and went limp at last, she called us one by one
to present our work. She made us stand beneath the body as she in-
spected what we'd done, taking her time. When she called my name,
I was very nearly sick. The only reason I didn't shake is because I
locked my joints, forced them forward like mechanisms. I held out my
offering and the first thick drop fell on my head.*

One.

*She tilted it this way and that, hoping to find a flaw or perhaps
making one up. She didn't need proof. Another drop landed on the
crest of my forehead and ran the scoop of my nose.*

Two.

*I bit hard the inside of my cheeks but that pain couldn't block
out the sound of Zach's groans. I tilted my head back in time to
see the third drop falling. It hit me square between the eyes before
dividing, two tracks that ran down either side of my nose, dipping*

beneath my eyes like tears.

Like war paint.

Three.

I lowered my head just as steadily and found those golden eyes upon me. She smiled.

"Perfect work Mallory."

* * *

Does she – does she see me? From whatever angelic field that has been blessed to have her in the afterlife. Does she see and hate me?

* * *

Come. Poor thing, you're all alone.

* * *

That mistake. The greatest mistake. It was to go in the first place. Don't listen to the lies dreams tell you.

* * *

Don't leave me. Promise you'll never leave me.

* * *

"Let me into the goddamn room Kyle!"

"No."

"She's going to die, you stupid piece of shit. Let Robyn in!"

You roar like him.

Scary.

* * *

I'm so sorry my little angel.
Please, everyone stop apologising.

* * *

Yes, we began to lay close together in the night, Zach and I. It was the most innocent of intimacies, an excuse to get used to holding someone. I rested my forehead against his chest and he wrapped his arms around me. His fingers were always climbing the ladder of my scar. We didn't speak anymore. Sometimes he whispered to me but I wouldn't reply. Sometimes I was the one who whispered. He would have frantic bursts of energy when he'd kiss my forehead, dotingly, as if I was something to protect and not to be protected from.

Then that morning came. The morning his family was to take him away. I woke to find him gone, as was usual. I dressed and, at a quarter to nine, I walked myself to class as I had begun taking the liberty of doing in my growing ease. The classroom was half full when I reached it. We still didn't acknowledge one another. Some of us were able to speak with ease to our professors, but even they could only just bring themselves to look at the rest of us. I was taking my seat when I heard the scream down the hall. By then the instinct to hide had all but been bled from me. Despite the hitch of fear when my heart beat doubled for a second, I was able to run towards danger. Not that I had had many causes to since Doctor Lindberg had arrived.

I was off down the hall in a second, closing in on the source of the shriek. I recognised Anya with a few of the younger students and a couple professors, who had clearly arrived there only moments before me. I don't know why, but my first thought was that, in the past two years, I still hadn't seen the little girl Doctor Lindberg promised would be okay. As I slowed, I realised we were outside the very room she had killed that man in. The same one Zach's brother had died in. I pushed my way into the doorway, though Anya hardly resisted having her view blocked. One of the professors reached out to me, falling short of grabbing my shoulder to pull me away. What I saw undid the past two years entirely.

Strung up, feet first.

Blood rain on a beige carpet.

When I think of it now, I remember it as if I were him, because it's the only way I can bear it.

Zach had woken up and seen me still sleeping with my head tossed to the side. My hair would have been splayed across my cheeks. It had grown long in the time the guards had gone, thick black tresses down to my rib cage. I wonder if he took a moment to kiss my forehead once more, to trace my scar, to say goodbye in some way, even though I wouldn't have the chance to reply. I wonder if he thought of taking me with him.

He left my room before the light came to bring colour to his ashen shadow. He was most at ease in the dark. In his room, he took no time searching the drawers for a fresh pair of clothes. Instead, he found the spare set of sheets in the bottom left drawer.

He had gone to that room where his ending began. Standing beneath the chandelier, he knotted the sheet around his ankles before looking up as I had done, his determination in his eyes like war paint. Jumping, he grabbed those chrome bars and flipped himself upside down. He hooked his legs over the metal arms and pulled himself up to secure himself to the light before lowering again. Tucked in the waistband of his trousers was a dagger. It wasn't the same one, such poetry would have been too generous for the likes of us. He drew it to his throat.

No, wishful thinking does not undo our past. But action can end our present and wipe our futures off the map.

* * *

The window is open. In the breeze, everything quivers as if it's about to fall.

Chapter XXVIII.

The next time I open my eyes, I am aware of things other than pain.

Like Kyle's body, pressed against the door.

Like the smell of wet rusty metal. Sweat. That's blood. I know blood. I'm still caked in it and the memories of it bathing my childhood are as fresh as a wound. Without moving anything other than my eyes, I look at a dark patch of flaking blood on my wrist. There's no way of knowing whose is whose. Inerea. Leora. Me. Yet I'm the only one who's still here.

I feel you watching me, Kyle. But I'm just not ready to look back yet.

Widely grown bruises flower like petals beneath blood stains all over my body. Look at me, an orchard of death. And yet he wouldn't pick me. I try to reconcile what I came to know of Thaddeus, the man who has taken my mother and grandmother, in the library, to what I have just seen but he keeps splintering. Is he not just like me? Driven to the point of doing whatever it takes to survive? Surely I understand that now I know my past. But I don't want to sink deeper into this abyss of comradery. Now I am ready to be found.

I look back into Kyle's deep eyes. Blue circles of ill health have spread beneath his eyes. All this wakefulness for me. He must not have slept in days.

"Thank heavens," he breathes, but doesn't make a move towards me.

Good. Please don't touch me.

"Did you say something?" a voice asks from the other side of the door and Kyle turns away from me.

This I cannot abide. I turn my head away in disgust. Never trust a voice belonging to a body you cannot see.

"Dammit Kyle what the hell is going on in there?"

It's Aaron. He sounds impatient and upset. But Kyle disregards his question.

"Robyn, can you get a change of clothes?"

"Of course. Come on Aaron, Leo."

"Like hell I'm going anywhere," one of them answers, and I shudder at the forcefulness of the voice.

"Ignore them," Kyle says softly, his voice drawing my gaze back to him. No words. I can't even bring myself to unstick my jaw from where my teeth are tightly clamped down. "I think it's a good idea for you to have a bath. We should wash the blood off," he adds, when I don't stir.

And take away the last traces of Inerea? I hug myself, rolling my head to the other side. These are my memories now.

"I won't make you, if you're not ready. I'll sit right here. As soon as you feel up for anything, food, water, just tell me." He brushes my hair from my face and I don't hate his touch. His hand is cool and makes me realise exactly how feverish my forehead feels. "I'm staying right here."

You're too good for me.

I curl my body into the foetal position, resting my head on his leg. He strokes my hair, running his fingers down from the roots to the tips. He gently prises the knots out before wiping the sweat from the back of my neck.

Your hand heals.

I unclench my arms from around myself and clasp his hand in my own. You who knows what I've just remembered and doesn't recoil at the sight of me. How are you so good? But touching him burns. I flinch, drawing my hand back as if I've touched a flame. My fingers are sore and bright red.

"Burns," he says, "I can bandage them up for you if you like."

I suck the tip of my index finger but the bitter poison

won't go. The heat of my breath only inflames it more.
Withdrawing it, I glance up at him.

"I."

His hand stills at the sound of my voice.

"I can take a bath," I whisper hoarsely.

"I'll go run one for you. There's a bathrobe so you
can put that on and give me your clothes to throw away."

If he gets rid of them, the memories will go with
them too, yes?

"And Mallory," he starts, a look of extreme discomfort on his face, "we really ought to heal the burns at least.
You're not going to be able to do anything otherwise."

I stare at him blankly. Do what? Everything I touches
falls apart. I shake my head.

"No magic."

"I'm not talking about Robyn," he says gently. Then
who? Leora is gone. "What about your friend Chloe?"

My heart melts at the thought of her. So much has
changed. I am not worthy of her friendship unless I tell
her how disloyal I have been, who I really am. That's not
a conversation I'm ready for. I shake my head fervently
and the effort makes me dizzy.

"No."

"The water will hurt you," he pleads gently. He stops
short of asking me to do it for him though I know that's
what he's thinking. And what wouldn't I do for him.

"Fine."

Just then there's a knock at the door. Kyle gets off the
bed and cracks it open, sighing a breath of relief when he
sees who's in the hall.

"I got Leo to distract him. He's not happy about it,"
Robyn says, passing him a pile of clothes through the
door.

Kyle opens it all the way, beckoning her in. She looks
slightly stunned for a moment before crossing the thresh-

old.

"Can you just heal her hands. The burns are pretty bad."

"Of course," Robyn says, and it is quite possibly the gentlest tone I have ever heard. "Hey Mallory."

She doesn't expect an answer as she crosses the room, crouching beside my bed and taking my hands in hers. I imagine her expression is unreadable to anyone other than the people in this room. She tries to soothe it with indifference, but the pain is apparent, the commiseration of my loss. Yet another parent figure gone. Only another orphan could understand that. She smiles at me, her face beautiful and softened in this moment of understanding. As quietly as she can, she murmurs the words for the healing spell and I am grateful for the quiet for I can barely stand to hear those words.

Kyle disappears into the adjoining bathroom as Robyn sees herself out of the room without another word. With both of them gone, I test my feet against the floor. They're the only part of me that doesn't ache. I walk over to the chair, with slow plodding steps, on which the bathrobe is draped. The design steals my thoughts, soft purple spirals against a lavender background. I can't gather the focus or the energy to remove my clothes. I hear water splash against the porcelain tub. In a few minutes, Kyle returns.

"What's the matter?" he asks, approaching me cautiously, "Did you change your mind about the bath?"

I shake my head.

"I can't."

"Can't what?"

I look at him, wide eyed, then down at myself.

"Do you need help?"

I nod.

He smiles, then slides my shirt over my head and lays

it on the chair. The way he hooks his fingers under the hem puts me in the mind of Alistair and I shudder. Kyle stops, breathing quietly and watching me, waiting until I nod again. Next, he unbuckles the arm sheath that has been left without its blade. He unbuttons my jeans, peeling them off of me. I step out of them and he tosses them on the chair.

"I'm going to turn around so you can do the rest. I'll be right here," he promises. Once his back is to me, I remove my underwear and bra. The silk robe slips over my body like cold water and I fasten the sash into a knot. In a jerky movement, as if my arm is weighted by lead, I lift my arm and tap his shoulder.

"Ready."

"Can you walk?" he asks and I nod.

He takes my hand all the same and I'm thankful for the support as we cross the room. My whole body is a dull aching mass of flesh. In the bathroom, the smell of sweetened pomegranates fills the room. Pink pearly bubbles form clouds across the surface of the water. Kyle turns off the faucet, so the room goes silent save for the dripping.

One, two, three.

I stare at the side of the bathtub.

"Here."

Kyle shuts his eyes and extends his hand to help me in. I let the bathrobe fall and push my weight onto his hand to ease myself into the water. It lights my skin like feather kisses, rising to consume me as I sink neck deep into it. When the water stops sloshing, Kyle opens his eyes and seats himself on the floor beside me. I rest my cheek against the back of the bathtub so as to look at him.

Don't smile to try to make me feel okay.

He does.

Why does it warm my heart when I should feel nothing but sorrow?

He looks even more exhausted up close. I can see he is only just keeping his eyes open, the warm steam having a soporific effect on him. He picks up a washcloth and dips it in the bath. Ringing out the excess water, he doesn't take his gaze away from mine.

"I'm going to clean your face first," he says.

I don't refuse so he runs the cloth down my cheek. The fluffy fibres have been matted down so they run frictionless across my skin. He rinses the cloth in the bath again before repeating the process until my face is no longer dried out by blood. Next, he takes a hairbrush from beside the sink and nudges my shoulders forward slightly so he can get all of my hair out from behind my back. I hear it dripping onto the floor.

One, two, three.

Sinking the brush's teeth into my hair, he runs it through as gently as he had done with his hand earlier. Even when he comes to fresh formed snarls of tangles, he takes care not to pull too hard. I think back to that new memory, the caretaker singing to me and I open my mouth. I want to share that with him, the little pieces of my history he cannot know because not everything about me was documented in a file. But my throat is too raw for that now. He places my hair over my shoulder.

Where did he learn how to mend people? Was it from Robyn? Is he how she was pieced back together after such a loss?

I feel my skin pruning beneath the surface of the velvety water. With my left hand I swirl a clump of bubbles around. I want to pretend it's a fluffy cloud of childish daydreams of heaven, sitting on a sorbet sunset sky. But I've seen heaven. Was it so idyllic? It doesn't make sense for Inerea to be in that cold, sterile place. She drove a car yesterday. She waited outside while I ran to try to save someone else's' life. I should have thought about hers.

The thought ties a knot in my chest.

"Do you want me to wash your hair for you?" Kyle asks.

I don't bother turning around for fear he'll see the expression of guilt on my face and try to comfort me. Instead, I nod my affirmation in the direction of the opposite wall. He unhooks the shower head from its stand before running the water, waiting for it to heat up.

"Scoot forwards a bit and tilt your head back."

He holds the shower head so close to my scalp it tickles with its warm jets. Small beads splash onto my forehead and roll down over my eyelids. He lifts my long tresses to dampen the hair on the back of my neck before letting them fall back down so they can be soaked too. Then he turns the water off. His fingers begin to move across my scalp, massaging in a shampoo with the same fragrance as the bubbles I'm immersed in. Making circular motions with his thumbs, he works his way through my hair until it's thoroughly covered. The repetitive sensation has a calming effect on my chest. He rinses it out before sitting back down beside me. For a while, he says nothing. He doesn't look at me either. The bath water is cooling and I know I could just fall asleep.

Though it feels as if my eyes are only shut a moment, when I open them again the light has gone from the window. Kyle hasn't stirred but he's now studying my face.

"Are you ready to get out?" he asks.

"Mhm."

He hands me a towel before taking my hand and helping me out. The surplus of water still in my hair drips all across the bathmat, some of it splattering the pale teal tiles. I dry myself off before wrapping the towel around my body.

"I'd like to get you something to eat if you don't mind me leaving you for a little bit."

"That's okay."

"I put the clothes Robyn brought on the bed so you can get changed. Do you feel like you could eat something heavy?"

I shake my head in response. The thought of food may make my stomach growl faintly but it also makes me feel slightly ill. I follow Kyle all the way to the door, wishing I could go with him. But leaving my little safe haven makes me feel dizzy, so I retreat back towards the bed. A pair of loose silky pyjamas have been folded and left on the pillow.

When he returns, I've curled back up under the blanket. He's carrying a plate with a sandwich and a big bottle of water in his other hand. Placing them in front of me on the mattress, he sits across from me, crossing his legs. I space out staring at the fluffy white bread puffed up by generous portions of peanut butter and jam.

"Sorry they're not Aaron's pancakes. This was always mine and Robyn's favourite growing up."

Picking off the corner of the crust with my finger nail, I chew it until the small bite turn to a mush in my mouth. The roof of my mouth feels raw and I lick the peanut butter off of it. I take one half of the sandwich and find myself devouring it ravenously within a matter of seconds.

There's a knock at the door and Kyle slips out.

"Robyn told me she's awake. Has she eaten yet? Do you need me to cook her anything?" Aaron's muffled voice asks on the other side of the door.

"I just brought he a sandwich but thanks."

There's a pause then I hear Kyle's hand rest on the door handle. I watch it drop beneath the pressure.

"I'd like to come in and talk to her."

The door handle rises again.

"She's hardly saying a word still. I don't think she

wants to talk about any of it yet."

"Robyn said she let her heal her burns but what about the cuts?"

My stomach flips and I put the last quarter of my sandwich down.

"I haven't asked but I don't think she'll agree to it."

"Why the hell not?"

"Whatever happened at the antique store, I'm assuming. Just let her heal normally. You'll do more damage but forcing her to do something she doesn't want to. I'm going to bandage what cuts I can and, if she sleeps long enough, the isuazko will do the rest. She'll be healed in a couple of days."

"I still want to see her."

"I know you do. As soon as she's ready I'll come and get you."

There's a moment of silence again and what comes next breaks my heart.

"This is my fault." He's crying. My eyes widen in shock.

"Aaron no it's not."

"I was right there and she couldn't wake me up. So she went to that fucking store alone. If I weren't such a Neanderthal I would have been with her. I could have kept them safe."

"There's no knowing that."

"Kyle, we both know I could have," he says, sniffing.

I can't help myself. I'm up and out of bed in a heartbeat, making my way to the door. I pull on it sharply and Aaron half stumbles into the room.

Aaron's eyes are red; this is clearly not the first time he's cried recently. His face is pale and he has the same signs of lack of sleep painted beneath his eyes as Kyle.

"Mallory," he steps towards me then hesitates, but I throw my arms around him.

"It's not your fault," I promise, digging my fingers into his back to hold him as tightly as possible. Suddenly I'm sobbing too, shaking in his arms. "It's not your fault."

He buries his face against my collarbone and I can feel his hot tears running down my chest.

"I'm so sorry. I wasn't there to protect you."

I want to answer him but all I can do is shake my head.

It is not your fault. Suddenly my head is spinning and my knees feel weak beneath me. Kyle puts a hand round my waist to support me as I step back from Aaron and give him a weak smile. It elicits no response of happiness, merely a further crumpling of his expression.

"Come on, let's get you back to bed," Kyle says soothingly. He nods at Aaron who backs down the hallway, unable to meet my eyes again before he goes. With slow steps, Kyle leads me back to the bed and lowers me onto it. "You should drink the water. We've barely been able to get any into you the past three days."

"Three days?" I croak. He opens the bottle for me.

"Drink," he commands.

I press the bottle to my chapped lips and take a long sip. When I put it back down, half of the water is gone.

"Why are you so good at this?" I ask, my throat cleared of dryness.

"Do you really want to hear another story about loss right now?"

His eyes are expansive oceans of sadness. I shake my head. I don't want to hear it and it would clearly pain him to tell it.

"I'd like to sleep now," I whisper.

"Do you want me to stay with you?"

"Yes but you should sleep."

I feel selfish asking him to stay when he's clearly been watching over me day and night.

"I'm not tired just yet."

"But-"

"Please, don't worry about me." I bite my lip and study the flower pattern on the blanket. "But of course, you can't help worrying about others. Alright. I'll get blankets to make up a place on the floor," he sighs.

"You don't have to sleep down there."

"I don't want to wake you if I get up in the night."

He leaves me again and I pick at a loose thread in the quilt, waiting for him to come back. It feels hollow inside again. The crying was not as cathartic as I thought it would be and not being able to see Kyle, even if for a moment, hurts. He returns with his arms full with a thick duvet, a blanket and a pillow. He lays the duvet on the ground before switching out the light and curling up beneath his blanket. Despite having said he wasn't tired, he falls asleep almost instantly, his chest beginning to rise and fall at a slower pace. I keep an eye over the steady rhythm until eventually it lulls me to sleep.

* * *

The wall is covered in dull yellow damask wallpaper that is peeling up at the corners. I hate the way it looks like the colour of fungus sprouting from a rotting log. I hate the way it clearly hasn't mattered since someone was paid to plaster it on. But I cannot look away. My body is that rotting wood, fallen on its side, never to move again, never to be noticed beneath bracken and moss. All I can do is think of that wallpaper's horrible pattern. If some-one crosses my field of vision, blocking my view of the wall, my mind simply goes blank.

"I thought you said she was better."

"She was! When I woke up this morning she was just staring at the wall. I tried to talk to her but she won't move."

"Fuck this."

The door slams open, banging against the wall. A body comes towards me. My mind draws a blank on the face and the voice.

"Mallory you need to get out of bed. You're not going to get better like this."

"Aaron!"

A pair of hands grab my shoulders and shake me aggressively. The world is blurry and I feel sick. I feel hungry too but that I can ignore.

"No, I'm done waiting. Look at her, she hardly looks human anymore!"

Now you see do you? Now I'm undressed of my human disguise. Now I have murdered and failed to protect those that mattered most.

"Aaron let go of her."

Leo is back. I feel the hands being prised off of my person and I am grateful to slip back into the bed.

"How can you two be so calm about this?"

"No one is calm," Leo snaps, "But what are your outbursts doing to help? She trusts Kyle, so let him help her. This isn't something you or I can fix, as much as I know it pains you."

"What the hell would you know about helping people. You're a fucking machine who just does the bidding of the Onyevaras without any concern for other people," Aaron yells. There's a crack and a thud. That's what flesh breaking sounds like. I used to undo people like that too.

"Get out," Leo orders in a voice, not only cool, but sharp.

The door shuts with a slam. I shudder. Silence. I prefer its silky texture to the rough edges of voices.

"Leo," Kyle starts, "He's out of his mind with guilt. He didn't mean it. I'm so sorry."

"Please don't. I don't need pity."

There's a shift of weight on my bed. Is he so close? I reach out my fingers and prod his side. My gaze becomes fixated on a belt loop of his jeans. He's not allowed to move, not now I'm finally distracted from the wallpaper. I hook my finger through the belt loop.

"That's the most I've seen her move all day."

The window is open. In the breeze, everything quivers but it does not fall.

* * *

The next day, Leo is allowed back in the room. Only today is different. I'm upright and drinking water.

"Good," Kyle sighs, as I drain the bottle, as if it is some sort of proof of my restoring sanity.

Leo is leaning against the wall watching us. I try not to look at him. I feel embarrassed by my infantilised state. Still, it's nice to feel something other than guilt and grief for a change, which is why I'm grateful for his presence.

"How's Aaron," I ask.

"Apologetic. He's a bit impulsive as you might have noticed. Still, it's rare for him to actually admit guilt over it," Kyle says, "I think this has affected him quite badly. He's still blaming himself for what happened."

He bites his lip, as if he regrets referring to the incident in question. And it hurts, to be reminded of it, but I am also able to feel it at a slight distance now. I set the empty bottle aside.

"I'd like to talk about it now, if that's not too much trouble."

Leo looks up from the floor, surprised, but Kyle's look does not change. He's known this would happen since they first found me outside.

"Nothing that might help you feel better is too much

trouble," he assures me, squeezing my hand.

I'm not sure it will make me feel better, but I know it is the first step to being able to function despite the loss. So, I start. From the dream all the way to how I made my way back to their house, I tell my story. I am able to recite it with a numb clarity. The events seem too farfetched for even my bizarre life to belong to me. I hear them as though I am a confused listener, who has no context of what we are or the events of the past week. When I've finished, none of us speak for some time. Leo is still leaning against the wall and Kyle is sitting beside me on the bed.

"You already knew about what happened at the antique store didn't you," I say.

"We guessed the part about the deabrueon. But yes. On the news the other day it was announced that two unidentified bodies were found. The police are crawling all over the place looking for a girl who was spotted running out of the store just before they were discovered but, fortunately for you, no one got a good enough look at her."

I furrow my brow.

"But Alex recognised me." The two exchange a dark look. "You used magic on him."

"We helped him forget the whole incident. Think of the trauma it spared him," Kyle assures me, though I know he did this only for me.

"We tried to get in touch with Leora after what happened and when we couldn't we assumed she was one of the two. But we had no idea," he falters for a moment, "we had no idea the other – I mean that it was Inerea. I'm so sorry Mallory."

I swallow hard, but the lump in my throat grows.

"I don't want to stop fighting just because Leora's gone."

"That's not really what we should be focusing on right now. You need to get better."

"And you think the deabrueon will just patiently wait for my recovery before attacking again? Killing Inerea and Leora was an escalation. Thaddeus has taken everyone from me. I want him to die."

Kyle stills, his pupils dilating. His face looks pained as he glances back at Leo, who shakes his head.

"Not at the cost of your life," he says.

"Why not? I have no family to live for. All I want is to prevent him from ever doing what he did to us to anyone else. He may as well have already killed me, so let me have my dying wish. Help me kill him." Kyle's face lights with conflicted anguish at my plea. "Please, if you're my friend you'll grant me this." He sighs, closing his eyes.

"I'll help you but there are a few conditions. First, this isn't a suicide mission. You have to be as willing to fight for your own survival as much as for his demise. Second, we follow Leora's plan: find the spell and use it to defeat him. And last of all, when it comes time to fight, you stay here."

"Yes to the first two, but I will not be left behind."

"He's right," Leo interjects, "without much combat training you're not going to be the one wielding the weapon. If we bring you along it just puts your life at an unnecessary risk."

I glower at Leo but he doesn't waver. Turning my gaze to Kyle, I open my mouth to speak. He knows, with my training from the Academy, I am better equipped than any of them to fight Thaddeus and yet he still prioritises my wellbeing? But he knows I won't object because, even if he agrees, the others won't without some explanation.

"Fine. I'll stay here."

"Then we're at your service," Kyle says.

"You two are getting a bit ahead of yourselves. We need to find the spell first and locate the Vaerdiexes stone before we can even think of facing Thaddeus," Leo comments.

"We'll get the first half of the spell from the store's office. That will make it easier to track down the other part."

"But I thought you said there were still police at the crime scene," I say.

"There are. But Robyn can get us around them easily enough."

Chapter XXIX.

"You can't park right in front of the store. That's suspicious," Robyn says to Aaron, as the car rolls slowly up the street.

"Well, I'm not circling around to find another parking spot. We've already been around twice. That's what's suspicious," he counters.

We take the parking spot across the street but none of the news reporters, on-lookers, or policemen seem bothered by us.

"Please take as little time as possible. I don't want you running the chance of being exposed longer than you have to," Kyle says to his sister.

She brushes off his concern with a pointed look in his direction.

"I'll be fine. Now, are you ready?" Robyn asks me.

"Wait, what?" Kyle and Aaron demand simultaneously.

"She agreed not to be there for the fight but you two are quite idiotic if you thought Mallory was going to let herself be left behind. Even I saw that coming," Leo intones, looking back at us from the passenger seat before taking a remarkable amount of interest in the dirt under his nails.

"I said no fighting! That was part of our deal," Kyle insists.

"You said I couldn't come when you fight Thaddeus. Until then, I'm going to do everything I can to help."

"Whatever we agreed, I still don't think it's a good idea for you to go in there."

I know he's referring to returning to the scene of Inerea's death and, though the thought of it has pained me for days, I am determined to be as helpful as possible.

"The-the bodies will have been removed by now.

There was never anything else in there that was going to break my resolve."

"I'm getting old," Robyn groans, "can we go already?"

"Fine," Kyle sighs, though he glares at Robyn.

It's the first time I've seen him openly display animosity towards his sister. I know, despite her laid-back attitude, she's only doing this to comfort me. She must understand what it is to need to affix yourself to a goal after loss. Ever since I found my way back to their house, she has shown little kindnesses that I would not expect of her.

"Don't mess this up with your stupidity," she huffs. Well, kind in relative Robyn terms. "Destoyar savis maiz letai aizkawa ni vanage sis a destoyara vanagemar kasun cituuka diravaz'noventa vanagemar savis."

She finishes the cloaking spell but neither of us disappear. I can still see her sitting beside Kyle.

"Am I supposed to be able to see you, or does that defeat the purpose of the cloaking spell?"

"As long as we're both under the cloak of sight created by me, we can see each other. To anyone else we're invisible."

"And never looked better," Aaron adds. "Ow!"

He rubs his bicep where Robyn planted a swift punch.

"We can still be heard though so keep the talking quiet and only when absolutely necessary. Let's go."

Kyle leans across me and opens the door, following us out on the pavement. The streets are busy and I stumble back into the road to avoid a pedestrian who is barrelling right at me.

"Where are you going?" Aaron asks Kyle, twisting round in his seat.

"I can't just sit here. I'm getting coffee."

"Like hell you are. You know it makes you jumpy and weird."

"But I'm tired," he groans, and I can't help giggling at his childlike intonation.

He looks around furtively in an attempt to spot me and his gaze settles a little to my left.

"Come on."

Robyn takes my hand and leads me across the street. Despite my resolve in the car, my chest is constricted with anxiety. I keep waiting for someone to turn around and spot us. But Robyn walks as confidently as ever past spectators, ducks under the police tape and waits until one of the policemen comes out so we can slip through the door.

I breathe a sigh of relief as we enter and Robyn gives me a warning look. Luckily, no one seems to think anything of the small sound. I cast a look around. The bodies' removal I had been certain would have happened by now, but I didn't know to what extent the rest of the store would have been cleaned up. Thankfully, the blood has been cleaned away. There are only two other people in the room, who seem to be finishing the last of the cleaning up. One sweeps up the shards of shattered vase while the other ducks behind the counter. I look at Robyn, who is ushering me into the office. She takes the risk of opening the door ever so slightly and shutting it behind us, but does so in near silence so as not to draw attention. Leora's spell on it must have vanished after she died, just as Inerea's did from my memory. Once we're inside the office, I feel panic uprooting itself from within me.

"They've finished investigating the scene and have made no announcements about suspects. That's good, it must mean they haven't found anything to link you to this place," she says, "it would be all over the news if they had."

"Good? I didn't kill anyone yet I'm being considered

the murderer. I would hardly consider that good."

I know she's just trying to comfort me but somehow her comments don't do anything to ease my mind.

"You did run out of a murder scene with a bloody sword," she points out, a sympathetic look crossing her face. I'm not sure I can take much more of her pity.

"Whatever, let's just find the spell." I start by trying to open the drawer Leora had kept it in before but it's locked. "She must have had the key on her. Shit."

"I've got this," Robyn says proudly, moving me aside. "Matkur."

The lock gives no sound of opening and when she pulls on the drawer it doesn't budge.

"It must be a more complicated spell binding it shut. I wonder why it didn't fade like the one on the door?" Robyn wonders aloud.

"Maybe she didn't cast it. Let me."

She raises her eyebrows but doesn't say anything as she steps aside. I place my hand to the lock and think of what Alistair said. All I need is the feeling of the spell. I try and call to mind the lock spell that was on the door. That was cold magic, but it could be undone had I known what to do at the time. I focus on picking the lock as if it were that one. There's no sound then, suddenly, a little click.

"How'd you do that?" Robyn demands, "you can cast without words?"

"Alistair taught me," I say grimly, and the jealousy blanches from her face.

I pull the drawer out. Inside is the same box. Lifting the lid reveals it to be empty, however.

"Damn it, where else would she have kept it?" Robyn mutters.

She hands me the box before going to look through the bookshelf.

"Maybe she left it in one of her books?" I suggest.

"Great, that's exactly what I want. To leaf through every page of every book," she grumbles, making a start.

I start to put the box back when I notice a gap between the base of the drawer and its side. Peeking from beneath, however, reveals the same space is gone. I try to get my fingers between to pry up the bottom but can't manage to get a good enough grip on the narrow space. Glancing around, I spot a ruler in the pencil pot on the desk. It should be just thin enough. I slot it in and bend the plastic top until the base lifts slightly. Now, with enough room, I manage to pull away the rest of the false base.

"I think I've got it," Robyn and I say at the same time.

She spins around. Each of us is holding a half sheet of torn paper. She crosses over to me and holds the two pieces together. They're a perfect fit.

"That's the other half of the spell," she says curiously, "I wonder what it was doing in there. Looks like you're not a complete idiot after all."

She nods at the disassembled drawer.

"Is that definitely it?" She examines it, translating the words under her breath.

"It looks like it. Let's go."

She starts towards the door but before I follow her, I spot something else at the bottom of the drawer.

"Hold on." Withdrawing the sheet of paper, I scan over it only to find it too is in the ancient language. "I can't read it."

"Thank god you can cast without words, it would be a nightmare to teach you the ancient language."

"Hey! I know a bit!" I reply indignantly as she reads over the paper.

"Holy shit."

"What?"

"Give me a minute so I can figure out if Leora left us a heaven send."

I follow her to the table, waiting while she reads the page. Once she reaches the bottom, her eyes flick back up and she rereads it.

"How did she find this?"

I hear footsteps coming towards the door. Hastening to put the false base and box back in the drawer, I shut it just as two police officers enter.

"There were no signs the perpetrator came in here. There's not even a window for god's sake," the man says, following the woman in.

"Listen, if it were up to me we'd be out of here already. But there's no forensic evidence to indicate a possible culprit so we've got to sweep the entire place. They made a mess of things by cleaning up the DNA too soon."

Robyn sits stock still in her chair. She's scooted it in close enough to the table that she can't slide out without moving the chair. As they walk past her, she looks at me frantically and mouths 'help'. I move slowly and silently around to the other side of the table. Sticking my foot out, I trip one of the policemen so he stumbles and falls into the table. In the moment of commotion, Robyn leaps up, knocking her chair to the ground as if it were the force of his fall.

"What is the matter with you today?" the policewoman sighs in exasperation.

"Just tired," he replies, rubbing his shin, "must have tripped on my shoelace."

We wait beside the door, hoping someone will come in or out. But the two seem set on staying in the room.

"What are we going to do?" I mouth at Robyn. She shrugs, biting her lip.

The papers are clutched tightly to her chest. I settle my gaze on the clock. We've already been gone almost fifteen minutes; the others will start to worry soon. In the next hour that seems to never end, the two police go over the entire room. When they reach the bottom drawer of the desk, I hold my breath. I don't know why, seeing as there's nothing in there to find. One of them inspects the box but shuts the drawer again without noticing the false base. Another thirty minutes is spent moving documents into piles to take with them. Twenty more flipping through the books on the shelves but, seeing as they're in the ancient language, neither of them is able to make heads or tails of them. When one asks the other if perhaps they're in Latin, Robyn's face contorts as she attempts to stifle her laughter.

"You two almost done in here?"

A third police officer peeks around the door.

"Shouldn't be much longer," the woman answers.

Please don't leave without opening the door enough for us to leave, I silently plead.

"Come take a look at this."

He comes in, leaving the door ajar. Thank god. We leave unnoticed as they examine the books together. The front door isn't such a problem. Just as we emerge from the office, someone is stepping out. Robyn rushes for the door but I pull her back. The door swings shut. Glancing around to make sure we're alone, she swats my hand away.

"What are you doing? Now we're stuck in here until the next person happens to wander through," she hisses.

"Robyn it's here."

Her eyes narrow.

"Noutsumar letai kokku ni saviski isuazko'caz makun."

Her crossbow materialises in her hand and she loads a bolt into it immediately.

"Where?"

"No, not the deabrueon."

I approach the flat display case that is adjoined to the desk with the cash register. I remember it now. Scattered amongst other trinkets the first time Inerea brought me in here. It had been insignificant then but now it hums with the blue aura Illarion imbued it with. This is it. I press my hand to the lock and hear a clicking sound. Prying it open with haste, I remove the object and lower the lid.

"I wasn't aware you were a jewellery kind of girl."

"Let's go."

"Wait one second. Dersutisanar."

Her crossbow vanishes once more.

We're lucky again for, at that moment, the three policemen leave the office and head out the front door. We follow suit, before darting across the street. Robyn pulls me into a crouch behind the car, waiting until there's no one around.

"Eskuler."

Our skin glows for a moment before returning to normal. We right ourselves, glancing around nervously to be sure no one has seen us.

"Let's get out of here."

She tugs the car handle but it doesn't open. Sheltering her eyes, she presses her nose to the glass.

"What's wrong?" I ask, as she stands back up, frowning.

"They're not here. What's going on?"

She takes her phone, scrolls through her contacts and holds the phone to her ear.

"You better have been eaten alive. That's the only excuse for leaving us behind."

Crossing her arms, she taps her index finger on the crook of her elbow.

"You did what?!"

She scowls, hanging up, and fury blooms in her eyes.

"Where are they?" I ask.

She ignores me and storms towards the café Chloe and I frequent about two buildings down. I go in after her, thankful we don't have to wait for people to open the door for us anymore. The three of them are seated at a table in the corner. The surface is cluttered with empty coffee cups, which the waitress piles onto her tray as she puts down another mug in front of Kyle. His eyes are wide and he drums his palms anxiously on the table. Aaron gives the waitress a half smile and she blushes as she returns to the counter.

"You went to get coffee?"

"Kyle wanted some and we couldn't leave him on his own. He gets strange when he has caffeine," Aaron explains to me, shrugging.

Kyle begins to stack the packs of creamer into a tower.

"Well you shouldn't have let him have any," Robyn snaps, snatching the bowl of creamer from her brother.

"I need those," he pouts.

"Don't be annoying."

We sit down at the table and Aaron instantly leans towards me. Out of the corner of my eye, I spot the waitress needling me with a glare.

"You want anything?" he asks. My body is still singing with the adrenaline rush of what I've just discovered. "We can get you some coffee or tea? Apparently, their scones are just delightful here."

"I might have some coffee," I say.

"It's good," Kyle interjects, staring me down without blinking.

"On second thought, maybe I'll pass," I reply, frowning at him. "Should we go?"

"But I just got my third cup!" Kyle exclaims.

"Third!" Robyn scoffs, looking up from the menu.

"No, that's actually his sixth," Leo sighs.

He seems to be drawing as much attention as Aaron from a nearby table of girls I recognise from school. Please don't come say hello. Thankfully, they take no note of me.

"Shh, the mugs are halves," Kyle whispers to me.

"Why didn't you stop him from ordering?" Robyn demands.

"Because I don't really care that much," Aaron says, shrugging his shoulders, before adding to me. "Also, we're fine staying here."

"We can discuss this in the open?"

"Why not."

"I'm assuming things went alright or Robyn would be throwing a tantrum right about now," Aaron chuckles, taking a sip of his coffee. He offers it to me but I shake my head.

"I don't throw tantrums. But yes, how could everything not have gone well with me in charge."

"So we have the spell now," I start, "um Kyle?"

Kyle's eyes have glazed over as he stares, entranced, at the creamer in his hand.

"It's hazelnut," he assures me.

"That's it."

Robyn takes the cup from him and promptly dumps the contents into the potted plant behind her.

"Hey!"

"You're not doing heroin, you have no right to act like a drug addict," she says, "yes, we have the whole spell. Leora must have found the other half. But that's not all I-we found. I'm not entirely sure what it means exactly but see what you make of it."

She takes out the paper she had stopped to examine in the office and hands it to Leo. He reads it once before a v shaped crease forms between his eyebrows. Twice more through, but he doesn't look any less confused.

"Could this possibly be," he trails off.

"Let me see," Aaron says, taking it from him.

"I think Leora found the resurrection ritual. That's why the deabrueon took her out. That's why she must have used such a strong spell on the desk drawer that it outlasted her death, so the deabrueon couldn't get it back."

I glance at the paper. She had managed to find it? She said earlier she knew a bit about it, but had she really managed to discover the rest since we last saw one another and her time of death?

"It's all a riddle though," Aaron says, frowning.

"I know. But once Kyle comes down from his high he'll probably be able to make sense of it," Robyn says.

Kyle crosses his arms and sinks in his seat.

"I can make sense of you!"

"If he can stop acting like a child for twenty seconds that is."

"This is great step forward," Aaron enthuses, swigging down more of his coffee.

"We still don't have the stone though. So, this is effectively useless until then," Leo says.

"Glass half empty."

"Thanks to Robyn it's completely empty," Kyle mutters.

"Oh calm down drama queen."

"So, not to take the pessimism out of the conversation, but I did happen to come across the stone," I interject.

"You're just mentioning this now?" Robyn demands.

"Well I did find it all of five minutes ago."

Reaching in my pocket, I pull out the item I had removed from the antique store. It's a milky blue stone set in an old ornate silver setting, with pinnacles like a snowflake. The other three stare blankly at it but Kyle perks up immediately.

"Shiny aura," he muses, taking it from me.

I exchange a concerned look with Robyn. But, as the only other one who met with Illarion, it stands to reason he can also see the blue aura emanating from the stone.

"The only problem is," Robyn starts reluctantly, "I've never seen a more complicated spell. I don't think we can manage it, no matter how powerful you are."

"Oh, suddenly Mallory's powerful? What happened to her being incompetent?" Aaron asks, amused.

"She's a wordless caster. Makes sense. Your half Thiel, half Ovira. Magic runs strongest in those families."

"Still, I haven't heard of a wordless caster in decades. They're incredibly rare," Leo says, suddenly interested.

"We're not specimens for examination," I sigh, though I can't help the flutter of pleasure at his interest. Luckily no one seems to notice it in my voice.

"Anyway, I was thinking, there's probably only one way we're going to get this spell done," Robyn says, looking darkly at the others. They all go still and silent, even Kyle.

"You're not suggesting...blood magic?" Leo asks.

I'm aware of how taboo this is, if only by the fact that even Leo seems to have reservations about it.

"We need at least a third for this. And unless someone's got a witch to volunteer, we need Leora."

"Small problem," I say coldly, "she's not exactly available."

"She doesn't strictly need to be alive for this to work."

They all look at me.

"What?" I ask when no one says anything.

"Well this is sort of your revenge mission," Aaron starts, "don't get me wrong, I'd love to see the sick fuck get what's coming to him. But like I said, it's your mission, your choice."

I look around at all of them. I'm not sure exactly what Robyn's proposing but it doesn't sound good. Still, at this point, what won't I do to avenge Inerea?

"Fine. What do we have to do?"

"We'll need to get some blood from Leora's body. That means breaking into the morgue."

The thought of draining Leora of her blood makes my stomach turn but I can't turn back on my word now.

"Let's go now then."

"Mallory, you don't have to do this bit," Robyn says quietly.

"Like you guys said, it's my mission."

Aaron bites his lip, clearly regretting his choice of words in the first place.

"Okay," Robyn replies, "we go now. The police station isn't far from here."

Fifteen minutes later, Robyn and I are cloaked again, and standing outside the police station. It's not difficult for us to get in; people are going in and out every few minutes. The incident at the antique store has seemingly left them very busy. I lead Robyn in. For some reason, having the Vaerdiexes stone tucked safely in my pocket puts me at ease. We follow the signs to the morgue and, moments later we've entered the room.

"So, what is blood magic?" I ask as we stand over the cloth concealing Leora's body.

"There was a time when magic began to fade from Sundalev. It used to exist freely within every man and woman but over time, it dwindled down to a handful of witches, dragoviks, angeleru, and artari. It's quite gruesome. People would kidnap them and drain their blood for spells. It was usually witches mind you. Artari hardly have enough magic to cast unless there are a whole bunch of them, dragoviks are far too powerful for your average

human to capture, and the angeleru live in the City Between, Miesarinda, which is in-between Earth and Sundalev. Not exactly easy access. That's why witches are so
mistrustful."

"That's horrible," I whisper, staring down at Leora.

Suddenly I don't want to have anything to do with
what we're about to do. Robyn takes a vial from the counter, and slides Leora's arm from beneath the sheet. I think
I'm going to be sick but can't look away.

"Don't worry, I can manage this bit. Marel."

A small cut appears on Leora's inner elbow. Red
beads to the surface quickly before rising out of her in
a delicate arch and pouring itself into the vial. When it's
full, the tendril of blood retreats back into Leora and the
pinprick wound heals itself.

"That's fucking disgusting," I say, breathing heavily.

My head begins to spin and I feel my chest heaving. I feel Robyn watching me but I don't care. It's as if
a bubble is lodged into my oesophagus, preventing oxygen from going either way. I grip the edge of the gurney
and the sheet slips from Leora's body. Seeing the gaping
wound in her chest, I stumble back, falling into a cart
which overturns.

"Mallory you need to calm down," Robyn urges me,
crouching beside me. There are voices outside the door.
I hear one say Inerea's name, say missing person. Holy
shit. "Mallory, you're making the cloaking spell slip!"

"I can't," I gasp between ragged breaths.

It feels like they're coming out from a pinhole in my
lungs, barely enough oxygen getting through to sustain
me. I see black spots cast in my vision. The voices are
getting closer. Suddenly, Robyn puts her hands on either
side of my head, dipping her head down so she's looking
at the ground.

"Nevosona imadiava etev si kauava udi tyesta couras.

Perova destoyar nevorsona baniraava avot."

The tightly wound ball in my chest begins to unravel instantly. I feel my breaths grow steady and my mind blank. Inerea seems to me wrapped in a distant fog, loved but safe from the tarnish of my last memory of her.

"What did you do?" I ask, but Robyn shakes her head, putting a finger to her lips.

The approaching footsteps have stopped right outside the door, which suddenly swings open. Taking my hand, Robyn yanks me out of the man's way as he enters then leads me out. We dart out of the building but, before she can lead me back to the café, I pull her down an alley.

"Robyn, what was that?" I ask again

"A calming spell, it temporarily removes the distress surrounding an incident," she explains before casting the decloaking spell.

"Temporarily?" I feel a pang of desperation. The ease I feel right now thinking back on that day is not something I want to dissipate. "Are there more permanent ones?"

Robyn goes still, suddenly less concerned about being noticed by passers-by than my question. She turns her eyes on me, wary and cold.

"What exactly are you asking me?"

"I-I want to know if there's a way to take away how I feel," I say quietly, my hope jarred by the expression on her face. Her nostrils flare.

"Never, ever ask me that again."

Turning away, she storms back the way we came.

Chapter XXX.

"No drug users allowed! You can come back once you've returned to normal," Robyn snaps, ushering her brother out the library door and shutting it promptly in his face. She slumps back down on the sofa beside Leo, who has started writing out a translation of the resurrection spell. "Why are you two in here anyways? You're useless."

"That's real cold, dry ice," Aaron says, flopping down on the couch beside me.

The force of his landing puffs my couch cushion up and I shoot him a look. I still feel the effects of Robyn's spell as if it's stilled me to the quieting of a ringing bell.

"You can take it." She smirks at him.

"Maybe it's best if we go so we're not a distraction," I suggest.

She eyes the pair of us, that distinct look of dislike returning to her face when her gaze comes to rest on me.

"Just shutting up would help," she quips.

"No can do on either front," Aaron says.

I lean back and let my head sink towards my chest, somewhat grateful we don't have to leave. Being one on one with anyone other than Kyle, when he's not suffering from a caffeine induced meltdown, still has me slightly unnerved. The only thing holding me together is being able to focus on the task at hand. Take me away from this scenario, even one in which I am being useless for a time, and I don't know what would become of me. I clench my hands into fists, pressing them hard against my thighs to prevent their shaking. Out of the corner of my eye I see Leo's eyes flicker up to look at me but when I glance over he's returned to translating.

"Unless you wanted to be alone with me?"

I jump slightly as Aaron leans towards me.

"I'll stick to public forums as far as you're concerned," I say.

"You could frost glass with that cold attitude of yours," he sighs, pouting. "What happened to the good old days of you getting all flustered when I teased you?"

"I realised you're just a creepy alien who shouldn't be taken seriously," I reply, rolling my eyes.

"Was that before or after we shared a bed?"

The stuffy windowless room seems to have filled with an atmosphere of tension during our conversation. I glance nervously at the other two. Leo takes no notice of us, squaring his shoulders and continuing his work. Robyn, on the other hand, may as well be shrouded by a deabrueon's dark aura. Her usually flat, emotionless eyes have been filled with dislike. She's not afraid to make clear that it's for me, holding my gaze briefly. Is she still mad about my asking about the spell? We seemed to have gotten along fairly well earlier today, considering it's us.

"It stands to reason you'd sleep with him eventually. Not very interesting are you," Robyn intones quietly.

Holy shit. I glance back at Aaron who's giving me a self-satisfactory smile. She's in love with this moron? Does he have any clue what he must have been doing to her every time he hit on me? Something tells me he does.

"What? No! There was no sleeping together."

"We did literally sleep in the same bed."

Snatching up a throw pillow, I dash him across the face with it.

"Keep your little lying mouth shut," I say, perhaps a little more harshly than I mean to, "fine you slept in my bed but I would never sleep with you."

Now it's Robyn's turn to look satisfied. It's a brief flash across her face before she resumes her usual look of indifference, snatching the pen and paper from Leo.

"I'll finish this, I don't want to wait forever for your

idiot brain to function," she snaps.

He raises any eyebrow but doesn't protest as she begins to write. Watching her work, he indicates something
on the page.

"I think that's actually an I, not an L, making that
word-"

"I know what it says."

I tuck my legs beneath me and shut my eyes as the
two begin to bicker.

"Tired? You can nap on me if you'd like," Aaron
says.

Without hesitation, he ropes me around the waist
with his arm before pulling me towards him.

"Wait a minute!" I protest, attempting to free myself
from his grip. Squirming within the cage of his arm, I
push against his side to make him move away. He gently
presses my head down, resting it on his thigh. "There's
nothing restful about this."

I feel his body shake with a tremor of laughter.

"There's that nervous look," he says, ruffling my hair
before letting me go.

"Charming," I huff, "I'm going to go find Kyle."

"I'll come with you-"

"No," Robyn and I say simultaneously.

I take a furtive look in her direction but she hasn't
looked up from her page.

"Keep your sexually harassing mitts away," I add.

His laughter follows me out the door. What is with
him? However playful he may be, the man's definitely
sharp enough to have noticed how Robyn feels, given
how close they seem. Does he not see the cruelty in doll-
ing out affection towards me the way he does, right in
front of her? Perhaps he's tried telling her no, but she's
unable to accept it. Either way, I've still not quite grown
comfortable with his attention. Kyle's reminds me of a

caretaker rather than any sort of advance, which was why when he took care of me the other day as if we were old, intimate friends, it didn't feel strange. I make my way down the staircase into the entrance hall before following the corridor on my right to Kyle's room. I knock on the door three times before it cracks open.

"Oh hey Mallory."

Seemingly relieved it's me and not Robyn returned to scold him again, Kyle opens the door completely. He looks embarrassed, his eyes averted and cheeks flushed.

"Did Robyn need me?"

"Nope, just came down to check on you," I say, smiling at him and resisting the urge to giggle at his anxiousness.

"Okay well, sorry about how I acted this afternoon. Coffee makes me-"

"Almost as weird as the rest of us," I finish for him.

He grins, relieved, as if he thought that could have made me mad at him.

"Are they done translating yet?"

"No, but I just couldn't sit still any longer listening to Leo and Robyn bickering. Besides, Aaron's being extra creepy today."

"Yeah," Kyle sighs, "he's like that with just about any beautiful girl. He does seem a bit fixated though. Anyway, want to get something to eat?"

"Um, sure."

I follow him, my mind suddenly occupied. Is it vain to think about the possibility of someone finding me beautiful? I know that coming from Kyle it would never be an admission of attraction, just something he's observed. The other day, when he helped me bathe as if it were nothing, wouldn't have happened if it was. Suddenly, my face is burning with a rush of blood. Holy shit, I was completely naked in front of him. How could I be so unaware? At the time I could hardly think of anything but, now that I'm looking back at it, it seems incredibly embarrassing. Should I be self-conscious? I don't feel self-conscious, but maybe that's a bad thing.

"What do you want to eat? I'm starving," Kyle asks as we enter the kitchen. "Mallory, what's with that look you're giving me?"

"You practically bathed me the other day."

His face lights up as brightly as mine, flushed a deep red.

"Where-where's this coming from all of a sudden?"

"Isn't that weird? Friends don't do that."

"It wasn't exactly under normal circumstances. Helping a person in pain with whatever they can't do on their own is necessary at such times. I guess I just didn't see it in that light," he mumbles.

"I didn't either until just now. But isn't it strange?"

He sighs and closes the fridge.

"My parents adopted Robyn when I was six and she was four. That night, my parents left her with me and our very, very drunk aunt, who passed out about as soon as she got there. They had gone to hunt whatever had killed her parents. They just dropped her off, covered in blood; I assumed it was her parents' but I never asked. She wouldn't say a word to me even when I asked her if she wanted water. So, I just kept asking whether she was okay with me assisting her and went ahead as long as she didn't shake her head. She was in the same state you were, completely shocked, physically and emotionally. When someone's that fragile, the boundaries of ordinary relationships shouldn't get in the way of keeping them together. And it's not like I was using the opportunity to creep on you," he assures me.

"I know. I trust you enough to know you wouldn't do that. You're not Aaron. I just didn't want things to be weird because I put you in that position."

Kyle comes around the counter and pulls me into a hug.

"It's going to take a lot more than that to make me abandon my friend," he insists.

He smiles before removing a Tupperware from the fridge and sticking it in the microwave. Can I really leave him behind once this is all over? The thought drains what little strength is left in me. I sit down on one of the bar stools and watch as he takes out bowls and cutlery.

"By the way, you won't mention to Robyn that I told you that, right?"

"We're not really close enough for heart to hearts like that," I assure him.

Now that's two people I'm keeping secrets for. I wonder if Aaron will ever tell the others he transformed. I sigh, propping up my chin on my hand. The microwave emits a small ping and Kyle distributes the contents into our bowls.

"What is that?"

"Don't look so suspicious, it's just curry," he says, laughing at my expression.

"But everything is absolutely drenched in sauce, how am I do identify what I'm eating."

I jab something fleshy with my fork and hold it up to prove my point.

"It's all edible."

"Humans are edible. A cannibal can attest to that."

"You are truly a bizarre woman," he chuckles, "besides, I haven't been able to get my hands on any human meat so we'll sadly just be eating chicken."

I scarf down about half my bowl before the burning sensation in my mouth produced by spice is too much. My nose has started to run and Kyle laughs as I begin sniffing.

"I never thought my cause of death would be weaponised food," I say, wiping my watering eyes.

"Element of surprise. Mind if I finish yours?"

I shake my head and he eats the remaining contents of my bowl.

"How…it's like you're eating hellfire," I remark, watching him in awe.

"Part dragon, remember. I can handle the heat." He puts the two empty bowls in the sink then leans on the counter across from me. "Mallory, there's something I wanted to talk to you about."

"Why do you look like you want to use my puppy as a sacrificial lamb?"

"No, it's not that," he chortles, "I've just been thinking. I know you're set on seeing this as a suicide mission, regardless of what you promised me. But I wanted to ask, if after we all survive, maybe you'd come and live with me in New York. I got you into this mess after all."

"You are never to blame for the danger I put myself in. Listen to me," I insist as he looks away. "You think I'm doing this because I hope I die? No. I'm doing this to protect you and the others. I am forever willing to give my life for you. As if I could have survived up until now without your kindness. You found my family for me. You came to my aid at the Academy knowing full well what I was. When Inerea died, you're the one who drew me out of my inner darkness. My desire to protect what is most precious to me is all that's keeping me from slipping back into that state. You're the family that saved me."

At last, he meets my gaze, his eyes reserving belief. Please Kyle, know that what I say is true. Know that living, right now, only means keeping you happy.

"You're my best friend."

In a heartbeat he's beside me, his arms wrapped around my shoulders. His dark curls blend with mine, the only difference being a bluish sheen that the lights leave on mine. Completely intertwined, there is no beginning and end with us. I clutch tightly at the fabric of his shirt. Letting go and leaving him behind hurts more than most things. The love I share with Kyle is irrepressible.

"You're my best friend too you know," he says, still not letting me go. "Even though you're a reckless muppit."

I laugh, burying my face in his shoulder.

"Who'd have thought I'd end up owing the entirety of myself to a drug addict?"

"And I to someone with a death wish." He leans back, interlacing his hands with mine. "So, what do you think?"

I hesitate before answering. I've had to let go of so much recently. What I thought I knew of myself, people I love. Can I let go of Kyle?

"Yes."

"Good. Because I want to hear about your life at university and how all your new friends at school don't measure up," he teases.

"Oh dear god, I forgot. I'm going to university! I'm going to have to make friends. What if everyone hates me?" I ask.

"Impossible. Just be as naive as you were when we first met and people will jump at the opportunity to help you."

"That would work were it not for the fact that Aaron has thoroughly corrupted my innocence."

I bite my lip before we simultaneously start laughing.

"Come on, let's go see if the others are done yet."

Back in the library, Leo and Aaron are gathered around Robyn, inspecting the final translation over her shoulder. They glance up as the door clangs shut behind us and Aaron grins.

"Back to normal?" he asks Kyle, as Robyn scowls menacingly.

"Yes, sorry about that," he says, ignoring his sister. "Mind If I take a look?"

Without looking at either of us, Robyn passes the paper to her brother, before crossing her arms. She must be livid with us if she's not even willing to offer a scathing remark or a dirty look.

"What do you make of this?" Kyle asks, offering me the page after he's read it.

The blood, the blood, the heart:
spilt thrice, carved out the price.
Beneath night's closed eye
unseen goes unlawful life
bidden to rise by unwise hands.
Summoned back from death
the body remade in part,
completed when the vessel lets depart
the final piece, its place shall find
and fill once vacant eyes with life
beneath night's closed eye,
where the old god cannot see the crime.

"The style of the wording is rather archaic, even for the ancient language. This spell must be ancient," Leo says.

"It's no easier to make sense of once translated," Kyle sighs looking over my shoulder.

"The blood, the blood, the heart," I murmur, frowning at the page.

"What's that?" he asks, looking back at me.

"It's just, I've heard that before…The fire of the blood. You sound like him. Except, you know, I don't eat the blood, the blood the heart. He has to consume it."

The memory of my first night in Aplin Hollow rears its head.

* * *

Following Doctor Lindberg out the door, I fold the piece of paper with her phone number on it and slip it into my pocket. I glance around for Kyle, hoping one passing look will fortify me before I meet my aunt and uncle, but he's nowhere to be seen. We cross to a door in the atrium and she twists the handle. The door opens, audibly grazing the too stiff carpet fibres. Doctor Lindberg steps aside, holding the door ajar for me.

I see the woman first. She's a lot to take in, full of too much boldness in colour for my muted vision. Her hair is a fiery shade of orange, yet it looks earthy, like terracotta. She seems about my height, but her narrow figure makes her appear smaller. As soon as I see the man behind her she seems tinnier still. He clears at least a foot and a half above her.

"I'll leave you for a while," Doctor Lindberg says, nodding her head as if to bow before leaving.

They stare at me openly while I hide my gaze behind hair. Neither of them look like me. Is it possible we're even related? The man, Milton, looks somewhat perplexed as if my presence in the room is unexplainable. No, just my existence. Her face is unreadable. It shifts between emotions, sometimes returning to one I don't understand. It makes me feel sick. Confusion. I know that. I hold onto that trace of what I know as it leaves her face. Why wouldn't she be confused? My parents hid a child from them all this time yet somehow they've ended up my legal guardians. It doesn't seem they weren't close to my parents or I would have been left to someone else. But that doesn't make sense either. Surely if they trusted my aunt and uncle to raise me they would have told them I existed? Then again, these are the same parents that entrusted my life to the Academy.

My brain begins to stir the muddled truths that are not be able to mix until I can't think on the matter clearly. I consider instead what makes sense in my mind. I am currently in the presence of people who share my blood. They are here to take me away from a place that is haunted by painful memories. And yet, all we do is hold our breath examining one another, the weight of it crushing me. After all these years of comfort in silence I accept the truth: it is a burden. I step forward to introduce myself even though I don't know how to do so.

But there's no need, the movement triggers everything. She darts forward and my body tenses, knees bending beneath me. I may not have fought in a long time but it's all still in my bones. I move my arms to defend myself, but her arms wind around me. She pulls me in too gently to be filled with the intent of harm. It takes me a moment to dig myself out of the confusion before I realise what she's doing. My arms go rigid by my side, unable to reciprocate.

"Mallory," she whispers, the sound of threatening tears cracking her wind-chime voice. "Mallory."

I don't remember how to fight. I don't know how to free myself or breathe. But then she detaches from me and air dives itself down my throat.

"Celia," Milton sighs, his hand guiding her a few steps back from me.

"I know. No emotional outbursts. But look at her Milton! She looks so much like her mother," Celia whispers.

My stomach flips at the notion of being likened to my mother. They study me. Even though this has been the basis of my interactions for my entire life, this feels different. It's far more personal. They want to know who I am, not just what I'm capable of.

"I'm Celia. This is my husband, Milton," she says, her face calm even if her voice is unable to hide its emotion.

"Hello."

Do I need to say who I am? Even though we all knew each other's names before meeting they still introduced themselves. I'm resolved to start again when Celia begins to speak.

"I know this must be a lot to take in so quickly. If you feel at all rushed we can rearrange our travel plans," she offers, "You've been at the Academy for a long time and we don't want to take you away from your home if you're not ready. We were just both so excited to meet you."

She smells of a natural sweetness, something a novice in fragrances of the world could not identify.

"No, it's alright. I'm ready."

Do I mean it? In this room maybe, but will I be too scared of those glass doors waiting for us?

"So determined," Milton chuckles, though I hardly meant to sound so. "She sounds like you almost."

He smiles at Celia. There's a cloudy look in his eyes, which I hadn't even noticed was there until it vanishes the moment he looks at her.

"Milton!" she exclaims, her soft composure vanishing.

Now she's a stubborn child standing in front of me, teasingly being infuriated. She looks back at me, the traces of embarrassment effusing red beneath her cheeks.

"We're so happy to have you as part of our family."

A smile holds the mask of happiness on my face. They're too soft, too kind. It is certain that I will break them unintentionally. The door reopens and Doctor Lindberg joins us once again.

"Are you ready?" she asks.

While I know she's speaking to me, her gaze is directed away

"I believe so," Celia replies.

"Goodbye Mallory. I wish you all the best," she says, opening the door for us. I follow Milton and Celia outside, where I have never dared to step before. We get in the car and, before I have a chance to look back at the building, we're driving.

Milton and Celia's car reveals the world through tinted windows too dark for the world to see back. I watch the way leaves move beneath the violent wind. Within the sheltered courtyard outside my room window trees were only subject to the meekest breath of air. This is no delicate dance of mere overlap. Leaves hit their siblings roughly, take beatings too, for the attention of their mother. She stands stony, skin battered and cracked by the gales that have struck before.

At first Milton attempts to strike up conversation by asking which radio station I'd like to listen to. I don't know any so I say anything is fine. Celia asks what restaurant I'd like to go to. Again, I've never known any food but that which was brought to me on a wooden tray and dispensed into plastic bowls. I tell her whichever is their favourite. I notice her roll her lip back and forth, bitten between her teeth. She and Milton exchange a look. He answers her worry by saying we'll decide about food later then turns on his soft music that doesn't try to soothe with human voices.

It's the archaic calls of the first machines that did battle with their sounds until they wrestled into harmonic overlap of one another. They're more graceful than the low engine of the car or the steady whir of an electronic device as it begins to feel overused. Yet in their gentleness instruments wield a more dangerous power than modern machines. They tick artificial emotions to life where they don't belong. As the interwoven threads of melody fall smoothly only to burst apart again I have to hold onto breaths that want to be ragged and panted after each note.

They speak in hushed voices, too quiet to distract me from the ethereal song. I attempt to latch onto an object out the window, but my pinpointed gaze is dragged through the passing scenery as we speed on. Either side of the road is lined with trees. Their appearance is so repetitive it wouldn't surprise me if each coming mile borrowed the previous mile's foliage. The world reiterates what it's already made when it's bored of creating and it seems we never go forwards though we're always in motion. I'm lulled from observation by a warm hum from the next song starting up. I feel my muscles slacken in my legs and the warm pin pricks in my stomach settle themselves. The cold window doesn't burn my cheek as I rest against it and give my mind over to sleep.

"You must be tired, all that fire burning you all the time." The voice has the same warm tonality of the song, assuring me I'll be safe from nightmares for now. "Why go to hell when it keeps coming to you?"

"The fire isn't what's to be feared," I say, watching the oozing magma accommodate my feet as I dip them in.

"Then what?"

I pause when he asks. I want to find his embodied voice, the sound concentrated as something soft and warm that can hold me safely away from this world I know.

"It's the blood. Why is there always blood?"

"Hell if I know," he mutters, "It's the fire of the blood."

Warmth may be stronger than the cold here but fear is stronger yet. I shiver.

"You sound like him."

"Except, you know, I don't eat the blood, the blood, the heart."

"I presume that's supposed to comfort me?" I ask.

"Do I ever try to do anything else?"

"You try to make me laugh," I reply, drawing my toes back towards me out of the velvet heat.

"Has it ever worked?"

"I don't know."

"Are you sure?"

"Are you sure?"

Celia's voice echoes, recalling me from sleep.

"Hm?" I ask hazily, still comforted by my dream and unafraid of speech.

"You're sure you don't have any idea where we should go? It's our first meal together," she asks looking over her shoulder at me.

I avoid her gaze, pulling my jacket tightly over my chest to shield myself.

"Not that dinner off exit 148 is anything special," Milton adds, switching lanes.

"I'm really not very hungry, but I'm happy to stop if you are," I reply.

"Well it is only about another half an hour from here to your mom's," Milton says to Celia, "should we just keep going?"

"Sure," she agrees, before beginning to tease her lower lip between her teeth again and glancing at me.

She looks so scared that I can't stop myself from smiling. I remember being so afraid that Saturday long ago until I saw my caretaker smile at me. Reassurance. That's what I felt. For a moment Celia's face darkens but then she returns my smile.

"Did you have a good rest? You went out like a light."

"The music helped," I manage.

Her phrase is noted. It's going to be difficult to learn

the colloquialisms an education in language never afford-
ed me.

"Finally!" Milton declares, causing me to jump and
stare wide eyed at him. My heart beats up its own frantic orchestra. "We find out what kind of music she likes.
You're a classical music fan?"

"Yes?"

He doesn't take any notice of my questioning intonation.

"Any composers in particular?" He catches my eye in
the rear view mirror, a triumphant smile on his face. My
breath hitches and I bow my head so my hair will cover
my face. Triumph, victory over the exploitation of my
weakness. Her lips had twisted themselves into a smile
born of that sickening emotion. I grab the door handle,
gripping it until my knuckles blanch. Milton is not the
person who hurt me. Feeling the same emotions as she
did does not make him a threat. Blood builds up and
roars in my ears like a tidal wave. He's happy he knows
me better. I cling still tighter to the door. You're safe.

"Mallory?"

"No anyone is fine," I manage faintly, the tail lights
outside my window fusing together into tracks of red in
my blurry vision.

"Don't say that or Celia will have you listening to her
MC Yogi," he warns.

"There's nothing wrong with MC Yogi!"

"All I'm saying is that he's a rapper who incorporates
yoga chants into his songs. A far cry from the classical
greats."

"It's innovative!" Celia argues, though she nurtures
a small smile.

A well worn argument that's broken through into
teasing. The effusing geniality in her voice grounds me
again.

"It's ear death," he mutters.

A warmth rises from my stomach into my chest. Unlike the settling weight of being nervous, this feeling does not electrify the skin but builds itself up through my body until I cannot help but smile at the two of them as they continue their teasing back and forth. For a while they converse and I am all too happy to sit by and listen, their banter almost as soothing as the music. I feel as if I am privy to a familial happiness that belongs to those who have lived together for years and there's security in its informality. But slowly Celia stops responding with words. Instead she replies with the steady drum of delicate fingers on the door handle and nods of her head.

We have moved from the four lane interstate onto a narrow, poorly paved road whose bumps have begun to wreak havoc on my stomach. My body responds poorly to the unnatural jerking motions of the car, which lack the fluidity of the human body. I focus on the windshield through which I see the spectre of a sign illuminated by our headlights. As we draw closer, I read the worn away words painted across it.

Welcome to Aplin Hollow.

It's followed by ragged pine trees clustered in thick bunches along the roadside, leading us back into darkness.

"Turn up here," Celia says, before pressing her lips into a thin line.

The wheels come into contact with a terrain that sounds both like a bursting bubble and a hiss as it's crushed and spat out. The night's inkiness hungers to swallow the space briefly illuminated by our headlights, but I can make out moss-covered roots of trees that have encroached further onto the road's edge. There's hardly any room left for the car to fit and low hanging branches periodically thwack the roof with such force I half expect it to crack open like skin.

A few minutes pass before I see an opening in the trees, a glittering island of forest refuge. The warm yellow twinkling reveals itself to be innumerable lights, strung up on the aged and sturdy branches of trees that surround a sizeable cottage. The front of the house is drenched in dripping bunches of purple petals whose veins have been coaxed up trellises. Each one is a purple shell, slightly curved to shelter their soft white and yellow bellies. In their bunches they loom over the windows like curtains that are as much for keeping away intrusive purveyors of nature on the inside as they are to hide the rooms within the house. The woodwork of the porch awning is entwined with the same lights as the trees, which are wound around the thin wooden columns that support it. They cling as tightly as the flowers to the vines. Rusty chains drop from the roof to hold up a wooden swing that appears newly veneered.

A slight woman sits on it, her legs tucked up beneath her. Her hair is ghostly white and appears both as soft as baby birds yet as wiry as the twigs of a nest. She watches us steadily with eyes that seem exceptionally large set against her small face. There's something alert and cat-like in her unblinking gaze, those eyes being such an unnerving shade of grey they appear as pale as my own.

Milton cuts the engine and climbs out to remove my duffle from the trunk. I notice Celia is doing her best to look anywhere but at the motionless figure. She opens my door for me with a tight smile.

"Thank you."

She doesn't respond verbally, but her eyes flash kindness. It's not until I get out of the car and follow Celia up the stairs to the porch that I hear the creak of the swing's chains.

"Cici."

Her voice sings the same way Celia's does, like pure air being whistled through a metal tunnel. But beneath it is authority, ready to be invoked. Celia's face flushes at the sound of her mother's term of endearment. Her expression doesn't change overtly, but I note the slight sucking in of her cheeks and the tension that makes her jaw go taut. She breathes out barely audibly before moving towards her mother, drawn in by the command of her tone or perhaps by some innate family bond. They embrace, Celia's stiffness fading as her mother's arms envelope her.

I step into the bleeding lamplight that pools across the polished wood deck and her eyes find me. To be taken in by those eyes is to be read from atom. I feel each molecule of DNA unwind and become a sentence in a book for her to read. Can she really see every fibre of me with one look? The chill on the back of my neck says yes even though I'm certain it's impossible.

She pulls away from her daughter and comes towards me. I'm too enthralled by the aura of strength that surrounds her to move or even be afraid. Her arms pull me into their circular net and I'm lit by a strange hum. Within me a light begins to grow, more of a dying ember than a roaring flame. But like a star, even in its nebular state, it is infinitely more powerful and full of potential were I only able to understand the scope of it.

As she steps back the feeling does not instantaneously diminish but I feel it waver. She brushes my hair aside and places her hand on my cheek. Her thumb presses gently against the top of my cheekbone as if to map out my face. Her eyes are drawn from feature to feature, inventorying my every detail.

"Mallory this is your grandmother, Inerea," Celia says, stepping towards us.

"Mallory," Inerea echoes. It's as if I am at last being given my name as a permanent identifier. Until now I could not be distinguished by it. "How like your mother you are."

She removes her hand from my face, unsmiling and curious. Celia gives a half nod before stopping herself, as if she's afraid to corroborate our likeness though she made the same remark earlier.

"Her hair was just like yours. I could spend an hour brushing it smooth only for it to work itself back into curls as soon as I was done."

"That sounds about right," Celia says, smiling warily at her mother. "Remember how upset she would get whenever you made her put it up? She said you were oppressing her wildness."

The words chill me slightly. The only thing I seem to owe to my mother is my savage appearance. Inerea makes no reply to Celia's comment. She's processing my reaction, if there even is a visible one on my face. I've dropped to a deadpan.

"Come sit, I'll make some tea," she says just as Milton steps up onto the porch. "How are you dear?"

"About ready to pass out," he replies giving her a quick hug.

"A long day I imagine. Made no easier by my daughter's stubborn nature." Her eyes light up with fondness as she squeezes her son-in-law's hand. "You're a saint for putting up with her."

"Mother," Celia grumbles, crossing her arms.

Milton just laughs, slinging my duffle over his shoulder.

"Only teasing Cici."

"Perhaps Milton can show Mallory to her room while I help make the tea?" Celia offers.

"Which is she staying in?"

"The one on your left just up the stairs," Celia says. She's engaged Inerea's gaze away from me and I fluctuate between relief and disappointment at not having a chance to speak with her.

"Come on kiddo."

We go into the house before the other two, who turn off into the darkened room on the right. Directly across from the front door is the staircase he leads me up. The walls are made of compacted pebbles that press against the thinly applied white paint as if the earth were ready to pour in on us. We step onto the landing, bathed in the lonely moon howl light. Through the ajar door I can see a bed before Milton's figure obscures my view. He drops the duffle, which makes a soft thud as it lands on the cushioned duvet, before he fumbles for the light switch.

"This is Celia's old room I think. I've only been up here a few times," he says, glancing around.

The air is full of recently stirred dust that makes if feel more disused than if it had been left unclean. Everything has been left in picture perfect placement to grow stale. I'm accustomed to unseen eyes watching me and can feel Milton's on my back now as I look around.

The bed is covered in a metal shade green duvet, pushed up against the left wall, which is painted the same pre-storm colour. In the far right corner is a large window seat that wraps around the walls just enough to form a cosy nook full of plush cushions. An excess of moonlight blanches colour from the pillows arranged against the windowpane. They form hunched shadows, pressing their faces against the glass to see into the meadow below. Across from the bed is a white desk with various chips in the paint that reveal the wood beneath. A slender throated vase of yellow centred flowers is all that sits on it. The blue petals fold curl back slightly towards the stem, shaped like inverted mouse ears. Where the stems have been clipped from the original source is still green, not yet yellow with sticky secretion.

I draw closer to the window to study the view. The proudly puffed clouds of this morning have vanished, leaving the moon to hang low above the surrounding forest.

"You can practically hear the werewolves howl," Milton jokes. I smile fleetingly without looking back at him. The traces of my face are reflected in the window just enough for him to be able to make out my expression. "Not so funny. I've been told I'm spectacularly good at dad jokes despite not being one."

I feel the tinges of coldness permeating the window.

"It was funny. I'm just," I pause, "a little dazed by everything going on."

"It's a lot of newness to take in," he agrees, "I'm sorry about your parents."

My nails find the place I know white scars camouflage themselves beneath my sleeves. I dig deep to drive away the thoughts that want to be reborn as words. My bitterness burns too bright and cannot be stopped.

"Why?" Behind me he stills, as if all the space were vacant and human compassion was not swelling. "I'm sorry I didn't mean to."

I trail off. I didn't mean to do what exactly?

"You don't have to apologise. We were told you didn't know about us either. You're probably mad at your parents for keeping secrets. Death will breed resentment, bitterness and grief. It's better to act on it and speak your mind. You did lose them recently."

"No I didn't." I lost them a long time ago, before memory begins. "Did you ever meet them?" I ask, turning back to him.

"Your mother and only once," he begins. His face is agitated and his words come out in patches of inconsistent tempos as if he's afraid to say it. "She ran away from your family when she married your father. There was disagreement as to whether or not he was suitable for her. I don't think any of their relationships recovered from that."

Perhaps Milton doesn't realise it, but he's just offered me the most information about my parents I've ever heard.

"Thank you."

He smiles, his worry not completely gone.

"We should probably go back down. Make sure those two haven't broken out into a fight," he says, his own joke flooding his face with relief. At least he can calm himself.

"Is that likely to happen?"

"Well not really. But I could tell the way Celia was looking at Inerea that she probably wanted to talk to her about how she, for lack of a better term, handles you the next month."

"Handle with caution," I advise as we descend the stairs.

"I do believe that was a joke," he says in mock horror. I smile at him. If only you knew how true it was. "Inerea has some superstitions and beliefs that she was all too eager to have her daughters believe in too."

"Religious beliefs?"

"Not religious per say. It was more folklore. Faeries in the forest and such," he says.

"And that's bad?"

"Celia doesn't really talk about it much but I don't think she likes her mother's fantastical beliefs and I think she'd prefer if they weren't brought up to you," he whispers as we reach the bottom of the stairs. 'Just going to grab a glass of water.'

He disappears to the left and I stand just behind the door, terrified to exit. I'm about to open it when I hear hushed voices outside.

"A murder? Mom, why didn't you tell me?"

"Keep your voice down Celia. I am perfectly able to take care of my granddaughter."

"Well do you think it was…you know."

There's a pause.

"That can't be possible."

* * *

"I'm sorry, was that English? And where did you get the idea he has to eat it?" Robyn demands, snatching the page back, "it doesn't mention anything about that."

"I had a dream about it."

"You want us to take the word of your unconscious?"

"Mallory's dreams have proven to be prophetic at times," Kyle replies.

"Still."

"The deabrueon carved out Leora's heart. Other than her, the deabrueon killed Theodore and one other person. I remember the night I arrived in Aplin Hollow hearing Inerea and my aunt talking about the murder. I didn't understand at the time but I think they both knew it was supernatural. That's blood spilt thrice."

Robyn looks at me in surprise, her mouth slightly open as if she wishes there were some point in my logic she could rebuke.

"So that's what, the necessary preparations? We can't exactly stop Thaddeus now that he's got what he needs from the deabrueon," Aaron says.

"So it seems we'll have to attack after he's been resurrected," Kyle comments, a look of worry crossing his face.

"Or right as he's resurrected. It's the moment he's most likely to be disorientated, which will give us our best opportunity to use the weapon imbued with the power of the Vaerdiexes stone. Perhaps the rest of the spell might indicate where and when this will happen," Leo suggests.

Again, Robyn looks like she's ready to argue but can find no fault in his comment.

"Beneath night's closed eye. It repeats it twice but that's not very specific."

"Unless it's referring to a specific part of the night sky," Kyle murmurs.

I gaze past them. Had I not, that day I collapsed outside their house, considered the sun to be the sky's eye? In that case…

"It's referring to a particular day, not the time of day. When's the next new moon?" I ask.

Kyle pulls out his phone and types quickly.

"Two nights from now." He glances up, worry etching itself deeper into his features. "If that's the case we hardly have any time to prepare."

"Be thankful then that Mallory managed to find the stone. We can cast the spell tomorrow during the day. Your magic is strongest when the sun is at its peak, the sun being the emblem of the phoenix," Leo explains to me. He comes to stand behind me, reading the paper over my shoulder. "The next part is simple enough. Someone has to raise him, which is the deabrueon. The vessel and the place the old god cannot see on the other hand."

"Who's the old god?" I ask.

Robyn gives me a wicked look, as if delighted to at last have something to complain about.

"Ignorant as ever new girl. Vaerdiexes. Supposedly, he's ruled the three hundred sixty-five spheres of reality since the beginning of time."

"Supposedly?"

"That's only according to followers of The First Principle. But most have lost faith in him now. When that happens a god's power dwindles so, apparently, before his could vanish completely, he divided his seven great powers into seven stones before passing on," Kyle clarifies.

"How sad," I breathe, and I feel the chill of the god's death, "In that case, doesn't there exist no place he can see, meaning this ritual can take place anywhere?"

"Not necessarily. When a god passes, it just means they lose contact with the mortal realms. He can still see what happens but can't prevent evil on Earth or Sunda-lev."

"Then why does it matter whether or not he can see the ritual?"

"Undoubtedly Thaddeus' new body is already in our world, but his soul still resides where Vaerdiexes is. If he were to see what was happening, he could prevent Thaddeus' soul from leaving," Kyle says, "the deabrueon would have to enter a place marked completely unholy in order to avoid Vaerdiexes."

"Or the territory of a living god," Leo comments, his breath warm on the nape of my neck as he leans closer to reread the last few lines. "Vaerdiexes wouldn't be able to see in there and a living god will be too busy interacting with the world, so they're likely to take no notice. Besides, there are a dozen malevolent forces that would look fa-vourably on Thaddeus' return."

"I'll research whether there are any temples in the area. It's got to be in Aplin Hollow, given his clear fixa-tion on the town thus far," Kyle says, "there should be a record of temples somewhere."

He leaves my side and starts removing books from the far bookshelf.

"In the meantime, Aaron and I will see what we can find regarding the vessel. Robyn, you should go over the property transference spell with Mallory."

"Why do I have to work with the moron?" she de-mands, glaring at me.

"Because she's the one who has the Vaerdiexes stone

and she'll also be helping you cast the spell," he sighs.

He takes the translation of the spell from me.

"Wonderful," she snaps. She seats herself on the couch. I go to join her but one dirty look and I relocate myself in the armchair, a relatively safe distance of five feet away. "Alright let's see the stone."

I reach into my pocket and produce the clunky chain. The blue light that has initially pulsed around it has grown fainter now.

"It looks like an amoeba," she says, taking it from me and putting it on. "That's so disappointing."

"It's not the actual stone," Kyle calls over without looking up from the book he's engrossed in, "it's just imbued with the power."

"Whatever."

The centre of the rock is indeed an amoeba shape, with a pattern of white veins. The shape is outlined by strips of colour, gradiating from maroon to burnt yellow, which gives it the impression of being a small tunnel.

"No wonder this was still in the store. It's an atrocious specimen."

"An atrocious specimen with the power of a god," I add.

This instantly proves to be a bad decision, as Robyn's nostrils flare and she grinds her teeth.

"Shut up lay person. If for some reason everyone died and you were the last person left alive, it would still take a miracle for me to give a damn about your opinion. Go be useless somewhere else." I stiffen.

With a mechanical rigidness and tightness in my chest, I go join Kyle at the table.

"Do you need me to look at anything?" I ask.

He clearly hears the underlying despondence in my voice because when he looks up his eyes are clouded with concern.

"Robyn?"

"Don't worry about it," I sigh, "I can take it."

"That doesn't mean you should have to."

"Please just let it go."

He resigns himself back to his book. I don't want to be the reason he and his sister fight, not when there's clearly already so much tension between them.

"So, could Thaddeus be resurrected in a Christian church? I know I've seen at least five in town."

"The Christian god is far too observant to let that pass in one of his churches. He'd bring the roof down on them," Kyle says, glad for a change of subject.

"What sort of temple then?"

"Any number of chaos gods would allow it to happen. Or gods that control multiple realms and can't dedicate enough attention to one temple on one planet It's just a question of which god actually has a temple here. For a hot bed of supernatural activity, Aplin Hollow is severely lacking in temples," he answers, skimming another page, "Got it."

"Who?"

"In 1893, there's a record of a Haovodachin temple being built."

"Chaos god?"

"A particularly disturbing set of twin gods. Their speciality isn't so much chaos as it is betrayal and malice. Vaina and Turoman are the worshipped deities. It's said their mother, Kora, was pregnant with a whole litter of children for one thousand years. Separately at first, Vaina and Turoman cannibalised their siblings. When it came down to the two of them, neither could defeat the other. They tore through their mother's womb, effectively killing her, and became lovers. They enjoy tearing apart relationships by having people turn on one another, usually by appearing in the form of the Trickster."

"People actually worshiped them enough to build a temple?"

"You can't imagine anyone cruel enough to devote themselves to such gods? Besides, they haven't passed because even without direct worship, the number of people who do their bidding without realising it is immense."

"That's disgusting," I say.

"All gods are. They've spilt more blood than mankind ever will and yet people worship them. Don't you think that says something about mortals? They disillusion themselves into believing that gods only carry out benevolent deeds, turning a blind eye on death."

"Not all gods directly cause death, surely."

"No. But they all allow it to happen."

"So what, they should make everyone immortal?"

"Perhaps I ought to rephrase. They allow cruel deaths by illness and murder, instead of letting everyone live a full life," he says.

"Now who's delusional? Not everyone's life is going to be happy or even okay for that matter. But how are we to know our strength and self-worth if we're not tested by suffering?"

"That sounds like the logic of a person who's trying to rationalise the pain she's been through," he whispers, shutting his book.

My body trembles, half afraid of the truth he's thrust at me and half furious because he doesn't have the slightest idea of what he speaks.

"Have you found anything?" he calls over to Leo and Aaron, effectively ending our conversation.

"No, but I can't say I'm surprised. I've never read anything regarding a resurrection spell being possible let alone how one would be cast," Leo says.

"That's unfortunate but I think we've found the place. A Haovodachin temple about four miles away."

"That certainly would be the perfect place. Chances are Vaina and Turoman would be thrilled to see the destruction Thaddeus would bring."

"Aaron and I can go scout it tomorrow. I'll be able to cast a spell to discover whether Vaerdiexes is truly barred from there," Robyn offers.

"Best to do that during the day. Though perhaps we should all go just in case there's any trouble," Kyle suggests.

"We don't need her. She can't even do anything."

"That's enough Robyn," Kyle snaps, "Mallory's going through enough without your childish pettiness."

"Oh? Looks like miss moron has an admirer."

"No, she has a friend, which is more than I'll be able to say for you if you don't back off." Robyn falls silent. I can tell by the way Aaron's back stiffens that Kyle losing is temper is not common. Even Leo's eyes widen in shock. "Mallory will come because I'm not going to leave her here unprotected where she might die, no matter how much you want her to."

"I don't want her to die," Robyn whispers, eyes widening.

"Just go please."

As he finishes, I see something I never believed could happen. Robyn's eyes begin to swell with tears. She dashes from the room.

"Robyn!"

I jump out of my seat ready to follow her but Leo holds me back.

"She really won't take kindly to you trying to talk to her, even if it's out of compassion," he says.

"How could you say that to her?" I demand furiously.

Kyle looks stunned.

"How? Because you never stand up to her even though what she says drives you closer to giving up on yourself."

"Stop Kyle," Leo warns.

"Maybe it's time we all go to bed. Everyone's probably just wound up over what's happening," Aaron suggests, "come on Mallory I'll take you downstairs."

"That's alright, I'll do it. You should probably talk to Robyn," Leo says, dragging me out of the room.

I look over my shoulder to see a bemused Aaron attempting to comfort Kyle.

"I need to apologise to Robyn," I insist.

"Trust me, if you don't want the entire world to end tonight, you shouldn't do that."

"Enough with the hyperboles."

"Why didn't you just stand up to her yourself? Why are you being so cowardly?" he demands, blocking the door to my room.

"I didn't say anything because I know, out of the two of us, I can take it. She can't," I say, staring him dead in the eye.

His flash dangerously before simmering back to their usual indifference. He lets go of my arm.

"Why do you care if she gets hurt when she clearly doesn't care about you?" he asks, his voice soft as it had been that day in the training room.

"Because I could never intentionally cause harm to someone for no reason," I reply.

"Would you really sacrifice yourself for anyone?"

I bow my head. Would I? Maybe not when I was little. But the pain of losing Lilth changed that.

"Yes. I'd even sacrifice myself for you."

He looks at me wildly, trying to detect the smallest hint of a lie in my eyes.

"I don't think you would. But thank you for saying that. I'll take my leave now. Goodnight, Mallory."

"Goodnight. Oh and Leo?"

"Yes?" he asks, already halfway down the hall.

"You're wrong and someday I'll prove it to you."

He smiles sadly.

"I hope you never have to."

Part VI

Chapter **XXXI**.

Morning yawns, easing me into its arms with a soft summer light. That's one fewer night until he comes. Not that I'll get the chance to see him. He'll be remade and gone in an instant. That's the hope anyway. The alternative is not something I can bear to think about. I want to be there when it happens but Kyle has made himself very clear on the matter. I roll over in bed, the thought of Kyle making my stomach sink. I need to apologise for getting him and Robyn into a fight. First thing this morning…as soon as I muster the will to get up. I pull my pillow over my head. Is there any way to prolong the inevitability of tomorrow night by never getting out of bed? Just to keep my friends safe for another day.

A timid knock sounds from the door.

Apparently not.

"Come in," I yawn.

The door opens and Kyle shuffles in, precariously balancing a very full mug of coffee in his hand.

"Tell me you're not back on the hard stuff," I say.

"It's for you," he replies, offering me the mug, "a sorry, for what I said last night."

"You're apologising with drugs? I was just going to use words and hug you," I sigh in mock exasperation, taking the proffered cup, "maybe I should try and get some cocaine for the next time we argue."

He rolls his eyes, sitting on the edge of the bed.

"Yeah the coffee is mostly because we're leaving in about twenty minutes to scope out the temple. When I stopped by earlier you weren't awake so I figured you might need it in order to live."

"That sounds like a really unhealthy human beverage relationship."

"Ours is a cruel love," he sighs, "but, like I said, I

did also want to apologise. Not for what I said to Robyn, because she did need to hear that. But when we were talking about religion, I said some pretty harsh things. I just wanted to make sure I didn't come off accusatory. I may know a lot about your past but I can't imagine the things you've been through, and it's not my place to tell you how to deal with it."

"To be honest, I'm only okay with what you said because you said it. That didn't upset me, it was just strange to hear because I suppose the past few days I have begun to try and rationalise my past but hadn't noticed until someone pointed it out to me. No one's really had the chance to," I say, staring at the brown oblivion in my mug. "I do think you should apologise to Robyn though."

"Absolutely not, she was totally out of line."

"Kyle, however much she despises me, we both know she doesn't actually want me dead. It was unfair to accuse her of that. I think," I say, frowning.

"Fine. But I'll just pull the old cower-in-fear-until-she-feels-superior-again. She hates indecisive anger more than she hates being called out for her bullshit. Apologising is out of the question with her."

I take a sip of the coffee and am almost inclined to spit it back out. Gagging slightly, I manage to swallow it.

"This is foul," I cough, grimacing, "it's so bitter."

"I probably should have added milk." I offer him a sip from the mug but he shakes his head. "Not today."

"That's probably for the best," I laugh.

"Alright there may be one more little thing."

"Oh?"

"I know we talked about you coming to live with me but I had forgot about your aunt and uncle, that you've already met them, until you brought them up yesterday. Are you sure you don't, you know, want to live with them?"

He says this last bit reluctantly and I can tell, despite his thoughtfulness, he's hoping I'll say no. The truth is I have thought about Celia and Milton, and at the end of the day I'm too conflicted to live with them.

"Not after what happened to Inerea," I whisper.

He wraps an arm around my shoulder and kisses the top of my head.

"I understand. I just thought I'd ask."

"And you're sure I won't be an imposition coming to live with you?"

"Are you kidding? I'd finally have someone to talk to about things other than the latest automatic cocking crossbow," he replies.

"One, is that really a thing and, two, how can that be a conversational topic of length?"

"Weapons and Robyn. What else would it equal?"

"Good point. Wait, have you mentioned this to Robyn yet?"

"Not as such, no."

"Don't you think it's probably important to do so before you ask me? I don't think you should incur her wrath anymore."

"I already know she'll be livid," he grumbles, "but it's not up to her."

"Do you two not live together?"

He shakes his head.

"She still lives at home. I've been a bit of a nomad lately but I'm planning to settle back down. So, you know what that means: apartment hunting."

"As exciting as that sounds, you should probably tell her, at least before I officially accept. I don't want to come between you two anymore."

"Fine. But not until after she's got to kill some deabrueon tomorrow night. She'll be in a better mood to hear the news then," he says.

"I don't know, I think you're missing a trick by not telling her before the fight. She could visualise our faces on all the deabrueon," I suggest. We exchange a look before bursting out into laughter.

"Okay fair that's a far better idea."

Just then there's a banging on the door that causes me to jump and slop coffee over my thigh.

"Are you guys almost ready to go or what?" Aaron calls from outside.

"Just a minute," Kyle replies.

I go to grab my clothes from yesterday but he shakes his head. Leading me to the large mahogany closet in the corner, Kyle opens it up. Inside are all my possessions from Inerea's.

"When did you get these?" I ask, fingering the hem of a camel-coloured jumper.

I remember getting this with her. It was winter, for which I was utterly unprepared. We drove two towns over to go to the decent stores and ended up getting snowed in. That night we stayed at a picturesque hotel on a lake edge. The moon was full and, even though it was freezing outside, we bundled up in the duvet from the bed and sat on the balcony, counting the stars. I don't know when during this recollection I begin to cry but I'm made aware of the fact when Kyle wipes a tear from my eye.

"I thought you'd feel more at home if you had your stuff. I hope it's okay. I didn't even think it might upset you."

"No, no, it's fine. More than. Thank you."

"I put all your books under your bed and there was this wooden box I put in the bedside table."

"That's the second time you've spared my books and me from separation. You're really wonderful, you know that?"

He shrugs but I can see the colour flushing his cheeks.

"Happy to make you happy."

I take the sweater off the hanger and, changing out of my pyjamas, put it on with a pair of jeans. I zip up my boots and don my leather jacket before following Kyle to the door. Aaron is leaning against the wall opposite my room, his hand resting on the pommel of the sword strapped to his hip. He tosses a sheathed sword with a long leather-bound grip to Kyle, who slings the strap across his torso.

"You'll probably need weapons too," he says to me, beckoning us to follow him back to the training room.

"Do you think we're going to be attacked?" I ask.

"Not necessarily, but you never know."

We go into the adjoining weapons room, the walls of which are covered in mounted swords, daggers, quarter-staffs, and bows.

"Take your pick."

I glance around, uneasy at the prospect of wielding a weapon again. The last time it didn't do anyone much good. I pick up one of the parrying daggers.

Outside, the sun has managed to permeate the clouds with a few beams, leaving scattered wraithlike shadows across the ground. Leo has foregone the passenger seat, which Robyn now occupies. He holds the door open for me and Kyle before getting in after us. Looks like even he knows when to take a step back and make room for Robyn. She doesn't look directly at us, but I can practically feel the raging residue of last night's anger as she seethes silently. The car rumbles to life beneath us and we're on our way.

This has to be the most excruciatingly uncomfortable car ride ever, and I've had my face bashed into a window by a bellatoja. Kyle's crossed arms take up part of my seat but I daren't say anything. Instead, I'm squished against Leo. I feel his body tense against mine as he glances over.

I want to apologise aloud but the heavy atmosphere of the car doesn't allow words to escape me. I offer him an apologetic smile.

Eventually, Aaron turns off onto a dirt path that has started to be recoated by grass and ferns. The back tires bump us up and down until we finally come to a halt at a dead end.

"We'll have to walk from here," Aaron says, "do you have the map, Kyle?"

Kyle nods, still seemingly unwilling to speak in Robyn's presence. We trample after him through the thick undergrowth of the forest. Robyn sticks close to Aaron's side, her crossbow already loaded and balanced steadily in both hands. Aaron's hand is wound around the grip of his sword, ready to go at a moment's notice. He said we shouldn't expect an attack, but everyone seems on edge. Sensing Robyn's territoriality over Aaron, I fall back to walk beside Leo. He's the only one who doesn't look ready to decapitate oncoming attackers. His arms are crossed firmly over his chest and he surveys the surrounding environment attentively. It takes clearing my throat to draw his attention to me though I sense it's not for a lack of his noticing me and more a wilful ignoring.

"Everyone seems extra on guard today," I say to him.

"There's a chance the deabrueon's keeping guard over the area. And, potential deabrueon attack aside, going into a Haovodachin temple isn't exactly a reason to party. If those gods notice us here they might decide to have their version of fun," he mutters in response.

"Far worse than a deabrueon's definition of the word I'm guessing."

"Vaina is known for taking on the form of a beautiful woman, usually to seduce unsuspecting men into cheating on their partners or committing some horrendous crime. After it's done, they still remember what they've done but not why. She has them do such awful things that, when they come around from her enchantment, they're often driven to madness. But Turoman's form is much more dangerous. He sees within you and becomes the person you love most. In that form, he can convince a person to do just about anything. See neither god wants to outright kill you. That's no fun for them. They want to see you destroy everyone who matters to you only to realise with self-loathing what you've done. Are you cold?" he asks, as I shiver beside him.

I wrap my arms around myself.

"No, just mildly terrified after hearing we're effectively walking into a murder death trap."

In what form might they appear to me? Growing up, there weren't many people I cared deeply for. Yet, now, Kyle, Lilith, Inerea, and my caretaker flash before my eyes. I would obey any one of them in a heartbeat. I look nervously at Leo but he's looking straight ahead. Honestly, I'm not too afraid of what would happen if one of them appeared to the other four. But now my training has come back to me, I don't think there's a damn thing they could do to stop me. My heart begins to pound.

"You're worried?" Leo asks.

"You don't strike me as the type to be perceptive of other's feelings," I say, perhaps more rudely than I intend to.

He doesn't look offended but raises his eyebrows at me.

"I choose not to express mine but don't confuse that for an inability to empathise."

I want to scoff when he says this. Empathy is not something I could imagine from Leo. He's cold and calculating. I learned that the day he put my life on the line to catch the deabrueon.

"I didn't mean that. And yes, I am a little bit worried."

"You should be. You're quite the catch even for a god."

"We're here," Kyle calls back before I can reply.

The trees open up into a clearing, revealing a dilapidated temple six columns across. There are entire chunks missing from the ridged pillars, and most of the noses are missing from the figures on the metopes. We ascend the temple steps and enter. The back of the temple has fared even worse over time. The roof has partially collapsed without the support of the back wall, which has somehow been reduced to something more akin to a fence. Moss springs between the cracks of the massive stone slabs tiling the floor. As we enter, I feel a chilled sickness enter my veins and I can't help shuddering. Leo draws closer to me.

"Kyle and I will take the perimeter," Aaron says, "Leo, stay guard while Robyn casts her spell."

As they leave, Robyn approaches the rough-cut stone altar. She flexes her palms and presses them flat against it.

"Nayrudir savis, marora Vaerdiexes vanagemar?"

A gathering whisper of wind answers her question. It starts low, hushed amongst the trees before sweeping over us through the temple. The sudden rush leaves me light headed.

"He's definitely not here, but, then again, the altar is the centre of the temple's power so he'd have no chance of seeing to it. I'll have to check the rest of the building too. It's weakest points especially," Robyn adds, heading to the back wall.

Leo nods and she begins to repeat the spell, moving from place to place.

As she does so, I feel the sickness in the pit of my stomach creeping through my limbs. They feel weak and leaden, as if they could drag me to the ground. Everything is harsh in this grey light. Lightheaded and disoriented,

I'm tempted to sit down on a nearby slab of fallen wall but can't remember how. My body is paralysed by the feeling. The air is so dark in here. It's feeding off my life force, which slowly pulses and dwindles. My heartbeat slows, its thumps audible in my ringing ears. The room feels static. Must sit down. I attempt to lower myself to the ground but end up stumbling, falling against Leo's turned back.

"Be careful," he warns, before seeing my face which is coated in a sheen of sweat. "Mallory?"

"He's not here, he's absolutely not here," I insist.

Leo's face becomes a blur as I begin to sink to the ground.

"I'm going to take her outside," Leo calls to Robyn.

My hearing is too warped to hear her reply in full but I catch the words 'of course' and 'useless'. I can imagine the rest. My legs are scooped out from beneath me. I rest my cheek against his warm chest, shivering uncontrollably in his grip.

"You're freezing."

"He's gone," I whisper, licking my chapped lips.

He presses a hand to my forehead.

As soon as his foot is off the bottom step I feel a flood of warmth heating up my body again. Leo kneels on the earth, laying me down. With a sudden thrum, my heartbeat begins to pick back up to a normal tempo. I sigh, tilting my head back to best catch the warmth of the sun. Above me, the foliage is at first just a mass of emerald clumps swirling in the breeze. A few minutes pass and the distinct shape of each leaf returns to my sight. I see birds flitting between the airborne highways of branches, singing different arias in harmony.

"How are you feeling?" Leo asks, still kneeling beside me.

"Better," I sigh, closing my eyes again, "I'm sorry

about that, I don't know what came over me."

"You said someone was gone, who was it?"

He's right, I remember saying that but I have no idea of whom I was speaking. One minute I was fine and the next thing I knew I was overcome with the sensation of losing something dear to me. A feeling I'm all too accustomed to. I hear the sound of footsteps pick up to a run as Kyle and Aaron approach us.

"What's the matter?" Aaron demands, crouching beside me.

I sit up, rubbing my forehead and blinking through the light to make out their faces.

"Just a dizzy spell," I say, "nothing to worry about."

"I'll return to Robyn."

Leo leaves my side and I watch him disappear through the temple archway.

"You're sure it's nothing?" Kyle asks nervously.

"Really I'm fine," I insist.

But as I stand up my body fails me again. I sag and Aaron catches me. Looping my arm over his shoulder and his arm around my waist, he props me upright. I lean my weight against him.

"Clearly. I'll take her back to the car," Aaron says to Kyle.

"Are you sure it's a good idea to split up?" he asks.

"She can't stay out here."

"Alright, we'll see you back there in a little while."

We begin to walk back the way we came, Aaron half carrying me. For some inexplicable reason, I'm overwhelmed by a desire to cry. I mentally implore tears to stream but all that comes of it are my breaths growing increasingly uneven.

"You have a pretty weak constitution. Do you always get so ill?" Aaron asks.

"I'm just not used to so much action-packed adventure time." He doesn't say anything so I roll my eyes. "Say whatever perverted thing you wanted to say."

"How do you know I was going to say something perverted? Get your mind out of the gutter Thiel."

"Of course you were. This is you we're talking about," I scoff.

"It wasn't that funny anyways."

"Not like you to doubt yourself."

He smiles but doesn't say anything. I see the car shaded by a canopy of leaves ahead. When we get there, Aaron hoists me into the passenger seat with ease.

"Jokes aside, what happened?"

"I don't know, it was just this overwhelming sense of an absence. I felt utterly alone and deserted," I say.

He doesn't reply at first, glancing absently back the way we came, watching for the others.

"I've got no clue what that was but I bet Kyle would be able to figure it out."

"No please, I don't want to worry him," I reply hastily. He gives me an exasperated look. "I'm keeping your secret, now promise you'll keep mine."

He looks mildly amused.

"Very well Thiel. Let it be known that you have hereby called in you one favour from me."

"Dammit, I was going to ask for one more."

"What's that?"

"Could you drop me off at Inerea's."

His eyes widen.

"Are you sure that's a good idea?"

"No but I just want a little bit of time there alone before I leave. If you could just drop me off there I'd appreciate it."

"Of course. We'll have to go at night though, it may not be a good idea to let anyone spot you going in," he says, "how about after you and Robyn cast the spell?"

"That's perfect. Thank you."

I rest my cheek against the headrest and close my eyes. The breeze sweeps into the car, ruffling my hair. It cools the slight sheen of sweat that had broken out when I felt faint.

"Looks like they're back," he says after a few minutes in silence.

Aaron shuts my door before climbing into the driver's seat. Robyn makes her way to the passenger seat door before spotting me, a sight that puts a murderous look on her face. The other three pile into the back seat.

"Anything?" Aaron asks Kyle.

"Nope."

In the rear-view mirror, I see Robyn lean forward and open her mouth to speak. At that moment, Aaron decides to turn the radio on, cranking up the volume until my body vibrates with the beat.

Chapter XXXII.

The sun has begun to shroud itself in the tree tops by the time Aaron comes to get us for the spell. Kyle and I are in the kitchen, huddled around the counter. I watch while he whisks a bowl of muffin batter before folding in the blueberries.

"Stress baking?" Aaron asks him, strolling insouciantly into the room.

"Mallory's not yet tried one of my baked goods," he answers, lifting the spatula and letting the batter run back down into the bowl to check the consistency. He seems satisfied. "It just seemed wrong."

"Yes, this is what troubles us the most right now," I say dryly to Aaron, who grins.

He sticks his finger in the bowl and licks it clean, dodging Kyle's swats. Kyle then puts cupcake liners in the twelve-hole tray before distributing the batter.

"Once we had to recapture a member of the Vernis Lanin who escaped custody and he baked us a three-tier cake," Aaron informs me, hopping up onto the counter.

"What a mother hen," I laugh, poking his cheek.

Kyle puts the tray in the oven, scowling at us.

"Well excuse me for needing an outlet in such circumstances," he huffs.

"Don't worry, it's cute. You'd make a great house wife," Aaron says, running his finger around the edge of the bowl to collect batter. "You want some?"

He offers his finger to me with his usual sly smile lighting up his face.

"Don't be disgusting," Kyle scowls. He sets the oven timer before taking off his apron, which I have refrained from giggling at this whole time. "What do you want?"

"Robyn's ready. It took a fair bit of convincing to have her agree to use Mallory's power. She seemed to have gone sour on the idea and thought she could do it with just Leora's blood," he sighs.

"She was never going to outright refuse, that would just be reckless. We only have enough blood to try this once." Kyle glances between the two of us. "Right?"

"She's your crazy sister, I'm washing my hands of the matter," Aaron says, shrugging, "She's ready in the library."

"Well, I can't just abandon my muffin venture now, so you two will have to go."

"You're just too scared of her to go," I accuse.

Kyle bows his head and his shoulders sag.

"Basically yes."

"In that case, can I also be a cowardly shrimp and stay here too?" I ask hopefully.

"Unfortunately, no," Aaron sighs, "you and I must suffer her rage."

Kyle gives me a reassuring look, but it does little to assuage my fear that Robyn will be in fine wrathful form. No doubt she's prepared a series of insults to bite my head off for this afternoon. Leo is waiting for us outside library, his hand gripped tight around his sword.

"Couldn't wait to see me?" Aaron asks.

"Even I'm at my limit with Robyn," Leo sighs, shaking his head.

"That bad? Maybe we should just wait out here when Mallory goes in?"

"What am I, a sacrificial lamb again?" I demand.

When neither of them answers or makes any sign of movement, I scowl and grab them both by the arms, dragging them through the door. Robyn is seated at the table, the pendant lying on its surface. While I take a seat opposite her, the other two stand skittishly between us and the door. I roll my eyes, beckoning them over. Finally, Leo approaches, unsheathing his sword and setting it down beside the necklace. He then backs away slowly.

"Is that everything? Seems a bit too easy," Aaron comments.

"There's nothing easy about it. In order to imbue the power of the stone into the sword, I have to act as a conductor, which if I'm not strong enough could kill me," Robyn snaps, "luckily for us, I am a powerful witch, unlike certain people."

"And you'd be referring to the girl who can cast spells with her mind and whose energy you need to cast this spell," Leo comments quietly, "yes I can completely understand the demeaning tone."

I look at Leo I shock. I do believe he just used sarcasm.

"Stupid, stupid Leo," Aaron murmurs, as Robyn's chest swells up with rage. Her eyes flash angrily at him.

"Oh look, a door. And you can get the fuck out by going through it," she says, glaring furiously at him.

"How come the Earth never opens up and swallows you when you want it to?" Aaron asks me.

"Enough! If you two aren't going to shut up, how about you try getting out," Robyn snaps.

My heart sinks as I watch them leave. Robyn hasn't said a word to me since I got in here, and now she busies herself rereading the spell, ignoring me. She reaches for my hands but I draw them away.

"Listen, I'm sure you're getting cold feet but I need you not to be a coward and do this."

"It's not that. The spell won't work. The energy in here is too out of balance. We have to restore it to equilibrium," I say. I can tell she feels it too, this strange pulsing in the air, because her face sags.

"Fine." She crosses her arms, glaring at me.

"Why are you so angry? Is it-is it Aaron?"

I regret asking the second question immediately. Her

face contorts in rage.

"What the hell is that supposed to mean?"

"Well, I just thought - never mind," I finish hastily.

"If you must know, I'm fucking pissed because ever since you came into our lives my brother couldn't give less of a shit about me. No to mention you wanted to use emotion magic like it was nothing. You're too much of a coward to face up to your emotions and deal with them."

I had wondered if it had been my request to cast a spell outside the police station since the day before. I've seen anger painted on her face before, but the look she had given me when I asked was like nothing I'd seen before.

"Robyn, Kyle loves you so much. And the past few days have been horrible."

"Mallory, when you lose someone you feel it, you don't let go of them forever," she seethes.

I'm taken aback by her, of all people's, lecture on how to feel.

"It's not just Inerea, okay? Inerea's spell broke after she-she died. It was so overwhelming to feel an entire fucked up childhood come flooding back. I still can't wrap my head around that person being me, but I know I have to reconcile who I am now to that past. I just wanted-I wanted to feel happy like I did for the six months before," I falter.

"Before you met us," she replies quietly.

"It's not you four. Please don't misunderstand me. But all of this fucked up stuff has started happening since I met you and it's so hard to keep going. I wonder if I'll be able to at all after Thaddeus is dead."

Robyn is silent when I finish. She knows something of the motivating anger of which I speak, this much is clear. She swallows hard, looking down at Leo's sword.

"Do you want to know why I got so angry when you

asked me? Because that was me. When I was a teenager, I started using emotion magic to cope with the pain of losing my parents. It seemed like a good idea at the time. But I became so numb and washed out in that year, I hardly remembered how to feel anymore. The sad bit is no one noticed the change. Not Kyle, not our parents. No one, but Aaron. He persuaded me to stop using spells to stem my feelings. He eased the suffering without magic. And that's what you need to do, find real reasons to be happy, not rely on magic. I've never fully recovered from that abuse; I struggle to control my emotions now."

She blinks rapidly and it takes a moment to realise she's fighting back tears. I know better than to try to hug her so we sit quietly, her retaining her dignity in the silence of our mutual understanding. Finally, she wipes a single tear from her cheek and clears her throat.

"Come on, we haven't got all day. Hold on to the sword," she instructs.

I pick up the hilt with one hand and she takes hold of the necklace. She pours the vial of blood in a circle on the table. Interlacing her fingers with mine, she holds my other hand.

"Tsi Vaerdiexes, lera okhim diradar siezata. Vema suyakur savis aka cri riekaik nevosor lera vane ni sav."

My stomach lurches as the pendant bursts into blue flames. It's as if someone is pulling apart the stitches of my being. Pieces of my memories flicker in and out of focus, then disappear for an instant as if they never existed. I feel my thoughts slipping away, whatever source they originated from taking them back. My heart accelerates with the shock of the power that has burrowed in me as a temporary home. In my grip, the sword turns ice cold, its blade glowing the same hue as the necklace. The light fills the whole room and then, in an instant, it's extinguished. The pressure of the spell lifts from me and my body sags.

I hear Robyn's gasps as she struggles to keep upright. The faint blue light that used to pulse around the pendant has vanished, its power now gone.

"Oh my god," Robyn pants.

"That was," I start before gripping the edge of the table, doubling over and vomiting on the floor.

Robyn leaps up from her chair and holds my hair back.

"Disgusting," Robyn groans, but then her body jerks and she's spewing sick as well. "Holy shit."

She wipes her mouth, sinking back into her chair.

"You okay?"

"It's fine now," she breathes, shutting her eyes, "I just feel like I'm dying. It felt like…"

"Like your soul was being ripped apart within you and the pieces were stolen or rearranged," I finish.

She nods.

"Bet the boys are happy not to be magic inclined dragoviks right now," she laughs.

"So you think it worked?" I ask, eyeing up the sword. It looks utterly unremarkable.

"The feeling of death in my stomach can attest to that," she answers, opening her eyes again, "Mallory?"

"Yeah?"

"I know my brother really well. And I'm guessing he's already asked you to move in with him. I just want you to know…I'm okay with it."

"Thank you, Robyn," I whisper.

She waves at me dismissively before rising from her chair.

"I need to sleep."

"Come on, I'll take you to your room."

"We should tell Kyle it went well. Why didn't he come with you and Aaron?" she asks.

"He's baking muffins."

"Of course. Will you let him know?"

"Yeah," I say, helping her back to her room.

I ease her down onto her bed and her eyes flutter briefly before closing. She falls asleep almost instantly. I make my way back to the kitchen which is filled with a sweet steady growing aroma. Kyle is removing a tray from the oven as I come in.

"Oh, how'd it go?" he asks, setting the tray on the stove and removing each muffin with care to put on the cooling rack.

"We threw up. And no, I'm not cleaning it," I say, watching Leo take one of the muffins and peeling back the lining. The smell has made me instantly hungry though I still feel sick.

"A success then?" Aaron says.

"Well that's disgusting. I'm not getting stuck with cleaning duty," Leo says. They both look at Aaron.

"Why me?"

"Because you're so domesticated." Aaron pouts. He disappears down the hallway.

"Are you okay though?" Kyle asks, bringing me a muffin on a plate.

He pours out a cup of tea from the teapot and I watch the rivulets of steam spiral up and sigh out the smell of camomile.

"Let me die and come back to life, then I'll let you know."

I eye the muffin. Smells so good. Must resist temptation or I'll probably throw up again.

"Well you'll have to be extra careful with the sword from now on," Kyle informs Leo, "the first wound it makes is the one that will cause soul fragmentation; we have no chance of defeating Thaddeus other than temporarily without it."

"I will," he sighs, picking off a chunk of the muffin.

"This means I'll have to leave the deabrueon to you three. Can you handle that?"

"I'm sure you didn't intend it this way, but that came off a little condescending," Kyle laughs.

"My apologies."

Unable to resist any longer, I take a bite of the muffin. It's light fluffy texture, contrasts perfectly with the sweetness. My eyes must light up because Kyle starts laughing at me.

"Looks like I've redeemed myself for the curry."

"Kyle, you're an amazing cook! This is the best thing I've ever eaten," I say before eagerly scoffing down the rest.

"That was fast," he says, watching me with a mixture of amazement and alarm. I lick a few sticky crumbs from my fingers before holding out my plate.

"May I have another please." He laughs, putting a second muffin on my plate. "I'm going to get fat when I move in with you."

"Move in with him?" Leo looks at the two of us with shock.

"I asked Mallory if she wanted to move in with me after we go back. I figured things will be difficult with her aunt and uncle all things considered."

Leo swallows hard on a piece of muffin.

"Do you really think that's a good idea?" he asks.

"Excuse me?"

I go tense, halfway through eating my muffin and watch the flat look restore to Leo's eyes.

"I mean do you really think it's a good idea to take in a Thiel? It's inviting chaos into your life."

Kyle takes the dishcloth from over his shoulder and chucks it on the counter. I half expect him to throw a punch. He puts a hand on either hip.

"Oh I'd love to hear this."

"I'm not saying this to be antagonistic. And I mean no offence by bringing this up but Mallory is connected to the death of the bellatoja at the Academy. If anyone ever finds out the Hirutere will want her head."

"All the better to keep her close."

"Not if they try and charge her with murder. You know the Onyevaras wouldn't stand up for us in that situation, much less someone who owes them no allegiance. Much less a Thiel, whose existence challenges their very right of being. If you take her in, you and anyone you're connected to may be forced to sever ties with the Onyevaras."

"If you're that's what you're so worried about no one's forcing you to stick around Leo," Kyle says acidly.

Leo approaches Kyle and I jump to my feet, ready to defend my friend. But Leo just puts his hand on Kyle's shoulder.

"You know I'm not going anywhere if that's the decision you make. I bear Mallory no ill will," he adds, looking to me, "I just want you to think through your choice."

Kyle sags, his chest deflating. I hadn't stopped to consider these factors, what it really meant for me to live with him.

"Kyle," I start, but he raises a hand.

"Whatever the cost, we protect our own," he says.

Leo nods.

"So I suppose I'll be seeing you around then," he says.

"Is it just me or did he not sound happy about that," I ask Kyle jokingly.

"I have no idea; I only understand his emotions forty percent of the time."

"That's a pretty harsh percentage for a friend."

Leo rolls his eyes at us.

"Vaerdiexes save us all from two more jokers in the

group. I thought that idiocy was reserved for Aaron."

"If I keep finding you two all cosy like this, I'm going to start believing you're cheating on me," Aaron whispers in my ear.

I squeal, swatting him away while I almost choke on the bite I've just taken. He chuckles taking the rest from my plate.

"Hey! That's mine."

"I just cleaned up your sick. I'll take what's owed."

"Why do you always appear out of nowhere?" I demand, clearing my throat.

"Because you make the cutest faces when you're startled." My face burns crimson. "So, when did you want to sneak off with me tonight?"

Kyle and Leo both eye us suspiciously.

"It's nothing like that. He's taking me to Inerea's," I clarify hastily.

"So quick to deny our love," he sighs, dropping the empty muffin liner to my plate.

"We should probably go soon if we don't want to be up until midnight."

"I don't mind being kept up by you."

"Please shut up forever," Leo intones.

"No way, you have a long day and night tomorrow. You need to relax."

"I can think-"

"Of a way to relax? We know," Kyle sighs, rolling his eyes, "honestly, you're grossly predictable."

Aaron grins wickedly.

"Shall we?" he asks.

"Just one thing. I meant to ask you after the Academy but with everything that's happened, it slipped my mind," I say to Kyle, "why did Robyn say that girl was better off dead?"

The three exchange a look.

"You just can't resist prying, can you?" Aaron teases, but I hear an edge to his tone. He's afraid.

"Let's just say even the angeleru have their demons," Leo answers.

"Okay you can't seriously expect me to be satisfied with that answer," I say but none of them reply. "What could be worse than what we've already been through?"

Kyle sighs, rubbing his forehead.

"Some angeleru are born different: bellatoja, praestinin, vyrium, and avikas. These mutations are rare but none so rare as the caeliti umea. Their a unique faction of angeleru that can sustain the power of angels on Earth. They appear on earth in pairs during times of great unrest and, when their duty is complete, their white wings turn to gold and they're allowed to enter the angelic realm. The caeliti umea are only allowed to breed with one another or not at all."

"Why, what happens if they have children with other angeleru?"

"A few centuries ago, a caeliti umea named Lailah Caelista ran away with a bellatoja. She became pregnant with quadruplets who, when born, showed the marks more of demons than angels. This species was named the jaieitsi bataruce. Their own progeny came to be known as deabrueon, complete mutations of the angeleru. As their parents, the jaieitsi were able control deabrueon. Just a few when on their own but, when the four of them were together, they could command armies. They're also able to manipulate their own dark matter."

"And that's what she was? The child of the caeliti umea?"

"The original four were. Now, much like the caeliti umea, the jaieitsi bataruce can be born to anyone, even a human. If you kill one, another will just be born. There must always be four. The Hirutere's aim is to capture and keep them alive, imprisoned, where they can't start an uprising. Because as bad as the Hirutere are, four jaieitsi bataruce is far worse. The Hirutere at least have some moral code, even if it's ambiguous at times. But the jaieitsi would wreak havoc on Earth and Sundalev."

"So that's what they wanted to do to her? She's just a child! She could be saved," I argue but even Kyle shakes his head.

"The jaieitsi cannot be redeemed, it's in their nature to destroy. They're the parents of all deabrueon after all."

"That's enough story time for now," Aaron says, "we should get going."

"I'm not sure, I might need a buffer to keep you from doing anything extra creepy," I say sceptically.

My mind is still wholly on the little girl. Though I know she is grown now I still can't help my concern for her.

"I second that. I'm coming with you," Kyle says. He puts my plate in the sink before joining us. "See you later Leo."

Leo doesn't seem to hear him, wholly occupied by the rest of his unfinished food and thought.

"Or not," Aaron says.

It's the first time we actually have enough room to sit comfortably in the car. Despite Aaron's persistent requests, I let Kyle take the front seat so I can be absorbed in my thoughts. Is anyone inherently evil? If so, surely I am too. What could make someone irredeemable even in the eyes of Kyle, who was patient with even me.

Outside, darkness lets us slip through its silken surface like a knife and the trees stand to attention. This will be my first time going back since that day. I wonder if the police have gone through the house, or declared her a missing person officially. Perhaps they've taken everything and I'll come in to find the shell of her home. The fairy lights won't be in the trees and the puddle of light the house sat in will have dried up. I shiver thinking about that. My first impression when I arrived was that of a safe haven. And Inerea was strength itself. She lit within me an innate trust and happiness I had not known in years, even before the spell. I wish I could purchase the past few months back. I would refuse to leave the Academy. I would never meet Inerea and she would never have come running into the antique store looking for me. I shut my eyes and dig my nails into my palms.

"Mallory?"

When I open my eyes again, Kyle and Aaron are looking back at me. We've come to a stop outside the cottage. The sight of the strings of lights still draped over branches soothes me. Not every piece of her is gone.

"Are you sure you want us to leave you?" Kyle asks.

"I'll be fine," I insist, "I'd like to do this alone."

"Alright. We'll be back in two hours."

I clamber out and watch from the porch as they drive away. I try to take in the surroundings as I had done that first night. Only now they are burdened with sentiment. The table where we had tea together, the path Inerea and I walked through the woods on spring days, and the porch swing we would sit on in the morning, even when it was cold, drinking coffee. Nudging the swing gently, I watch it roll smoothly back and forth through the air. I push the front door open, still unlocked from that morning, and stare down the hallway. Nothing has been moved. Even her shoes are still in place on the shoe rack. But that's exactly what's wrong. Life hasn't bothered to stir her possessions with daily interaction, while those of us living must keep moving. My chest beings to feel swollen with an aching sensation. I press my palm over my heart, as if to still its pounding. But my ribcage prevents such interference, allowing my heart its erratic, emotional beat.

I ascend the stairs Milton had led me up. My room is as it was, the duvet still rumpled as Aaron must have left it that morning. I open the cupboards and drawers but they're all empty. Out of habit, I remake the bed. I survey the room, the little vase of wilted flowers Inerea must have put on my desk while I was off with the others. She had tried so hard to make her home my home and I took it away from her along with her life. I close the closet doors and leave the room before the sight of the flowers makes me sick.

Then, with nothing to do, I cross the landing to her library. There, I leaf through her books, waiting for the end of these tiresome hours to come. I come across the book with the images of the dragons. It no longer seems frightful, now I know the story behind its pictures, but something hopeful. I flip it open and come to find that note in the front. I open it up and try to make out what it says but can make no sense of the ancient language. I pluck from the shelf a dictionary and pull out a pen and sheet of pencil before setting to translating.

It must take me at least an hour to make sense of it but finally I set aside the paper and read over it.

He's in New York. He doesn't know about her yet. The box is the key. The phoenix fears the moon.

Frowning, I reread it a few times but am not able to make any sense of it. Were Mr Bowen and Inerea exchanging notes in these books or were they a means of communicating with someone else? Who is he, and who is the her? Could it be me?

Overcome with exhaustion, I slip the original note and the translation into my pocket. I tuck myself up in the corner of the room and, before long, weariness droops my eyelids. I rest my head on the floor and tuck my knees to my chest. I'm not sure if I fall asleep or if I'm only comfortably curled up for a minute before I hear a creak. I bolt upright, my heart fluttering. The lull of silence has already returned but my heart is beating fast. Perhaps I'm hearing things? Just as I'm about to lie down, the floorboards groan again. I reach to my waist. I still have the parrying dagger. Moving stealthily to the door, I peek between the small gap between it and the door-frame. Expecting to see either Aaron or Kyle, I find that there's no one on the landing.

"Weird," I whisper to myself, hoping the sound of my own voice will reassure me.

But a persistent churning in my stomach tells me to look again. I glance back out and, sure enough, the door to Inerea's room is now ajar. My blood goes icy within me. Could it possibly be?

"Inerea?"

I hear the self-chastisement in the back of my mind, telling me to stop being foolish and run. But this is blotted out by the impossible possibility that has just presented itself to me. With increasingly hasty footsteps, I rush across the landing and burst into her room. My heart sinks. The bed is unslept in, and there's no one here. How delusional I have become in my desperation to have the past recti-fied. I turn to leave but find the door shut. My head cries out in sudden pain as I'm knocked to the ground. I roll onto my side and attempt to raise my head but all I see is -

Chapter XXXIII.

One, two, three…
Wake up!
Don't leave me. Promise you'll never leave me.
I don't want to yet. But I know I must.

My eyelids, as if coated with a wax sheen, struggle to flutter open. I beat my lashes against the non-existent weight. I hadn't expected to see Inerea's house when I awoke but, still, the sight of the night sky above me strikes panic in my heart. Still, this is better than the possibility that had swam through my subconscious, that I may never wake at all. I breathe deeply, the cold air stinging my lungs.

I am the dark corners you've always lingered in.

Why are the voices so loud? It's only ever been like this once before, that day Kyle found me in my room. They shout directly into my ear, roaring their sentiments at me. It's a jumble of words I cannot extract a single coherent thought from. My body shivers against the icy, damp grass I'm lying on. I hear someone whispering, too hushed for me to decipher their words. Footsteps approach my resting place and I shut my eyes again. I'm lifted up and carried a short distance before my body comes into contact with a stone surface. Its delicate grooves turn their peaks into weapons, jabbing through my thin shirt.

"She seems to still be asleep. That was quite a blow she took after all," a quiet girl's voice says, in a near whisper.

"Indeed, but I believe our little angel is merely playing dead."

I know that voice. His voice, from my dreams; it must be. A hand strokes my cheek and I feel the stir of the air around me as he leans over me.

"Isn't that right?" he asks in a soft tone.

I open my eyes, unable to stem the fearful curiosity blooming in me. I'm held in an instant, bound as I was that day Theodore died, by those sharp golden eyes. His face is centimetres from mine, his hand still resting on the side of my face. Tendrils of his shoulder length brown hair brush my chin. He smiles, more fully than I have ever seen. But his lips disappear when he does, giving the appearance of a gash in his face.

I breathe a sigh of relief and throw my arms around him, sitting up to do so.

"John, thank god, I thought-"

"You thought I was Thaddeus?" he asks, wrapping his arms around my waist and pulling me close to him.

"Yes, but how do you know about him?"

"Never mind that. How are you feeling?"

His face is pained with concern.

"My head still hurts but otherwise I'm okay. What happened? Did he come for me? Did you rescue me? Are you a dragovik?" I barely whisper the last question. What if he thinks I'm mad? But he merely smiles and brushes a curl from in front of my face.

"Yes, to all three."

"How, how did you fight him? And how is it possible? I thought the resurrection couldn't take place until tomorrow."

"It was a decoy," he says, sitting down beside me, "the spell was supposed to occupy your attention. But see, Thaddeus never died. He had simply grown weak and required the blood of other dragoviks to cast a spell to become strong again."

"So, you stopped him, before he could cast the spell?"

He smiles sadly.

"Mallory, I do love you dearly. Your faith in me is truly endearing. But I thought you would have realised when you woke up, recognised me at last."

He speaks with such a calm ease, the phantoms of overbearing thoughts gone from his eyes. He is still holding me, rubbing my back as if to comfort me in the face of the blow he has just delivered. He is still looking at me with more love than I have ever known before and, yet, he is not the same man.

"Thaddeus."

He smiles as I squirm in his grip, trying to escape.

"Now, now don't you want to hear the whole story? We have all the time in the world, your friends won't think to look for you here tonight. And I'd appreciate it if you'd hear me out, as you did in the library."

I go still, my eyes widening.

"How did you know?"

"Do you really think, I ever let you out of my sight? After that night when I killed your mother, I transformed and went on a rampage. When I awoke, I found I was bound to my human form once more. To be sure, I was severely weakened. Having got my revenge I saw no point in going on until I heard of Regan's other child, the one who had escaped me that night. I vowed to find the girl and kill her, end the Thiel and Ovira bloodline once and for all."

"But you, you were not what I expected. Raised in the most deplorable of circumstances, you still retained all the strength and dignity of a dragovik. I fell in love. I watched you grow up at the Academy, unable to rescue you, unable to get close for fear Diane would know me and expose I was still alive. At last the Academy was freed of that horrible woman's control. Still, I kept my distance, knowing if anyone found out I was alive there would be a manhunt which would mean I'd never meet you. You began running at night so I joined you. Do you remember? Keeping perfect pace, never drawing close. It took every ounce of my self-control not to take you then.

But see, I had a plan."

"I never had interest in the Vernis Lanin's more destructive plans until after my imprisonment and torture. But then I saw the Onyevaras for what it really was: the Hirutere's lap dogs. If I was ever to live freely in this world, with you by my side, I would need to rid the world of both of them. I didn't know how I was going to manage that until one day I saw someone at the Academy who changed everything. Clara."

He calls out the name and from the shadows of the forest emerges a petite girl of about Robyn's stature. She can't be more than fourteen or fifteen. When at last she gets close enough for her face to be revealed in the light of the nearby fire, I gasp. The young girl from the Academy who the bellatoja had searched for, the jaieitsi bataruce, stands before me. Her hair is a pale blonde, almost white, her eyes a peculiar shade of green-blue. She smiles at me, so sweetly, like a friend.

"Hello Mallory. It's been a long time since I met anyone from the Academy," she says in her demure voice.

"Why," I ask, "why are you working with him?"

"I think the more pertinent question is why are you not? He stands for everything we should: the fall of the people who allowed our childhoods to happen. The fall of those who stood by while we were enslaved and our powers used for selfish means."

I turn to Thaddeus incredulously.

"Yes Mallory, Clara and I have been working together to avenge her, and you. One day, she was playing outside and I approached her. She was young yes but she knew that a life as one of Doctor Lindberg's pet projects wasn't for her. She is how we rescued you from the bellatoja, how we enlisted the deabrueon to do our bidding."

"You? That was you at the Academy?" I ask, blinking in horror at Clara. The image of those bodies flashes through my mind and I feel ill.

"They killed children, innocent children, and you lament their death? I saw what they were going to do to you too. I was halfway on my way to save you when you saved yourself. That's when I knew you could join us; so much like Thaddeus. Be part of our family. I'll admit I was reluctant to let you in before; the last person who joined us was an annoying lump."

"I could never be like him," I say, before turning back to Clara, "it's not too late to change. We all did horrible things at the Academy to survive, but you can have a new life. You don't need to be what they made you. I'm not."

"Aren't you? You killed that bellatoja without hesitation. For the past few days you've worked towards killing Thaddeus for revenge. You're just what they made you, as am I. As Thaddeus is what the Onyevaras made him," she replies.

"I know you felt it when you heard my memories," he whispers, "you understood how I became what I am, how I was abandoned and betrayed by my friends, my father and my government. How was I to become anything other than what they made me?"

"I can understand without accepting," I say.

I'm not sure I mean it though. Looking at Thaddeus' face, the face of the man I had slept with just days ago, all I want to feel is anger. When I saw his memories, my own feelings went beyond understanding to commiseration. What my mother had done to him was sick. His own father, tearing his son apart. How could he not become mad in the face of all this? Who has the constitution to withstand such betrayals and not desire revenge? I know I don't. Clara's right, as soon as he took someone dear from me I sought to kill him, not unlike why he killed Regan. But my understanding of his plight is all too strong. So much so that I must defy it. That, and the desire to subdue the love that had begun to grow for him, causes me to lunge forward and rake my nails across his cheek. Caught by surprise, he doesn't manage to stop them from cutting through. He grabs my wrist twisting my arm over my head and pinning me down to the stone slab. I cry out.

"Forgive me angel, for causing you pain, but I need you to understand. Your grandmother, Inerea, I never meant to hurt her. You see Leora was working for me, another witch seeking revenge for her exile from Sundalev. She helped me plant the resurrection spell to confuse you. But when she found out about you, she saw you as a threat to my claim to lead the Vernis Lanin. You, a Thiel and an Ovira, would be the only one who had a stronger claim to the throne than I. She was insistent we needed to kill you. Poor girl, I do believe she was slightly in love with me."

"Slightly? I think she'd lick your shoes if you asked her to," Clara snorts. She tosses her mane of hair over her shoulder and crosses her arms.

"Either way, I couldn't allow her to pose a threat to you. And I needed the heart of one more magical creature so why not her? It wasn't until you and your grandmother arrived that I realised my mistake. But it was too late. Clara lost control of the deabrueon in her attempt to calm my panic and it killed Inerea. She only just regained control in time to save you. I would never have hurt Inerea, she was like a second mother to me growing up."

"Don't you dare," I snarl, "speak of her as if you knew anything of her love."

A look of panic strikes his face.

"I did. She was a good friend of my parents and I knew her from the day I was born. But don't you understand that all I've done is for our life together?"

"As if I want a life with you."

"But didn't you? In those moments we spent together you were falling for me. I didn't think it was possible, to have such good fortune as to get your attention amongst all these boys constantly vying for it. But that night you were most in distress, you came to me." He lowers his gaze, running his thumb across my collarbone and tracing the contour of me down to my hip. "It's why I took you. See, together, we would have an unbeatable claim to the throne. No one would dare question the birth right of our child."

"Our child?"

I panic, thinking back to that night. But we hadn't been safe. In my haste I'd been reckless. And him the father of Regan's other child. My half-brother. No matter the circumstances into which that child came into being, him wanting a child with me is still beyond perverse. My stomach spins. I feel as though I'm going to be sick. I can't look at him as he says it. I look over his shoulder, out at the forest but instead see the Haovodachin temple.

"If you don't need the resurrection spell, why bring me here?" I ask, suddenly changing my tactic. I need to buy time until Aaron and Kyle realise I'm missing. They'll find me. Robyn will find me.

"As you might have noticed, several parts of the spell held true to the restoration spell I do require. The blood thrice spilt and the heart of a supernatural creature to have enough isuazko. And, let's not forget, the unwise hand which bid me rise. Rather foolish of Leora to help me, knowing I could never love anyone but you. And she feared me greatly. But I'm beginning to believe that we seek that which we fear."

"No, Leora wouldn't betray us," I insist. Wouldn't she though? I remember those cold green eyes.

"Oh no? You didn't find it odd that a witch of ordinary means happened to be able to uncover a spell that had never existed in order to give you the exact details of my resurrection? Sometimes your trusting nature was disappointing, even while helpful. You even led me right to the place where my body could be healed."

"You used us to find the temple."

"Would you really have put such trickery past me? I pretended to be an ordinary librarian just to be close to you," he asks, looking at me with sad eyes.

Fury sweeps through me again that I cannot control the manifestation of. A guttural growl comes from deep within me.

"You're disgusting."

His eyes widen.

"To see thoughts of violence stir within you. My how you've changed."

"You fell in love with the picture of a melancholy girl you thought was like you, but I am not," I hiss, "you have no idea who am."

"No?"

I seethe, unable to believe the arrogance of his assumptions after all he's done to me and the people I care about.

"I knew exactly how to convince you I am worth saving," he says.

"You're beyond saving."

"That's not what you really think. I have bared myself to you, my past, and you know I am not the monster they make me out to be but that they made of me. If I could just have you," he sighs, "maybe I could find that balance between fire and water once more."

I spring towards him again but this time he catches me before we can make contact.

"Get off of me."

"I am under your skin. Admit it."

"And yet, I'm capable of acting of my own freewill."

I drive my nails into his hands. He doesn't flinch but twists my wrists until the ache.

"You are light, yes but you are also dark enough for me."

"My madness will never be akin to yours."

"You're wrong. Whatever Inerea did to ease your suffering over the past few months, you have still been trained into the belief that you're a monster. Your hope for the future may be bright, but you will be by my side in darkness. Even if you hate me at first, you will have your place there. I will prove my goodness overtime."

He pins me down and I writhe beneath him, sickened by his proximity. I remember the way his body felt on top of me, his forehead pressed against mine as our breath mingled.

"You are everything Regan could never be to me."

"You killed her yet you speak of proving goodness?"

"She brought it on herself. Do you have any idea?" he roars, and I flinch. I have not seen such violent wretchedness before. I knew it to be in his character but this face, it still belongs to John in my mind. I did not expect to see it so marred. "Do you have any idea what she did to me? She tore my life apart, cost me my freedom, my divinity. She took my son from me. No matter, even in death I will make her suffer. I will have what is dearest to her, what she sought to protect over my son. Her precious daughter."

He rests his head on my abdomen, breathing slowly.

"I have a brother." I breathe, the realisation finally sinking in. I should have put it all together back in the library or moments ago, but only now does the extension of my family tree bloom in my mind.

"Isabrand. If you think you or I have become a monster you should see him," he sighs. I close my eyes and tears stream down my cheeks. "You two are not so different in many ways. I think he'd love you dearly, as he never could me or his mother. He sacrificed a great deal for you as a child."

"You took his mother from him, how could he love you?"

He goes quiet for a moment, and all I can hear is the thrum of my heart and his soft breathing.

"You reminded me of Regan when I first saw you. The same long hair, the shape of your face. But your eyes are two bright doors leading into a void at the end of which there could be more light. Hers were warm and good from the day she was born, yet she bore a mark of malevolence neither you nor I ever did. She could never be for me. How blessed I am that she left you behind."

A sweeping wetness spreads from my collarbone along my neck as he lifts his head and licks my skin. He moans into the dark space of my throat.

"Get off!" I cry.

"Shh, no please don't be scared. You weren't afraid of me before. This time, I'll send shivers down your spine, but not out of fear."

He lifts himself up and I hear Clara retreating to the forest. Restraining my wrists in one of his hands, he uses his knee to wedge my legs open. I choke on the acidic liquid burning my throat as I realise what he's doing. I raise my leg but am unable to contort it into a position to kick him off. His irises have been all but completely swallowed by his pupils. With his free hand he strokes my jaw, then dots kisses across my throat.

"Please, don't. How could you after what Regan did?"

He hesitates, holding his weight just above me.

"Forgive me my little angel. I don't want to hurt you but I can't see straight around you." He presses his thin lips against mine, invading my mouth with his tongue before biting my lip and drawing away. I twist in his grip, turning my head away from him. "Now it's time to cast the spell. Be not afraid, I will not do to you what was done to me. But I will have you one day."

"Never," I hiss from between my teeth.

"You will be mine, and I'll be yours forever."

"Like she said, you'll be having her never."

We both turn out heads in the direction of the speaker. Leo steps out of the darkness, his sword raised and the other three behind him. Relief floods me at the sight of the four familiar faces, weapons already drawn. But in a heartbeat, it's flushed out by a wave of fear. I know what he is capable of, and I don't underestimate what he'll do for love. He massacred an entire household of dragoviks on his own and yet here they are, believing they can fight him? Especially not with Clara by his side.

"Run!" I scream, panic stricken, "He has a jaieitsi bataruce with him."

He snarls at them, his back dipping like a cat's.

"Keep her bound," he calls out.

"Yes sir." Clara has remerged from the forest. In the instant between him springing from me and landing on the ground, thick black tendrils wrap around my wrists and ankles, rendering me immobilised. "Come."

I hear a howl from the woods and watch in horror as five massive hounds emerge. They have the same dark demonic eyes of the deabrueon we had faced in the crypt. The one at the front rears on its back paws, howling up at the sky and extending its tattered wings. Then it drops to the ground, barrelling towards my friends.

"I'll take the bitch," Robyn says.

She charges at Clara as Aaron and Kyle nod, launching themselves at the onslaught of deabrueon. Thaddeus slides his hands beneath me, throwing me over his shoulder.

"Now we take our leave," he murmurs, holding me by my lower back.

"I don't believe you will be."

Thaddeus leaps aside just in time to avoid Leo's flashing blade.

"Clara!" he yells.

I see her from over his shoulder, directing a deabrue-on hound that is protecting her from Robyn's attacks. She looks over at Thaddeus, but there is no fear on her face. She knows she can best her opponent and help him.

"Noutsumar letai kokku ni saviski isuazko'caz makun."

Just as Robyn's crossbow had done in the antique store, Thaddeus' sword emerges from shimmering darkness. He grips the hilt and takes a swing at Leo, who fades back. During this time, Clara's control over the deabrue-on has faltered. Her hound backs off of Robyn for a moment, in which a bolt narrowly misses Clara's shoulder. She shrieks, conjuring a shield of black matter in front of her to stop a round of bolts.

I try to find the others but the invisible rivets that keep my body in place prevent me from doing so. Inhuman yowls of pain fill the air and I pray that they are those of the deabrueon. Robyn and Clara move back into my line of sight. In the instant it takes Robyn to reload her weapon, Clara sends a whip of energy forward that hits Robyn square in the chest. She goes soaring through the air.

"Robyn!" I scream, throwing my weight to my left.

My useless body rolls off of Thaddeus' shoulder, hitting the earth with a thud. Turning my head frantically, I manage to relocate the pair. Robyn is raising herself up on her elbows. Staring at Clara, whose hand is wrapped around a bolt Robyn has managed to plant in her leg.

"Destoyar elean kay dare lean tora," Robyn commands. My limbs go slack, loosened from their bindings. "Get the bitch."

She raises her crossbow again but a black tendril shoots through the darkness and wraps around the weapon. With a sweeping gesture, Clara knocks it from Robyn's hand. I scramble to my feet. Leo is holding his own against Thaddeus, parrying every blow, but Kyle and Aaron are pressed back to back, surrounded completely. My dagger is still sheathed at my side but there's little I would be able to do with it in the face of these four beasts.

Help, I plead.

A recollection answers my call.

Before you go, I give you one more gift. It will not save you, that is something you alone must do. But it will be of help during the first of many tipping points in your fate.

Illarion's last gift flashes through my mind. Staggering at first, I run towards Kyle and Aaron.

"Mallory don't!" Kyle calls out.

Temporarily distracted, he allows a deabrueon to slip past his guard. With one of its brutish paws, it knocks the sword from his hand before pouncing and pinning him to the ground. It bares its teeth, inches from his throat.

"Dersutisanaraava'noventa callanedo lera aleve vema dersutisanaraava callanedo saviski vanage, destoyar kaisma korevezinarava, destoyar oelanus darava izjumar," I say calmly, raising my hand.

Light roars from it, sweeping into a gust of wind that pushes against the swarm of deabrueon. They howl, clawing at it, but it drives them back. Flicking my hand once, I land the final blow, throwing them from the ground and out of sight. My spell dies, and I gasp. It's not as much pain as the power imbuing spell, but I feel lightheaded. Aaron and Kyle begin to rush towards me but I shake my head.

"Help Robyn."

Clara has her pinned to the ground with her dark magic. As she approaches for the kill, Aaron takes a swing at her. She lets go her power over Robyn in her shock. Stumbling away, she narrowly avoids the blow. The world caves in on itself in my fading vision for an instant. When it's clear again, an unknowable amount of time has passed. Clara is being backed into a corner, but still manages to fend Aaron off as Kyle drags Robyn to safety.

Leo. I've left him alone. I stagger to my feet and spot Leo and Thaddeus locked in intense combat. They bear down on one another with swift movements, neither able to lay a blow on the other. All it will take is one cut of Leo's sword and we'll be free. My heart stings at the thought of the man I thought I could love dying. This was not how it was supposed to be. I wipe a tear from my eye then begin to move towards them. Perhaps I can distract Thaddeus long enough for Leo to get the upper hand. Only a few feet away now, I slip my hand behind my back and wrap my hand around the grip of my dagger.

With one steady hit, Thaddeus jerks Leo's sword from his hand, the effort causing him to lose grip on his own. Thaddeus slams into Leo, knocking him to the ground, his hands around his throat.

I slip the dagger from my sheath and press it to my throat. I know, after all, what he really wants.

"Let him go."

Thaddeus looks up, the rage in his eyes dissolving into fear.

"Mallory, no!" Leo says, struggling against Thaddeus' grip.

I see, out of the corner of my eye, Kyle moving slowly towards them as Aaron and Clara battle on.

"You wouldn't do it. You think you've lost it all but you have so much to live for," Thaddeus whispers, rising slowly. Leo rolls over, gasping for breath, unable to get up.

"Not if you kill a single one of them." I feel the sting of the blade as I press it harder. "You watched me all those years in the Academy. You don't think I have the drive or desire to take my own life?"

"I've let him go, now please, stop."

In that terrible moment, the worlds of fear, pain and death collide. Kyle, holding Leo's sword, pounces upon Thaddeus. Clara cries out, distracted by her master's predicament. Aaron raises his sword to deliver the final blow. She dodges before sending a thick tendril to wrap around Kyle's sword wielding arm. I hear a sickening sound of flesh being torn, Kyle's scream as his arm is ripped clean from its socket. He drops to the ground, so much blood pooling around him. Clara jumps on the back of the remaining hound, comfortably situated between its wings. It bats Aaron out of the way before galloping towards Thaddeus. He rights himself, armed with Leo's sword, standing between Leo, who is now kneeling, and the other blade.

"No!"

My body moves in a flash. A shorter distance from them than Clara, I reach them before she can reach out a hand to Thaddeus. The cold bite of metal in my shoulder sends me stumbling backwards into Leo. We tumble to the ground.

"Mallory!" Thaddeus screams, his eyes widening in horror. But Clara's hand has already pulled him onto the back of the hound, and it launches itself clear into the sky.

In an instant, every memory, every fragment of my being contracts. They're too small to see. I clutch at Leo, looking up into his terrified eyes. He cradles me against his body and I try to take his hand, to feel something real, but it feels like a phantom. What if all these seconds are fiction, happening in my head? What if he's not real?

Who's not real?

My chest heaves rapidly, each breath drawing out pieces of me. Is there such a construct as myself? The world is snatched away from my sight.

Tell me what you see.

Nothing.

Yes. And what are you?

Nothing.

Those long-nailed fingers press themselves to the tender flesh beneath my chin. She tilts my head up, eyes looking into mine. They are gold eyes. I am not sure if they are Leo's or Thaddeus' or if they are even real.

"Siezata dvesmeel nar rahissor, destoyar siesta keh-pas artier yeda cits."

I fade.

Chapter XXXIV.

The time spent in unbroken sleep is full of splintered thoughts. Shards of myself find the jagged edges they broke from and fuse themselves. My inside becomes a glassy reflection, cool and smooth. Dancing across its water surface are images of moments I had long forgotten or had hardly thought mattered. But when I see them now I remember how they made me, even if just by altering one cell within. They diffuse through the reflective exterior, concentrating themselves into one entity. The glass shatters and I free myself. The past clings to me like drops of water, but they are not all I'm made of. I blink into darkness.

* * *

Lilith pulls me into a shrub to avoid the searching light of a patrolling guard. She straightens the collar of my dress and smiles reassuringly at me. We have never been given coats and I shiver against the icy night air. Our breath comes out, foggy like a dragon's.

"We're going to be okay," she mouths.

This is it, the night we tried to leave. And it's all my fault we got caught.

When the guard is out of sight, she pulls me after her, running towards the treeline. There are shouts in the distance, no doubt someone has noticed we are gone. I thought we'd have more time, but it seems we are too important to let slip away.

"We're almost there," she assures me, pointing to the edge of the forest.

I see the dark shape huddled on the ground before she does. It sends her sprawling as she stumbles over it, falling face first into the grass.

"Lilith!" I say in a hushed panic.

Rushing to her side, I glance over my shoulder at what has tripped her. Sprawled on its stomach, a creature with massive grey wings, which have been broken, writhes on the ground. It groans, pushing itself upright. It tries to beat its wings twice, and I can see the traces of magic on them, keeping them deformed. I see an arrow sticking out of the creature's back just below its shoulder blade. Despite its immediate monstrous appearance, I see it has the face and body of an adolescent boy.

"Who are you?" he hisses, noticing me watching him.

"Mallory," I reply. I can see the arrow tip sticking through his torso. "Who are you?"

"You're not one of them?"

I shake my head.

"You're trying to escape."

I nod. Blood drips steady from the wound in his chest and he heaves ragged breaths between his words.

"I'm Elias."

"Come on Mallory we need to go," Lilith says, trying to pull me to my feet. I resist her strength with my own and she lets go of my hand. "It won't be long until they find us."

"We can't just leave him here Lilith," I whisper, crawling towards him. He flinches and I hesitate before starting on my course again. "I can help with that."

He looks down at the wound as if he hadn't noticed it was there until I pointed it out. He grunts in agreement and I sit beside him.

"Don't be silly Mallory we need to go."

Ignoring Lilith, I snap off the back of the arrow. Elias grunts with the force but doesn't flinch. Going behind him, I pull the arrow out. Suddenly the blood comes out thick and fast. But, though I am often the last in classes to try a spell, I am currently imbued with a sense of calm.

For once, I will save a life, not take it. I press my hands to his back and close my eyes. In an instant, the wound closes beneath my touch.

"Now these, you'll need them to escape," I say, laying a hand on one of his deformed wings.

"Mallory! Those have been cursed by magic, there's nothing you can do to reverse that," Lilith hisses.

"I'm not leaving him," I insist. Placing my palms on either wing, I shut my eyes.

Think of your happiest moment.

Think of what it is to be whole.

I have little of either to cling to but still I feel my hands warming beneath my magic. I feel the ground rumbling beneath us. Suddenly Elias cries out, his body jerking forwards. I hold him fast, aware that, if I'm not successful, this boy's blood will be on my hands.

"It's okay," I whisper, cradling his body in mine, "it's okay."

There's a brilliant burst of gold light, beating back the darkness before receding to nothing. I hear voices cry out in the distance and Lilith looks around nervously. With a terrific gust of wind, his wings flex out to their full span. He beats them twice. Lilith looks at me in awe and I open my mouth to ask how he's feeling. Just then, I hear the sound of running footsteps approaching. I spin around in time to see a group of guards rounding the corner of the Academy. They spot us.

"Mallory we have to go now," Lilith urges.

She grabs my hand and pulls me to my feet.

The first arrow misses her by an inch. The second imbeds itself in her shoulder. She screams, dropping to her knees.

"No!" I cry out, kneeling beside my friend. I look up at the angel who is rising to his feet. "Help us, please."

His steely grey eyes meet mine but not a single emotion flickers through them. He turns, spreading his wings and bounds forward before launching himself into the sky.

I bend over Lilith, tears streaming down my face.

"I'm so sorry," I sob as the guards approach us.

"It will be okay, Mallory," Lilith whispers, "it will all be okay."

How? Hands grab me by the collar of my dress, wrenching me from Lilith. I scream, clawing madly but strong hands subdue me. They put handcuffs around my wrists which are attached to a collar that is buckled round my throat. I try to struggle, command my magic, but it won't come. The collar and handcuffs are blocking it somehow. I watch in horror as they attach the same contraption to Lilith before one slings her over his shoulder with little care for the fact that it pushes the arrow deeper in. She groans.

"Don't hurt her!" I scream, but the guard steering me by the shoulders just laughs.

Soon, we are back in the warmly lit halls of the Academy. They take Lilith down one corridor and march me down another. I know where we're going. I know this path all too well. Opening the door, one of the guards tosses me by the scruff of my neck onto the floor of the mirrored room. He rips my dress from me before stripping me down entirely. Then he leaves me, standing stock still in the middle as I know to do without being told. The floor is concrete, cold on my feet.

The door opens again. Two sets of footsteps enter the room. One is the heavy trudge of a guard but the other is lithe, hardly makes a sound at all.

"Hello Mallory," she sighs. Diane. "I heard you tried to leave me tonight."

My body begins to tremble, knowing what will come next. She comes towards me and I can just make out her shape in the mirror's reflection. She stops right behind me and lowers her face so her lips are beside my ear.

"Tell me what you see, Mallory."

"Me," I answer, and the mirrors that panel every inch of the room's octagonal walls answer the same.

"Yes. What are you?"

"Human."

* * *

I blink into the blinding light. It's so cold and sterile I wonder if I am not in the afterlife that Illarion showed me. But no, I know this room. It is the room I have been staying in at the Caverly's. I groan, rolling onto my side. My body does not ache as much as I thought it would. Raising my arms above my head to stretch, I test my limbs.

"Everything in working order?"

I jump at the sound of a voice. Suddenly scrambling to sit up, I look around and spot Aaron sitting in a chair in the corner of the room. He has a few days stubble and is slightly slumped over, a posture so unlike his usual poise.

"Aaron? But how."

"How are you not shattered into a million little soul fragments? Honestly Mallory, I don't know. But you were in a restorative sleep for days."

He crosses the room to sit beside me. Gone is his usual bawdy banter. He looks tired and concerned.

"What happened? The last thing I remember was Thaddeus attacking Leo and-shit." My eyes widen and I try to get out of bed. Aaron clearly knows what's on my mind and he calmly eases me back into bed.

"He needs to rest Mallory."

"He's alive though? Kyle, he'll be okay?" I demand, concern coursing through me.

"He's lost his arm. I don't know if he'll ever be okay but, yes, he's alive. As for what happened, that bastard escaped, that's what. The jaieitsi used a deabrueon to get them both out of there. Now it's your turn. What happened before we got there?"

I swallow hard, trying to think of how to explain John to Aaron before deciding to leave it out. Instead, I tell a modified version of the story. The one in which Thaddeus had watched me all those years, had bided his time to take me with him. Had never needed the resurrection spell in the first place. When I finish, I find I'm quite parched, and drink down the entire glass of water at my bedside.

"You sure do attract the crazy ones don't you," he sighs, and I think it's the first attempt at a joke since I've woken up. It relieves me, to hear his sense of humour restored, even if it's weak. It means hell can't have entirely frozen over just yet.

"Would you count yourself among that number?" I ask, hoping to elicit a smile, and I do.

"Definitely. Sanity is overrated."

We sit in silence. It is impossible to continue in a humorous way, thinking of Kyle, though it was a nice respite from the reality that is setting in.

"I should go get some sleep," he murmurs, rubbing his eyes, "it's been a couple days."

"Okay."

"Will you be alright on your own?"

"I think on my own is what I need to be at the moment."

He nods, complete understanding pervading his expression before leaving. I look down at myself, and see someone's changed me into pyjamas. Climbing out of bed, I make to the wardrobe to find a change of clothes. Discarding my pyjamas on the floor, I slip a sweater overhead and a pair of jeans over my hips. I dig through the hamper in the corner of the room and fish the note and translation from the other night out of my pocket, grateful they survived. I'm about to close the wardrobe before I notice that box again. I remove it from the bottom of the wardrobe and stare down at the carving. A phoenix under a full moon. But I know now how wrong that is. We do not thrive in darkness but in light.

The phoenix fears the moon. The words from the notes drift back to me and I frown. The box is the key. But to what?

I try again to shift the lid of the box but it won't budge. For the first time it occurs to me that the box may be spelled shut. I should ask Robyn. As I start to make my way down the hallway, I am aware that I am clinging to this new goal to avoid thinking about what has been bothering me since I spoke to Aaron. That it's my fault what happened to Kyle, my desire for retribution that put him in that situation in the first place.

I'm so absorbed in my own thoughts I don't notice Leo until we're about to collide. He's looking down at a small book in his hand, oblivious to his surroundings. As I spring out of his way, he jumps, slightly startled.

"No monsters; it's just me," I say, tucking the box under my arm and holding my hands up in surrender. "See?"

He stares at me in that way only he does, only half in this world but still seeing so much more than anyone else.

"Really?" he finally breathes in response.

The comment stings. I know I am a monster. After the risk I put us all in, between my vendetta and forcing their hand so they had to come rescue me, I can't even think to be upset with him for pointing this out.

"I guess I could be considered one, yes," I say, swallowing the lump that's fast forming my throat.

"That's not what I meant."

"Oh?"

The single word teeters on the edge of the air, hoping for an answer but doubting it will ever get one. Then he steps forward, so we're standing only inches apart.

"How could it ever be just you?"

"What do you mean?"

"I mean stop devaluing yourself," he says.

"I'll try to, but it's hard after what happened the other night."

"How so?"

"It's my fault. If I hadn't let my guard down you would never have had to show up there to save me."

"Mallory, we would have faced off with him regardless of whether he took you that night or not. And I don't think we would have fared nearly as well without you."

"But-"

"Who stopped the deabrueon from killing Kyle and Aaron? Who kept Thaddeus from killing me? It was all you."

"So you forgive me?"

"There's nothing to forgive silly girl," he sighs, smiling slightly before a frown crosses his face, "but."

And I already know where he's going with this. It has played on my mind too, ever since he had first brought it up in fact.

"You still don't think I should live with Kyle."

"I bear you no ill will Mallory. But after what's happened, I'm scared for him. I don't think he would hesitate dying for you and I can't lose a friend."

His impassioned plea takes me aback. There's a look of desperation and fear on his face that strikes a chord in my heart.

"Don't worry, I've been thinking the same thing," I whisper looking down. "I'm not made for this life. I can't stand to watch people I love die or get hurt anymore."

He nods, chewing his lip.

"What will you do?"

"I can't go live with my aunt and uncle," I say, "but Thaddeus told me something. I have a half-brother, and maybe, I can go find him."

"So, this is goodbye then?"

I don't answer immediately and he shakes his head, pivoting on his heel and pacing away from me. He leans on the edge of a windowsill, staring out at some unknown horizon. Words rise up in my throat but fear pushes back down. And then I realise the reason I cannot say it now; the reason he never will. We've both been conditioned to be afraid of one another. We've rationalised our fear of closeness with our personal skewed logic. And the sad truth is, I know it hurts him just as much as it does me. So, I make my way to his side and pull him gently by the arm so his face is once again turned towards me.

"I told you I'd prove you wrong," I whisper.

He smiles but stops on the verge of laughter.

"You did. And I hate that you had to. I'm so sorry Mallory," he replies, but he doesn't move back to my side.

"There's nothing to forgive silly boy," I reply, smiling.

He holds my gaze as intensely as the day we were first introduced, but I can see now in his eyes a sense of yielding. The black cores, hard as stone, which have hung so long within us are breaking and cracking. This is the closest we will ever be. I know now that I must go and that, after today, this chapter of my life will be over. I have chosen to leave behind this image of who I could be. I am not a Thiel. I am not a warrior.

"I made my choice to protect you that day, and you let me in just a little bit. But I see how much it hurts you to do so and I can't bear the sight of it," I say, "I know you'll never be able to forgive yourself for letting me endanger myself for you, even though there's nothing to forgive. So, I can't be near you as long as it hurts."

"So, that's my goodbye."

"That, and this."

I look down at the box in my hands. I don't want whatever legacy Regan left me.

"What is it?" he asks, inspecting the proffered box. The phoenix stares blankly back at him.

"An assurance you'll never see me again. My mom left it for me."

He reaches to touch my arm as if to comfort me but stops just shy of my shoulder. A dark look crosses his features and he lets his arm fall back to his side. Something unknown unfurls in my chest. Why couldn't we have been brought up differently? Brought up in a world where such emotions didn't cause pain. But I let the thought go because I know it doesn't do any good to hold too tightly to could have beens.

"Have you tried opening it?" he suggests, his tone the best attempt at teasing that he can muster.

"I have, but I don't really want to anymore," I sigh, running my hand over the top of the box.

"So?"

"I'm leaving this world behind. I can't handle this secret and a normal life. This is something I have to leave in the past if I'm ever to move forwards."

"Are you certain? I know you don't want our lives but this isn't just part of our world. It's part of who your mother was."

He doesn't know what she did. To him she is as she was to everyone else: an innocent victim. I clench my fist.

"She was never my mother. Not really. She was consumed by her secrets and the horrible things she did. If she ever really loved me, as I can't be certain she did, she wouldn't want the same for me. I never want to know what it is she left for me."

He closes his hand around mine. In an instant, I feel the sentiments I am hiding ready to come to light. But there's a torturous barrier between us that words cannot penetrate. I pull my hand back.

"Right," he says, stiffening as he takes the box, "is that all you want to say to me?"

"What exactly do you want me to say?"

"That you'll come with me to New York. I can take care of you. Thaddeus will still be looking for you."

I look at him, completely startled by his proposal. So, he won't let Kyle risk his life for me but he'll risk his own.

"You don't owe me anything for what I did the other night," I mutter, stepping back.

"That's not why I'm asking."

"You don't mean it," I say softly.

"Don't I?"

"You wouldn't be acting like this if you weren't certain this was goodbye," I say.

"You're right," he sighs, stepping away from me.

"Goodbye Leo."

I wrench myself from where my feet wish they were planted. I can't remain here forever. Each step I take is leaden, weighting me down.

"Do me one favour?" I stop to ask.

"Anything."

"Don't tell Kyle I'm gone until he's better."

He nods.

"As long as you have that box, I'll never come near you again."

"Can I count on that?" he calls after me.

I don't reply. He'll just have to trust I want my future more than my past. I keep walking, my heart already sunk. This goodbye will be the hardest, most of all because I must be selfless and not actually have a goodbye.

I make my way to Kyle's room, where I find him sitting upright in bed, staring out the window. His right shoulder is bandaged and he has a mug in his other hand. There's no more steam rolling off the top; he's let it go cold.

"I hope that's not coffee," I say, shutting the door behind me. He turns around, alarmed by the intrusion.

"Tea. I'm four days clean," he replies, smiling dully at me as I sit on the edge of the bed.

"That's a celebratory milestone if you ask me."

"Funny how I don't exactly feel like celebrating," he mutters. My heart contracts. How can I leave him like this?

"Kyle-"

"Please Mallory, no more pity. I can't take anymore pity. Even Robyn is tiptoing around me."

I nod, staring down at my hands.

"Thank you for coming to rescue me."

"You did most of the rescuing in the end," he reminds me, but I just shake my head. Taking the mug from his hand, I set it aside and interlace my fingers with his.

"Not enough."

He studies me.

"You think I'm mad at you?"

"You have a right to be."

"Damn right I do. You go off on your own, knowing it's better to keep us close. You get yourself kidnapped and then you almost get yourself killed," he says, before lowering his voice, "is that what you want me to say?"

My eyes go blurry with tears.

"I hate this. He gets away and you," I start before dissolving into sobs.

"Come here."

I crawl beside him and he rests his head on my shoulder.

"This is an occupational hazard Mallory. It's shit, yes

but I'll learn to live with it. Besides, I've got you to open jars and stuff when we get back to New York."

The smile he then offers me breaks my heart. I close my eyes and lean against him. This safety. This is what I'll miss most.

"Yeah you do," I lie.

"I'm thinking Soho for the apartment. We can start scouting online tomorrow if you really want to cheer me up."

"As long as we have our own bathrooms, I'm happy," I say.

"You have no clue about New York real estate, do you?"

"Not a bit."

We talk about the future we'll never have a bit longer before, eventually, Kyle falls asleep and I steal out of the room. It's dark by this time and no one else stirs in the halls. I walk out the door without a moment's hesitation, without any of the possessions Inerea bought me aside from the clothes on my back. I walk and don't think about where I'm going until I arrive at Inerea's house.

The inkiness of the night hungers around the house, waiting to swallow it as I switch off each strand of fairy lights. What will become of me without Inerea, without Kyle? Their names, even in my thoughts, bring back tears to my eyes. I stumble up the porch steps as if drunk in my grief, steadying myself against the wall as I enter. I wipe my eyes but no ground is gained against my loss. Closing my eyes, I rest my forehead against the wall, hoping to calm my erratic breaths.

That's when I hear the soft breaths beside me.

By now, Kyle may have woken to wonder where I am.

By now, Inerea has been declared either missing or dead.

By now, Leo will be looking at that box, half hoping he will see me again.

Whatever is here can have me.

But where I expected Thaddeus or Clara, I see only the face of someone from long ago. Whether he's here to kill me or help me, I throw myself into his arms. They wrap around me and I feel his nose against the top of my head as he dips his face to kiss my forehead.

"What are you doing here?" I whisper.

"Did you think I wouldn't keep my promises?" he asks in reply, his voice low and warm.

He steps back, sweeping his thumb across my cheek as he cups my face in his hand. They're soft and hot, the only certainty that this isn't a hallucination.

"I didn't know if there was a you left alive to keep them. After they split us up at the Academy-"

I can't finish the thought. After Lilith and I attempted to escape, Dominic, Lilith, and I were forced to go our separate ways. I worried for them both, endlessly.

"I couldn't very well up and die on you when you're so often getting yourself into life and death situations. Who would have kept you alive?"

"It was you," I say, putting the pieces together. "The restorative sleep Robyn put me into was never enough to heal me after the sword cut me."

"Of course, it was me," Dominic whispers and I press my face to his chest.

"Why didn't you come to me sooner?"

"I didn't know if you'd want to see me."

"Always," I whisper, "always."

His hands run the length of my back, coming to rest on my waist.

"Mallory," he murmurs, "we can't stay, it's not safe here."

"I know, but I have nowhere to go."

"Yes, you do. I'll keep you safe."

I know he can. Better than Aaron, Leo, Robyn, or Kyle ever could. Not one of them, not even Thaddeus would be a match for him.

"Where will we go?"

He breathes audibly and only then do I realise he doubted my answer would be yes.

"You know who to ask for help."

I stare blankly at him for a moment until the answer dawns on me. I pull my phone from my pocket and scroll through my contacts. It takes a few rings before she answers, clearly drawn out of sleep.

"Hello?" the tired voice says.

"It's Mallory."

Silence. And then-

"What do you need?" Doctor Lindberg's voice is restored to business as usual at the sound of my name.

"What you promised. A way out, a new start."

"Done."

I sigh a breath of relief. Dominic pulls me to him and I'm home.

* * *

"They're taking awfully long to get home," Lilith yawns, reclining on the sofa. She has no fear of draping herself around a crime scene. We'll never be caught no matter how much evidence we leave.

"Lilith take your feet off the sofa," Dominic says, ignoring her comment.

He draws back the curtain and glances down to the darkened street. Even though he's vigilant, they both seem so at ease. While Dominic's been at this a few years longer, Lilith and I have been doing it as long as one another, but I have still yet to master their nonchalance. I stand in the corner of the room where no one can creep up behind me. Not that anyone entering this house would stand a chance. I pity the common criminal who might break in and come upon us three.

"Mallory what's the matter?" Lilith asks from her perch, heeding Dominic's request. She moves her feet to the coffee table where the soda she's opened sits. Beside it is a half-eaten pack of cookie dough. It's often her way to raid the fridge of our victims for foods we could never dream of having back at the Academy.

He drops the curtain and glances over, a worried expression on his face.

"Don't worry, you won't have to do anything," he promises.

Still protecting me, after what we've already done.

"It's not that," I lie, my soft voice wavering.

"Come sit with me," Lilith says, patting the sofa cushion beside her. Her voice has softened. I cross the room and tuck myself next to her. She wraps her arm around me and draws me close. "Someday, I'm going to get you away from here."

"Lilith," Dominic says warningly but she just shoots him a nasty look.

"The Academy, Diane, all of it."

"Where will we go?"

"Anywhere you want."

This is the game we play while we wait. Anywhere but here. Lilith promises to steal me away from the Academy and Dominic humours us to put me at ease. I know he disapproves. He would rather protect me from the inside than risk Diane's wrath if we tried to escape.

"A diner in New York with big pancakes full of chocolate chips and walnuts," I say.

"A park in Paris when spring has just started and it's sunny, you with a book me with some ice cream," she replies, grinning at me.

I feel safe, wrapped in her notions of the future. But then the front door downstairs clicks shut. In the blink of an eye Dominic is by my side. I don't need protecting I want to say but it's not true. I'm so terrified of what's about to happen.

I hear the murmured exchanges of husband and wife downstairs.

"Where's the babysitter? She was supposed to wait until we got home."

"I'll go check on the kids, you know sometimes they get her to stay with them while they sleep."

"It's okay," Dominic whispers, taking my hand.

None of us move another inch as the man comes upstairs and turns into a room further down the hallway. He doesn't notice us three, small child sized shadows still in the dark. More murmurs, soft and loving to his children, tucked in their beds. Then comes the puzzled voice, unable to fathom what it's found. Finally, the broken cry, the stumble and thud of a body falling out of sheer horror at what's been done. Two children, tucked in, throats slit. They would have grown up to be a danger, Diane had said. Lilith slinks around the other side of the sofa and we follow her down the hall to stand in the doorway of the children's room. The man looks up, shocked further still by what he sees.

"You. Diane had you, oh god."

He crawls to the other side of the room, cowering in our presence. Lilith glances back at Dominic, raising her eyebrows. She may be leading the charge but she always asks his permission. He nods, then turns to me. Lilith creeps forward, her hand reaching for the knife sheathed on her hip.

"Look at me," Dominic murmurs, gently turning my face away from the scene about to unfold. "Close your eyes."

I obey.

"Sweetie what's the matter?" I hear his wife call from down the stairs.

Dominic draws me close to him so my face is buried against his chest.

"Think of home," he whispers.

I'm already there. I hold him tight.

Chapter XXXV.

Isabrand is silent on the walk back from the restaurant. We hardly touched our food in the end, though the wait staff scarcely seemed bothered. It's not long before we arrive back at my apartment. The dogs have gone quiet downstairs and even the street seemed silent.

When we get upstairs, he sinks onto the sofa, clearly bothered by the story, his eyes fixed on to a point in the distance. In his mental absence, I take the opportunity to make a cup of tea. I'm exhausted from the day. Even before Isabrand showed up. I close my eyes. How many more people will have to die for me to survive?

"But that still doesn't take us to the present," he says thoughtfully.

I feel his eyes on my back as I pour the hot water over a tea bag.

"No," I sigh, "but hopefully it helps you understand how I came to be here."

"So you...you and my father," he begins, his face wrinkling in disgust. My heart sinks. I had so desperately hoped he wouldn't bring that up.

"I had no idea who he was."

"It's sick."

I flinch at the vehemence in his voice. Of all the things the two of us have done, that perturbs him most?

"I suppose it is."

"And you, you're no better than I am. One of the Academy's assassin dogs."

I narrow my eyes at him.

"That's rich coming from the man who showed up to kill me tonight. I didn't choose that life, and I left it as soon as I had the chance."

He hesitates.

"You're right. I did come here to kill you."

Before I can move, he's sprung to his feet and sent me spilling across the small table. He presses his forearm against my windpipe and a dagger to my throat.

"Isabrand," I say calmly. But my heart is pounding. If I don't leave here tonight so many people will die. Dominic needs me. Kyle too.

"I'm sorry sis, but see Regan stole something from me and gave it to you. I want it back."

"What? What are you talking about?"

"You still don't remember?" Grabbing me by the hair, he drags me across the room to where the box Regan left me lies on the sofa. "Maybe this will help."

He presses his thumb against the moon and small triangles pop up around it, transforming it suddenly into the sun. He turns it like a combination lock, and I hear it click each time it stops. On the final turn the box emits a small popping sound and I see a crevice appear, the place where the lid can be removed from the top.

"Time to remember sis," he says. He pulls the lid off.

Several things happen at once.

The door bursts open and whoever bounds in throws Isabrand's body from atop me.

There's a rush as at last I remember everything. What happened before I came to the Academy. How I died.

Someone extends a hand to help me to my feet.

"Are you okay?" Killian asks, pulling me up before decking my staggering brother clean on the nose. There's a dull thud as he hits his head on the corner of the table before he slumps to the floor.

"Isabrand!"

Acknowledgements

If my dedication did not say it enough, than, again, I must profusely thank my wonderful grandfather, not only for helping me pursue my writing, but engendering the curiosity in me that helped me explore the world in which *Fire of the Blood* is set. Without him, I would be a creatively poorer person, and possible still an accountant. I'll try not to think too hard on what might have been though, for my own sanity.

To my mother I am endlessly grateful, for instilling in me my love of reading and writing. To this day I still have the collection of Shakespeare inspired short stories she gave me at the age of four and, while I admit reading those were some lofty aspirations for a mother to have for her four-year-old, I wouldn't be where I am today without her. Her own passionate pursuit of writing has inspired me, and our conversations have always left me with a desire to better myself as a writer, reader, and a person.

All the love to my incredible godmothers, B and Ronni, who encouraged me to pursue every interest and opportunity. They endlessly opened doors to me in a world which so often seeks to close them.

Thank you to my sister, Camille, whose support and praise of my writing gave me the courage to keep working. No one made me feel prouder of my work than you. Whenever I faltered or had doubt, I need only have thought of your kind words to keep me writing.

To my father, I am eternally indebted for making me the woman I am today, one capable of understanding and creating the characters I do.

For my lovely Anthony, who was the one who finally got me off my lazy ass to finish this book, and see its merits as well as its faults, when I am so often uncertain of my capability as a writer. You are one of the most supportive people I know, and your love for the creativity I have inspires me daily.

This book was edited to the incredible work of composer Ludovico Einaudi, without whom my characters and story wouldn't have come to life, or been half so dramatic.

And on one last note, thank you to my crazy little shiba inu, Cleopawtra Queen of Shibgypt, for waking me up early every morning so I could work on my writing. You're an absolute demon.

About the Author

Jasmina Coric was born and raised in London, where she currently resides. At present, she is completing a master's in Contemporary Literature, Theory, and Culture at King's College London. She is the author of *Gallery Tour Through Grey Matter*, a collection of poems about love, family, and mental health. *Fire of the Blood* is Jasmina's first fantasy foray and the first in a series she is developing.

Printed in Great Britain
by Amazon